DEACON'S PROMISE

A NOVEL

ROGER BURGRAFF

DEACON'S PROMISE

Adventure/Thriller

Roger I. Burgraff

ARPress
45 Dan Road Suite 5
Canton MA 02021

Hotline: 1(888) 821-0229
Fax: 1(508) 545-7580

Ordering Information:
Quantity sales. Special discounts are available on quantity purchases by corporations, associations, and others. For details, contact the publisher at the address above.

Printed in the United States of America.

ISBN-13:   Softcover   979-8-89389-147-8
              eBook   979-8-89389-160-7

Library of Congress Control Number: 2024914637

In praise of Deacon's Promise

Spurred into action by a letter received from a murdered bush pilot friend, Roger Burgraff's unlikely hero, a church deacon, whisks us away from Chicago to South Africa in another Deacon Adelius thriller. Deacon is commissioned to rescue his friend's innocent daughter from imminent peril from drug dealers bent on recovering drug money he absconded with, intending to exterminate all those in the know or in the way. Full of twists and turns, the chase takes us through a world of good and evil: church fathers, a powerful femme fatal, rescue missions and luxury resorts, lovers and killers while Burgraff explores the relativity of morality and value in an exotic Africa. A wild ride indeed!
–Barry Crawford Ph.D.

Roger Burgraff has done it again. Another suspenseful thriller! With lightning rod speed, he spins us past another murder and intrigue to greed, power and lust. A riveting, racy read.
–Jan Fowler, Columnist and author. "Hot Chocolate for Senior Romance – How Great it is"

You've gotta love Deacon. He's a tough guy with a heart of gold and a soul in torment. He is called to South Africa to rescue his friend's children. There he must encounter a villainous drug dealer, child slavery and murder. He is hunted and hunter.
–Donna Kennedy, writer, editor and teacher

In addition to spinning a first-rate story in an engaging exotic locale, Burgraff delves between the lines into some basic human issues of good and evil, inner strengths and weaknesses. The most chillingly villainous of his characters is still driven by emotions we can all related to, while one of the most likeable and sympathetic of the lot turns out to have succumbed to a temptation with horrific consequences.

-Bob Winter, Writer

An absorbing adventure that captures the battle between good and evil in the world and in the psyches of its characters. Deacon is an intriguing tough guy with a conscience. His psychology rings true. And the villain-a delicious depiction of depravity.

-April Wursten, Ph.D. Psychologist and writer

Prologue

Still sitting in the cockpit, the pilot, a good man who had not always done good things, waited on the dark landing field trying not to feel the fear. Once again, the tryst was in the dead of night, in a remote location—tonight, the vast windy wilderness of the Karoo, the bulls-eye center of the province, an hour's bumpy flight north of Cape Town.

The tightness of his khaki bush clothes--which got worse with every month—made his heart hammer even more, reminding him that he needed to lose weight. He knew his health was at stake. He didn't want his kids to see him turning to fat. And it was uncomfortable as hell. The cockpit of the Alteris SP 45, his little workhorse, felt more and more claustrophobic every time he struggled into it, and tonight it made him want to scream.

When he could endure it no longer, he climbed out of the plane to stretch his legs and back and lean against the warm fuselage. Waiting, so common in South Africa and tedious, gave him time to think. The night wind carried the tart sweetness of jasmine and sage, but this did nothing to relieve the fear. The sky was another matter. It was clear, and the blinking stars looked hopeful. Who had said it—Inkosi or Father Godwin? "The light shines brightest against the darkness." When he squinted, the constellation of the Southern Cross looked like a sparkling necklace, twelve-carat Orange River diamonds - something you'd give to a woman you loved, to keep her with you, to make her happy.

The other weight he'd been living with would lift soon, he told himself. He'd be able to get in shape again. He'd be able to tell stories with a laugh, play the practical jokes he was known for, spend time with friends, and stop being afraid. He was fed up with the bad people and their ugly lives. What mattered, he knew now—he'd seen the truth two weeks ago, simple and sentimental, love above all. He had a family, and he would be of no use to them dead. This would be his last flight.

One way or another that was certain. He'd made enough, skimming from the profits of the old cracked ivory. Along with his life savings, he had enough to take his daughter and stepson out of country and begin again. An experienced pilot could find work anywhere. It wouldn't take long.

He'd been careful, he told himself, but he wasn't sure he believed it. First, he'd convinced the man he called Inkosi, his Xosa friend, to keep the stamped, sealed letter safe and mail it only in the event that he was killed. He sweated, actually sweated, writing it, but you did what you needed to do in life. The last lines had been the hardest. The words had frightened him, writing them out, but they'd also made him laugh. How do you put on the page things like "forgive me for dying like this" and "sorry to ask?"

He'd hidden what he'd accumulated – about R 2,000,000, ($200,000) in the safest place he knew – in God's hard red earth. It insured their future—his and the kids. He wouldn't have a woman with him—he'd lost her to disease three years ago—but he would have the kids, his family who loved him. Love enough.

He rarely prayed, but he did so now. He prayed that his fear would prove groundless. That they'd live and escape, and the letter would never be sent. Prayer was like a letter too, but somehow easier. "Dear God...."

In the beginning he had no inkling about the drugs, and some time in the future he'd make sure the kids knew this. He'd choose a moment a month from now, a year, to tell them. *"Feliz Colmillo—Happy Tusk"*—had been, he'd had every reason to assume at first, a simple ivory smuggling operation of the SADF (South African Defense Force). All the tusks from animals long dead, were sitting in Pretoria warehouses owned by apartheid-army front companies for thirty years, waiting for a chance to move and make a dozen levels of middlemen rich. Later when he'd been part of it too long, he learned what the tusks were really for, what was in them. Though he wanted to believe that Father Godwin hadn't known either, he was sure that the doctor and that Boer, Marais had known.

Startled, he looked up to see the two bouncing fireflies of a Land Rover's headlights approaching the road to the airstrip. He felt his pulse quicken, and steady again. *At last,* he told himself.

He'd load up one last time and be done with these people in an hour, two at the most. He'd smile, act like he always had and it would be over. Back at the Hands of Hope Mission in Muldersdrift, he'd breathe again, his pulse would slow for the first time that day, and he'd begin the task of getting the kids ready to leave.

As always, the Land Rover pulled up in front of the plane, leaving its headlights on for the loading.

The first sign that a problem was brewing was when the squat, husky man with the pockmarked face who alighted from the driver's side and with a bounce in his step moved into the light. He had seen the man only once before briefly, and they'd never spoken. He didn't know the man's name, only that he was Peruvian like the woman. Why he hadn't thought of drugs when he'd first met them, he couldn't imagine. Sometimes stereotypes were accurate. He was a bush pilot and therefore friendly and a former bar fighter. They were South Americans into bad business and therefore must be *narcotrafficantes.* True, too, it had turned out. The man had a scar on his upper lip that twisted his mouth, making him look cruel— probably true as well.

From the passenger side came the woman with the dyed red hair, the transplanted Peruvian, the one in charge, walking carefully on the rutted earth in her silly high heels. She was short and curvy—

beautiful in a brassy way, he'd always thought. Tonight she wasn't smiling.

"Evenin' all," he said, offering a smile and a salute from the brim of his well-worn flying cap. No blacks stepped from the car. An even worse sign. Usually there were two of them, friendly men, Ndebeles from the Southern Transvaal who helped transfer the cargo from auto to plane.

He now wished he'd stayed in the cramped cockpit with the sawed-off Ithaca shotgun behind the pilot's seat.

As the two of them reached him, the woman started shouting in her abysmal English.

"You are a *ladron, senor*. You know what that mean? It mean you have stole from us and you must pay us."

The pilot put up his hands placatingly, trying hard to think. He hadn't imagined they'd want to talk about it. If they discovered what he'd done, they'd simply kill him, he'd assumed. He had no idea what to say. "Please *senora*, I can explain to you how this happened...."

The woman laughed—it did sound stupid—and he knew it was pointless.

"*Ahora,*" she said quickly to her partner, and just as quickly the man answered, "*Sin duda,*" pulling something from his belt.

Feeling more foolish than afraid, the pilot made himself see the faces of his daughter and stepson, their faces now, older, their faces when they were little, standing on the patio of the mission as the rain fell, ruining that birthday party, and he made himself send another prayer—that the letter he'd written would somehow reach a man he hadn't seen in years—as the sound of the handgun took the stars, the hopeful stars, away.

As the body slid to the ground, leaving an arc of blood on the fuselage, the red haired woman spat, *"Esta hecho."*

Her partner walked over, put the barrel of the pistol against the pilot's forehead, and fired one more time. The skull came apart and the man swore.

The red-haired woman looked at her compatriot, smiled and in the slurred *espanol sucio* of her childhood, whispered seductively, "Now, the hands. I will wait in the car."

Chapter 1

AS I DROVE TO DELIVER THE ULTIMATUM to a sexually perverted priest, I felt my nervous energy ramping up. The pile of letters I'd hastily tossed onto the car seat would have to wait, even the letter from Mike Thompson in South Africa. My take-out coffee had cooled and I threw the rest out.

I recounted my recruitment by the secret society of the Gabrians two years ago while still at seminary. I had the right background to suit the goal of the Gabrians described succinctly by Archbishop Laine – "To remove the garbage from the clergy." When they told me I was an "angel," I almost laughed. Then I learned that "angel," meant "messenger." Unlike Gabriel, *My* messages nobody wanted to hear. The public could never know about the Gabrians.

This cloudless bitterly cold night I'd be visiting Father Grozak at Saint Joseph the Worker parish in Arlington Heights. The evidence against him - irrefutable. I had the *prie-dieu,* kneeling bench, in the back of the parish station wagon. It would follow Father Grozak wherever he chose to relocate.

The rectory adjoining the modern church had double front doors with Greek-like columns on each side. *Some sleazy attempt at class?* Father Grozak answered the bell. He was fairly short. I'd guess about five feet six inches tall. From my vantage of six four, I wasn't a very good judge of height. He had short curly brown hair that was thinning. His close-set eyes, slightly hooked nose and receding chin completed the picture. He looked comfortable in a maroon sweater, dark trousers and slippers. I would change that shortly.

"Father Grozak?"

"Yes, can I help you?"

"It is I who may be of assistance to you."

"Really," he said lifting an eyebrow. "Do come in."

As I entered, I said, "This is a gift for you from some of your brother priests. I'm Deacon Adelius." I set the *prie-dieu* down in the foyer.

He gave the personal kneeler a casual glance. He did not look thrilled with the gift. "Well, this is a surprise. Please join me in the parlor."

The rectory parlor was sparsely but tastefully furnished. I sat in a high wing-backed chair. He sat behind a small ornate desk. I didn't waste any time with preliminaries. It made my skin crawl just to be in his presence and converse with him. As always, I felt the urge to bash his face in. *Control, control.*

I recited my well-rehearsed introduction. "I'm here on the authority of the hierarchy in this diocese to give you this *prie-dieu* and deliver an important announcement."

I could see I had his full attention. I wondered if he had an inkling of what I was about to say.

"I have in this folder the names of three children you have abused. You stole their innocence, and you will be held accountable."

Father Grozak's face went pale. "I never did any such thing. This is an outrage."

I raised my voice over his. "You're an outrage. The evidence against you is overwhelming. The children will receive the best of counseling and free Catholic education for the rest of their lives. We all pray they recover from your depravity."

"Get out of here!" He said, trying to muster some authority.

"I'll leave when my task is finished."

Father Grozak rose and rushed toward the door. I blocked his way. He lost his balance and fell to the floor. *Control, maintain control.*

"Sit down and listen until I'm finished."

He flopped down in his chair, hands folded as if in prayer.

"Understand me -- you will be leaving tonight."

"Leaving? Going where?"

"Where you will not have any contact with children and will be given a chance to pray, continue to be of some use to the church, and repent of your sins."

Father Grozak called up some courage and raised his chin. "I'm not going anywhere. This is bullshit!" He growled, "I'm the pastor here."

"You have no choice. Your life as you knew it is over. Be glad you haven't been turned over to the police. That is still your choice. You *can* turn yourself in. The Gabrians I represent offer you a choice to relocate to one of three remote cloisters to live out your life in work, contemplation and pray to Christ our redeemer for forgiveness every day. I have a list for you."

He quickly perused the list. "The Gabrians? I've heard rumors." He gazed forward unfocused. "Suppose I choose not to turn myself in or be sent to one of these remote places."

"Then we'll turn you in. And if you run, we will find you, take you to a clinic where you will be surgically castrated and then we will turn you in to the civil authorities."

Father Grozak croaked "Oh no," as his eyes bulged, his breath came in gasps and blood left his face. He slowly went over the choices presented in the folder. They were remote and austere.

"Someone will be along shortly to escort you on your way. Pack lightly. You will take the *prie-dieu* with the carved Gabrian crest with you to pray and beg for forgiveness."

Father Grozak was in shock. His face ashen.

"Do you understand my message?"

He nodded and almost whispered, "How long must I stay in one of these places?"

"Until you die."

I left him sitting there, the pig. I would waste no pity on him. I had fulfilled my purpose as the announcer.

As I walked back to the station wagon I reminded myself of the four- fold purpose of the Gabrians: To hold wayward clergy accountable, protect the innocent, compensate them and give perpetrators a chance at redemption from a loving, all-forgiving God.

Chapter 2

THE TIRES OF OLD STATION WAGON crunched on the dry snow. Leaving the windows open slightly helped me to savor the night air and clear my head. I tuned the radio to an oldies station. Familiar songs usually lifted my spirits but not tonight.

The *Gabrian visit was unsettling*. They always were. I felt on my way to nowhere. My sense of being adrift had been too real for too many months. *God, show me the way.*

I pulled into the driveway and shut off the engine, listening to it click and sputter before it died. I climbed the ruddy brick steps to the front door of my diminutive digs adjoining Saint Sebastian's Catholic Church. I tossed the mail on the kitchen table. Only then did I remember the letter from South Africa. I thumbed through the stack of envelopes twice. Not there.

Irritated, I trudged back to the car, opened the driver's side door and reached in. Not on the front seat. I knelt down and patted the dusty burgundy carpet, feeling stupid. Nothing. I stood, glanced around and spied the pale blue envelope with its colorful stamps peeking out from under the car just in front of the rear tire. As I bent down to retrieve the letter, the tower bell from Saint Sebastians's Church began to ring. A glance at my watch showed both luminous dials pointing straight up. A midnight letter.

*   *   *   *   *

I took a frosty Sam Adams out of the fridge, popped the top, took a healthy swig and sat down heavily at my glass-topped kitchen table. I slit the envelope with a steak knife and read the first few words.

Dear Deacon,

If you are reading this, it means I'm dead. I've given this letter to a trusted friend to post to you in the event of my death. He knows nothing of the contents. Boyo, I feel very weird writing this.

My first reaction – shock. I said, "Oh, God." Mike's death hit me like a body blow. Then it occurred to me that this had to be some kind of a joke. After all, Mike Thompson took the prize as a world-class prankster. I read the rest of the letter and soon realized it was no joke. This was deadly serious stuff. Mike had obviously spent a lot of time crafting the document.

My friend, I'm writing to ask you for a big, big favor. I've hidden away some money, and I want you to take my daughter to it. It's there to secure her future. There is a letter of explanation to her and a few other items. The thing is, old boy, she does not know that I'm her father. I'd like you to break this news to her. Her name is "Kalina Sangweeni." She thinks of me as one of her four uncles. By the way, she knows that none of us is really an uncle at all. It's more of an honorary title, because we've all sort of taken care of her as she's been growing up. I want you to get her to that hidden packet without anyone knowing about it. Then, if you can, my friend, please help her to get the hell out of South Africa. I've grown to love this country, but it's no longer safe for my daughter and her half brother, Jaylin. Convince them to leave with you.

Make no mistake, both youngsters are in grave danger. Deac, for countless reasons, you are the only one I can ask. You aren't directly connected to me, or the other players in this insane game.

I got mixed up with some truly evil people. The unholy scheme that we hatched began as a good and noble cause even if, strictly speaking, it had an illegal aspect to it. As soon as I discovered what was really happening, along with my fees, I began to skim some money off the top. I planned to get the hell out with my family. Obviously, I didn't make it.

You can find Kalina through the Hands of Hope Mission in Muldersdrift. It is run by Fr. Frank Godwin. A great name for a priest, huh? He runs the mission and infirmary with Dr. Gideon Ngubane. They're two of Kalina's other "uncles." The fourth is Johannes Marais, an Afrikaner, who also works at the mission. You can't miss him. He looks like a gargoyle on steroids. Don't be deceived by his looks; his heart is soft gold. They are all involved with the scheme, but I doubt if Fr. Frank knows the full truth. By the way, the other "uncles" know that I am Kalina's father. They also know I deeply loved her mother Alisha, who passed away two years ago.

Beware of someone called, "Rosenmoon," or Rosenbloom." I'm not sure of the spelling or his involvement, but I know he is a killer. I know I'm rambling, but be careful. I hope that your friend Robbie at Misty Hills can give you a hand with some of the logistics while you're here.

That's it. My dear friend, please get in here, get the packet, and get my daughter and her half-brother out of South Africa any way you can. What is death if not the chance to die better than we lived? I died too soon Deacon. Please do this for me. I'm counting on you.

Mike

P.S. The packet is due north of the Tropic of Capricorn monument along the great north road in the Northern Transvaal. From the monument, follow the compass heading due North about 100 meters, until you come to a huge Baobab tree. You'll find three notches cut into one of the main roots. Dig down to the right of this root. There is also a little something in the box for your trouble.

"Damn." I said aloud. "Unfucking believable." It wasn't possible, was it? I sat back, closed my eyes, then rose and slowly paced the floor. "*Unholy scheme. Evil people.*" I read the letter more slowly, the voice in my head repeating, "That jokester. This is a put-on." But deep down I knew this was as real as anything could be. And a killer to worry about. What else?

I lost track of how many times I read the midnight letter, stopping between each reading to think hard about Mike's checkered past, our adventures together, and what the letter meant. Glancing at the wall clock, I realized I'd been at it for two hours and three beers.

My heart sank when I thought of Mike as gone. He was still present to me.

Like Ann. Not since opening the letter had I thought of Ann. I didn't know whether that was good or bad. She was gone too.

*   *   *   *   *

I would never forget the first time I met Mike. My hotel shuttle had broken down somewhere near Pigg's Peak Resort, outside of New Orleans. I'd been scheduled to do a training course for seminarians. The uniformed resort driver, who'd picked me up from the airport, glared at the useless vehicle, his professional smile gone.

He mentioned there were a few shops and a bar down the road where I could wait for his return. I had the choice of waiting in the van or trudging down the road in the misty rain to wait until the driver could summon help. I opted for the wet stroll to the local bar.

It was a dimly lit, gray, cinder block building with a corrugated metal roof, which resounded with the patter of the rain. It had the distinctive bar smell of beer, smoke, and sweat somewhat muted by the clear smell of rain. The clientele was mostly Black except for a heavyset white man sitting in the corner wearing an aviator's peaked cap at a jaunty angle. The man had a broad face that needed a shave, and a goofy smile. He returned my nod.

After ordering a bottle of the local brew, I sat at a small table near the front door, looking out at the rain to wait for my driver to return with the rescue car. Fatigued, wet, and frustrated, I felt pathetic as I sipped the cold beer at a dirty, wobbly table. For a while no one paid me much mind.

Then two Cajuns and what I thought might be a Creole, poorly dressed in faded tee shirts, shorts and sandals like most of the indigenous population of the bayous, sauntered up to my table. I knew the look of trouble coming.

The tallest said, "Dis here's our table, mon."

The lanky, emaciated-looking leader was staring down at me. He had large expressionless eyes with yellow where the white should have been. His nostrils flared above a crooked smile with bad teeth.

"There are lots of empty tables around." I said. The trio stood there silently. "Okay, look," I offered, "I'll move if it makes you happy."

The leader of the trio said, "All dese tables's ours." At that, several other patrons quickly slithered out of the bar or pinned themselves along the walls to watch. "Not only dat, you gots to pay for sittin' in one of our beau chaises. It goin' to cost you all da *argent* you have, mon." They all smiled showing discolored, crooked teeth.

As I sized up the situation, the leader leaned forward, spoke once more, softly, his smile instantly gone. "Y'all want ta die today?"

I tensed right down to my testicles. Despite the fact that I usually repressed my old MP reactions, they kicked in now, and I readied myself.

The leader raised a K-Bar, he had been holding at his side. "Stick him now," the young Creole yelled. The blade slashed down and stuck into the edge of the tabletop where my arm had been a split second before. I pushed myself backward to avoid the blow. In one motion, I jumped to my feet, picked up my beer bottle by the neck, and side-armed it into the attacker's head, as he struggled to pull the blade from the table. Blood, beer, and bits of brown glass flew in every direction. He went down. I held the jagged end of the bottle at the ready. I was in a spot I'd been in before while in the Middle East.

A big booming voice rang from across the room. "*Y'all* will surely die today if you don't get the fuck out of here right now." It was the man with the jaunty flyer's cap. He was standing in the middle of the barroom with his legs wide apart, pointing a strange weapon at the three young men before me. It was a stubby, single-barreled Roentgen shotgun with no stock, just a handgrip.

The threatening trio mumbled something like, "Oui, Oui, Cher, we's just goin' now for sure." They left, and my heartbeat slowed to a canter.

"Hi," said the gunslinger, shifting the weapon to his left hand. "I'm Mike Thompson. I fly, but as you can see, weather has me grounded in this dump. What are you drinkin'?" He waved to a barmaid who was wearing a pink blouse with a very low scoop neck and no bra. Mike took a long admiring look and said, "We'll have two more here. The Yankee's buyin'. So, what in God's holy name is a dandy like you doin' in a bloody armpit like this?"

"Name's Deacon Adelius and thank you."

"You looked like you might be able to handle the situation by yourself."

"Nevertheless, thanks. My resort shuttle-van broke down and I'm waiting for the driver to take me to Pigg's Peak for a conference."

"Nice place. I'm staying there myself. I'll cancel the drinks and tell the barmaid where we've gone. She'll relay the message to the driver. You come along with me. If we get there soon enough, they've got a topless Zydeco show on tonight. You'll see." He laughed heartily at a private joke.

The show was entertaining, as promised, but the topless performers were all men. Thus, my introduction to Mike Thompson's particular brand of humor, and the start of a close friendship renewed several times.

Whenever he was in Chicago, Thompson would show up unannounced to crash on my couch and raid my refrigerator for a few days. We'd talk all kinds of stuff, religion included. He claimed to be Christian-Lite with a touch of agnosticism. He sometimes came to Mass. Occasionally, he'd fly us out of the city to interesting places I'd never heard of. His surprise visits could be a bit off-putting, but somehow I not only tolerated the intrusions but enjoyed the hell out of them. I counted the quirky pilot among my few close friends and always would.

As I tried to sleep, thoughts ricocheted all over the memories of good times with Mike Thompson. The short breathtaking flights around the Great Lakes, Canada and Las Vegas. Rock climbing, fishing and kayaking. Mike sleeping one off on the couch. The memories projected themselves like a movie on my brain until fatigue overtook me like a warm blanket.

*   *   *   *   *

After assisting at morning Mass with my alcoholic pastor, Father Posjena, I poured myself a cup of French Roast coffee, sat at my table and reread the letter. I formed a plan of action. I always liked a good plan to point the way. One problem was that I'd promised to finish the academic year working at Saint Sebastian's. I thought I could spring free for a week or so with the Bishop's permission. He owed me. Father Posjena would just have to get along without me for a short time. He wouldn't like it. Tough.

Next, I would call my friend Robbie Forrester in South Africa to ask for his help and for a place to stay at his country hotel, Misty Hills. I calculated the time difference and decided it wasn't too late to reach Robbie in South Africa. I got through quickly.

"Robbie Forrester, here."

"Robbie, you magnate of South Africa, Deacon calling. How are you?"

"I'm fine, fine. Good to hear a friendly voice from the colonies. Howzit with you?"

"I'm okay. Say, I really didn't call to chat or catch up on things. I'm calling about another matter that has me...very concerned."

"Well, what is it? Hold on. Let me shut my office door."

I began to pace with my cordless phone in one hand and the coffee cup in the other.

Robbie returned. "There, that's better. Go ahead."

"Do you remember Mike Thompson?"

"Of course; I've even flown with him. He's been at the Carnivore restaurant many times, especially at the Simba bar. Shame about his passing."

My heart stopped for a second. "What do you know about his death?"

"Nothing specific, ole boy. Just that he died out in the Karoo."

"The Karoo?"

"A vast, remote area of the country north of Cape Town."

"I see. Anything else?"

"No, not as I recall."

"Would you do me a favor, old friend?"

"Certainly, if I can."

"Please nose around a bit and see if you can find out anything about his death. Then call me back as soon as you can."

"What's this all about?"

"I received a disturbing letter from Mike." I found myself saying, "I'm planning on coming to South Africa very soon."

"I am delighted to hear you'll be coming down. Our light is always on for you. I've got an old friend just retired from the police force, Colonel Stewart Marshall. He may be of some help. I won't promise anything, but I'll try."

"Right. Talk to you tomorrow."

After he hung up, I sat and brooded. What the hell had Thompson gotten into? How could he put his kids in danger like this? I didn't even know he had kids. He'd always been adventurous and self-centered, but he could always be counted on.

I spent the day in a state of agitated depression. I knew the symptoms well. It was an oxymoronic state understood only by those who experienced it first-hand. I considered taking something to soften the edge, but talked myself out of it. I read. Took a short frigid jog around the neighborhood. But nothing helped. The situation gripped my mind like tentacles. I helped set up equipment at the school gym, followed by punching the body bag hanging in the basement of the church. Later that evening while watching the news, my phone rang.

"Hello, Deacon Adelius."

"Deac, its Robbie. I have some news. I was on to Colonel Marshall and was able to pry a few things out of him. Cops are as tight lipped as Durban clams. I'm not sure this is going to help."

"Go ahead please."

"It's certain Thompson was murdered."

"What. How?"

"They found him next to his plane on a landing strip in the Karoo. Two gunshot wounds. The Colonel told me that from the evidence it was definitely a professional hit."

"My God." The letter was now frighteningly real. "What was he into?"

"I really don't know. I did hear once, some time ago, someone say that he wasn't above doing a little smuggling. Nothing big, I don't think."

"Yes?"

"I don't know if it was true. There are certainly lots of opportunities for a bush pilot to earn a few extra bucks. But Deac…"

"Go on."

"There was something else the Colonel wouldn't tell me— about what they found at the crime scene."

"What, any guesses?"

"The colonel hinted that something horrible was done to the body. The kind of thing the police don't make public for their own reasons."

I paused trying to absorb what Robbie had said. "Thank you, Robbie."

"How soon can we expect a visit from you?"

"I'll let you know. But soon."

"Right, well, got to get to work, I have people waiting."

I knew I had to go to South Africa. When you knew, you knew. *Yes, Thompson, old friend, you screwed up royally and dragged me into it.* My next step was to visit Archbishop Laine and get permission to travel to South Africa.

Chapter 3

I PARKED SEVERAL BLOCKS from the Archbishop's residence to avoid the exorbitant parking garage fees. I pulled my father's battered fedora down on my head and raised my collar. The old hat was all I had from my father who died doing missionary work in the Middle East when I was a kid. I liked how the hat made me feel connected to him.

The howling wind off Lake Michigan sliced through my coat. I pushed forward trudging through the dirty packed snow.

Crossing an alley, I saw a small bunch of teenagers standing roughly in a circle. I recognized a few from the parish. Curious, I approached the group. They didn't notice me until I was close. Four of them recognized me and took off. I heard one say, "That's the Deacon. You don't want to mess with him."

I was blessed to have a reputation like that in this neighborhood.

Something felt wrong. I opened my coat to have quick access to a weapon I'd dubbed Bat. I often carried an aluminum youth baseball bat with me. Sometimes it helped me dispense justice; sometimes it provided defense. I adapted its use from the moves I'd learned from the baton I had used as an MP.

Bobby, a mentally handicapped boy from the parish was kneeling down in the middle of the circle. He was crying. I knelt next to him. "Bobby what's going on?"

He answered in his inarticulate speech. "Dese guys said I … I gotta eat dese here breakfast sausages. Dey're not… sausages are dey?"

I looked down at a couple of dog turds. "No, Bobby, and you don't ever have to eat them."

"They're dog shit, right?"

"Right. Now get up and go home. Say hello to your brother for me."

As Bobby walked away, I rose and looked around the small group of teenagers trying to look tough. "What punk thought this up?"

Nobody spoke-up but a few looked to a young man with a studded leather jacket, and tattoos visible beneath his black tee shirt. Long black hair, pimples and the premonition of a moustache. The leader, the alpha male. He smiled a crooked smile, saying, "Just having a laugh with the retard."

Control, control. "I don't think it's fun to take advantage of anyone who can't fight back."

"Fuck you care."

"I make it my business to deal with bullies like you."

"Fuck off." He flicked open a stiletto and pointed it at me.

My stomach knotted and energy pulsed through my body. "Put that away before you get hurt."

"Fuck you, who's gonna hurt me?"

The time for reasonable discussion was over.

I grabbed his right wrist and twisted outwardly. He dropped the knife and groaned. As I let up the pressure he swung at me with a roundhouse left. I parried the telegraphed punch easily and put two hard jabs into his nose in quick succession. Blood spurted and he dropped to his knees.

I pulled out Bat from my belt and glared at the others. "Anyone else want to dance with me today?"

They looked down and muttered to themselves as they dispersed.

I knelt beside the wounded leader of the pack. "I just did you a favor. You should thank me. If Bobby had done what you asked, word would have gotten back to his brother, 'Tony Two Fist.' He's an ex-Golden Gloves middleweight champion. He'd have found you and you'd be lucky to be in the hospital on life support." I picked up the stiletto and put it in my pocket.

"What you were doing was just wrong. I'm sure you can understand that. I want to never see you again, got it" No answer. I tapped him lightly on the head with Bat. I said, "Got it?"

"Yeah, yeah, I got it."

"Then go with God and don't disrespect yourself by being a two-bit bully. You can be better than that." I helped him to his feet.

Mumbling an inarticulate "Fuck you" he shrugged me off, held a handkerchief against his broken nose and staggered away.

There was always God's work to do.

*   *   *   *   *

Archbishop Laine's office was located in a renovated old brick building just north of Chicago's loop. Outside, the sparkling granite with the tall slim windows gave the building a regal elegance. Within, Persian carpets, a few Victorian side tables complete with ornate vases and moldings added to the grandeur of the place. Pretty damned impressive.

After two security checkpoints, a rather stern looking assistant ushered me into a comfortable waiting room with colorful religious paintings adorning the walls. A portrait of Pope Francis I was prominently displayed in the entry hall. *The boss.*

I'd made an appointment stressing urgency. I felt the pressure to get to South Africa as soon as possible.

I didn't have to wait long. As I entered the Archbishop's office, he rose to greet me with a warm handshake and hug. We sat around a small mahogany coffee table.

The Archbishop referred to my being shot a few months earlier. "How are your wounds healing?"

"Just fine, thanks for asking."

"Great. We've all been praying for your swift recovery."

"I appreciate it."

"I hope this visit is an indication that you want to resume your studies for the priesthood?" His eyes widened in positive expectancy. "You'd make a helluva priest."

I'd become disillusioned by the clergy scandals and dropped out of my priestly studies after receiving the Deaconate. "No, Father, I'm still in limbo on that decision. I came to see you on another matter of grave concern and to ask for permission to travel outside the country for a while."

"Please reconsider your decision to join the priesthood, but until then tell me about your concerns and your need to leave the country."

"I think the best way to explain myself is by having you read this letter." I handed him the midnight letter.

He took it, put on his glasses and began to read. In thirty seconds he looked up at me. "This is extraordinary." He kept on reading to the end, periodically shaking his head.

He put the letter down and was quiet for a few minutes. "I think I know what you want to do."

"Father, I have to go to get these children out of harms way. I know I'm committed to working at Saint Sebastian's until the summer but I've got to take some time to do this."

"Of course, you must. I have a positive coincidence for you. Father Godwin at the mission in Muldersdrift is a Gabrian like yourself, so he may be of great help to you. Likewise, you may be able to help him. Perhaps a speaking engagement or two would provide a cover story for your presence. There are very few Gabrians in South Africa. Of course, you have my permission to go. I'll square it with your pastor. How long do you think you'll be gone?"

"Thank you. The cover story is a great idea. Probably a week to ten days at the most." I really hadn't a clue. "One other favor. I need a loan for the ticket and expenses. I'll pay you back. It seems my friend has some compensation laid away for me."

The Archbishop rang for his assistant. A young priest experiencing premature baldness came in silently. "Yes, your grace?"

"Bring me my checkbook with the red cover." The young man did so and the archbishop opened it and began to write. "We owe you so much for your recent services to the Cardinal and the church. If you can pay it back – fine, if not, don't worry about it."

I hadn't thought of asking for a specific amount. When I saw the check, I was sure it would cover my travels and any other expenses easily. "Thank you, your Grace."

"My pleasure. Thank me by bringing me the children to meet when you return. Your quest is a holy one to be sure. My prayers go with you for a successful outcome. Take care of yourself and try not to get shot. One good thing – its summer down there."

On the way back to the parish, I made one more stop. I felt I had to share what I was about to do with someone—with a friend. I stopped off at Rabbi Mel Cohen's home. He greeted me warmly as always with a bear hug and smile to warm my heart.

"So, what brings you to the dark side? Are you ready to convert?"

"Nice try. No, I'm still a Papist. I'll be traveling overseas soon and I wanted you to know." I handed him the letter. "Check this out and tell me what you think."

He sat in his leather chair, put on his reading glasses, adjusted the desk lamp and began to read. He made little noises as he scanned the page. "Well, well, well, quite a challenge. Is this the same Mike Thompson you've told me about before?"

"The same."

"It sounds dangerous. But of course, knowing you and how danger seems to follow you around, you've got to go. But what a story you'll be able to tell when you return. How can I help?"

You could lend me your private jet and send your attractive secretary with me."

Cohen didn't miss a beat. "The jet is in for repairs just now. The entertainment system is on the blink. Mrs. Bulgelski, who just celebrated her sixty-seventh birthday, is going in for a hip replacement."

"I'll just have to rough it." We had tea and raspberry tarts.

After a half hour of lively discussion, I got ready to leave. "Go with God, Deac, I'll look forward to your safe return."

Chapter 4

ROSA GARCIA, WHOSE LEGAL NAME in South Africa was Ginger Rose, sat on her balcony finishing coffee laced with brandy. As she often did, Rose turned to survey her rooms with a glowing sense of satisfaction. It had been a tortuous climb for a half-caste mestizo girl from the barrios of the river port city of Iquitos, Peru. She had been born less than one hundred miles from Colombia. Now she enjoyed an expensive apartment suite in exclusive Santon Hills, a tony suburb of Johannesburg.

She phoned another, less elegant apartment on a lower floor in the complex. "Vicente, I'm back. I'll be down in twenty minutes." She slipped out of her lilac silk robe to dress. Rose favored a wardrobe of brightly colored blouses or sweaters with tailored black slacks or a black skirt. Today she selected a scarlet V-neck sweater, ribbed at the waist. While working at the newspaper, she always wore a blazer, her mark of professionalism. When not working, Rose preferred to display her femininity. She appreciated the fact that she had been blessed with an hourglass figure. Her ample breasts shaped the sweater fabric, which also outlined her torso beautifully. She shook out her wild red hair, still damp from the shower. The black heels she'd chosen would bring her 5'4" height up to 5'7," nearly the same height as her partner, Vicente Luna. He would leer, she knew. Let him. Let him drool and develop blue balls, if necessary. He knew he could have none of her except what his eyes and imagination could provide.

She recalled the one time Vicente, who was built like a fireplug, had lost control and groped her breasts as he tried to force her into his bed. Her threat to sever his masculinity from the rest of his body had been graphic and totally believable. He would never try again. Since then, they'd maintained a companionable, businesslike relationship. But poor man, he couldn't help himself. She well understood his urges, as she well understood all men. She was careful not to dent his ego again.

Rose had promised not to tell Luis Salazar of Vicente's indiscretion. That would have been enough to end Vicente's existence…painfully. Salazar considered her his own, when it suited him. Still, she thought, Luis was her hero *de la revolution*. He had begun as a young idealist under Bermudes, then switched his loyalties to the Shining Path movement, and finally the FARQ.

Unfortunately for Luis, he'd been assigned the task of raising funds for the guerrilla freedom movement. Rose expected that once in that position, he'd become vulnerable to the corruption and greed rampant among the freedom fighters, a corruption she'd already accepted as universal among men. At first, he abhorred the misuse of funds. But, as so many before him, he learned to tolerate it, accept it, and, finally, embrace it.

Rose accepted him as he was and would be forever grateful to him for taking her in, making her his mistress, providing for her higher education, recognizing her ruthless cunning and streetwise judgment, developing her talents, and eventually making her one of his trusted lieutenants. She relished the power, well aware that no woman had ever risen so high among the scattered, violent guerrillas of Eastern Peru. She loved Luis deeply and knew at some level he loved her in return.

Luis had assigned Vicente Luna to her as partner and protector. Despite the one indiscretion, Rose felt safe with his loyal muscle to support her. He would not let any harm come to her. His own life depended on it.

She took the executive elevator down to his floor preferring to discuss business in his room, keeping her apartment private. Making sure that no one was in the hall, including the roving security men, she knocked softly on apartment number, 318. The door opened and she entered quickly.

"*Hola*, Vicente."

"*Buenos tardes*, Rose"

"Whew!" She said as she sat down. "I just got back from a long day in a place called Muldersdrift. I found where the boy works."

"*Bueno, bueno.* Would you like a drink?"

"*Si*, a Shandy over ice." Rose didn't really want a drink, but she enjoyed having Vicente or any man serve her.

"Right away," he promised.

As he prepared the drink, she scanned his apartment. Vicente was neat to a fault. The place was immaculate. Impersonal. She caught the faint scent of sandalwood incense in the air.

"So, what did you find?" he asked, handing her the cool amber drink.

"From the old photo you took off Thompson, I blew up the sections of each person. I showed the pictures of them at different post offices in the area where Thompson lived. The boy was recognized in one of them. He works at the Van De Veldt Royal Cheetah Institute. The woman, in the shadows with a scarf around her head, is the boy's mother. I discovered she's dead. No one knew the young colored girl in the photo, but she must be around. I think it's a family photo. The girl may well be Thompson's daughter."

Vicente poured a glass of Cabernet Sauvignon for himself, and sat almost delicately on the couch. He studied the photos. "So, the boy is next?"

"*Si*," said Rose. "And, finally, the girl. Of course, I want to know what Thompson did with the money he took from us. I figured it comes to many thousands of American dollars. I want it back."

Vicente frowned. He balked at killing girls. He had a soft spot for girls because he had two daughters back in Peru, one of whom was handicapped with a hearing loss. "The girl in the photo looks so young; she couldn't know anything."

Vicente watched Rose's forehead tighten. She spoke with an odd accent, a blend of American English softened with a Spanish flavor. "In the first place, she *is* young in the picture, but the photo is old. She's probably a young woman now. In the second place, we have no idea what she knows. And finally, Luis has his methods. Thompson was a disloyal pig of a thief who had to be taken down. When his family also dies, it sends a strong signal to others." She waved her hand in the air and scowled. "Why am I talking like a fishwife. You know all this."

As she spoke, Vicente found himself thinking, *This is a hard woman.* But she is *muy erotica.* But worth dying for at the hands of Salazar? No. He wouldn't put his hands on her. He merely said, "*Si, claro.*"

"While you track down the boy, I'll discuss the next shipment with the doctor. The others have gone well. Two of the last three were intercepted as expected, but one actually got through." She smiled with her mouth and eyes and threw her arms out. "*Viva, Feliz Colmillo!*" (Happy Tusk). Vicente remembered coming up with the code name for their smuggling operation. "Stupid *Americanos.*" She paused, changing the subject. "Now we have to find another pilot."

"*Si*, a great shame we have so many complications because of one gringo pilot with sticky hands."

"I think it was more than that. I have a feeling he wanted out. Well, now he *is* out, but our money has gone with him." Vicente watched her kick off her shoes and tuck her legs beneath her body on the overstuffed chair.

Vicente leered at her legs as he replied, "*Si*, it could be so." He could not share her bed, but she was a pleasure to watch.

"I'll e-mail Luis about our current situation," sighed Rose.

"Perhaps the *padre* or the *medico* know of this girl?"

"*Si*, maybe, but we must proceed cautiously with them. We do not want them to know about how we handle such matters. I think we have pushed them as far as their consciences will allow. They would rebel at a direct elimination; especially of one of their own."

"I'll see to the boy."

"While you're about it, try to find out where the girl is. The boy must know. He may also know something about the money."

"If he knows, he'll tell me," Vicente said.

Chapter 5

THE 747 BEGAN ITS FINAL DESCENT into Jan Smuts airport. From the small oblong window I saw low rolling hills, red earth, and rock outcroppings unlike anything in Illinois. Despite my fatigue and discomfort of being cramped in the ridiculously small seat, I was excited to see my friend Robbie.

I'd first met Robbie Forrester when we were introduced at a fund-raising charity function in Chicago. He was attending postgraduate studies for the ministry. He came from a well-to-do family in Rhodesia (he didn't like the new name and regime of Zimbabwe) and had started a first class restaurant and hotel complex in Muldersdrift, outside of Johannesburg. (now renamed Gautang).

We'd hit it off immediately, due to the fact that we both enjoyed anti-establishment humor. Our backgrounds and even our statures couldn't have been more different. Robbie, short and stout, I, tall and rangy. He had a thick beard and bushy eyebrows while I was clean-shaven. But we both had strong moral principles and family values. Both of us were conservative. I showed him around the haunts of Chicago. He soaked up information greedily. He was especially keen to see how hotels and convention centers were run. Being politically astute and extremely well-read, he was a worthy foe in our grand arguments.

He was proud of his new enterprise in Muldersdrift and invited me down as his guest several times. I had not been able to take advantage of his offer until now. I sensed his joy of my impending visit. I knew he would be a great help.

I emerged through the large opaque glass doors from the customs area into the main terminal of Jan Smuts airport, jet-lagged to the extreme but eager to see my old friend. I was met with a cacophony of sound jarring my eardrums and glaring lights making me squint. There was kaleidoscope movement everywhere. The public address system blared information in Afrikaans and English. Total sensory overload.

Hundreds of black people waved signs and banners, singing, and shouting. Many clapped while enjoying their own dance routines. A short distance away separated from the crowd by airport security forces, stood a group of white skinhead types. They held Nazi-like banners and chanted in a staccato rhythm. The bright lights from the TV cameras added to the surreal atmosphere of it all.

I forgot my weariness when I located my friend in the crowd.

When I spotted him, Robbie wasn't wearing his usual smile. His eyebrows were knitted and he had a determined glare in his eyes. I was alarmed by his serious look of concern.

"Greetings, Deacon," Robbie shouted. "Helluva show for your welcome to South Africa." We hugged briefly amidst the chaos. "Now, let's get the fuck out of here. Follow me."

We plowed our way through the crowd; Robbie, dragging a wobbly luggage cart, yelled at people, "Come on, you buggers--get out of the way—move!"

"What the hell's going on?" I shouted above the din. The crowd jostled me as I pushed the cart from behind.

Robbie shouted back as best he could, "A war of sorts, my friend. Some bloody tribal dignitary is arriving. One of our president's associates. Then there's the ultra-right wing of the Terre Blanche radicals. There have been threats of bombs and violence."

I didn't feel threatened--just overwhelmed. I stayed focused on Robbie.

We broke clear and made our way outside the terminal. In the passenger embarkation area the hot dry air roiled with car fumes. The warmth seeped into my Chicago winter bones. I felt like stopping and just sitting somewhere on the grass to soak up the sun's rays.

There was a phalanx of South African Police, impeccably uniformed, standing at port arms and looking grim.

Robbie approached one of the SAPs, speaking to him animatedly. The policeman took one look at me, then waved to one of his colleagues. A big, blond, freckled-faced young man bounded forward. After an exchange of a few guttural words in Afrikaans, the young policeman said in English, "Follow me, quickly now." Somehow, I found the accent very pleasing.

With my friend barking directions, the young officer led us to Robbie's champagne-colored Mercedes. The policeman stood tall, carrying his machine pistol at the ready and watching in all directions while we packed my bags into the trunk. As we slid into the car, the young officer banged on the hood and said, "Straight out now, doors locked and no stopping—go!"

Robbie reached down and removed what I guessed was a .38 revolver from an ankle holster and placed it on the seat next to him. Robbie scanned the lanes in the parking area. Once we were through the parking tollbooth and on a freeway, he relaxed and reholstered the pistol.

"Your timing is shit, Deacon," he teased.

"Of course. I planned it that way."

We both smiled.

"Besides the danger of a riot, thieves will take advantage of what's going on inside the airport, to mug passengers and steal their belongings in the carpark. Well, we're out of it now. So how the hell are you?"

"Fine. Thought I'd never get here."

"Do you mean the long flight, or your visit to this country?"

"Both, I guess. Thanks for picking me up—especially under the circumstances." I felt awkward about the drive. "Strange, driving on the wrong side of the road."

"You'll get used to it. We're quite civilized here, rather like the UK, not like you chaps in the colonies. Driving on the right side of the road—indeed!"

We both laughed in relief. I recalled that while together in the US, we loved our great dinners together with all the lively conversations about the differences between the Americans and the English. Robbie had spent much time in the UK as well as the US.

We'd discussed and dissected world politics, movies, women, current events, and even religion. Our religious ties were close-- Robbie was Church of England, and I, Roman Catholic. I had once asked Robbie if it was difficult being a South African and living in England. Robbie answered, "Not when you've graduated from Cambridge and your father is the ambassador to Kenya." Clearly, I had grown up on the wrong side of the tracks.

In recent years Robbie had developed the Carnivore restaurant—very ethnic—specializing in game meats. He had been impressed by the Carnivore in Kenya and had decided to develop his own Carnivore restaurant with full consultation of the Kenyan owners. He added a hotel, conference center, and was continually expanding to develop his place as a five-star country resort outside of Johannesburg.

"You're a sight for sore eyes—literally. Married life treating you well, I think."

"Too well," Robbie said patting his belly. He'd put on twenty pounds since I'd had last seen him and now sported a neatly trimmed black beard with a lot of gray streaks beneath the corners of his lips.

His hair was also speckled with gray. He had a plastic face over which expressions shifted continually.

Once on the freeway, Robbie gave me my first day's itinerary. "First I'll drop you at your rooms in Misty Hills to get settled. It's a nice cottage actually, not far from the pool. Relax. Take a dip. There's a buffet lunch on at poolside. I think you'll like the accommodations. Mind, just a short nap this afternoon or you'll take forever to get on our time schedule. I'll pick you up at half past six and take you to my home for dinner. Very casual. Del is looking forward to meeting you."

Del was Robbie's wife of two years, I remembered. They now had a daughter, Sarah. "Can't wait to meet your family."

"You'll love my lot. They're smashing. To change the subject, how goes your progress to the priesthood?"

"We'll have to have a long talk about that. Right now, I've suspended my studies. I really don't know if I can go back."

"Sounds serious. Yes, we'll talk when your head has caught up with the time difference."

"How's your empire coming along?"

"Fantastic. We just won two prestigious restaurant awards. The spa is nearly finished. I can't wait to take you on a tour. We're about to change the name of the entire complex to 'Recreation Africa.' You can stroll around the grounds and get an idea of the place on your own this afternoon. Tomorrow evening, dinner at the Carnivore--you've never had anything like it. I'd like you to meet some of my executive staff and friends. I even have a lady dinner companion for you. It will even the table seating, according to Del."

I closed my eyes for a moment. They felt scratchy.

Robbie noticed. "Eyes bothering you after your trip? Mine always feel sore after flying. I have just the meds. I'll get some to you after we arrive."

We drove for the better part of an hour with bits of catching-up conversation. Though beat, I was taking in the profusion of Jacaranda trees, colorful flowers, and billboards with products that were totally foreign to me. I saw women colorfully dressed walking with perfectly balanced large bundles on their heads. I couldn't help think of Oz—*"We're not in Kansas anymore."*

I didn't know how much to tell Robbie. It wasn't that I didn't trust him. But I didn't want to put Robbie or his family in any danger. I knew I'd have to be careful. I'd decide that later.

*   *   *   *   *

My cottage at Misty Hills was decorated with total African influence. I slowly took in the creosote poles with their unique, almost astringent odor, supporting a high-peaked thatched roof. Black slate tiles on the floor, artistic prints of animals and colorful, carved masks decorated the white stucco walls. The large, tiled bathroom had all the amenities of a five-star hotel including an indoor and outdoor shower, enclosed in a patio of greenery. Bright blossoms and lush green plants were everywhere. The whole complex was dotted with very tall eucalyptus trees. There were rustic walkways among water features and African statuary. It was impressive yet comfortable and informal. There was an animal skin on my king-sized bed.

As promised, the eye drops were delivered to my cottage by a neatly

uniformed housekeeper. The mini-fridge was filled with drinks and snacks. The long, hot, shower was positively rejuvenating. While nursing a cold Amstel, I sat on the small veranda in my shorts reveling in the sunshine. As I began to doze, I returned to the interior of my cottage. I hit the comfortable bed as I was stretching out directly under the ceiling fan. I soothed my eyes with the drops that had been delivered and just managed to phone the front desk for a wake-up call in two hours. It would be all I would allow myself so I could go to sleep on schedule with the rest of South Africa. Despite my immediate concerns about Thompson's stepson and daughter, fatigue won easily. I dropped off in two minutes.

*   *   *   *   *

Dinner couldn't have been better. Del was an accountant with her own clientele and kept the books for the Misty Hills complex. She was attractive with large expressive eyes and was as chatty as Robbie. It was rather surprising how Robbie was besotted with his daughter, Sarah, since I had known him at a time when he didn't seem too keen on having children. The charming child sat on my lap, giggled and wiggled. I was glad I'd thought to pick up a stuffed bunny for her at Heathrow Airport during my four-hour layover.

There were two unobtrusive black women wearing colorful headscarves in attendance to help with the dinner, the house, and the child.

After a hearty dinner, with impala steaks as the main course with an incredible fruit salad, lively conversation, and lots of laughter, Del went off to put Sarah to bed.

Robbie and I were nursing our lagers and sitting quietly on the huge wraparound stone veranda behind the house, which overlooked the slowly meandering Crocodile River.

"God, it feels wonderful here," I said.

"Good, my son," Robbie answered in his best God-like intonation.

"You've built an extraordinary kingdom. Thanks for setting me up at Misty Hills and for arranging the lecture at Zahl ministries.

"Well, I've got to make sure you can pay your hotel bill."

"I don't know where to start, but I've got some important things to tell you." I lowered my voice several notches. "You may not want to share them with Del."

"She's pretty strong—let me be the judge of that. What is it, ole friend?"

"First tell me about Mike Thompson."

"He loved to dine at the Carnivore and ran up quite a bar tab. Always paid though. Did you know he used a small runway at the nearby mission to ferry in business people here to the hotel and conference center?   I even went flying with him once up to Windhoek, Namibia to purchase some of the large stone carvings you see around the place. I liked him."

"So did I. Before he was murdered, he wrote to me, as I told you, and asked me to come here to do a favor for him."

"A favor?" Robbie focused intently.

"Do you know a young woman named Kalina Sangweeni? She works at a mission."

"My boy, there are not many people in this whole area I do not know. She lives and works at the Hands of Hope Mission. It's headed up by Dr. Ngubane and Father Godwin. They've built up a clinic, church, and school. Quite an enterprise. She has even worked here part-time when we get overwhelmed. She catches on quickly to everything. We'd like to have her fulltime. Why are you interested in her?"

"I'll fill you in on the details later. For now, know this, she and her half-brother Jaylin are in grave danger according to Mike. He begged me to get them out of the country. I need to spend some time with her as soon as possible, somehow. I've got to get her to trust me. Then I've got to tell her about her Dad."

"Her Dad? Are you saying Thompson was her father?"

"Yes."

Robbie's eyebrows rose quickly. "They were very clever to keep that a secret."

"Who was so clever?" I asked.

Thompson and Alisha, Kalina's mother. She was black, you know."

"They were so clever, in fact, that Kalina doesn't even know."

"Well, now." Robbie raised his eyebrows thoughtfully.

"How can I see her tomorrow?"

"That shouldn't be hard. I'll call the mission right now and ask Father Godwin." Robbie picked up his beer, went off and came back a few minutes later. "I had a word with the priest. He'd like to meet you, but unfortunately Kalina is off traveling with Dr. Ngubane somewhere in Swaziland. She'll be back the day after tomorrow."

"Shit. Look, I thought I could use an assistant to help me at my seminar to register attendees, make arrangements and act as an interpreter if necessary. Could you help me arrange for her to work for me while I'm here? That would give us the time together I need."

"Well, I'll certainly try. Her 'uncles' will have the final say."

"I know of them from the letter I received from Thompson. But I'd like to know more."

"Dr. Ngubane is Zulu and a brilliant Harley Street physician. Father Godwin, a Brit, runs the mission and school. They're always traveling about doing fundraising and expanding their services. The doctor also has a leper colony in the Chimanimani Mountains of Zimbabwe, and Kalina accompanies him there on occasion. Johannes Marais is their overseer, mechanic, and chief of maintenance. They're quite a team."

Robbie sighed and continued, "You could hardly do better than have an assistant like Kalina. She speaks English, Afrikaans,

Zulu, and Xosa. Probably bits of a few more of the tribal languages. Many blacks here have a gift for languages. But of course she's not black. She's 'colored.'"

"Colored?"

"With Thompson as her father, she's of mixed race, what we call 'colored.' You didn't know? They've always had their own representatives in our Parliament, they vote, and live in their own areas, away from the black townships *and* the white neighborhoods."

"What a system. So her mother…."

"Her mother was Alisha. Xosa. Beautiful, I've heard. Her marriage to Thompson--strictly illegal. She also worked at the mission. I never met her. I think she's dead."

I was learning a lot fast.

"Besides working for you, what else? Are you going to tell Kalina about her father?"

"Yes. I need to keep some of this to myself at the moment. I'll let you in on everything as soon as I can."

Robbie leaned forward, his eyes intense. "When you can, please."

I felt gratified to have Robbie's complete trust. After a long pause, I said, "And, by the way, it's been on my mind, who's the feminine companion you've fixed me up with at dinner tomorrow night?"

"You'll love her. She's stunning. Her name is Ginger Rose."

Chapter 6

THE AMBER EYES WITH OBSIDIAN CENTERS fixed on the man. The broad spotted head was low to the ground—ears down and back. The massive shoulders rose in relief like twin peaks behind the long muscled neck; the haunches raised and twitching.

One second the royal cheetah was crouched twenty-five yards away. In an eye-blink the claws of the right foreleg raked the thick chain link fence horizontally, making a grating metallic sound.

Vicente nearly flew backwards in shock. He stumbled falling hard on his rump.

Two children started crying. One boy screamed in panic, and repeatedly yanked down on his mother's dress, exposing her pink brassiere.

Vicente had been standing too close to the fence and the cheetah had charged. If not for the protective thick chain link, he would have been instantly disemboweled. The worst of it was that he had done the very thing he didn't want to do. He had called attention to himself.

The father of the panicked boy shuffled over to Vicente. He stood with a menacing look, and raised his voice in a thick Afrikaner accent. "You shouldt know better. Can't you read de signs dere? It says not to go inside the white rocks near de fence. See here." The ruddy faced fat man thrust his jaw forward and said in a lower tone, "What de fuck is de matter wid you!"

Had he known the kind of man he was shouting at, he would have run for his life.

One of the guides rushed over and intervened. "Are you all right, sir?"

Vicente could act the dumb, humble tourist if required. He bit back his anger and turned away mumbling that he was very sorry.

The Afrikaner went back to his brood and clipped the boy on the back of his head for crying, embarrassed to have his son's panic displayed in public.

Vicente sat on a bench in the shade. He had been looking so intently for the lad in the photograph he didn't notice the boundary rocks or the warning signs. Rather than walk through the rest of the cheetah reserve, he decided to wait in one place to see if he could spot the young man.

Hours went by--no luck.

He knew now he'd have to wait a few days before returning to the reserve. He was frustrated by his careless self-exposure and seething from the insult he had endured. The loud-mouthed Boer had made the incident much worse. He'd wait. Perhaps there would be an opportunity to deal with Boer later.

To make himself less obvious, he buried his face in a colorful brochure explaining how the royal cheetah was larger than the plains cheetah, with dark stripes down its back. He read and glanced up occasionally to see if he could spot the boy.

The reserve was primarily an institution to breed the extremely endangered royal cheetahs to the more common buff-colored plains cheetah, and thus preserve the species. The brochure indicated the reserve was also involved in preserving the endangered large hairy hyena and studying the habits of wild African hunting dogs.

*   *   *   *   *

Jaylin loved the animals—especially working with the cheetahs. Several, he had helped to hand rear, would happily allow him to come into their enclosures and stroke them behind the ears. This, of course, was never the case with the captured wild cheetahs or the larger more aggressive royal cheetahs.

The one job Jaylin disliked was his "side project" of collecting wild dog urine. Its smell was so pungent that it nearly flipped his stomach every time. It was also dangerous.

While the dogs were wolfing down their food at the other end of their enclosure, he used a pole with a makeshift hook at one end to pull the flat aluminum pan, which held their urine, to the fence. While holding his breath, he carefully tilted the pan to pour the contents into a small blue bucket he held along the edge of the fence. Then he quickly put a lid on the bucket and pushed the pan back into the enclosure. Having watched the very social wild dogs urinating in the same area, Jaylin managed to place some urine filled dirt into a large flat pan and push it back into the enclosure. It was good enough to entice the dogs to routinely urinate there.

He explained this odd activity to his superiors as an experiment he was conducting as part of his training to be an official game ranger. He told them that his collections were being used to test their ability to ward off certain insects. They believed him and encouraged his scientific investigations.

Jaylin made as much money from his urine collections as he made from his Institute paycheck. In reality, he wasn't quite sure why his uncle Johannes wanted the foul stuff anyway. He had seen his uncle mix it with ground elephant tusk and other chemicals into a paste which hardened like cement. He was told that the urine was added as some sort of a bonding agent.

Just about enough of the stuff was ready to take to his uncle. He relished spending time in his uncle's workshop at the back of the mission grounds. Jaylin – and everyone else who knew Johannes Marais - knew without exaggeration that he was a genius fixer-upper. He always made time to fix the children's toys.

And he was by far the strongest man most people had ever seen.

Jaylin completed his chores then took the sealed blue bucket to an area above the animal enclosures, where he stored it in his locker. At the uppermost portion of the path, used by employees only, he stepped out on a large, overhanging, flat rock to look over the edge. Directly below was the enclosure housing the hairy hyenas.

God, he thought, they were ugly brutes. They had huge teeth and jaws powerful enough to crack any bone. He looked over the entire campgrounds and saw a short swarthy man sitting on a bench and looking around. The man rose and walked to the exit among the other visitors leaving at closing time. A chill ran down Jaylin's back. He didn't know why. It was as if he suddenly felt a cold breeze tingle his skin.

*   *   *   *   *

Vicente stayed in the shadows as far away from everyone as he could. He slowly made his way toward the exit to the carpark. He waited for most of the people to get through the gate so he wouldn't be stuck in a bottleneck.

While waiting, he saw the Afrikaner who had insulted him publicly, drop his family off into an old white van and return to the compound. Strange, Vicente thought. The reason soon became obvious. He was headed for the restroom to make a pit stop before the ride home.

Vicente walked over and peeked into the toilet area. The heavy Afrikaner was at the urinal. No one else was in the toilet.

Vicente crossed the floor quickly and silently in his rubber-soled shoes. He punched the man in the back with powerful right and left blows to the kidneys.

The Afrikaner arched backwards and groaned piteously as he sank to the damp cement floor. The man's face was a picture of agony. He would be painfully pissing blood for some time.

Vicente walked out of the reserve and slid into his car before the Afrikaner's family even realized their patriarch had been gone for a while.

Vicente Luna felt better. He would return soon, find the boy, get information about his sister and the missing money, then eliminate him.

Chapter 7

Echoes reverberated off the towering Gothic pillars. He was surrounded by men wearing dark brown robes with large cowls hiding their faces. Torches provided the only light creating flickering images on the walls.

The Gabrian inquisitor began: "Why do you turn your back on Christ, your God?" A whip cracked and flying rat-like creatures with fangs dripping gore dove at his head from lofty perches.

"I don't reject Jesus! I just wanted the woman!" he cried in shame.

"The woman! For the sake of your lust and carnal desires you reject the Lord your God, who suffered and died for your sins. The same Lord you vowed to serve."

"I'm sorry. I didn't realize...."

Fires blazed behind the human shapes moving around him, making them stand out in silhouette.

"And she betrayed you, like Eve betrayed Adam, eventually murdering the innocent soul within her."

"I'd have done anything to stop her. It was horrible."

"Horrible? You made it possible. You acted like a willing instrument of the devil." Bass drums pounded and the place shook as in a violent earthquake.

"Now tell us everything, as your brothers have confessed before you. Omit nothing if you expect any mercy on your black soul."

"I was a deacon." The drums increased their beat and volume. "I met her working at the local parish church. We went for tea and talked. Then later, after meeting at the Guy Fawkes bonfire, we went to a pub and had a few drinks. We smelled of smoke from the fire and gawked at the fireworks."

"Hear brothers, what insignificant pleasures this vermin was drawn to." Thunderclaps raged on and on.

"One night she invited me to see the furniture store where she worked, long after closing hours. Then with the drink, her perfume, her softness, and her wanting me as a man, I was weak…helpless."

"No one is helpless in the Lord. How did she seek you as a man?"

"She kissed me, touched me, slowly shedding her clothes."

Suddenly Gloria O'Connell appeared there on the stones, then on a bed, and on a series of beds stretching to infinity. She writhed in sexual arousal, her tongue flicking in and out, her full breasts heaving, nipples erect, her pelvis thrusting spasmodically.

A chant began in rhythm with the drums.

"We did it again and again, every chance we had." I knew then I had no vocation, so I left the seminary in Salisbury. We married. I took a job teaching and coaching basketball at a nearby public school. It was all I could get. She hated my meager salary, and the relentless dullness of our lives. She grew tired of me, spent all the money I made, and began to betray me with other men."

"So you're a real Hosea with your own Gomer."

"Yes…no." Suddenly Godwin looked down to see he was naked, and with an erection.

"See, brothers, how his lascivious thoughts still control him." Now the flying creatures laughed at him and pointed with their little talons at his turgid cock.

"So you were shamed and betrayed. Tell us of the murder."

"She fell pregnant and I thought she'd be happy and that she'd change with motherhood. But one night she came home with a man in tow. They reeked of cigarette smoke and whiskey. She laughed at me and pulled him into our bedroom. She said, "We've already done it once tonight, but we'll do it again. It's a celebration. No brats for me. She announced without any distress – I got rid of it.'"

"I was beyond shock. My face felt like cracking apart. I fell to my knees but I couldn't pray. An innocent life I helped create was thrown away like some inconvenient garbage. I descended to a deep dark place inside myself."

The thunder, chanting and drums increased to a deafening crescendo.

"I screamed over the noise. I left her. The seminary wouldn't take me back. On the advice of an old sacristan, I sought out the Gabrians. They took me in and helped me finish my studies for the priesthood."

"Unworthy, unworthy," came the rhythmic chant from all the shadowed figures. They removed their cowls to reveal hideous, puss-oozing, skin lesions and horrible facial disfigurements.

Father Frank Godwin drenched in sweat shuddered awake screaming from his nightmare. He spun out of bed to his knees. He prayed for forgiveness. He prayed in thanksgiving that it was only a dream. His shaking slowly subsided in the pre-dawn's pale light. The dream was far too real, as always.

After celebrating morning Mass and having some coffee and rusks, he went out to his hardened earth basketball court to work off the tension from his past, from his dreams.

*   *   *   *   *

I borrowed Robbie's Mercedes and drove to the Hands of Hope Mission to meet Father Frank Godwin. I was glad it was a short drive because suddenly driving on the left side of the road was unnerving. I kept turning on the windshield wipers when I wanted to use my turn indicators. In addition, my habitual driving habits were backwards. I kept feeling that I was going to get into an accident because of being on the wrong side of the road.

I arrived very early hoping to have a talk with Father Godwin before he started his workday. I pulled into the red dirt carpark. As I approached the nearest building I could hear singing from the women working in the kitchen. They weren't just making music together but blending their voices naturally in three or four-part harmony. The melodies seemed to welcome the new day with positive elegance. Brightly colored birds added to the chorus.

The surrounding countryside was serene, with low-lying areas canopied in a cotton mist. The warmth of the morning wrapped around me like a fuzzy blanket. I began to thaw from the Chicago winter I'd just left.

I found Father Godwin at his makeshift basketball court. A weathered basketball bounced off the rim and shot sideways to me. I caught it in mid-air and couldn't resist taking a shot. I took a few dribbles jumped and arced the ball through the hoop. *Probably more luck than skill.*

"All net—very impressive." Godwin picked up the bouncing ball and passed it back to me as I drove in for a layup.

"Thanks." Without speaking or introducing ourselves we played an energetic one-on-one game. A guy thing.

The priest was good. At six foot six and probably under two hundred pounds, his stick-like shape and long pointed nose made him look taller. His slam-dunk appeared effortless. He had long fingers, huge feet and sported a Marine Corps–type crewcut.

After working up a sweat, Father Godwin beckoned me to the side of the court. He threw me a clean towel as he sat on a crude bench to dry off. We both drank deeply from water bottles he took from a cooler alongside the court.

I spoke up, "Name's Deacon Adelius. Robbie Forrester loaned me his car to come and meet you. I'm staying at Misty Hills."

"I thought it was you. Robbie called to tell me you might be coming along. You caught me at one of my two passions--outside of the mission and my work, of course."

"And the other one?"

"Jazz. Mostly of the older variety."

"Well, officially then," I extended my hand, "I'm pleased to meet you, Father Godwin."

"At your service." We shook hands. "You're pretty good with the round ball, college?"

"No, high school. Then a lot of intramural ball in the Army."

The priest rose in stages and arched his back. "Let's go into the house. I'll show you around and later I'll try to get you to empty your pockets for the mission--fair warning."

I laughed. "Nothing new. The church has been pulling at my pockets for years."

"What a blessing that you've been given so many chances to help do God's work."

I smiled. I liked this priest.

As I sat and waited on the stone porch of the large stucco house with the shiny tin roof, the priest went in and came out again wearing fresh shorts, a black Nike T shirt, and sandals. He carried a tray with a large pitcher of juice and glasses with ice.

"My own concoction. I love the fruit juices here in South Africa. Do try one of my favorite drinks--passion fruit juice and sparkling mineral water. Very refreshing."

I gulped down the beverage and smacked my lips in appreciation. "Thanks, it's delicious. Father, I'd love a tour around the mission, but first I'd like to tell you something. Can I do it under the seal of the confessional?"

"Not unless you're confessing your sins," he smiled. "So, unless it's a crime you're *planning* to commit, go ahead and tell me your tale; I'm pretty good at keeping things to myself."

I told him about my friendship with Thompson and his commitment to care for Kalina. I explained about the letter and my mission to help her and her half-brother get out of the country. "I'd like to hire her as my assistant for a short while so I can get to know her better." I left out the part of Thompson's buried stash.

Father Godwin, like a lot of priests, was a good listener. When I finished, he stood up. "Walk with me and we'll talk. First of all, I know Thompson and Alisha were married. I married them myself. Strictly illegal of course, mixing the races, but when things change and the lingering Apartheid finally dies—as it soon must-- such marriages will be sanctioned by the state. Only the couple themselves, Dr. Ngubane, Johannes Marais and I know of this."

I said, "The four 'uncles,' I've heard about."

"Quite so."

"Now I hope to be added to the list," I said. "I told Robbie Forrester. He'll keep it to himself."

"I'm sure he will. He's a good man. Let me tell you of Alisha Sangweeni, Jaylin and Kalina's mother. We are talking about a 'saint'—truly an angel of God." Godwin sat on a stump in the shade of a large acacia tree, looked skyward and sighed. He nodded reflectively as he weighed his words.

"Alisha joined Dr. Ngubane and me shortly after we opened the mission. Our initial projects were the chapel and the clinic. Did Robbie tell you he sold us this land, with the abandoned air strip, for next to nothing?"

"No, he didn't." I wasn't surprised.

"Of course, there were a few small strings attached."

Again, I wasn't surprised. Robbie was nothing if not a good negotiator.

"One was that we had to maintain the runway for small planes. This suited us fine, because we used it ourselves, especially after Thompson joined us. The other was that he could send any of his workers here for free emergency treatment for minor burns or other injuries. The arrangement has worked out well for us all."

He finished his drink. "Anyway, Alisha joined us as a trained midwife, but soon became indispensable in many areas. She helped to recruit the best staff, kept our books—I'm hopeless at that—and in her quiet way, she got everyone to work together as a team.

"We had a driver and mechanic named Bashi. He was a good-looking young man with a quick smile who loved to sing and dance.

"Alisha fell for him, and they eventually married. They lived in a cottage right here on the grounds. It was only after they'd married that Alisha realized he had a drinking problem. A mean streak emerged when he was drunk. They had a few fights, but also happy times, and Alisha was able to temper most of his drinking."

I listened to his narrative carefully.

"While he was away and detained by a storm, Alisha gave birth to their first child, a boy, named Jaylin. Unfortunately, he was born with a partial cleft of the upper lip, webbed fingers, and a 'lazy eye,' with a drooping eyelid. Dr. Ngubane assured us all that these were relatively minor deformities and could be remedied as the child grew older. He would see to it that the boy got the best of care, from specialists if necessary."

"However, when Bashi returned and saw his son, he was repulsed. Bashi's superstitions and fears were exacerbated when he consulted a witch doctor, who came to see the boy and proclaimed the baby was born of the devil, and had the 'evil-eye.' He told Bashi the boy was evil and to be feared."

"As if to reinforce these fears, every time Bashi picked up his son, the baby screamed and squirmed to get free. Bashi felt that he'd lost face by having a deformed child. Such a thing had never happened in his family before. He blamed his wife for bearing an 'evil son.'"

Godwin paused and looked disgusted, "Eventually he took their few valuables, beat Alisha one last time, stole one of our trucks, and disappeared into the night."

I shook my head. I'd heard many tragic stories. This one moved me more than usual.

Godwin stood and stretched. "We all thought he'd gone for good. Alisha eventually divorced him for abandonment. She continued to work here. Dr. Ngubane saw to it that the boy's lip was closed and the eye and fingers made normal.

"During this time, Johannes Marais and Mike Thompson joined us. Jaylin grew up thinking of the four of us as his 'Uncles.' He was a loving boy, and we all in our own way, taught him and encouraged him. He does well at school, and has a great outside jump shot, I'm proud to say. He's quite a young man now, studying to be a government game ranger."

I could feel the support the boy must have had from the "uncles." I looked forward to meeting him.

"Anyway, Thompson and Alisha fell in love. When she fell pregnant, they came to me and begged to be married. Never have I seen a more loving couple. I said no, at first, knowing that their interracial marriage was illegal and would bring trouble. They would be ostracized. But I finally agreed."

Godwin paused seeming to look around for words to explain his story. "They had to be careful, to keep their union a secret. So to keep up appearances they maintained separate living quarters on the compound. Alisha continued to be our angel, especially with the new mothers and their babies."

"Kalina was born to the delight of everyone. You should've seen Thompson." Godwin gave an exaggerated eye-roll. "Because he couldn't openly acknowledge fatherhood, he saved up his feelings until he was with one of us 'uncles'. Then he would unload his happiness, and tell us of every little thing Kalina did. She was a beautiful child. She's a wonderful blend of black and white, as if someone had put as much cream as coffee in their cup. She is tall like her father and has her mother's regal bearing.

"While Alisha was still nursing Kalina, Bashi returned. He'd been drinking as usual. When he walked in and saw his wife nursing a mixed race baby, he went crazy and was going to kill them both. He cut up Alisha badly, and raped her. In his fury he cut baby Kalina from the corner of her left eye to her earlobe.

"We'd heard Alisha's screams and several of us came running. Thompson was off flying somewhere at the time. Johannes Marais arrived first, followed by the doctor Ngubane and myself."

Godwin paused looking out into the distance. "We threw Bashi out and took care of Alisha and her daughter."

I picked up on the dark cloud that came over the priest's face. Something wasn't right. I sensed Godwin was lying, or at least leaving something out. As if to punctuate my suspicions an angry birdcall screamed across the valley.

"Bashi was never heard of again. When Thompson returned, he nearly went insane with grief, anger, and guilt. Afterwards, he was unbelievable with Alisha. He did everything he could to help Alisha to recover. He got rid of all the mirrors in her house and slowly helped Alisha to see her beauty through his eyes."

I nodded, feeling a shiver of pride for my friend's behavior.

The priest dropped his voice. "But it gets worse. During her long convalescence, Alisha seemed to sense something was wrong with her. She requested some further testing be done, and discovered that Bashi had given her AIDS. Eventually, she died of the disease.

"Thompson stood by her to the end, and vowed to take care of her children and he did with all the skill and love he had. He told them countless stories of the wonders of their mother and all she had accomplished at the mission."

A fragrant breeze swirled around us. I was grateful to hear the story. It helped me understand Kalina. But the words from Thompson's letter haunted me. What was the "unholy scheme?" Why were the children in danger? Was it Bashi or someone else? Was there something Father Godwin wasn't aware of?

Changing the subject, Godwin asked, "And do you have a family?"

I told my own story as succinctly as I could. No family. The military, schooling, and finally the seminary. I told him of the horrors of priest pedophiles and why I left my studies after receiving the Deaconate. I left out my recent encounters with the evil and political corruption of men in Chicago politics, and of course, my falling in love with Ann. Despite all of this, I continued my work as a Gabrian.

I was pleased that the Gabrians maintained their secrecy in South Africa and were active in rooting out sexual predators from the church.

Godwin nodded and put his big hand on my shoulder. "God be with you. You might not believe it, but I do know how you feel. I've had my doubts and still do."

He frowned and began walking in small circles, kicking at the ground obviously contemplating something serious. "If you're willing, an important Gabrian mission is brewing in Capetown." He looked at me sideways, his facial muscles taut, the corners of his lips drawn down. His voice was barely a whisper. "We could use another Gabrian warrior. It will be dangerous."

"I'll help any way I can."

He nodded in thanks and switched topics abruptly. Godwin told me that he would check with the other 'uncles' to see if they would allow Kalina to travel with me as my assistant. But they would have to meet me first. "I'm confident I can convince them to allow Kalina to assist you while you present your training seminars at the local seminaries."

I had Bishop Laine to thank for providing cover for being in South Africa. "Certainly. How about tomorrow? You'll be my guests for lunch at the Carnivore restaurant?"

"Thank you. Dr. Ngubane will be back by then, and we'll all join you for lunch, one o'clock all right?"

"Great."

Father Godwin said, "It's time for Kalina to know the truth about her father. We'll entrust you with this task since it seems Thompson wanted it that way."

*   *   *   *   *

We continued the tour of the clinic, the school and the airfield. The buildings had peaked tin roofs, and the insides were immaculate, modern, and extremely well equipped. From the stainless steel kitchen to the laundry to the lab, everything was top of the line—very expensive, well organized, and spotless. At the back of the compound, I asked about the fenced-in buildings.

"Those are for the lepers Dr. Ngubane brings down from his clinic in the mountains of Zimbabwe. They live separately from the rest of the people here. Behind those buildings are the workshops where Johannes Marais performs his magic."

"One more thing, Father. Have you ever heard of anyone named Rosenmoon or Rosenbloom?"

"No, I can't say that I have."

Chapter 8

FROM MY VANTAGE POINT on the upper deck entrance of the Carnivore restaurant, I could see Robbie and Del. Seated next to them, a striking woman with red hair was smiling broadly. She had a vacant seat next to her. I surmised it belonged to me.

As I descended the steps, I took in the great room with its huge roasting pit on one side, its wooden trestle tables and its chairs upholstered in a zebra-skin pattern. Dark slate stone covered the floor. The walls were dotted with multicolored carved masks, backlit for effect. The Simba Lounge bordered one side. A large outdoor patio wrapped around the entire dining area. The restaurant looked busy.

Del rose as I approached and led me to my seat. "Deacon Adelius, I want you to meet Ginger Rose. She works for the Johannesburg *Sun*. Ginger, this is Deacon, our good friend from

America. Ginger has been good enough to do feature articles on the Carnivore and Misty Hills."

Ginger didn't rise. She extended a hand with at least three or four glittering rings and said in English with a faint Latin accent, "How do you do, Deacon. Is 'Deacon' your given name or your title, may I ask?"

"It's both actually," I answered automatically as I took in Rose's dark eyes and flaming mane. Her lips were covered in a high gloss reddish-orange lipstick. The emerald green V-necked blouse she wore showed just enough cleavage to reveal freckles between her breasts.

"Oh, do I have to be careful of what I say, to a man of the cloth?" She smiled coyly.

"I'm usually pretty tight-lipped about what people reveal to me. Besides, I'm not on official duty right now."

"Nice to meet you. Robbie has told me about you and your times together in the States, but you must tell me more."

"Maybe I'm the one who has to be careful of what I say. It could wind up in the morning paper."

"Not to worry. Like you, I'm not on official duty this evening."

I liked her easy smile at our repartee. "What department are you in?" I asked.

"Here in South Africa, many of us cross department lines. I enjoy freelance. I write feature articles, editorials, crime reports, and anything else the chief will pay me for."

Robbie recommended me to order a "Dawa," the specialty drink of the house; vodka and lime with a thick stir-stick coated with honey at one end. I ordered a second for Ginger Rose. Waiters with boater hats, big smiles, and red-white-and-blue striped aprons, came around with four-foot skewers of meats. They carried the ordinary meats like sausage, chicken, and Kariba lamb, as well as specialty game meats like waterbuck, ostrich, hippopotamus, and gazelle. They held their skewers vertically and sliced the meat on to the individual plates. The waiters kept coming until you placed your little toy flag down on the table to show you had surrendered your appetite.

The dinner conversation ranged from politics to gender differences to movies and the similarities of South Africa to the United States. I enjoyed the lively, animated discussion. I could have had an even better time with my dinner companion if I could have stopped thinking of my promise to get Thompson's kids out of the country.

Rose, an experienced interviewer, artfully pulled a good deal of information out of me. I let it go on anyway. When she asked if I knew anyone else in South Africa and I mentioned Mike Thompson, she went silent for a few moments. I felt a definite change in the atmosphere. She looked down and folded her arms.

"Did you know him?" I asked.

"Yes, slightly. We met when I was doing a local story. He was a bush pilot, yes?"

"He was that, and a good friend." I didn't want to go into any details, so I felt it best to drop this subject.

As we stood to leave and goodbyes were exchanged, Ginger leaned closer to me and asked, "Buy a girl a drink? One of those special Dawas for the road?"

I couldn't refuse. I didn't want to refuse. We adjourned to the Simba bar and found a small table on the patio. The evening was rapidly bringing on a refreshing coolness in the air. Rose pulled a soft black sweater over her shoulders.

I asked, "Would you rather sit inside?"

"No, thanks, but you're a dear for noticing. I'd rather be out in the night air."

Robbie winked at me as he waved goodbye.

As we chatted, Rose crossed her legs, absentmindedly giving a small tug on her short black skirt. She leaned forward and said, "Robbie told me that among all your talents, you also paint."

"I'm going to have to speak to Robbie about revealing my secrets. Yes, I dabble when I have time."

"What do you paint?" She began swinging her crossed leg and twirling her swizzle stick between her fingers.

"A variety of subjects. My own brand of Surrealism, I guess."

"A Dali devotee? I happen to like Dali myself. Do you have the strong erotic streak in your work that he has?" She licked a few drops of honey off the tip of her swizzle stick.

"Perhaps, down deep somewhere."

"I'll have to ask you more about that sometime. But I'm a working girl and I have to leave soon." Finishing her drink, she tilted her head. "I wonder, would I be totally out of line if I asked you for a favor?"

"Go ahead, I can always refuse."

"Tomorrow night, I'm to speak at the Directors' Club. It's made up of the MD's of major corporations in and around Joburg--I still can't get used to 'Gautang'."

"MD's?" I inquired.

"Ah, 'Managing Directors' as they're called here, not-doctors. After standing in a receiving line, I need an escort to walk me in, believe it or not, in a short procession. Would you be my escort? You'd be saving me from having to listen to boring, rich, old businessmen all evening."

"Tomorrow evening?"

"Yes. Are you free?"

"Yes, I am," I said without thinking. My reason for being in South Africa did not, I reminded myself, include dinners with attractive women. Still, I reasoned, I might learn something more about Thompson. And there was nothing I could do until I met Kalina anyway.

"Great," she said with a warm smile. "I'll pick you up here, at about six."

"Sure." I felt a bit uneasy, but I couldn't renege now.

As we strolled to the carpark, I asked, "I hope you don't mind my asking, but I couldn't help notice your accent. Where is it from?'

"From all over. My father was a diplomat. We spent time in Europe, South America and South Africa." As she answered, I noticed that her shoulders and neck tensed, and she averted her eyes. Was it her past that made her uneasy or something else?

As we reached her silver Jaguar, she gave me her keys to unlock the door. When I bent down to open the door, she looked up into the moonlight, rose up on her toes and kissed me. It was a soft kiss, full of promise.

"Thanks for a lovely evening, and please thank Robbie for inviting me. See you tomorrow."

"Should I meet you down at the front gate?"

"That'll be fine. Goodnight." As she slid into the leather seat, her skirt slid up to reveal more than half of her thigh in the door's courtesy light. She smiled when she saw me looking.

"Goodnight," I said. Though I felt played, I didn't mind. *When in Africa*, I told myself.

Chapter 9

BORDER CROSSINGS BETWEEN ZIMBABWE AND SOUTH AFRICA were always a bit unnerving when Dr. Ngubane transported his contraband. Being well known to the soldiers and the border patrol insured his safety. As the official GMO, (Government Medical Officer), he often treated their illnesses and injuries. That, and the fact that he carried patients with Hansen's disease in the back of his truck assured him a swift border passage. The soldiers were instructed to inspect his vehicle, but they avoided it. Very bad *muti*—lepers. Few were brave enough even to look inside from a distance...until today.

As the young Afrikaner lieutenant named Van Haughton met him on the front steps of the border station house, several things happened at once. First, there was a loud commotion as the border guards yanked two men out of their car and dragged them with lots of shouting and hand waving into the police station. The people in the waiting column of vehicles watched with a mixture of fear, fascination, and fatalism.

Van Haughton spoke above the din nervously. "Good evening, doctor. We've got a situation here only you can help us with." There was an odd look in his eye.

"I'll do what I can."

Just then another officer came out the station door and collided with the soldiers and detainees trying to get inside. Van Haughton introduced him quickly to Ngubane as Major Trechert, who was on a border inspection tour.

"Good to meet you doctor," Major Trechert said, "I've heard good things about you helping our men as you come across the border." He didn't offer to shake hands with the black physician.

"Thank you." The doctor nodded. "I'm happy to offer assistance."

The major touched his swagger stick to the peak of his cap. "You two carry on. I'll have a look in the truck."

Ngubane's heart sank into the pit of his stomach and his mouth went dry. Would the major actually go into the back of the truck? Would he search diligently enough to find the packets?

Van Haughton kept interrupting his thoughts. "When you came through here a few days ago, you gave one of my top sergeants some medication, yes?"

"Yes, I did....a sample. It was a private matter, but I tried to help." Ngubane stretched his neck trying to see what the major was doing around his truck.

"We're all grateful for your medical attention."

"What's the matter? I must be on my way."

"The sergeant you gave the medicine to is in our little infirmary room. Perhaps you could take a quick look at him." The lieutenant had a wry smile and jerked his head toward the interior rooms of the station.

"What? Yes of course." He felt he had no choice but to follow the young officer. He would just have to wait it out. They walked single file down the dingy corridor to one of the back rooms.

The sergeant lay under a sheet in great pain.

"So Sergeant Mugalu, what seems to be the problem?" Ngubane already knew. He said to his young military escort, "Please leave us alone now."

Once the door had been shut, Ngubane's face turned angry. "So you didn't listen to me did you?"

The man had tears in his eyes. "No, doctor, I didn't. I am very very sorry, doctor."

"I'll bet you are." Ngubane removed the sheet. It was a terrible case of priapism. The persistent and painful erection was without any pleasurable sensation.

"And are you proud of yourself now? You really didn't need help to stiffen your member, did you?"

"No, I didn't. I lied for sure. But I wanted to service three women in one night, so I thought I could use some of your medicine to help."

"Three, you randy goat!" To insure maximum effectiveness, Dr. Ngubane combined modern medicine with ancient, psychologically soothing primitive remedies.

Along with the Viagra tablets and careful instructions as to the dosage, Ngubane had also sprinkled some chicken blood on the man's penis and mumbled a few incantations to convince the man that this was indeed strong medicine.

"How many tablets?"

"All of dem, boss. I made love to all three women and dey did all dey could, but it wouldn't go down. And boss, I know it sounds crazy, but everything I see looks blue."

"Now see what you've done to yourself. How would you like to go about like this for many years?" The blue visual haze was one of the odd side effects of taking too much of the drug.

"Oh, no!" The man pleaded.

It was important to scare him. "I have a good mind to leave you like this."

"No, no, please, doctor!"

"This is powerful *muti*, I don't know if I can help. I'll try, but it's going to hurt." While he slipped on his white powdered gloves, he bent down until he was six inches from the man's face. "Never disobey me again." To make his point, Ngubane flicked his finger against the swollen penis.

The sergeant inhaled sharply and his stomach muscles tightened.

"Now I will try to fix you, but you must bring a calf or pig—a good one—to my clinic in the Chimanimani Mountains and you must not lay with a woman for one month. You must wash-down there-two times a day with strong soap also for one month."

The doctor began his own invented tribal chanting as he prepared the needle and syringe. His mind kept flitting back to the major and his truck, but he forced himself to concentrate on the patient before him. "I expect to be let through the border without delay as I pass through in the future, yes?"

"Oh yes, yes, boss, *nyabonga*, no delays at all, and I'll wash and get good meat to your hospital."

The doctor took a small clean towel and rolled it up. "You will have to be strong now. Take this and hold it between your teeth. Pray to your gods for strength. It will hurt, but won't take long. And one important thing....*don't move!*"

"*Yabo baba.*"

Ngubane inserted the needle into the sergeant's penis from the tip downwards and drew out blood. He did this three times to relieve the pressure. To his credit, Sgt. Mugalu stoically endured the painful ordeal. Relief was immediate. He swabbed the area and applied a light gauze dressing. "You will have soreness down there for three days. You are a brave soldier."

The man could only nod and smile gratefully as tears rolled down his cheeks. The doctor smiled and wiped the tears away.

As he left, Ngubane bathed the infected eye of another soldier and left some sleeping pills requested by the lieutenant.

When Ngubane emerged from the building, the queue to get through the border had lengthened. The rising exhaust fumes sickened him.

Ngubane was devastated to see the short fat major coming out of his truck. No one had ever entered with the lepers there. Major Trechert clutched a packet wrapped in brown paper.

The major marched to the station red-faced and puffing from his exertions. He had small sunken eyes and a shiny bald head. He walked like a penguin, his uniform fitting him like the skin of a sausage.

"Dat's your truck, yah?"

"Yes, it'mine."

"Den come wid me."

Ngubane followed the major to a small sparse office. He trembled a little, his mind racing.

"Leave dis office now!" the major barked to a few black officers. "And close the door." He sat down heavily and lit a cigarette.

Exhaling a cloud of bluish smoke, he said, "So, let us not waste any time, yah? I went into your truck dere and look what I found. You been passing through here many times carrying this stuff, eh?" He held the wrapped packet as if weighing it. "The lepers were a good idea, but I knew the lepers in your truck were 'dry lepers' and not contagious. In any case it would take long exposure to catch the disease, correct?"

Ngubane risked a bluff. "I'm the regional medical officer here. Of course I sometimes transport medications."

"Medications! Oh, come now, let us not play the games." The major's congenial manner vanished. "A dozen packets of uncut heroin? My God, what do you take me for an idiot? I know it when I see it, smell it and taste it. We're not all fools, you know. We're trained in such things. Oh, it's jail for you, my medical friend. Have you ever been inside the South African prisons at Rustenburg or Stellenbosch? Not very pleasant, I can tell you." There was a long pause. His pleasant manner returned. "Of course, maybe we can work something out?"

Ngubane recognized the unmistakable sound of impending negotiations.

The major spoke slowly in a hushed staccato voice. "So what might it be worth, say, on a periodic basis, if I didn't notice your contraband?"

Ngubane thought it best to be direct. "I can start off with one hundred thousand Rands now. I'll have to speak with some other people to determine future payments, but I'm sure they'll cooperate."

The major's pupils dilated with greed. "You have dis money wid you?"

"Oh, yes, but it's well hidden. May I be permitted to open my medical kit?"

"Yah, go ahead." The major put his hands together as if in a prayer of thanksgiving, and couldn't suppress a smile.

Ngubane had only a few moments to act. He knew the major would have to go. He'd helped people pass on before—a few he helped to start their journey. He would help the major.

He opened his medical bag on the empty desk and started emptying its contents.

"What's all dis?"

"Please be patient. I have to get to the compartment at the bottom of the bag."

"Yah, of course. I see."

The doctor took a long time setting out bottles and other paraphernalia all over the desk.

The major's impatience drove him to stand and look over the doctor's shoulder.

When Ngubane had what he needed, he whispered, "Why don't you lock the door."

"Yah, good idea."

Ngubane poured chloroform on a 4 X 4 gauze pad. Major Trechert stood at the door, his back to Ngubane. Before the major could turn around, the doctor reached from behind and pressed the gauze pad over his mouth and nose.

The major arched backwards violently, nearly hitting Ngubane in the face sending both men to the floor. But as the major relaxed Ngubane turned him on his stomach and knelt on his back, keeping the gauze over his face.

Just a few seconds more, Ngubane thought.

The major's breathing gradually slowed.

Ngubane inhaled deeply. Methodically he went back to the desk, put the chloroform away, placed the packet of heroin in the bottom of his bag, and piled in the rest of his supplies. No hidden compartment existed and no money.

Now, for something clean and simple. He removed a large bore needle, sterilized it with an alcohol swab and filled it with epinephrine. Turning the major over, he opened the shirt and eased the needle through the chest wall into the heart. He pushed the plunger down until the syringe was empty, then gave the heart a second dose. The body flailed a couple of times and then went still.

No one would question his report. His reputation as Dr. Gideon Ngubane, government medical examiner, philanthropist, and one of the most respected men in the region insured his credibility. He relaxed, took a deep breath and began the great charade. He shouted for Lieutenant Van Haughton.

The lieutenant charged into the room. "What's going on here?"

"The major had a heart attack. I noticed he was overweight, no doubt out-of-shape, smoked heavily, and probably had significant stress in his life. There were probably other factors as well. Heart failure was inevitable." The doctor stood and spoke in a low voice seeming to talk to himself. "I did everything I could when the arrhythmia started and he collapsed. When I couldn't get a pulse, I injected the heart with epinephrine to get it going. But to no avail."

The paperwork avalanche began. Calls were made to higher authority. Condolences all around.

The precious white powder was safe again. He would get the heroin to Ginger Rose for payment, and operation *"Feliz Colmillo,"* (Happy Tusk) would continue unscathed.

An extraordinary amount of money came in from this venture. It allowed him to keep his two commitments in life: to help his people, and to live the luxuriant lifestyle he had coveted while growing up and observing his mother at work.

She had an elegance about her, and with a cultured English accent and knowledge of Afrikaans, Zulu and Xosa. She secured receptionist positions at several upscale South African hotels and resorts. Little Gideon Ngubane, while there observed the lifestyle of the wealthy American and European guests. He vowed someday he would live this way.

His father, an exceptionally bright financial officer in a small bank passed on his love of books and learning to his son. He instilled in Gideon a sense of ambition—even destiny. Blessed with an incredible memory, Young Gideon eventually entered medical school at UK's Cambridge University. Studies came easily and he graduated with honors.

He cared deeply for his people, patients and the impoverished blacks in surrounding villages. Even with his extensive medical training, he realized he could have only a limited impact. With money—big money—he could have a proper clinic and an expanded staff to care for the physical, emotional and spiritual needs of many.

This was the lofty purpose of the Hands of Hope Mission. He and Father Godwin had begun a great, shared vision. They flew around the country on fundraising tours. But it was not enough. Modern equipment, supplies and pharmaceuticals were outrageously expensive.

Ngubane learned of the lucrative underground ivory trade.

Elephant tusks filled warehouses all over South Africa and fetched a high price on the black market. Many custodians and police officials could be bribed easily to part with some of the ivory. With typical sloppy bureaucratic recordkeeping, no one would notice some missing tusks. No one would care.

Father Godwin also appreciated the needs of the people and saw the absurdity of the valuable surplus ivory gathering dust in government buildings. Persuaded by Dr. Ngubane, Father Godwin agreed to bend the rules and deal in ivory sales for the good of the people.

Mike Thompson had flown for them, gathering and delivering tusks. Whenever he'd collected a full cargo, he transported it by air to a flat deserted beach in Namibia, north of Cape Cross on the Skeleton Coast. Money exchanged hands in desolate areas. From there boats transported the illegal cargo to waiting ships and on to world markets.

This scheme worked well, but Ngubane lusted for bigger money. Then came the proposition by the red-haired Peruvian woman, named Ginger Rose, whom he met at a fundraiser in the toney Santon Hills suburb of Johannesburg. Profits would skyrocket. Only one small alteration had to be made to the tusks prior to shipment--a genius stroke--known only to Johannes Marais and himself. It was possible Thompson their pilot had guessed, but he couldn't have been sure. Father Godwin had to be kept in the dark. He never would have agreed to this part of the scheme.

Ngubane would drop off the lepers at the mission and get the powder to Ginger Rose for payment. Her partner, Vicente Luna, then returned the heroin to Johannes Marais at the mission to specially prepare it for shipment.

*   *   *   *   *

When he wasn't transporting lepers and heroin or working at the clinic, Dr. Ngubane spent as much time as his busy schedule allowed at his retreat—the *Eagle's Lair*. With his share of the incredible profits, he had built himself a grand walled estate on his own kopje. It had a gorgeous 360 degree view of the surrounding countryside. He'd installed an elaborate security system complimented by his own trained guards and dogs.

The house was modern/Afro-ethnic. Carvings from Zimbabwe were surrounded by a profusion of exotic flowers. The house was shaped like an "N." The diagonal stroke of the letter was a glass hall that went over a pool with a waterfall to one side and a large patio and braii area on the other. Beautiful stonework in red earth tones surrounded the pool.

He often had fashion models of different races well paid to prance around in the barest of bikinis or even go topless around the pool area. Their function--to add to the eye-catching décor and to mingle with his guests.

Ngubane loved to give small dinner parties, especially with politicians, artists and writers whose sparkling conversations were lively and thought-provoking. He treasured every minute he spent at *Eagle's Lair.*

Chapter 10

"I DON'T LIKE IT. WHO IS DIS AMERICAN? We don't know him," said Johannes Marais as he alighted from the car.

Kalina looked up at him, "Oh uncle, give him a chance. Mr. Forrester is his good friend, and the American was a good friend of Uncle Mike's back in America."

"Yah, my princess, we'll see." His expression immediately softened as Kalina smiled at him.

Father Godwin stretched his tall frame out of the car like an erector set building itself. "Well, at least we'll have a great lunch at the Carnivore. I met this Deacon fellow and I like him. He's well-educated, friendly and a man of God."

"All Americans are friendly," said Dr. Ngubane with liberal sarcasm.

"And," added Fr. Godwin, "He's a good Catholic boy."

Dr. Ngubane looked skeptical. "Like Johannes here, I'm not so sure I like it either." He turned to Kalina, "You'll be traveling alone around the country with a man none of us know. We only want what's best for you. You know that."

"I know and I love you all caring for me." Kalina put on her best soft smile and raised her elbows so Johannes and Dr. Ngubane took one on either side. "Lead on, Father, lead on."

They all smiled. She charmed them like no other. All three helped raise this lovely girl and were finding it hard to let her grow into womanhood. Father Godwin led their little procession across a bridge into the entrance of the Carnivore.

*   *   *   *   *

I sat nervously at a table near the open patio doors, nursing an Amstel, waiting for them to arrive. I'd been jumpy all morning from jetlag, too much coffee, and from the anticipation of the day; lunch with the "uncles," meeting Kalina, and a dinner date with Ginger Rose.

On the one hand, I felt apprehensive for not totally focusing on Kalina and her brother and getting them out of the country. On the other hand, I accepted the fact that I was moving as fast as I possibly could.

This trip excited all my senses. I kept noticing new things. The trees and flowers, the musical language of the Zulus, the odd accents of English and expressions peculiar to South Africa. I learned that "now," meant "very soon," and "now-now," meant immediately. Strange to hear adults say, "now-now."

Of course, Rose was the most exciting surprise in all of this. When I closed my eyes I could just make out her image in the moonlight and feel the gentle touch of her parting kiss. *Not exactly holy deacon thoughts.*

Kalina and Jaylin being in great danger, from Mike's letter kept snapping me back to my mission in South Africa. I had seen plenty of the sick elements of society during my life, but people who were actually targeted for murder jolted me. Especially young, innocent people. God knows there's enough evil in the world.

If her uncles approved, Kalina and I would be off to a speaking engagement in two days to the town of Thondyandou in Venda, a small homeland at the northern tip of South Africa just south of the Zimbabwe border. Robbie had advised me to fly to Pietersburg and rent a car for the rest of the journey, but I was determined to drive. I wanted to get to know Kalina. I also wanted her to get to know and trust me. Finally, I preferred the freedom of movement a road trip offered. On the return trip, I planned to stop at the monument marking the Tropic of Capricorn and dig up what Thompson had left for Kalina. That, would be a moment—real buried treasure, like in the pirate books I enjoyed as a boy.

I had already planned my full-day seminar on the challenges of a committed religious life. My conference attendees consisted of the management team and students from Zahl Ministries, a faith-based multi-national charity organization.

I looked up, and there they were--coming down the entry steps into the Carnivore. They were easy to spot, led by the tall priest in black, looking like some great condor. Behind him was a black man in a black suit, white shirt, and natty electric blue tie. Average in height and build, he had a moustache running down into a well-trimmed, graying goatee. He wore his hair short and glasses with square tortoise-shell frames. His nose was narrow and his nostrils wide set. I correctly identified him to be Dr. Gideon Ngubane.

Next, came an elegant young woman wearing a wheat-colored cotton dress. She had a long neck and hair cropped as short as the doctor's. She was tall, I guessed about five foot nine. For me, she epitomized the natural native beauty of South Africa. Her smile seemed warm and genuine as she observed the waiters and cooks scrambling around the roasting pit. She was lithe with small pointed breasts, long limbs, and large beautiful almond- shaped eyes. Her lips - wide and aubergine. I could just make out the thin scar on the side of her face. I thought it gave her a dramatic look. Walking gracefully, she exhibited no self-consciousness. As she turned behind the hostess's desk, I spotted the last of the entourage.

If Kalina looked striking, Johannes Marais looked startling. He appeared to be a man made up of two different bodies. From the waist down, he looked like most men. His legs were short and bowed. But his upper body compelled your attention. His shoulders were like round melons; his upper arms, massive and bulgy. Large square pectorals pushed against his shirt. He was nearly bald and had a neck of greater circumference than his head. He had small deep-set eyes in a ruddy face. His arms flared out from his sides and were attached to his hands seemingly without the benefit of wrists. His fingers resembled stubby sausages.

I rose as they approached. Fr. Godwin made the introductions. Kalina's handshake was very light and warm. I was almost afraid to shake hands with Johannes Marais.

After they had ordered drinks, Father Godwin brought up my proposal. "I've told Gideon and Johannes of your request. Correct me if I'm wrong. You wish to take Kalina with you to help register attendees at your seminar, provide interpretation if necessary, and be your all-around assistant. Is that about it?"

"Yes, I need someone exactly like Kalina. Robbie Forrester recommended her highly."

Dr. Ngubane said, "I'm sure she can be of great help to you, but understand, she is like a daughter to all three of us and we do not know you."

Johannes Marais, who had been nearly silent, while eating the equivalent of a split-side of beef, added, "And you will be with her overnight, yah?" He didn't smile.

I could readily understand their concern. "Gentlemen, maybe my only hope to convince you is to say that I was an old and loyal friend of Mike Thompson, who I know also felt toward Kalina as you all do. Robbie Forrester is also a dear friend who will vouch for my integrity. I assure you I will take care of her –protect her."

"But you will be alone, yah?" asked Johannes.

"Yes…." I paused, "How about this?" I had to assure Johannes Marais that Kalina would be safe with me. "I'll have Kalina call you every night and check in."

"Dat would be good."

Kalina interrupted, "I'm sorry, I can't go with you to help at your seminars."

They had all assumed that she had wanted to go along. "Why not?" They all chimed in, looking at her.

She looked down into her lap. "I do not have the necessary business attire."

"Oh" I said, "That is easily remedied. I'll ask Del to take you on a shopping trip tomorrow. From what I hear from Robbie, she'd love any chance to hit the mall. Consider it part of your wages."

Kalina looked down and said, *"Nyabonga kukulu*, thank you very much."

Frowning, Dr. Ngubane asked, "And what is the remuneration involved?"

I knew I'd have to be careful with my response. If I offered too much, they'd be even more suspicious. If I offered too little, they might think coming with me wasn't worth the risk. I'd discussed this with Robbie and we settled on a figure. "Six hundred Rands per day plus, of course, all meals and hotel rooms."

The priest and doctor responded together. "Well, that's more than reasonable." They both looked at Johannes.

Johannes Marais said, "Yah, I think it's *lacker*. If she wishes it and if you two agree, I agree also. But I want dat phone call every night."

After their lunch, Robbie came across the dining room to join us. He was delighted that an agreement had been reached. "Shall we adjourn to the patio for some champagne and sorbet?"

While the others were walking away, Johannes held back a bit and turned to me. "Walk wid me over here a minute."

"Okay." We walked to a quiet corner of the restaurant.

"I do not know if I like you yet or not, but know dis, American, if you touch her, make her unhappy, or if she is harmed in any way…." his voice dropped to a whisper, and a big hammy fist came up in front of his face, "I will crush you, hard. Make no mistake about dat. Dere, I said it, and I won't take it back. No more now. Just so you know, yah?" Johannes's eyes widened, expecting a response.

I didn't appreciate the threat, but tried to be empathetic. I nodded and said, "Yes, I understand."

"Okay den, we agree."

As we joined the others on the patio, I observed Kalina smiling at people she knew in the Carnivore, and speaking to them in different languages with ease. Her face lit up when I joined the group on the patio.

"I hope I know what to say to the important people at your seminar."

"I'm sure you'll do just fine. They are no more important than you. I'll give you a little coaching on the drive up."

"Thank you. I'm saving up money to go to a good nursing school. Dr. Ngubane has spoken on my behalf and helps me with my studies and savings."

I noticed that Dr. Ngubane found this amusing. He said, "She already knows more practical nursing than most qualified nursing sisters I've met. It will just be a matter of the bookwork. You will excel, my dear, we all know it. You will help many people."

Fr. Godwin raised his champagne flute, "To nurse Kalina."

We all joined in the toast, "To nurse Kalina." She lowered her eyes, and smiled, perhaps a little self-conscious.

Del was consulted about the shopping excursion and Robbie reported that his wife was gleeful about helping Kalina purchase some appropriate business attire. I asked her later to include undergarments, shoes, casual clothes for travel, a travel bag and any other personal items she needed.

After they left, I said to Robbie, "I think it all went off quite well."

"It seemed so. Did I glimpse Johannes talking to you privately?"

"Yes, you don't miss much around here. He's about as subtle as a charging rhino in a red cape. He threatened me but I just think it's his way to tell me he loves the girl and wants her safe. From the way he looked, I pity the man that ever harmed that girl."

"I'm going to order another Dawa and tell you a bit of history I learned from Mike about *Meneer* Johannes Marais."

*   *   *   *   *

Robbie propped up his feet in a comfortable position, sipped his Dawa and began. "As I understood from Mike, Johannes was orphaned or abandoned—I don't know which—somewhere in Germany. He speaks fluent German, Afrikaans, English, and some Romany dialect. Anyway, he worked in a foundry, then, as a stevedore loading ships. He performed hard heavy work his whole life -- and through his work, and probably his own internal hard wiring, he became very strong, as you have seen." Robbie lit a panatela, blew out a thin smoke stream and continued. "The story goes that one day, a Romanian circus came through his town. Dazzled by the lights and the music and the excitement of it all, he immediately signed on as a roustabout."

"The classic story of a lonely boy running away to join the circus."

"You got it, my friend. Well, one day he got into a brawl with a couple of other workers and one of them threw a sledgehammer at Johannes. He caught it and threw it back. He missed his target and the sledgehammer went right through the wall of one of their wagons. A member of the flying troupe noticed and got an idea. Their catcher, getting older, and taking more and more to drink, had become a liability and danger to the troupe. So they developed Johannes into a catcher for their trapeze act."

I leaned forward with focused attention.

Robbie went on. "While getting fitted for a glittering costume, he met Hannalore who was the head seamstress for the circus. She also took tickets and helped with the cooking. Well, anyway, they were married and had three daughters. Their oldest was Steffi who became a wonderful acrobat, but eventually joined the flyers against her mother's wishes.

"During a performance—I think it was outside Heidelberg—the daughter developed a terrible crush on a boy, and during the performance she was distracted by his presence. She actually tried to wave at him while making a transfer in mid-air. Evidently her lack of concentration caused her to flip sideways instead of straight into her father's arms. The bottom line was they missed each other. Tumbling to the side, she missed the safety net, and impaled herself on a supporting stake."

I shuddered, identifying with the pain of the girl's family. "God, what a horrible tragedy." I had that hollow feeling, experiencing others' pain.

Robbie paused to give some instructions to one of the waiters then continued, "They left the circus, took their savings and their other two daughters, and moved to Namibia, where I think his wife had relatives. Evidently they couldn't recover as a couple from the tragedy. His wife blamed him, and he blamed himself."

Robbie put his feet down and sighed. "Johannes began to get odd jobs while his wife opened a café. She was a good cook and catered to the German population in the town. Johannes was very good at fixing things. They struggled along until he met your buddy

Mike while helping him fix his airplane. Mike told him that they could really use a fixer-upper and over-all handyman at the mission. Johannes seemed interested so Mike flew him down. He met Father Godwin and was hired.

"Thompson used to fly Johannes back to Swakupmund periodically to see his other two daughters whom he loves dearly. As a matter of fact, he seems to love all children like his own. He's forever making toys and fixing bicycles and dolls. He also loves to help with the sick children at the clinic.

"Because of how he looks, some of the women around the hospital worried when he carried young children. I heard Alisha convinced them that the children were as safe as if they were in the hands of God."

Chapter 11

"YOU WHAT?" ROSE HISSED.

"I couldn't find the boy. It's a big place. But I will go back again in a few days."

"And why not tomorrow?"

"Because there was an incident and I was noticed. Next time I will make myself look different. Don't worry, I will find the boy get the information and finish him."

"Very well. We need to know about the girl *and* the money. Have you found a pilot for us yet?"

"No, no one I can trust. We have some time. The next shipment is not quite ready anyway."

"I see. Well, I know you'll do your best." *Always do I have to massage the ego,* she thought. "I have to go out tonight—late. A dinner where I am speaking. I convinced Deacon Adelius to accompany me. I want to find out more about why he's here. Something bothers me about him." Her mind slipped away--*maybe what bothers me is that he is an attractive Americano devil, and it's been a very long time since I've enjoyed the company of a man.* "Anyway I'm going out shopping now."

*   *   *   *   *

I had learned a lot in my short time in South Africa. The culture set my mind racing in all directions. I felt frustrated by not being able to take more immediate action. To keep things straight, I spent a good part of the afternoon putting events and people on paper. Through Father Godwin, I knew of Kalina's mother and half-brother. And thanks to Robbie, I knew about Johannes Marais and his past. Father Godwin had related his own story to me very vividly.

"Rosenmoon" or "Rosenbloom"--still an unknown. I hoped that I might learn something more from Ginger Rose later this evening. I didn't know much about Dr. Ngubane except that he had a leper colony in Zimbabwe and helped establish, run, and fund the Hands of Hope Mission and Clinic with Father Godwin.

On the plus side, I anticipated going off with Kalina in another day and a half to tell her of her real father and pick up what he had left for her. Then somehow I'd convince her to get out of the country. The nursing school opportunities in the States might be persuasive.

100

I filled up about ten pages of a notebook with details of the people I'd met and questions that needed to be answered. Later I went for a swim and a nap. I was still catching up to the time difference. My thoughts frequently downshifted to Ginger Rose. A Latina newspaper reporter in South Africa. Unusual to be sure. *Where the hell am I going with that?*

I shaved again and wore my only suit with a white shirt and gold and black regimental striped tie. It was, after all, kind of like a date. Every time I thought of Ginger Rose I remembered her kiss when we'd last departed. It held promise. I had also garnered some information from Robbie, who likes to share a bit of gossip. Evidently, Rose, after a few drinks, had bragged about having a tattoo that only one man outside of medical doctors had ever seen. It was her naughty little secret. To me it made her all the more desirable. *Nothing like a bit of mystery to stimulate one's imagination.*

*   *   *   *   *

Ginger Rose pulled up in her jag only ten minutes late, which according to Robbie was tantamount to being early in South Africa. I waited, as we had planned, at the stonewall entrance gate to the Misty Hills/Carnivore complex.

"Ride mister?" she asked playfully as she leaned over to greet me.

"Don't mind if I do, ma'am," said I continuing the role-playing she had started. "I don't know where we're going, but I'm at your service."

"Really," she smiled at my unintended double entendre. The evening was balmy with a slight breeze. Ginger drove fast making me uncomfortable as she came dangerously close to people walking along the roadside.

"The event is at a lovely country restaurant nearby called Casa Colina. How do I introduce you?"

"Just my name will suffice."

"No, that won't do, how do I use your title—Deacon, professor, what?"

"So, Deacon Adelius, 'semi-professional escort,' won't do?"

"It certainly will not," she chided humorously. "You have to realize that these people place a high value on titles and protocol."

"Well then, add 'Religious Consultant.'"

"Okay, that should do."

We chatted freely as she drove. Rose was wearing a black dress with spaghetti straps. The bodice was dotted with tiny rhinestones. As she breathed, her breasts swelled slightly over the front of her dress. Her curly red hair was pulled back on one side exposing her ear with its dangling, ornate gold earring.

Once at the restaurant, we stood together in a receiving line and met the guests. I smiled patiently at each meeting. Again, I enjoyed the cultural tradition of this country. We waited with several other "Dignitary couples" in an anteroom until everyone was seated.

Then the entire group stood and each of the dignitaries was introduced as they entered the room and proceeded to the head table. I was introduced as, "Deacon Adelius, lecturer and Religious Consultant to Bishop Tutu." Ginger had added a few bits to enhance my status. I found this all to be quite formal, but sort of old world charming as well.

To my disappointment, I had to sit at one end of a long head table and Ginger Rose sat at the other end. My dinner companion who had been somebody's wife, was an elderly, chatty, woman with a mole alongside her nose. Again my thoughts wandered to Kalina and how I'd tell her of her real father, and get her out of the country.

The food was superb. Fish and lamb were the main course items, served with a superb attention to the details of presentation. As a starter, we had a tasty ginger soup. An abundance of tasty, colorful fruit, fresh salad, and wine from the Cape completed the menu. After dinner we had chocolate almond mousse, coffee, and a selection of liqueurs. I thoroughly enjoyed my meal.

Rose's speech was polished and well received. She had just enough information, humor, and current event stories to be entertaining, while sharing a few important concepts having to do with the freedom and the investigative nature of journalism in South Africa today. I had a tough time concentrating on her message; my mind racing in many directions.

People left quickly afterwards. It was a weeknight.

Rose came over to me and took my arm, "Let's have a nightcap in the lounge. As I recall, they have a wonderful pianist. We haven't had a chance to talk at all tonight."

"Fine with me. Your speech was brilliant."

She shrugged and smiled, "I did all right."

We sat comfortably in a semi-circular booth in a quiet corner of the lounge. She ordered a Pina Colada, I had a beer. God, I thought, she looked ravishing in the candlelight. The music was light classical and subdued.

One drink became three or four.

She asked, "How did you know Mike Thompson?"

"We met in the States and saw each other from time to time."

"You know, I covered his murder for the paper."

"No I didn't know."

"There were details that were purposely withheld from the public. They often do that."

"They?"

"The South African Police. I can tell you one thing, it was determined to have been a professional hit."

"Really? A professional hit," I repeated, although I was already aware of it.

"Yes, and there was something wrong with the body."

"Please define, 'Wrong'?"

"It was mutilated or marked in some way."

"Sick bastards." I thought, that must have been what Robbie's friend, the Colonel had meant.

"That's for sure. But I've seen such things done before as a signal to others."

"Really, what kind of signal?" I needed to get more information.

"I'm not privy to everything in the investigation. Sometimes mutilation could mean: 'betrayer,' or 'thief' or, 'no one messes with my woman,' etc." She changed directions quickly. "Did Thompson have a family?"

"No, no family I ever knew of," I lied. "Not in the States for sure. He never mentioned any family here."

"No family. Strange. Someone at the crime scene saw a photo of him with a woman and two children. From what I could gather, it looked like a family photo."

My guard went up quickly. "Did you get any names?"

"No it was a dead end."

I was relieved. There was no way I would talk of this to her. Why did she ask? I put it down to a journalist's incessant curiosity.

Ginger sighed. "I'd better get you back," she said rising from the booth.

On the ride back, I again felt the frustration of not being able to act immediately to accomplish my mission. *My impatience— another character flaw.* Until now I felt I had done all I could. Gathering information about the players involved would help me to rescue Kalina and change her life forever. I had to convince myself I was moving forward.

"A penny for your thoughts?" Ginger asked.

"Sorry to get distant on you. Just the jet lag, I think."

After another harrowing ride, we pulled into the Misty Hills Hotel. She tossed her hair back, smiled and said, "Can I ask you one small favor?"

"Sure."

"It will only take a minute. Could I see the inside of your cottage? I have friends and co-workers who've asked me about staying here. I'd like to be able to describe the rooms to them."

I showed her where to park.

Entering my room, she opened her arms and beamed, "It's beautiful in here—I love the native rustic look, great nature prints, skins, and I love the masks with lights behind them." She wandered around the room touching things. She picked up a stone carving from Zimbabwe of a man and woman embracing. She smiled, caressed the stonework and set it back down on the side table.

"Do you have music?"

"That I do." The room had a boom box with radio, and CD player. I had brought along some of my CDs. I chose the group, "Enigma" and hit the "play" button.

"Ooooh, I like it. It's strange, but I like it." Ginger went into the bathroom. "Oh, this is very nice—black tile and indoor and outdoor showers. Give a girl a minute to powder her nose?"

She shouted through the closed door. "Would you have anything for a nightcap?"

"I can manage that." I rattled off the choices from the mini-bar. She selected a Bailey's. I chose another beer and prepared the drinks.

As I turned around, glasses in hand, she was standing in the bathroom doorway, arms akimbo, wearing only black panties, a smirk on her lips, eye lids at half mast.

I gasped. "Gorgeous." Not very original but totally sincere. I wasn't expecting this. Her olive skin was covered by a spray of freckles on her torso and arms. Her breasts were full with dark nipples surrounded by generous brown areolas. She had a hint of a round belly. Her hips were slim and flat—almost boyish.

She walked over to me but stopped short, letting me make the final move to bend down and kiss her. It was long and slow and she pushed hard against my lips. She tasted sweet.

Suddenly she pulled away, snatching the Bailey's from my hand. "Thank you, Mr. Deacon." She took a small sip of her drink. "What do your friends call you?" she whispered.

"Just Deac."

"May I, 'Just Deac?'"

"Certainly." I was mesmerized by her silky movements; her naturalness. I couldn't get enough of looking at her. I felt drawn downwards by a hypnotic spell. I'd come to South Africa on a quest and now....

She interrupted my thoughts by strolling over to a full-length mirror on the bathroom door, pirouetting to evaluate herself from different angles. Turning away from me, she slipped out of her panties then turned back to face me, keeping her legs a shoulder's width apart. "Well, 'Just Deac,' what do you think of the artwork?"

Vines with thorns sprang upwards from her dark triangular bush to envelope a small, perfect, ginger rose tattoo. The tattoo artist had used colors from deep rust to peach sherbet to highlight the petals of an exquisite delicate rose.

"It's beautiful." I was transfixed.

She watched me, looking at her. I knew she enjoyed my surprise and excitement.

As our mouths, lips and tongues invaded each other, she moaned heightening my excitement. As she pulled me towards the bed, I inhaled the exotic, spicy aroma permeating her hair. The music, the lighting, the booze and sensuality of the evening combined making a powerful aphrodisiac. Her movements and breathing screamed she was ready. I was ready. It had been a long time.

She stripped off my shirt. "So many scars." She touched them and kissed each one tenderly, including the most recent puckered scar on my shoulder. I didn't want to think about anything else. No yesterday, no tomorrow, just the insistent now.

"Oh my *grande Americano*, come to me, *querido*." She took me, and slowly increased her rhythmic movements until after a while, she arched and cried out. I let go as well. In a few minutes, as she relaxed, she said playfully, "Oh D*ios*, I needed that."

"Me too." I laughed.

We kissed gently letting our breathing normalize and held each other for ten minutes and drifted off to sleep for several hours.

My sleep was fitful. I woke often during the wee hours, staring at the rotating ceiling fan, thinking of the quest in front of me and the woman beside me.

What the hell was I doing? Not exactly deacon-like behavior. I'd deal with some guilt later.

*   *   *   *   *

I woke to see her dressing and applying makeup. I felt an intimate privilege watching her prepare herself for the day. Leaning up on one elbow, I asked, "Do you have to go?"

"Unfortunately. I'm due at the paper in an hour and a half. I wish I could stay for breakfast and… an encore." She kissed me goodbye and dallied with me playfully under my terrycloth robe as I made coffee.

"What a lustful wench, you are."

"Thanks for the memories, and for being such a good escort. Last night was extraordinary. I'm off." She gave me a quick kiss, took a cup of coffee from my hand, and slipped outside.

It was barely light and the birds were already clamorous. I sat on a low wall of my veranda and enjoyed my steamy mug of French Roast as I watched her drive away: a red dust cloud following her. I lingered, savoring the day come to life. Streaks of brilliant color filled the Eastern horizon. *Ginger Rose, thanks for the memories.*

Would I ever see her again? Unknown. For the tenth time during the past few hours, I thought—I've got to get Mike's kids and get the hell out of here.

My feelings about last night—disturbing, exciting. Was I sorry? Did I feel I guilt? Did I use her? Was she playing me? Was anyone hurt in our encounter?

I knew one thing--*South Africa, you are certainly full of surprises.*

Chapter 12

"SO, YOU THINK YOU CAN BEAT ME TODAY?" Johannes pulled out a small sturdy table and sat on a stool alongside. He smiled expectantly, ready to play one of his favorite games with the young man.

Jaylin, Kalina's half brother, pulled up a chair and indulged Johannes. They both put their right elbows on the table. Johannes extended a fore-finger which Jaylin grabbed. "Ready, go." And so the strange arm wrestling match commenced. Even this lanky teenager using his hand and arm—even two hands against the fingers of Johannes, couldn't budge his opponent's arm. Jaylin actually was developing some upper arm strength as he played this game over and over. Johannes laughed good-naturedly at the boy's efforts. After a while, they went at it with their left hands.

"No, not today, Jaylin, my boy."

"One day I'll get you. I will."

"I know it, I'm sure. You make me work harder each time. So, did you bring me more 'perfume'?"

Johannes enjoyed his little joke. Jaylin carried the bucket of wild dog urine into the workshop. And even though it was sealed and had been washed off, the pungent scent was still noticeable.

The workshop had a security door with strong locks and a peephole. There were no windows, but there were two large skylights and air vents in the corrugated tin roof, and a large exhaust fan. Along one side was a well lit solid workbench. On the opposite, shelves held a wide assortment of tools and other equipment. A stunning watercolor of a magnificent Cape Buffalo graced one wall. It seemed out of place in the workshop. Johannes kept his sanctuary very private. He worked here mostly in the cool of early morning or late evening. The only other person Jaylin knew for sure had been inside, was Dr. Ngubane.

Johannes took the bucket and handed the boy a hundred Rands. "Well deserved. You are being careful, yah? Take no chances, Dere is always more where dis came from."

"Thank you, Uncle."

Jaylin had been sworn to secrecy by Johannes, on the grave of his mother, never to reveal to anyone what he saw inside the workshop. Besides the water buffalo painting, the only really odd and out of place things were the elephant tusks which Jaylin had noticed on occasion. Johannes winked and said that this must be kept a secret.

Johannes put the bucket into a box with a tight fitting lid. "Here lad, now don't tell anyone." He handed Jaylin a pack of cigarettes. Johannes didn't smoke but once caught Jaylin smoking, and it pleased him to secretly supply the boy with tobacco.

"So, tell me, are you studying hard?"

As they walked together outside, Jaylin told Johannes about his wildlife studies and his work at the cheetah reserve. Johannes, to his credit, gave the boy the favor of being a good listener. He didn't talk much anyway.

Johannes was a severe taskmaster with the blacks who worked at the mission until they proved themselves to be trustworthy and hard-working. Then there was a quiet acceptance. He knew he could never really be friendly with a *Kaffir*. The blacks who lived and worked around the mission stood in awe and fear of Johannes. Alisha, Jaylin, and Kalina were, of course, exceptions. He had fallen deeply in love with Alisha, although he couldn't admit it to himself or anyone else. Ever since that day on the road, when they had come across the accident, he believed her to be a very special, holy woman. He loved Jaylin and Kalina as his own.

Jaylin sat talking to his "uncle" for a while, and finally they exchanged their silly secret handshake, and parted.

It would be the last time they ever saw each other.

*   *   *   *   *

"So how did it go last night?" Robbie asked.

113

I'd slept late and had taken a leisurely stroll around the grounds winding up at Robbie's office. "It was about as good as it gets." I wanted to keep the intimacy with Rose a secret for now.

"You old devil. One of my security guards reported that a Jaguar with a lady driver with flaming red hair raced out of here in the wee hours."

"Oh, oh. I'm busted. Let's just say we got on very well."

"Really, my boy, you should be thanking me. But don't worry, I'll keep it to myself. You know, for some reason Del doesn't much care for Miss Ginger Rose. She can't even explain why—it's a female thing I guess. Who can understand them? Myself, I admit, I find I am attracted to Rose in a seriously lustful way, and am more than a bit envious of you. But, never mind, happily married am I, but I can still look. No harm done, eh?"

"Rob," I said, wanting to change the subject, "Did you ever hear of someone called Rosenmoon or Rosenbloom?"

"No, I can't say that I have."

"Oh well. Keep on the alert for that name would you?"

"Sure, I'll keep it in mind."

"Del is taking Kalina out shopping today?"

"They've already gone. Can you believe it? So, tomorrow is to be the big day, is it? You and Kalina off to the wilds of Venda."

"Yes. I thought we'd get to know each other a bit during the drive up, before I tell her about her father. I plan to break the news to her on the following day."

"It's up to you, of course. It will be a shocker for her. Hell, it was for me and I thought I was beyond being shocked. I don't envy you having to tell her." Robbie shook his head.

"You know, Ginger Rose has asked me several questions about Mike Thompson. She seemed to be especially interested to know whether he had a family."

"Really, I wonder why?" asked Robbie.

"Well, she *is* a journalist, and she covered his crime scene. Another odd thing; she mentioned that Mike was mutilated or marked somehow, probably as a signal of some sort."

"Just as Colonel Marshall had alluded to. How was he marked?"

"She didn't say. I'm not sure she knew. She also mentioned a photo being recovered, showing Mike in what looked like a family pose with wife and children."

Robbie thought about this for a moment. "I never saw one. Why, is that important?"

"I don't know. It could be."

Chapter 13

JUST BEFORE LUNCH, I DID SOME LIGHT EXERCISE and jogged around the grounds with its amazing assortment of plant life and flowers. I didn't recognize any of them, but I'm not much of a Botanist anyway. These plants probably couldn't grow in Chicago. The colors were dazzling from bright reds, oranges and yellows surrounded by large deep green leaves of various shapes.

One of Robbie's employees came running up to me out of breath. "I been lookin' for you, boss. Mistah Forrester wants you come his office now-now." His wide eyes and head-nodding indicated urgency.

"I'm on my way."

The messenger ran off.

I hurried back to Robbie's office. Father Godwin and Robbie sat side- by-side; their facial expressions like tombstone engravings.

Father Godwin began, "Deacon, please take a seat. Thank you for coming." He sighed and stiffened his back. Robbie stared into the dregs of his coffee cup like a gypsy fortune-teller reading tea leaves. Godwin continued, "Remember I said that I might need your help while you're here?"

"Yes, whats up?"

"I just received a call from Father Trang in Capetown. He discovered where some children are being held by slavers. He could use some manpower to help rescue them. Would you be willing to help?"

"Yes, of course, but what about the police?"

"The men we're after have enough money to have spies among the authorities. We can't risk telling anyone. At the hint of a rescue mission, the slavers will move the children. God knows if we'll ever have a chance of finding them again. Father Trang thinks we must take this action on our own. We will be in harm's way, no doubt about that. Are you in?"

Robbie added, "It's dangerous, my friend."

"Thanks Rob. I'm in."

"Great stuff, old chap."

"When?"

"It's got to be now. If all goes well, we should be back early tomorrow morning."

Robbie pitched in. "I'm coming along as well. We'll get you back in time for your road trip with Kalina."

Robbie raised his bushy eyebrows, "One more thing, as far as Del knows, this is an important business meeting." He winked. "If she finds out what I'm doing, it'll be my guts for garters. So, Mum's the word. I've arranged for a quick flight from nearby Lanseria International Airport to a small airfield outside of Capetown. It should take just over four hours."

Another surprise. I quickly changed into comfortable black clothes and brought a jacket. I wished I had Bat with me.

*   *   *   *   *

Within the hour we boarded the waiting Cessna. We flew close to tree top level. Robbie was up front with the pilot. Father Godwin and I were literally squashed into the rear seats of the aircraft. Luckily it would be a short flight.

Godwin beckoned me to lean towards him.

"I thought I'd take this chance to tell you about Father Trang. I'm sure Robbie and the pilot can't hear us over the engine noise. First, you need to know that Father Trang is one of our Gabrian brothers. He makes Announcements like we do, ridding the church of sexual predators, but he is also deeply involved with rescuing children from human traffickers. I'm proud to call him 'friend'."

"Tell me about him."

"Well, to begin with, he's a diminutive Vietnamese priest. His age is a mystery to me. He's probably the first guy a bully would pick on in a bar fight. Big mistake. He was a Montagnard jungle fighter for years. He probably knows twenty ways to kill you with his hands. I'd say he's about five feet seven inches tall and probably weighs one hundred thirty pounds soaking wet. He rarely shows emotion except a mild pleasantness. He wears rimless glasses and has straight black hair that comically sticks out from his head in all directions. The man is part warrior, part priest and totally dedicated to the suffering children of the world. He had four children of his own about whom he never speaks. They, along with his wife, were tortured, mutilated and killed by the Viet Cong. He found what was left of them."

"What a tragedy. How does he live with it?"

"God only knows." Goldwin continued. "After a year-long one-man killing spree to make an Army Ranger puke, he realized he had become like those he most hated. He entered a mountain monastery and after two years of reclusive meditation, self-denial and prayer, he emerged from the jungle highlands and entered a seminary to study for the priesthood. How he got to South Africa I don't know. He was a perfect candidate for the Gabrians. They recruited him and that's how we met. He now has his own parish in Capetown."

Father Godwin went silent, leaving me to my own thoughts. I felt a deep sorrow for Father Trang. *God help him.* My thoughts drifted from his story to several others I'd become aware of, back in Chicago. After a few minutes wallowing in these tragedies, I shut them out by focusing on the world speeding along beneath us.

South Africa looked as bedazzling from the air as it did from the ground. The first thing I spotted were some giraffes loping along. I gaped at wild herds of all kinds of hoofed animals. Passing below us, a muddy stream meandered through a village with its distinctive roundaval huts. We flew over a large gathering of baboons moving in their highly structured pattern. Dominant males in key positions on the perimeter, other younger males on an inside ring and the females and youngsters in the center. As we approached Capetown, the blazing sunset caressed the vineyards of the Cape. The scene was absolutely stunning to this Chicago boy.

I was grateful for feeling the bumpy landing and the ground beneath us. It was a pleasure to get out of the noisy flying sardine can and stretch. By the groans he made, it looked like Father Godwin felt the same. An old rusty beige station wagon waited for us, panting in the setting sun.

"There's Father Trang with the parish transport," Father Godwin said.

As I approached him, Father Trang bowed, thanking me several times for joining his expeditionary force. He said, "Now we retire to my parish, take refreshment and prepare for evening." He remained quiet for the rest of our trip.

After a spicy noodle dinner topped off with luscious fruits, half of which I'd never heard of, Father Trang took me aside. He lowered his voice and said, "I want to tell you my plan tonight to save the innocents. Child slavery, especially using young girls, is more rampant than people can imagine. Large number of children filter in through Capetown. It's pure evil. Young girl and boy are sold to do the bidding of sexually depraved men. Many forced to perform in videos, become drug addict. Many wind up commit suicide. When some no longer useful, they set up for "snuff films.'"

"It's disgusting. What about the authorities?"

"Useless. We can never be certain who to trust. Some take bribes to look the other way. And the slaver are slippery – always moving the children around. The children, even if asked, too afraid to speak out."

"My God." I'd heard of child slavery but never had been directly confronted by the problem. As the priest spoke I could feel my gut clench.

"Do you know how many we saved and recovered in the past three years? Over one hundred forty. Most have been reunited with their families."

"That's remarkable."

"Not enough." Father Trang stood and his face tightened. "I recently learned of a holding place where we have chance to rescue large group at once."

"May I ask, who is 'we?'"

"Just few trusted friends and one parishioner. You agreed to join us but I want you appreciate the danger. Slavers well-armed and ruthless. One of my helpers still in hospital. Others have been injured. The children guarded as precious commodities."

Father Trang sat on the edge of a battered desk. "I know you are on an important quest to rescue the children of your friend. I will pray for your success. But if you find it in your heart to help on this raid, this old priest and many children and parent will hold you dearly in thought and prayer forever. I know this a lot to ask of you and if you refuse to join us, I'll understand. Father Godwin told me your background. I could use another warrior strong arm tonight. We have to deal with several armed men. It a blessing you showed up at this moment - Divine Providence?"

"How many children?"

"We not sure. We think over twenty."

"Where are they being held?"

"On upper floor of old dockside building along the quay."

"When do we leave?"

"Not until midnight. We like to catch the kidnapper asleep if possible."

"Count me in."

"Thank you, my son." The old priest bowed.

*   *   *   *   *

As darkness fell, I asked Father Godwin, "How will we get them out?"

"I don't know the exact details yet but there's our transport." He pointed to a sunflower yellow school bus parked in the alley behind the church. All identifying marks had been painted over in black. It looked like a crazy bumblebee on wheels.

"You've got to be kidding."

"Nope, that's it. This will be a rather large bunch of kids, after all."

"Of course."

Beyond the bus, the gloaming brought on an array of orange, red and violet rays reflected off Table Mountain. Only God could create colors like that. I couldn't believe I was looking out onto the historic Cape of Storms, where the Atlantic and Indian oceans come together, and where countless ships had gone down. I felt exhilarated by the scene and the pending action.

Father Trang came in and introduced me to a strange-looking man named Etienne, who would be another member of our entourage.

"What you want coming *avec nous?*" He asked.

The man was blunt to the point of being aggressive.

"I want to help." I replied.

Etienne was thin and angular with wild gray hair, beard, and hairy forearms. The most striking thing about him was that the sides of his face didn't match. It was a sculpture that the artist hadn't quite gotten right – Piccasoesque. The eye on one side was lower than the other and had a droopy eyelid. The left side if his jaw was not aligned with the right. As if to emphasize the point, he had one blue eye and one brown eye. He wore a floppy hat and kept a wicked-looking machete with a bone handle in his belt. His hands were gnarled and scarred.

He said, "You know these *merdes* no give up *les enfants sans combat.*"

I could just make out his French, having sweated through two years of classes at DePaul University. "I understand. Why do you come?" I asked.

Etienne inhaled sharply. His eyes glazed over. *"Ma fille,"* then he abruptly walked away.

Father Trang approached and explained, "His nine-year-old daughter was snatched about a year ago. His wife run off and left him to raise the girl by himself. She became his whole world. She never been found. Helping to rescue other children is his way of dealing with pain and guilt."

"Poor bastard," said Robbie, shaking his head.

*   *   *   *   *

Father Trang gathered our small strike force near midnight. He laid out a crude map of the neighborhood and the route our team would take going in and out.

The final member of the team showed up– the bus driver. Her name was Lucinda but she went by "Luce." She had been a school bus driver all of her life. With jet-black skin, her hair cut short, she looked like she might have played guard for the Chicago Bears. She made it clear that she, "Don't take no shit from nobody." To emphasize this fact she brandished a small crossbow. Her eyes pierced mine. "I am knowing how to use it, man."

I didn't doubt her for a moment.

Father Trang also laid out a hand-drawn floor plan of the inside of the warehouse. "They only post one armed guard at front door. We not sure how many other guard. Maybe five or six. The bottom floor is not habitable. The children are kept in room on the second and third floors."

He looked up at everyone and continued, "The front room here," he pointed to the largest room on the second floor near the stairs, "is where the guard sleep and eat. We don't know which room the children are in. Godwin and I check them all." He looked at Etienne and me.

"If you two can keep the guards in this room, we get children out and down to the bus. After, we follow bus back to the parish."

Etienne wordlessly sharpened his machete and chain-smoked as Father Trang continued. "Because of our Roman collar, we hope children listen to Father Godwin and me. Robbie stand guard at front door and help load children onto bus."

Etienne paused, his eyelids at half-mast.

I was relieved to hear Robbie would be standing guard. I didn't want him in harm's way any more than necessary.

"And their guard at the front door?" I asked.

"With God help, I take care of that little chore."

I could just detect a twitch around the priest's eyes. "Now we go to church to pray for success."

We prayed with our arms stretched out from our sides, like Father Trang. The Montagnard priest went behind the altar and emerged carrying two, twelve-gauge over-and-under shotguns -- one for me and the other for Etienne. "From Capetown Rod and Gun Club. Their president is a faithful parishioner with four daughter. He know what we do. These should help you hold guard at bay." He passed out extra shells. "Use only if absolutely necessary—-you both understand?" He stared at us for a long minute. He thrust his face close to Etienne's, *"Comprend-tu?"*

We both nodded. He went over the plan again.

*   *   *   *   *

In the moonless night we mounted up: Five of us in the old beige station wagon, and Luce in the bright yellow school bus. Two blocks before we reached the warehouse, Luce pulled into an alleyway to keep the bus out of sight. Later, she would bring up the bus and park it directly in front of the warehouse to take on the children.

A block away, Father Trang slipped out of the parish wagon. He wore an old shiny black suit with a Roman collar.

The dark street with three and four story buildings on either side felt like an urban canyon. The dockside smelled fishy-sour and trash blew everywhere. As soon as the guard was out of the way, Godwin would pull up and the four of us would enter the building.

Father Trang shuffled about forty yards to feed the stereotype of the humble coulee. I saw a fat man with a seaman's cap and handlebar moustache seated on the loading dock watching the priest's approach. When Father Trang stopped at the bottom of the steps and looked up, the guard slid off his stool, waddled a few steps forward, put his hands on his hips and said, "What do you want, priest?"

Father Trang said, "Maybe you help me, I seem lost."

"What do I look like to you, a friggin' travel agent?" The man jerked his thumb towards the end of the street. "Fuck off."

Father Trang pulled a map from his jacket pocket as if he hadn't heard the man "I think I here," he said pointing to a spot on the map. "But I can't find church I look for. It Saint Gerrard. You know it?"

"Can't you hear, old man? Get the hell out."

"What? I no hear so good. What you say?" The priest went up two steps and the guard came down a few steps so he was right above Father Trang.

The guard snarled, "Do I have to shout in your ear, dink priest. I don't...."

A lightening, stiff-fingered strike to the guard's throat abruptly cut off his voice. As he gasped for air, the priest swept the guard's legs out from under him, turned him over and put zip-tie cuffs to secure his hands behind his back. Strips of duct tape around his mouth and ankles rendered the guard quiet and immobile. Father Trang rolled the man off the side of the loading platform behind some dented garbage cans. There had been no sound. The whole episode had taken less than a minute. Father Trang was very good.

We pulled up to the warehouse and the school bus followed. As we emerged from the car, Robbie looked at me solemnly and murmured, "Take care, Deac."

I nodded in return, "You too, old friend. I don't want to face Del if anything happens to you." I sent up a prayer. *Lord, we could really use some help here.*

Etienne and I joined Father Trang and Father Godwin following them silently up the stairs, leaving Robbie at the door. Father Trang held a small flashlight to guide our way.

My nerves were like so many electric charges coursing through my body. The stairwell was obsidian black, smelling of rotting garbage and mildew. I hated being in a closed dark space during an operation. In the army we referred to this situation as a deadly funnel – a closed in space that made it impossible to move or take cover. Maximum vulnerability. It felt like the warehouse in Chicago where I'd had some trouble recently. We were bunched together and exposed to anyone looking down the staircase.

Using hand signals and touch, Father Trang indicated the door Etienne and I were to enter and hold the guards at bay. He signaled that he and Godwin would go after the children.

Etienne and I carried our shotguns at port-arms. Surprise was on our side. I turned the doorknob very slowly. Unlocked, as expected. We entered the room and spread out. I noticed the snoring followed immediately by the stench of stale smoke and body odor. When Etienne found the light switch, he nodded to me and clicked it on. One small bare bulb hanging from the ceiling provided only dim light. The room contained a kitchen table, assorted chairs, a couch a floor fan and a small TV in one corner. To one side of the room, three men sprawled on mattresses on the floor.

I thumped the butt of my shotgun on the floor. The men stirred and looked up at the sound. I said, "Quiet now, everyone up and over to the wall." The men in their underwear sobered into alertness quickly when looking down our shotgun barrels. They were all short, with dark beards.

Etienne, his face a mask of restrained rage said, "Slowly, no sound to make."

I said quietly, "Kneel facing the wall and put your heads on the floor. While Etienne kept them covered, I put my shotgun on the kitchen table and started searching for weapons. Looking over the room, I saw a problem. There were seven mattresses with piles of clothing near each one. The three men in the room and the guard outside made four, leaving three men unaccounted for. *Not good.*

Near the mattresses I found five knives and three handguns, which I shoved into a pillowcase to take when we left. One of the men mumbled something and Etienne kicked him in the side. "Silence."

As I knelt to cuff the men with my zip ties, another man burst into the room shouting. Naked, he had his arm around the neck of a young girl who also wore no clothes. He had a handgun pointed at Etienne. "Put it down," the man ordered. Etienne had no choice. He slowly laid his shotgun on the floor. "Now kick it over here."

I realized the gunman had all of his attention on Etienne and the shotgun and not on me. It had to be now or never. But my gun was out of reach. When the man loosened his grip on the girl to reach down to pick up Etienne's shotgun I grabbed the only thing near me and side-armed the pillowcase full of weapons sending it whirling into the man's chest. Knocked off balance, he released the girl. Regaining his equilibrium, he shifted his attention towards me and raised his handgun. His eyes were murderous.

Etienne's machete whistled down and all but severed the man's right hand. Blood spurted even hitting the lone light bulb. The wounded man's scream of agony reverberated in the small room. I bolted for my shotgun and pointed it at the men who had regained their feet. "Back on your knees as you were. Now!"

The girl scampered to one corner of the room, curled up and sobbing. She clutched her knees to her chest to cover herself. Her face resembling that of a trapped animal.

I went back to my chore of cuffing the men's hands behind their backs. I duct-taped their mouths and ankles. I came back to the man with the nearly severed hand. He'd passed out. I quickly put on a tourniquet and taped a pressure dressing on the wound. I heard myself speak my thoughts aloud. "I'll call paramedics once we're safely out of here." I kept half an eye on the door. I wanted no more surprises. Two men were still unaccounted for. *A worry.*

I heard the beautiful sound of small footsteps behind me in the hall. Sticking my head out the door, I saw a queue of children hustling down the staircase, eyes as wide as saucers. Father Godwin had two kids clinging onto his neck and he carried one in each arm. Etienne threw a blanket around the naked girl shivering in our room and gently helped her join the procession in the hall.

When Etienne and I exited the building I saw Father Godwin and Robbie on the loading dock directing the children onto the bus and into Luce's waiting arms. Father Trang appeared. "We have them all, we go."

Etienne appeared to be in a trance. He said to no one in particular, "You see dat asshole with his prick hanging out, holding *le juenne fille?* She 'bout *neuf ans, n'est pas?*"

"Yes, I saw her but now she's safe. You did it. You saved her." *Oh shit.* I could see my partner teetering on the far edge of sanity; his eyes wide, pupils dilated and his jaw muscles pumping. I remembered his daughter had been about nine when abducted.

"Yes, now we've got to go and take care of the children." I kept nodding my head to convince Etienne to comply before he did something bat- shit crazy.

"You go help *avec les enfants,* I be along *a bientot.*"

He shoved me aside and ran back into the building. I ran behind him up the stairs, shouting, "Stop! *Arrete',* we have to go."

When I entered the guard's sleeping room, Etienne began to systematically stab each of our prisoners in the buttocks with the point of his machete.

"They no run after us so well now, *eh bien?*"

Blood stains covered each man's rump. They'd all be walking with a limp for months. I thought they were probably lucky that Etienne hadn't castrated them or killed them. "For God's sake, Etienne, let's go, *alle' alle' vite.*"

As we emerged into the open, we saw two men running down the street towards the bus. We had no line of fire. I realized we were too late. One of the men had jumped up through the front door and onto the bus. A second later, the man shot backwards into the street looking incredulously at the bolt from Luce's crossbow sticking out of his gut. He was alive, squirming on the dusty street. *Six down.*

The other man started shooting. Godwin and Robbie shouted at the children to stay down. The shooter ran and shot wildly. I heard a shotgun roar and saw the man fall flat on his face, his legs twitching and spurting blood. Etienne had shot his legs out from under him. When I hustled over to retrieve the man's gun, Etienne came running up with his machete raised high about to decapitate the man.

"No," I screamed, and dove to grab Etienne's arm. He struggled, and finally dropped his machete. He was raving in French, English and Afrikaans. Father Trang came running up. He, Robbie and I wrestled with Etienne and held him until he was still. We half-dragged him back to the station wagon.

To the wounded men in the street, I yelled, "You assholes thank God you're alive."

I ran back to the bus to see if everyone was all right. Luce was sitting in the driver's seat facing the open door, the crossbow on her lap, her eyes blazing and lips quivering, "He asked for it, stupid pig, trying to get on my bus with dese childrens. Jesus, Mary and Joseph, can we go now?"

Godwin ran past me to get on the bus.

"You okay?" I asked.

He responded, "Yes, Robbie and I will stay on the bus with the children. You drive behind us" After he mounted the bus, I could hear him speaking softly to the frightened children.

"Great." I said.

I turned to Robbie. "How you doin'?"

"Fine, just a little shaky. Bloody hell, I've never been shot at before. I nearly pissed myself."

"Could you call for an ambulance or paramedic? Some of the kidnappers need medical attention."

Miraculously, none of our rescue team had been injured. *Thank you, Lord.*

I jumped into the driver's seat of the parish wagon. Like yesterday, driving on the "wrong side" of the road was a harrowing experience. My brain screamed at me that I was going to die in a head-on collision. I concentrated on following the school bus back to Father Trang's parish.

Had anyone bothered to look at the school bus closely they would have been surprised to see several fresh bullet holes in the side and one window shot out. No one followed us. The kids were safe and unhurt.

Father Trang and Robbie squished in the back seat of the station wagon, hugging a blood-splattered Etienne who shook badly. I looked back to the priest, "How's he doing?"

Father Trang nodded in the affirmative, his face impassive.

I had to ask, "How many children?"

"Thirty-four. Praise God. Thank you, my son. You were a godsend."

Yep, that's me I thought. An angel sent directly from God.

*   *   *   *   *

As soon as our mini-convoy returned to the parish, Etienne faded into the night without a word. Some people are like that. They blow into your life like a sudden squall, release a load of energy, then, just as quickly, leave taking their dark thunderclouds with them. And we're never the same afterwards. Etienne--a tortured soul. *God grant him peace.*

Once back at Father Trang's parish, we gathered the children for tomato soup, cookies, milk, prayer and bed in that order. I watched with admiration as Father Trang moved among the children speaking in comforting tones, giving them the gift of his touch, and blessing each one.

Robbie helped relax the kids with his upbeat and positive attitude. He reassured them that they were safe.

Many of the children still various stages of shock, stared about wide-eyed. Too frightened to speak, they remained quiet.

Tomorrow Father Trang and his staff would begin the arduous task of contacting agencies to find their parents, and for some, foster homes. Of the thirty-four children there were twenty-nine girls and five boys.

I felt pride in being part of a successful mission. A feeling I'd almost forgotten.

Was this part of God's plan for me? Helping people in trouble? This seemed to be a big part of my life in the past year. Finally, should I resume my studies for the priesthood? The questions haunted me.

Too wired to sleep, I snatched up a couple of bottles of frosty Asahi beer from Father Trang's fridge and slid onto an upholstered chair on the porch with my feet up on a brightly striped ottoman. I needed to wind down. As I stared into the indigo night, I again saw the children scrambling into the safety of the big yellow bus; their chariot to freedom. Invariably my thoughts returned to Kalina and her brother. *Could I help them escape as well?*

Father Godwin came up behind me. "Oy mate, want some comp'ny?"

"Sure, Father, how about a beer?"

"Don't mind if I do." He opened a bottle and took a long swig, his pronounced Adam's apple bouncing as he swallowed.

"Couldn't sleep?" I asked.

"No way, old chap, too charged up." He sat heavily in an old wicker chair, stretching out his long legs. "Thanks for coming along tonight. Robbie is still helping the urchins settle in."

"It was well worth it."

"Yes indeed." His face clouded over. "What happened back there at the warehouse?" The screaming and…."

"Nobody died. There were a few injuries. The specifics don't matter."

Father Godwin nodded and was silent for a while. Then he said, "Father Trang is really something, eh?"

"Amen to that. I'm glad we belong to the same club. Remind me not to piss him off." I held my beer high, "Cheers for the Gabrians."

Godwin did likewise. "Hear, hear."

An hour later, we clambered into our Cessna for the return flight to Muldersdrift. Somehow, the plane didn't seem so uncomfortable this time. I drifted off as soon as we were airborne.

Chapter 14

THE NEXT MORNING AFTER A BRIEF NAP and hot shower, I joined Robbie at the Simba lounge for a full English breakfast. We were both ravenous. I ate heartily but couldn't get used to kippers in the morning.

Del and Kalina strolled in while we were finishing our coffee. "Good morning you two night owls. Did we have a day," Del said triumphantly. "Let me tell you what we bought for Kalina." She plunked down on Robbie's lap, kissing him on the forehead. "I got myself something too. A really beautiful red dress—on sale. Aren't you proud of me?"

Robbie groaned. "You'll put me in the poor house, woman."

Del totally ignored his comment. "That's not all, I also got two outfits for our lovely daughter."

Another groan.

Kalina and I smiled at their banter.

Del continued, alternately looking at me and at her husband. "But most importantly, for Kalina, we got four blouses which can be interchanged with two suits to make seven or eight outfits. Wasn't that clever of us? One suit is a plum color, and the other is a cream-colored pants suit. Kalina looks smashing in both. Oh, to have a figure like hers again!" She rolled her eyes. "And we got matching shoes and a few other bits."

Robbie's voice took on a melodramatic tone. "I'm glad Deacon here is footing that bill. And for your information, your figure is just fine with me. You can take that to the bank."

Del smiled all over herself and gave Robbie a big hug and a wet kiss on the cheek, rubbing off a lipstick smear with her thumb.

Kalina's eyes sparkled. "I'm happy with my new clothes. Thank you Deacon," said Kalina, looking a little embarrassed.

"You're welcome. I'm glad you like them. It's all part of the plan. You'll look so sharp and give such a good impression that the seminar participants will be glad they came, just to have you register them in." I realized I'd never shopped for a woman. Later, I'd have to thank Del.

Kalina smiled and looked down.

Del said, "Well, I'll drive Kalina back to the mission so she can eat and finish packing. Then, my darling, I'm going home. When may Sarah and I expect you?"

"I've got a few more things to do. Probably about five. I'll call you as I'm leaving the office."

"Maybe you'll get lucky and I'll model my dress for you tonight."

"Just don't show me the bill," said Robbie looking skyward.

I couldn't help feeling envious of their relationship. Their love for each other, blatantly evident. They felt pleasure just being in each other's company. Undoubtedly, they had problems like everyone else and I was probably idealizing their relationship. Nevertheless, their interaction brought me a sense of joy.

Chapter 15

GINGER ROSE GLARED AT DR. NGUBANE. "Get them out of here, you old voyeur."

"You want my attentions all to yourself, do you?" Ngubane teased. He guessed Rose didn't relish the competition from a couple of nubile young beauties languishing around his lavish pool at the Eagles's Lair. The pool was beneath a glassed-in causeway between two parts of the house. He loved having beautiful young women around.

While Ngubane shooed the young models back into the house, Rose slipped out of her caftan and admired her reflection in the still waters of the swimming pool. She wore a bright floral bikini, leaving little to the imagination. She had wonderful posture which seemed to naturally thrust her breasts forward. The string bikini bottom covered very little and exposed her derriere nicely. Sitting on the edge, she splashed her feet in the cool aquamarine water and sipped a glass of chilled chardonnay. She smiled staring up at the star filled sky.

On his way back, gin and tonic in hand, Ngubane drank in his opulent surroundings, accentuated by carefully placed lighting and floral arrangements. Not bad, he mused, for a man who spent half of his time in the squalor, stink and illness of his country's people. He respected the work he did and he respected himself, but had no respect whatsoever for Ms. Ginger Rose and her lackey, Vicente.

Ngubane accepted himself as a complex man, overly formal, neat to a fault, and dedicated to his own causes. And to his own pleasures. Why not?
Financial success provided for it all.

He returned to sit at the poolside table behind Rose. Ngubane could see how men found her attractive. The word that came to mind—voluptuous. He wondered if she and Vicente were more than companions. But for him, she was too long in the tooth, a little too heavy and certainly too brash for his tastes. A man–eater. An aura of danger enveloped her.

"So my dear Ginger; if you have something for me, I have something for you."

She turned from the pool to face him, "We're being very direct tonight, doctor."

"Why not?"

He couldn't decide up to this time whether to tell her of his little difficulty at the border. He chose not to. She could never be trusted. The less she knew about his farm/leper clinic in Zimbabwe and his operation at the mission, the better.

He slid a small black duffel bag toward her. She didn't bother to open it. He had already told her how much poppy powder it contained. He had always been meticulous about such details.

She nodded to a small, beaded, purse. "In there."

He reached in and pulled out a beautifully wrapped packet. It was the size of a brick and covered in gold lame' cloth. Receiving cash in such a fashion seemed especially gratifying. Ginger Rose had style, he reflected. The transaction had always been made this way.

Vicente would take the powder to Johannes later. Johannes would then prepare it for shipment. The "Happy Tusk" operation would continue. It couldn't fail, even if it "failed." That was the beauty of their plan.

"How about a pilot to transport the tusks?" Ginger asked.

"Godwin and I have found a few who might be suitable."

"Good, keep them handy. We must be careful to choose one who can keep his mouth shut."

"It's terrible about Thompson," said Ngubane.

"Yes, it is," Rose said.

Ngubane saw Rose turn away. He suspected she knew more about Thompson's death than she was telling. As far as he knew, it was a random killing, probably a robbery gone sour. It was too bad. Ngubane liked Mike Thompson.

"What of the American?" she asked. "Why is he here?"

"I met him at lunch. As far as I know he is here to present seminars to seminarians and to vacation in our beloved country. Evidently he and Robbie Forrester have been friends for a long time." Ngubane realized he walked on shaky ground.

"Your beloved country, not mine. Isn't it interesting that this 'Deacon' knew both Robbie and Thompson?"

"An interesting coincidence. He's off tomorrow to present some sort of seminar in Venda."

"Venda? There's nothing there," she said, looking surprised.

"Well, I guess someone is there who hired him. I think it might be Zahl Ministeries."

"Is he going alone?"

Ngubane didn't want Kalina and Rose to be on the same continent. "He is taking an assistant from Misty Hills." True enough. No need to bring Kalina's name into the discussion.

"I see. I dined with Deacon yesterday." She smiled wickedly thinking of their time together after dinner. Men were so easy. Deacon had proved to be more than satisfactory. Much more. "By the way, was Thompson married, or did he have a family?"

"Not that I know of. Of course, he travelled a lot. Who knows where he spent his time?" Ngubane was glad Rose faced the pool so she couldn't detect the lie that might have been obvious on his face. He wondered about her interest, but decided not to ask.

"Our business is completed," she said rising from the pool, slipping into her sandals, shaking out her mane of long red hair and drew on her colorful caftan. "I'll have Vicente bring the goods to Johannes to prepare for shipment tonight."

Ngubane knew she didn't want to be seen at the mission—ever.

As Rose left, the slap of her sandals fading, Ngubane figured out how to split up the money. He would donate an ample portion to the mission—"from a generous donor." He'd keep some aside for operating the clinic and the poppy farm in the Chimanimani Mountains. And of course, he'd take a healthy cut for himself and the Eagle's Lair.

*   *   *   *   *

Near midnight, Vicente entered through the back gate of the mission. He cursed the darkness stumbling along one of many paths that crisscrossed the mission grounds. As arranged, he delivered the powder to Johannes at the workshop, the handover conducted without discussion. No one had ever witnessed them together. To say the two men did not like each other would be an understatement. Johannes saw Vicente as a thug in the service of a woman. Vicente thought Johannes was a muscle-bound simpleton. They maneuvered around Johannes's workspace like two boxers in the opening of round one. They had always conducted their exchange with minimal conversation and eye-contact. It was all business.

After Vicente left, Johannes hid the contraband in a safe in the floor of his workshop. The trap door was directly under a leg of his heavy workbench. It was unlikely anyone would ever conceive of moving it.

Johannes justified his involvement in the illegal and dangerous scheme. The poison would bring a high price and be used by the rich and foolish in America. So what? Let them get high and die. The money would allow Father Godwin and Dr. Ngubane, to minister to the children at the clinic. The children he loved and protected.

He got misty eyed as he sometimes did when alone, thinking of the children. His thoughts would naturally shift to his own daughters--and the one missing forever. His beautiful Steffi. He began to weep silently. He could see her now as vividly as he did on the day she died. She wore the bright emerald costume with glittering gold trim, her natural blond hair tied back in a ponytail. She wore theatrical make-up which made her look older.

He relived the "miss" again in his mind as he had done thousands of times. How could she be so far off center? And how could he miss her? He *never* missed a catch. In his mind's eye he saw her fall, narrowly missing the safety net. For a few agonizing minutes, a guilty ache consumed him as his stomach churned in agony.

Yes, he thought as he put the powder away, the money from their happy tusk operation would certainly be put to good use. He had to force himself not to consider what Kalina's beloved mother, Alisha, would have thought of their little operation. Of course she never would have approved.

Chapter 16

"HALT", A TALL, BROAD-SHOULDERED white South African Police officer barked. Most of the other South African police at the roadblock were black.   All had impeccably, pressed tan uniforms, shiny Sam Browne belts and boots that reflected tiny spots of sunlight. From my previous soldering I remembered well how to bring up that kind of spit-shine. They carried a variety of weapons. The S.A.P.s took their jobs very seriously. They knew the face of violence they could encounter at any moment.

The officer spoke to me in deliberate, staccato Afrikaans.

From the passenger seat, Kalina spoke softly to the police officer in Afrikaans, deferentially not making eye contact with him. "He's an American. Doesn't speak Afrikaans."

The officer switched to heavily accented English. "Ach, well den, American, where you going?"

"To Venda. I'm conducting a conference there."

"What kind of conference?"

"It's a educational seminar for the students and seminarians at the Zahl Institute"

"Ach, I see. And who is dis?' he said, pointing to Kalina.

"She is my assistant."

The officer looked at Kalina, "Name?'

Kalina told him.

Then back to me. "Do you have a gun?"

Not wishing to get into trouble, I said nervously, "No, I don't have a gun. I don't own a gun. I'm not carrying any gun."

The officer flushed red, his neck veins prominent. "Are you mad? You travel here wid dis nice car, and money in your American wallet, and you don't carry a gun? Where do you think you are? Dis is not America. You must have a gun to travel on dese roads. I take you to my brother-in-law's shop down the road. We get you a proper gun." He turned away and spoke in Afrikaans to the other policemen. The only words I could make out were "crazy Amerikaner."

"Now, follow me, if you please."

"Wait," I said as he walked toward his car. "I don't want to buy a gun."

He looked back at me with a frown. "You must have one--and papers too. You make me mad. It's for your good I give dis advice."

Kalina said quietly, "Maybe he is right, Deacon. Cars are sometimes hi-jacked on the roads, and people are robbed and beaten."

"All right, all right. I guess I'd better play by your rules." *When in Rome...* Besides, I thought, it was a dangerous game I was playing as Thompson's letter indicated. Maybe it would be best to have a gun.

I reluctantly followed the officer in his funny little car with orange, green and black markings. I wondered how he managed to fit into it. Within ten minutes, his driver pulled off the main highway onto a dusty dirt road. I followed as we rolled into a small town, stopping in front of a gun shop. Two serious-looking armed guards stood out front. One of them had to be six feet eight inches tall and weigh three-hundred pounds. A buzzer sounded and we entered through a heavy steel security door. The interior was very neat and organized. A variety of guns were displayed on the walls in patterns. Well lit, ceiling fans dissimilated smells of metal and oil. After a half hour of animated discussion, I finally chose an Astra .38 special, with an ankle holster, a box of ammunition, and a cleaning kit. The officer and his brother-in-law were pushing me to get something larger and with more firepower, but I held fast. I didn't want to lug a cannon around.

I test fired the Astra on a small range in back of the shop. Nine out of ten practice shots hit the silhouette target at forty meters. I'd shot handguns before. I reloaded and placed the pistol in the olive drab holster on my left ankle. After the shooting exhibition, the officer treated me with more respect. "You shot a gun before I see. Dat's good shooting, Meneer." He raised his eyebrows, looking pleased with my performance. He turned to one of his men. "See dat?" He lowered his voice to an intense whisper. "Dat's how to fire your weapon."

Once outside, the officer pointed the way to Venda. "Dis is much better now, yah? You be safe." He smiled broadly, looking proud of himself.

"Thank you for your help." I felt like saluting. There was a cloud of red dust as the policeman wheeled his car around to return to his roadblock. I had no way of knowing how soon I would need to use my new purchase.

"Well, that was an unexpected turn of events." I said to Kalina as we resumed our journey.

Kalina smiled, "Life is full of surprises"

"I'll certainly go along with that." The gun, Father Trang and the children, and of course, Ginger Rose.

Continuing our road trip, Kalina spoke more openly. The incident at the roadblock helped to lower some barriers between us. We had an "experience" in common. I felt I was winning her over, or was it the other way around?

Kalina spoke freely of her uncles and how each in his own way had influenced her life. "My mother had a special friendship with uncle Johannes." She paused abruptly, suddenly sat upright and her eyes widened as if in response to a memory.

Seeing her expression change, I encouraged her to speak. "What is it?"

"When I was very young - my mother - Alisha was her name, told me a story I'll always remember. She and Uncle Johannes were driving back to the mission in the pickup truck. They had just purchased some supplies when they came across a car accident."

She rolled her eyes as she remembered the story. "A car had rolled over into a ditch. It was upside down. My mother raced down to the overturned vehicle and reached into the car to feel the driver's pulse. There was none. They were going to leave the scene and call it in to the police at the next place where they could find a telephone. But before they left, my mother heard something. They went back to the car and looked more carefully. They found a young girl who was hurt and scared, but very much alive, trapped in the rear of the car. There was no way to pull her free. My mother said she looked at Johannes and said, 'Johannes you must raise this car so I can free the girl, now.'"

"But Ms. Alisha," Johannes said, "Dis is a big automobile."

"My mother said, 'I can see that. If you will lift it off her please, I'll pull her out and tend to her injuries.'"

"Johannes looked at the overturned vehicle and hesitated. My mother told him, 'Why do you think God gave you the muscles of a Cape Buffalo? Was it not to help people like this girl here? I know you can do this. Now, if you please.'"

"Uncle Johannes took a few deep breaths and grabbed the rear bumper. He squatted and began to lift. My mother said the muscles and veins in his neck, arms, and shoulders stood out like tree roots. He turned very red and began to pour sweat. The car inched upwards enough for my mother to pull the girl to safety. Johannes dropped the car and sat down hard, puffing like an old farm truck. My mother went over to him, put her hands on each side of his face and stared into his eyes. 'You saved this girl's life. God sent you here today. No one else could have done this thing. You are my hero, Cape Buffalo Johannes Marais.' She touched her forehead to his."

"Later, she asked Mr. Forsyth if she could buy one of his fine watercolors of a Cape Buffalo. Her request surprised him but without hesitation he sold it to her for ten Rands. A ridiculously low price for such a piece. She presented it to Johannes who has it hung proudly in his workshop."

Kalina paused, "How much does a car weigh?"

I shook my head and shrugged—"A lot."

* * * * *

We found the Venda Valley Hotel in town. Our rooms had been reserved for us. The country hotel also had a casino. Gambling although forbidden in South Africa flourished in the Homelands. The casino adjacent to the reception desk reminded me of a "B" movie shot in Las Vegas in the 60's. The orange shag carpet and black ceiling with psychedelic colors and flashing lights provided a startling visual dimension. A heavy layer of cigarette smoke and the smell of beer permeated the room. I registered in and followed the bellman with our bags to our rooms.

We were taken to a detached cottage with two separate mini suites. I was glad we were well away from the noisy casino. The room décor was an attractive blend of traditional Africa with modern touches. The tall bellman with a basso voice explained the amenities. I tipped the bellman and thanked him for his information about the room.

I suggested to Kalina, "We can rest up for a while and I'll see you later for dinner. Will you be okay?"

"Oh, yes." I could see she was looking around, impressed by her lodging. A ceiling fan rotated lazily above the bed. Two vases of red and yellow flowers gave off a sweet natural scent. The floor consisted of black slate with colorful throw rugs. A queen-sized bed with radio and TV completed the picture.

I took advantage of a refreshing shower and stretched out on the bed to relax after the long drive.

*　　*　　*　　*　　*

Three hours later, we shared a pleasant dinner at the buffet. In addition to assorted fish dishes and chicken, they served some game meats. I had the ostrich. Kalina had an enormous salad and curried fish. The food was presented with a lavish flair. It took a lot of man-hours to put on such a spread. As usual with such an abundance of great looking food, I overate. We shared a bottle of Reisling. I kept the conversation very light. Perhaps a little shy at first, Kalina became more comfortable with me as the evening wore on. That would be a big help later.

After dinner we retired to our rooms to get ready for the next day. I reminded Kalina to call Johannes at the mission as promised. No way did I want to get on Johannes' bad side.

I paced and ruminated, my thoughts far from the seminar I was to present the next day. I stared at the handgun on my night table. I kept going over in my mind how to tell Kalina that Mike was her father and that she and her brother were in danger and I had promised to take them out of the country. That was a load. I even made a few notes. It didn't help. Sleep was slow in coming.

The next morning we had a quick, light breakfast with fresh rolls, mango juice and rich coffee. I also snatched a few rashers of bacon. Kalina looked very elegant in her business attire. She had the classic lithe appearance of a fashion model. Also efficient, she remembered everything I had told her about registering attendees; checking their names, handing out nametags, distributing workbooks, and evaluations. She was assertive with the hotel staff about removing the first row of tables and chairs to give me more room, re-supplying the drinking water and orange squash, and changing the room temperature as needed. I admired the way she flipped easily from one language to another.

The seminar went very well. This could only happen because I had given similar versions many times before, and was operating on semi-automatic. The managers and staff from the ministry seemed to need reassurance that they were up to date in their practices. They appreciated my self-deprecating humor. Some of the attendees told me that it was great to hear that they were reading the same books as their counterparts in America and were familiar with many of the concepts and techniques I discussed. Lively class participation made the day fly. I enjoyed the interaction and fielding questions. These young people would be the vanguard of Christianity in South Africa. But I found it difficult to talk about a religious life dedicated to helping others when I was in a crisis about my own life in the church. *Was I going to continue my studies for the priesthood or not? And then what?*

Dinner with Kalina after the seminar was more relaxing and leisurely than the previous evening. She was delighted with my approval of her performance. I think she was also proud of herself. After escorting Kalina back to her room, I sat by the hotel pool nursing an Amstel, thinking and praying. The starscape was incredible. I looked up and there it was – the Southern Cross. I thought it was cool to look up and see this ancient Christian symbol blazing in the night sky.

Kalina promised to call Uncle Johannes at the mission again and report the events of the day.

We had another half day to finish the seminar before heading back to the mission.

If anything, sleep was slower in coming than the night before. I had to break the news soon. How would she take it? Would she and her brother actually believe me and go off with me? Hundreds of questions—few good solid answers.

I wouldn't have slept at all if I'd known what was coming my way the next day.

Chapter 17

THE DAY OF REVELATION ARRIVED. It almost felt biblical.

The morning session at the conference went well. I felt a very positive response from the audience who closed the session with a standing ovation. Kalina and I took our time leaving. We thanked the attendees and I answered a few more questions about preparing for the priesthood. We checked out by noon.

Before we drove off, I felt a bit foolish strapping my new pistol to my left ankle. During the drive home, Kalina opened up even more about her life at the mission with her four uncles.

"Dr. Ngubane was very patient with me as he taught me nursing. I know I have much more to learn but I do love taking care of people as my mother did. As a matter of fact all my uncles helped teach me things.

"Father Godwin taught me to be compassionate and loving to all the patients. He brought them spiritual peace."

She smiled broadly, "Even Uncle Johannes taught me to fix things and to be practical in figuring things out.

"Did you know Uncle Mike used to take me up in his plane and actually let me fly? Now that was scary but what a thrill. He was wonderful."

I was glad to hear she was close to Mike. *Good, that might make things a bit easier.*

We stopped at a roadside café for lunch and dined *al fresco*. A beautiful sunny day followed us. It was time. Despite finishing my large Stella Atrois, my mouth was dry.

"Kalina, I'm glad that you love your uncles, especially how you loved Mike. He was my good friend and I know that he loved you and your mother very much. I have something very important to tell you."

She looked at me wide-eyed sensing the importance of the moment.

"Before Mike Thompson died, he sent me a letter. He told me some things which had to be kept secret from you for various reasons, and asked me to do him a big favor."

"What kind of favor? What secrets?"

"Well, here goes—this is difficult for me. Mike Thompson was not your honorary uncle, but your true father."

"No, Uncle Mike...." She was obviously stunned. I had expected that.

"You can check. He loved you and your mother very much. Your mother and Mike were married by Father Godwin. Johannes and Dr. Ngubane were there as witnesses."

Kalina, expressionless, got up and walked away from the outdoor tables to sit alone on a grassy rise and stare into the bush. I let her go.   Relieved I'd made "the announcement," I shuddered at what I had to say next.

After a while, I followed and sat down on the grass next to her. She sat with her arms around her knees, tucked up to her chin. She had been crying and looked helpless and frail, with tears running down her cheeks. I didn't stare but looked off in the distance with her.

"But why didn't they tell me?"

"I don't really know all the reasons. They probably wanted to avoid trouble for you with the authorities and perhaps other children."

"I always wished Mike to be my father. I felt he was very close to my mother and me."

We sat in silence for twenty minutes. It felt longer.

"There's more," I said.

"What else?"

"Shortly, we'll stop by the monument of the Tropic of Capricorn. Your father asked me to take you there. He left things buried for you. I don't know exactly what's there, but we must get it. And, finally, he told me that you and Jaylin are in great danger and the big favor he asked was that I help you both to get out of the country and to begin a new life elsewhere.

"Leave South Africa? Leave my home? The mission?"

"Yes. You know your father was murdered. That was shocking enough but it seems that you and Jaylin are also in deadly danger."

"Why? We have done nothing."

"I know. I don't even know exactly what it's all about. The world can be cruel. But somehow, as Mike's children, you have also been targeted for assassination."

"How did such people even know my father?"

"I don't have all the answers. Let's go find out what he left for you. Maybe then, we'll learn more. He made me promise not to tell anyone of this."

"Oh. God, I don't know what to think. She buried her face in her arms. I want to talk to Father Godwin."

"Yes, of course. That's a good idea. You must do that as soon as we return." It felt natural to put my arm around her shoulders as we strolled back to the car.

*   *   *   *   *

The monument of the Tropic of Capricorn stood as a tall dark monolith of some kind of carved granite. I could see it easily from the Great North Road. We pulled off and parked. Luckily, no one else was in the small parking area. The cloudy sky put a grayish pall over the landscape. The wind had picked up noticeably.

From the trunk of the rented Delta, I retrieved an old military entrenching tool that doubled as a pick and as a shovel. I had borrowed it from one of Robbie's workshops. As we walked up to the monument, I pulled out a compass.

Standing at the base, I found north and said, "Well, Kalina, here we go. You can help. We need to go one hundred meters. So let's both try to count one hundred paces of a meter in length. That should get us to a Baobab tree. Will you help?"

"Yes, I'll try."

We paced, counting silently. Once we had walked north an estimated fifty meters, I began to have doubts. No Baobab tree in sight. However as we got to eighty meters, a gully opened before us containing the only Baobab tree in the vicinity. "There it is. Now we have to find a root with three carved notches on it."

We approached the tree. Kalina spotted the notches easily.

I began to pick at the earth to the right of the marked root. The hard red clay made for heavy going. I had only gone down about a foot when Kalina screamed.

I spun around and encountered a terror I would never forget. Rising about two feet off the ground, the head of a dark snake moved quickly, straight for us. It seemed to be suspended in the air or flying. "Kalina, run, get back." I threw the entrenching tool at the snake. The handle hit the snake's body and it stopped. The head went down--only a momentary pause—striking at the offending tool. The head rose up again with the tongue darting in and out of its mouth. The reptile kept coming.

I scrambled back toward the car. My attention was divided between Kalina running ahead of me, and the snake steadily gaining on me. I wasn't watching where I was going and stumbled and fell.

Kalina shouted, "The gun, the gun." I had been reaching for it as she screamed. I extracted the handgun from the holster. I thought this had to do it. I can't outrun the damned thing. I took a kneeling firing position. *Keep a steady head, boyo. Remember your training, it will keep you alive.* Slow, steady breaths now.

I clicked off the safety, took aim with arms outstretched, left palm supporting the handle grip and the right forefinger squeezing off a shot. The damned narrow target kept moving and swaying from side to side. Two shots…three…, the fourth shot punctured the snake just below its head and it fell dead, writhing on the ground. I had only one shot left.

Kalina approached slowly. "You killed it. You did it." As I rose, I could see she was shaking. I held her in my arms for a long minute. The shooting habits I had cultivated while in the service were still there. *Bless you forever, roadblock police officer and your gun-selling brother-in-law.*

As I dusted myself off and knelt to return the gun to my ankle holster, I became acutely aware of my rapid breathing, and the perspiration running down my forehead into my eyes.

While I caught my breadth, I saw two men about thirty yards away approaching quickly from the direction of the monument carpark.

They came close to us. "We heard shots. You two okay?" The shorter one said.

"Yes, we had a close encounter with a snake."

The two men walked over to it. "Yah, you was lucky. Dis is the black mamba—very fast and very poisonous. It kill you for sure."

I didn't like the look of the rough-hewn pair. As they got closer, they smelled of old body sweat and stale beer. They wore shabby clothes and beat-up boots.

"So what you doin' out here for fuck's sake?"

I said, "Hey, easy on the language."

They frowned.

"We saw the monument and wanted to stretch our legs from driving, that's all."

"Well, American huh. Dis here be a black mamba," one of the men repeated. Then the other one with the floppy hat, pointed at Kalina and said, "and dis be a black mama." They laughed heartily. They stopped laughing, looked at Kalina and me with contempt, and shaking their ruddy heads said, "We take it, yah?" I nodded my head. They picked up the dead snake for some reason and walked back towards the monument. They conversed in Afrikaans. I felt sure they spoke about me and Kalina.

"Let's go back to the car and wait until they leave. Then we'll get back to Mike's tree."

By the time we returned to the monolith, the men had driven off. After a short break, I said, "Well, shall we try again?"

We walked quickly back to the tree. I found my entrenching tool and began to dig once more. About three feet down, I hit the top of a metal box wrapped in several layers of tough plastic. I pulled it out of the hole and handed it to Kalina.

She opened the box to find two business envelopes. One marked for her, one for me. There were also two larger manila envelopes with our names. Kalina's large envelope contained some jewelry from her mother and cash in rands, euros, and dollars. There was also a delicate black velvet sack. Kalina loosened the top strings and peered inside. It contained several diamonds. Unsure of their value, I estimated it to be several thousand dollars.

My own large envelope contained ten thousand in American currency and a smaller envelope marked "Jaylin." An awesome discovery!

Kalina stood very still – in shock. Mike certainly considered the practical side of getting his daughter started in life.

Kalina handed me the money and jewelry to keep for her. Sitting cross-legged on the rough ground, she opened her letter, totally immersed in its contents. I watched her eyes skim across the page as she gently bit the side of her lip.

From downwind, I sighted the two Afrikaners we had encountered earlier, hunched over, approaching in a stalking gait. One wore binoculars hanging from his neck and the other gripped a tire iron alongside his leg.

Seeing they'd been spotted the lead man smiled. "Hello again. We got to thinkin,' why you two out here? We stopped down the road and watched you. Digging by a tree, way out here? What's dis? We thought. So we come by to see what you dug up. Maybe we let you take something. The rest might be for us. Who knows? Things of value can be found by anyone near a tree, neh?" Their smiles vanished. They looked determined. They looked murderous.

I held down my panic and considered alternatives. Options from my past military training and the streets of Chicago started to kick in.

The taller Afrikaner said, "Hey, its okay. We share. It's the right thing to do. We take some, you take some—a little." They laughed without mirth. One of the men approached Kalina, reached out suddenly and grabbed her buttocks. She twisted away from him, her face in terror.

Although my blood went way over the boil, I remained in control. "Leave her alone."

"We share the girl also, no? Dis kaffir girl looks like she needs to be broken in. Dey love to fuck, you know. Like animals dey breed. First, let's see what you got in de little box."

"You know," I said as calmly as I could, "If we can share, it might be a good thing. Besides, the girl's no good to me anymore, I already broke her in for you boys."

The men looked at each other. The shorter one with a lower missing incisor broke into a grin. The taller one with the heavy eyebrows and binoculars looked quizzical.

Before they could discuss anything further, I went down to one knee, and opened the lid of the metal box towards them. I looked beyond them and shouted, "Oh, Jesus, is that another snake?" They were distracted for about three seconds. It was enough time to pull the pistol from my ankle holster. I pointed it at them and stood. "Now, step back. You, drop the tire iron. Kalina, get behind me."

They stepped back. The taller man dropped the tire iron.

"But you won't shoot us."

"I have an advantage. Has either of you cowardly bastards ever shot a man? Probably not. I have. So, yes, I will shoot. Start walking." I pointed away from the direction they had come.

"I don't think so," said the man who had grabbed Kalina. He took a step forward.

"Enough." I aimed the pistol quickly and placed a grazing shot into the man's right thigh. The man screeched and gripped his leg. Blood seeped through his fingers. "God damn, God damn!"

"The next one will be in your balls—move."

The men didn't hesitate. They turned away and started walking, the wounded man limping while leaning on his companion.

"Faster, or I'll blow holes in your fat asses."

They sped up.

"And don't look back." Then softly to Kalina, "Hand me the tire iron. Run back to the car. Bring back the box of shells for the gun. You'll find it under the front seat. Go now quickly, run."

Kalina did as I asked without question.

I started walking backwards slowly following Kalina without ever taking my eyes off the two men walking away.

Kalina came running back out of breath. She handed me the box of shells. I squatted in the tall dry grass to avoid being seen, reloading at ground level. "Now we can go."

"You had no more bullets?"

"No, but I know how cowards operate. They had to be convinced I'd pull the trigger."

"But, what you said, you scared me. You said you killed before."

"All an act." I lied. "Please don't be frightened of me. I was a soldier once, a hundred years ago. I learned to fight."

Kalina walked calmly to a stunted acacia tree, bent over, and vomited.

*   *   *   *   *

As we drove around a bend, I spotted an old car parked in a layby. I pulled in behind it. I was still jumpy and thinking in flashes--Adrenalin flooded my system. I thought the car probably belonged to the two men. No one was around and it seemed to be in approximately the right place. I got out and saw the dead snake on the floor of the back seat. Without hesitation, I shot the two front tires. I also took their tire iron and hit the windshield. It spidered out like a sunburst. Now that I'd started, it felt too good. When I remembered how one man put his hands on Kalina, I continued until all the windows, rear lights, and headlights had been smashed.

I came back to our car panting slightly. "They won't be following us. Are you okay?"

She stood straight. "I am not," she said evenly. Suddenly she screamed at me in staccato bursts. "I thought the snake was going to kill us. Then I thought those two men were going to kill us. And what you said about me scared me, then you shot one of them and I learned of my real father and...." The rest retreated into an incomprehensible gibberish.

I approached her softly and spread my arms to enfold her. A slender young girl enfolds so easily. I didn't know what else to do. She collapsed into me and sobbed, her slim body shaking in spasms. I knew I had to protect her, like a precious daughter.

After she settled down, I said softly, "We'd better go now."

"All right. I'm sorry. I feel better now."

We got into the car and roared down the road. Kalina dropped her head, curled up in the seat and drifted off, emotionally and physically spent.

I couldn't help feeling relieved and being grateful about getting her out of a dangerous situation. She had resources now--her father's legacy. It felt like retribution and vindication.

I'd faced that black part of myself; the rage against man's evil nature—and the violence that inevitably followed. This time I'd managed to exert some self-control. *Thanks be to God.*

Kalina looked serene in sleep—trusting me to take her to safety. I felt good about that.

As I drove, the bright sunshine retreated a few octaves towards sunset. The adrenalin staved off any fatigue. I relived the incidents at the baobab tree. Couldn't help it.

As we drove back towards the mission, neither of us knew of the horror awaiting there.

Chapter 18

OBSCURED BY DARK FOLIAGE, Vicente waited patiently with the intense gaze of a bird of prey. He wore baggy clothes of earth tones and a bush hat with the entire brim turned down. He covered his eyes with large sunglasses and carried his favorite cane.

He had spotted the boy earlier in the day. The Van DeVeldt's Royal Cheetah Institute would be closing soon, at which time he would confront the lad.

As the setting sun painted long shadows, Vicente eased himself through large green metal doors marked, "employees only." The path beyond the gates rose up above the animal enclosures toward the employees' lockers and sundry equipment. After waiting five minutes in the shadows, he heard a footfall approaching. As the sound got closer… it suddenly stopped. Vicente peered out and saw the boy standing on a flat rock outcropping overlooking the animal pens below. The boy was still—meditative--a National Geographic classic picture of a lanky, muscular, young black man surveying the African landscape, like thousands of his ancestors before him.

Vicente approached smiling and trying to look safe. "Hello, there." He called softly with a smile.

Jaylin turned and said politely, "Sir, this is a restricted area—employees only—and now we're closing. If you'll follow the path to the right, it will take you to the exit."

Vicente smiled, "I know, I know. Let me introduce myself, my name is Dr. Frederico Andiamo. I'm here at the Van DeVeldts' invitation to observe and learn about your breeding techniques to take back to our zoo in Tuscany."

"Oh, I see, I'm sorry, no one told me."

"Would you indulge an old professor for a minute. I won't keep you. What is your name please?"

"I am Jaylin Sangweeni."

Vicente repeated the name, committing it to memory. "Just a few questions, if you don't mind. Do you have other family members working here?"

"No."

"Ah, do you like it here?"

"Yes, very much."

"I'll wager you sometimes bring your family here to show them the animals, and give them a special guided tour."

"No, my parents are dead." Jaylin added for no apparent reason, "I'm studying to be a game ranger."

"Ah, *excelente'*, very good. We need such as you. Admirable. Admirable. Do you have any brothers or sisters?"

"Yes, I have a sister, but why are you asking me about my family?"

"Just curious. It's actually part of my studies—the people who work with animals. As you know, it takes the right sort of people to do your type of work. I will use the information for recruiting purposes. What is your sister's name? Does she work here too?"

Vicente had pushed a little too fast. The boy spooked.

"I'm going to get the manager and maybe he can help you." Jaylin tried to circle around Vicente, who moved laterally to block his way.

"I'll go in a minute. Your sister's name?"

Jaylin tried to pass. Vicente hit the boy with a hard right in the solar plexus. Jaylin sagged to his knees, doubled over.

"Now, back up, boy. Where is your sister? And where is the money?"

"Are you crazy?" Jaylin gasped.

"Yes, I am. Now, tell me and this will be over and I'll leave."

Jaylin scrambled back to the rock's edge, very scared now. He had never been hit so hard.

"Now, once more," hissed Vicente.

Jaylin faked a movement to his right and darted left.

Vicente was much too experienced to be fooled. He moved sideways and threw a right hook into the center of the boy's chest. Jaylin fell back with an unbelievable pain in his sternum. He didn't have the air or energy to scream. Glancing over the precipice he saw two of the huge hairy hyenas looking up with curiosity. Each had his lips pulled back in a hideous grimace, revealing strong pointed teeth capable of crushing any bones.

Once more Jaylin stood, and gulped air. He reached deep, and summoned up enough energy to charge the strange man in front of him.

Vicente popped a hidden spring-catch in the handle of his cane releasing a six-inch blade out of the bottom. He plunged it like a picador into the charging boy's left thigh. The boy dropped at Vicente's feet but managed to reach up and snag the man's belt buckle. He pulled back, taking Vicente' down on top of him.

Vicente chopped down with a rabbit punch into the bridge of Jaylin's nose, breaking it easily. He rose to look down at this helpless, stubborn young black. "Now, for the last time you can end this. What is your sister's name and where can she be found? And one more thing, what did Mike Thompson do with the money he stole?"

"Money? Mike? What are you talking about?" Jaylin saw life through a dense fog of pain and shock.

Jaylin staggered up to a standing position and backed away— too quickly, loosing his balance. He slipped on loose gravel, falling toward the edge of the outcropping. Vicente dove after him but he was too late. The boy fell silently, his arms windmilling, his eyes wide, looking skyward. His fall was broken by a jagged rock, shattering his spine. His supine body lay draped over the rock like a cloth doll.

Vicente looked over the edge carefully. Clearly, the boy was dead. The hyenas moved forward, ears back showing their interest.

Vicente had mixed feelings. On one hand, he had accomplished his goal of getting rid of the boy. It would look like an accident, preventing an investigation. But he felt upset with himself, because he hadn't been able to find out more about the girl, or anything about the money. He knew Ginger Rose would be disappointed and angry with him. He didn't look forward to reporting back to her.

However, he now knew the girl's last name was Sangweeni. Vicente repeated the name several times, so he'd be sure to remember it. He looked around to make sure no one had seen the altercation. No witnesses. Breathing a sigh of relief, he knew he was in the clear.

Vicente mixed with the others who were leaving for the night. No one paid the slightest bit of attention to the heavyset man with the bush hat and sunglasses. If someone had looked carefully, they might have wondered why there was blood on his shoes and the bottom of his cane.

Chapter 19

KALINA AND I PULLED INTO THE MISSION shortly after nightfall, exhausted from the drive and our encounter with the Boer thugs. To our surprise, a small entourage greeted us. Father Godwin came out to the car first, followed by Dr. Ngubane carrying his black bag.

Before I could get out of the car, Kalina rushed out to meet the priest, eager to tell him of our day and ask him about her newly discovered father. I'd cautioned her not to tell anyone about the cash and diamonds. I hoped she would listen, but I couldn't be sure. I kept them safe for her.

Father Godwin looked very grave. His furrowed eyebrows and downcast eyes immediately told me something very, very wrong had happened. With a nod to me, Father Godwin smiled a thin smile, put his arm around Kalina and gentled her inside.

Dr. Ngubane came over to the side of the car.

"What's going on?" I asked.

"We have very bad news. Kalina's brother Jaylin is dead."

I couldn't believe I would be experiencing more jarring emotions today. Now this. I hadn't even met the lad, but I felt heavy inside. I had counted on talking to Kalina first and then soliciting her support to convince Jaylin to come away with us. Perhaps, I thought, I should have done it the other way around. *God, I wish I'd spoken to him sooner.*

"How did he die?"

"Apparently, he fell from a high ledge onto some rocks. It happened at the Cheetah Institute, where he worked. It's tragic. We're all in shock. I've left it to Father Godwin to break the news to Kalina."

Just then, a keening scream pierced the African stillness. Some birds and other creatures of the night screeched in response, seeming to identify with the painful sound.

Dr. Ngubane said, "Now she knows." He sighed deeply. "I'd better go in. I'll give her something."

I mumbled, "Of course." *How much can one young woman take?* The events of the past twenty-four hours were stressful enough, but now, her half brother—dead.

Although I hadn't met Jaylin, I felt incredibly sad, and guilty. It was my responsibility to get both brother and sister out of here to safety. I hadn't done enough, fast enough. I failed.

Was his death an accident? In my gut I doubted it. Young men just didn't fall off high ledges, especially in areas familiar to them. I suspected he was murdered. *I've got to get Kalina out of here.*

I rose and felt the impulse to charge into the room, drag her out, and drive like hell to Jan Smuts airport, and get on the next plane to the States. As I went up onto the porch I heard her sobbing. *Lord have mercy.* For the second time today she had broken down. I stopped in my tracks. I felt grateful Dr. Ngubane medically had eased her pain. I wanted to ease her pain as well—somehow.

I turned back to sit on the porch steps, drained, bewildered as to what to do. I hated that feeling. I hated myself for feeling that way, feeding my rage. To whom should I confide? I felt I had to tell someone what I knew.

*   *   *   *   *

Thirty yards away, I saw Johannes Marais in the moonlight, pacing the grounds in hard purposeful strides. I could hear him making guttural noises; he may have been saying something in some language, but I couldn't make it out. I could see his massive shoulders twitching. Johannes was raging inside and ready to burst. He had lost his daughter in a fall; now Jaylin, a boy he had loved, in an obscene coincidence, had also died in a fall.

Watching the hulk of Johannes striding in and out of the shadows, I decided it was best not to approach him. My mind raced around possibilities. Mike Thompson had warned me about the danger to his family.

I had to focus on Kalina. From what I'd heard of Jaylin's father, the thought struck me that maybe he had come back and somehow confronted the boy.

Dr. Ngubane returned, his face rigid with his own grief over Jaylin's death, then Kalina's breakdown. I knew that any of the men present would have gladly taken on her grief. Ngubane sat heavily on the steps next to me. "She'll rest now." He removed his glasses and rubbed the bridge of his nose. Seeing Johannes pacing in the field, he said, "I wish I could do something *for him*. He loved the boy like a son. I'm afraid he'll hurt himself or have a stroke."

We sat in silence, lost in our emotions in the stillness—a night filled with sounds of life and death. I watched as Johannes disappeared from view. Shortly, he showed up again wielding an ax and a pick. He started hacking at the roots of a large jacaranda tree stump with powerful strokes. He had often used that stump as a stool while conversing with Jaylin. The ax blade glinted in the moonlight rising up and descending. Something or someone had to absorb his rage. He punished the stump mercilessly.

I said, "What he's doing is probably best for him. He looks like a man who has to act out his grief. By the way…. I told Kalina that Thompson was her father."

"How did she take it?"

"Shocked at first. Wondering why it was kept from her, but also pleased."

"I see."

I had to tell someone of my concerns. "I learned about Alisha and Jaylin's father, Bashi, I think his name was."

"Yes?"

"Could he have come back and somehow... fought with the boy?"

"What are you saying?" Ngubane asked.

"I'm saying that I don't think Jaylin's fall was an accident."

"But who...?"

"I don't know. But from what I heard of Bashi...."

The doctor's forehead tightened as he interrupted me. His face turned to stone. "Bashi couldn't have had anything to do with this. Bashi's dead. I helped bury the bastard myself."

I was surprised to hear the usually very formal and proper doctor talk this way. "I see."

"No, you don't. You can't possibly imagine. What have you heard about Alisha and Bashi at the end?"

"That he came back after years of being gone, went crazy, and cut his wife up and raped her, and passed on the AIDS virus to her. He even managed to give Kalina the thin facial scar she carries on the side of her face."

"And then?" asked Ngubane.

"I heard from Father Godwin that you all arrived, threw him out, and attended to Kalina and her mother."

"Yes, that's all true as far as it goes. I'm going to tell you something in the strictest professional confidence. All right? Do you agree? I need your word as a man of God."

"I agree. I can keep a confidence."

"I think you should know, since it seems that Thompson has entrusted you with so much concerning his daughter." The doctor paused and lowered his voice to a whisper. "Out here, sound carries very well, especially to ears that are interested." He sighed deeply.

"I'll never forget that night," Ngubane continued in hushed tones. "Alisha's screams brought Father Godwin into the cottage first. He did what he could to stop Bashi and sustained several defensive slash wounds. But he was too late. Bashi had already done his worst. Johannes arrived next. He took in the situation and how piteous Alisha looked. He loved that woman deeply, whether he could admit it to himself or not.

He picked up Bashi and threw him against the wall, like a rag doll. Then he picked him up again and threw him against another wall—again and again—even long after he was dead.

That's when I arrived. Father Godwin and I jumped on Johannes and I finally managed to give him an injection of a powerful tranquillizer—enough to sedate a horse. Nevertheless he threw us off and continued picking up the bloody lifeless body and throwing it around. After smashing in Bashi's skull, Johannes finally succumbed to the drug and collapsed."

I had listened intently. I could appreciate the risk the doctor was taking. "I can see how you'd never forget that night." I hadn't been around so much violence since my last encounter with an assassin in Chicago. The story ricocheted me back into the reality I'd considered often: violence and murder seemed to be lurking close to the surface of civilized life, ready to burst through at the slightest provocation. Sometimes I felt evil stalked me, ready to emerge at any moment, testing my faith.

Ngubane finished his tale. "So, we attended to Alisha and Kalina. Then Godwin and I buried Bashi at the rear of the property. The grave is unmarked. I'm not sure to this day if Johannes realizes what he did that night. We never talk about it."

I wondered how many more such stories and secrets were part of the tapestry of the Hands of Hope Mission. We sat in silence watching Johannes hack away at the stump. *So it couldn't have been Bashi who killed Jaylin. But who? and why?*

*　　*　　*　　*　　*

At this late hour, nothing more could be done. I felt helpless. Kalina slept. I drove back to Misty Hills, dragged myself to my cottage and opened the door. The bed never looked so good. As I kicked off my shoes and began to unpack a few things, I noticed an envelope with the Misty Hills logo propped up on the middle of the small writing desk. I tore it open.

Dear Deacon,

Please come to my office as soon as you get in, no matter how late. I'll be waiting.

Robbie

Oh Jesus, what now? When I got there, Robbie had a hang-dog worried look. He said, "Come in, come in, my friend. I want you to meet someone. This is Colonel Stuart Marshall, South African Police. He's the one who gave me some of the information you requested about Mike's death. Given recent events I invited him here to ask for his help."

The Colonel stood, offered his hand and said, "Stuart Marshall, recently retired, how do you do." His handshake was firm, his tan skin like warm bark.

I estimated him to be six feet tall. Narrow at the waist, looking whipcord tough, he stood straight as a Zulu assegai. He had a huge drooping moustache, like the horns of the Cape buffalo, salt and pepper in color. His hair looked like white wire combed straight back. Dark bushy eyebrows completed the dramatic-looking pockmarked face.

I said, "Colonel," as we shook hands.

Then to Robbie, "What's going on?"

Robbie answered, "I know you're bushed. We'll talk later about Kalina and Jaylin. I'll let the Colonel explain."

"I'll be brief, Mr. Deacon; it's like this. I was in the process of retiring when Thompson's body was discovered. Technically, he was killed while I was still on my last day of active duty."

"I see." My fatigue ebbed as I listened to the Colonel's staccato delivery.

"My successor, rather understandably, didn't want me in on the scene, but the high commissioner wouldn't hear of it. As a compromise I consulted on the case. You see, it presented some unique circumstances." He paused and switched gears. "I understand you were a friend of Thompson's."

"Yes sir, I was."

"May I ask, what brought you to South Africa?"

"Well, that's hard to explain exactly. Robbie here and I became friends in the States and he frequently invited me to come out. My schedule allowed me the opportunity to come for a visit and conduct a training seminar for the Zahl Institute."

"Yes, yes, I see. But was Thompson instrumental in bringing you here?"

"We'd kept in contact; he also had asked me to come to South Africa." I was hedging carefully.

"You're a deacon of the Catholic Church, correct?"

"Yes."

"You are accustomed to keep secrets?"

"Yes, of course."

"In my line of work we learn to be secretive, too. To speak plain to you, sir, so we're not beating around a thorn bush, I don't think you're telling me the whole story."

I was trying to size up the man. He was obviously not easily fooled. *What was he after?*

He sat back, crossed his legs and continued. "I'll tell you what–to begin with, I'm going to tell you about our investigation of Mike Thompson's death, then maybe you'll open up to tell me more."

Robbie interjected, "I'll get some coffee and sandwiches sent up for us, all right?"

We nodded in agreement. I realized I was famished. Robbie made a call.

The Colonel squinted as he continued. "First, Thompson's body was found next to his plane on an abandoned emergency airstrip in the Karoo, a very remote area. One fact, not let out to the media–his hands had been cut off—mercifully, the M.E. tells us, post mortem. Our forensic team went over the inside of his plane thoroughly. They discovered two unusual items. To be specific, a small fragment of an elephant tusk and traces of wild dog urine. Really foul smelling stuff. What do you make of that?"

"I have no idea. What conclusions have you come to?" I felt really lost.

"Well, the severed hands is something we've seen before. It's usually a signal that the victim had been stealing. The bits of elephant tusk in the airplane out in the middle of bloody nowhere, indicates transporting ivory—no doubt illegally. We have no idea what to make of the wild dog urine. But yesterday, we found a connection. I shall get to that presently."

I tried to take it all in. The information piled up fast. First Thompson, now his stepson, Jaylin. The hands cut off, ivory tusks, wild dog urine--In my fatigued state, I had trouble connecting the dots.

The Colonel continued. "I'm convinced young Jaylin was murdered."

"But I just learned he fell."

"Let me tell you why I'm convinced he was murdered." The Colonel sat back for a moment and looked up to collect his thoughts. "Mind you, I have no official standing in all of this, being retired, but my contacts on the force told me about the boy's death and I invited myself in to see if I could be of assistance. First of all, he died of a broken back in the fall, an indisputable fact. However, our medical examiner discovered he had a large contusion on his sternum, a few cracked ribs in the front of his chest, and what appeared to be a knife wound in the front of his right thigh. According to the ME's report, these were pre-mortem injuries and could not have been caused by the fall."

"Now, for the interesting connection I just mentioned. As we interviewed his employers and fellow workers at the Cheetah Institute, we were told that Jaylin participated in a school project which necessitated the collection of wild dog urine. None of his teachers nor anyone at his school knew anything about such a project."

"Why the hell would he be collecting dog piss?"

"That, we don't know. But the fact that they found traces in Thompson's plane and the facts that Thompson and the boy knew each other well—both had spent time living and working at the mission—defies coincidence, wouldn't you agree?"

"Of course…I agree. Robbie, what do you think?"

"I haven't a clue, old son. But the connection is compelling."

"Have you interviewed the people at the mission?" I asked the colonel.

"No, I haven't, but I have to be careful. Remember, I'm out of it now. I have no official standing to do that. I shouldn't even be here talking to you."

"Then sir, may I ask, why you are here?"

"It's complicated." The colonel put his face in his hands and sighed.   "Thompson's murder happened while I was still on the force. I feel I need to clear it up to leave with a clean slate. I have the time. Also, let's say I don't approve of my successor's handling of the matter. I know the cases are connected, but he doesn't see it that way—the plank. I've got a feeling that there's a much bigger issue involved." Shaking his head, he said, "No one seems to agree with me, though"

I considered the facts. Jaylin was connected to Thompson and both had been murdered. Kalina would probably be next. While sitting in an easy chair in Robbie's office I felt the stab from within my pockets of the material inheritance I had dug up earlier. Was it only hours ago? It seemed like days.

"Colonel, before we continue, I'd like to have a word in private with Robbie."

He hesitated. "Certainly." I could see his jaw thrust forward.

Robbie and I left his office to speak in the hall. I spoke rapidly in a whisper. "Robbie, I'm in way over my head. I realize I've got to have some help. What about this Colonel?"

"Deacon, next to Del and you, he is absolutely the most trustworthy person I know."

"All right then, time to get some things out in the open. But first, I noticed you have a large safe in your office."

"Yes, it's a good one."

"I have some valuables to put in there. It's got to be now." When I handed my friend the envelopes, Robbie nodded, "Valuables, you said?" He looked inside the envelopes, noticing the wad of folded bank notes. "Bloody hell, did you rob a bank? Shall I count it?"

"Later, and here's a little purse to put in there as well."

Robbie opened it and saw the diamonds. "It's a small fortune!"

"Yes, it's for Kalina, from Thompson, except for one envelope with my name on it, and another for Jaylin." I paused to collect my thoughts before going on.

"Look, I'm going to tell the Colonel why I'm here, but not this part. We've got to keep this for Kalina's future."

We went back to join the Colonel. The coffee and sandwiches were brought in by a very young black girl in a kitchen uniform.

Robbie quietly put the valuables in the safe. The aroma of the grilled ham and cheese sandwiches with warm German potato salad sent my taste buds into a frenzy. I dug in, and spoke between mouthfuls. "Colonel, I'd like you to keep what I'm telling you to yourself, as much as possible."

The Colonel did not respond immediately. "I'll do my best, but I can't make any promises until I've heard what you have to say."

"Fair enough." I told him about the letter I'd received from Mike, the danger to Kalina and Jaylin, and my pledge to get them out of the country. I told the Colonel that Thompson said he got mixed up with evil people in a project that started out well, then morphed into something else. Something bad.

"Of course, Kalina didn't know Thompson was her father until I broke it to her yesterday."

"I failed with Jaylin, too slow–too late. I'm sure Kalina is the next target. There's no time to waste. We must get her out of harm's way."

The Colonel didn't interrupt. He remained focused and quiet, sitting ramrod straight, apparently digesting the material until I finished.

"Things become a little clearer now," he said. "I'll tell you more of what I suspect. Lately, we've gotten wind of a possible connection with a South American drug cartel operating here. It's all very vague at this point. I tell you this because it is their practice to mutilate bodies as a warning sign for others. And, more to the point, they dedicate themselves to killing the entire family of an enemy, or someone who betrays them, or…steals from them."

"So you think Thompson was involved with a drug operation, and crossed them somehow and now the dealers are out to eliminate his whole family?" The orbit was widening. Certainly this explanation fit the facts so far. Still, I found it hard to believe Thompson's involvement with drugs. I considered the proposition, then rejected it. Perhaps he didn't fully realize what was going on.

The Colonel nodded. "We're not certain, but a bush pilot like Thompson would be indispensable to a smuggling operation."

I said, "Maybe he didn't know drugs were involved. Initially he could have just been a courier. Then how does the ivory fit in?"

"Perhaps it doesn't fit in. It could be a separate issue. One thing for sure, if our suppositions are correct, his children wouldn't be safe anywhere in Southern Africa. Is there anything else you can tell me?"

"A couple of things. Have you heard of anyone with a name such a Rosenbloom or Rosenmoon?"

"No I haven't, why?"

"Well, in Thompson's letter he told me to be aware of such a person—a killer. A question. Was there a photo—like a family photo of Thompson and his wife and children at the crime scene?"

"Not that I'm aware of. Where did you hear that?"

I wondered if I should tell. "Is it possible there was such a photo and you didn't see it? Maybe it was put into evidence later."

"No, I'm sure no photo was found at the scene. My team, or should I say my former colleagues and I went round and round discussing everything about the murder investigation and the clues at the plane. No photo was ever mentioned. I repeat, where did you hear that?"

"A reporter for the Joburg Sun told me that there was such a photo."

"And that would be…?"

"A Miss Ginger Rose."

"I know her." He raised his eyebrows. "She's hard to miss. And I do remember her being at the scene. If she or one of those reporters found a bit of evidence and kept it from us, I'll have them locked up for obstruction of justice. Of course, she could have misunderstood, or perhaps the murderer was there, had the photo, and mentioned it to her for some reason."

After a period of silence, a bold plan sprang to mind. "Look, Colonel, now that I've told you so much, I'd like to offer you a proposition." I paused to consider my words carefully. "How would you like to help us get through this, and help me get Kalina to safety. You can name your fee."

"Private work, eh? I never thought I'd see the day." He paused, stroking his moustache. I could see him considering my proposition seriously.

"It's an interesting case I'd like to clear up. And I'm not ready to retire, by God I'm not!" He pounded his fist into his other palm. Another pause. "It would be nice not to be hampered by the bureaucracy." He took another long quiet moment. "I'll do it. We can discuss my fee later." We stood and shook hands.

We all agreed that the main thing was Kalina's safety. Well into the night, we discussed how to protect her and eventually get her out of the country.

I felt a lot better having allies, people in whom I could confide. No longer was I in a helpless situation—out of my control—like that night in Chicago when I took a bullet when a gang of thugs broke into my digs to pick up a madam who had entered the church looking for sanctuary.

Chapter 20

"SO, ITS DONE." GINGER ROSE SAID. She and Vicente Luna were enjoying sundowners on the balcony of his apartment. The sky flamed with improbable pinks, purples, oranges and reds while the Jacaranda trees splashed their violet flowers against the cityscape.

"Si, but I didn't get any information from him about the money or his *hermana*."

"Mmmm, that's too bad." Rose said.

"What about the American?" Vicente asked, blowing out a roiled narrow stream of smoke from his thin panatela.

"I'm still not sure. Possibly he knows nothing." But, she thought, now he knows me—a lot better. She briefly recalled their night together in delicious detail. Delighted with her brazenness, and Deacon's reaction, she relished her power.

Vicente interrupted her thoughts. "I found out one thing by talking to the people at the cheetah cages."

"Oh, and that would be…?"

"The boy used to live at the mission. Isn't that where Thompson lived also?"

"Yes, it is. An interesting coincidence, no? If that's the case, then it's likely the girl may live there too, or at least they might know of her whereabouts." Energized, she jumped up from her chair and started pacing barefoot, gnawing on her knuckles—an old unconscious habit.

Ginger's face brightened, "I have an idea. We'll attend the boy's funeral. I can get the details easily. It will be for a story in the paper." She looked up, her eyes closed, thinking. "We will observe the mourners carefully. I'll be close by. You'll have to observe from a distance. Use those high-powered binoculars you love so dearly." Folding her hands as if in prayer, she said, "With her father recently dead, and now her brother, she'll be devastated and grieving. As we both watch, we can pick out such a young woman. Others will be offering her their condolences.

"The mission is the link to Thompson's family. I should have thought of it before. We're very close. We'll do this and be finished. We may have a chance to recover the money yet. Then back to business. Once we get another pilot and have things running smoothly again, perhaps we can go on a vacation or even go home for an extended visit."

"*Si', bueno.*" Vicente smiled broadly.

*   *   *   *   *

Colonel Marshall, Robbie, and I arranged to have a conference with the uncles the first thing the next morning. I knew they needed information if they were going to be of help, and plans had to be made for Kalina's safety.

Despite the warnings in Thompson's letter, I decided to trust these men. Maybe I had missed something, but they all seemed to love Jaylin and Kalina. I decided to take a chance—a big one. I told them patiently, sensitive to their reactions, how Mike had been murdered and possibly why. How Mike's body had been mutilated, with his hands having been severed sent a message. One that said as clearly as any words could have, that Mike had been caught stealing. Stealing from the wrong people. That he had probably been involved in illegal ivory trading, and even, perhaps not intentionally, drug smuggling as well.

As I watched the men, Father Godwin began to twitch nervously—perhaps over the mention of the illegal ivory trade. But when I said "drug smuggling," Godwin looked as if he would implode.

Ngubane perspired profusely and cleaned his glasses over and over again.

Johannes remained as still as a granite statue. I noted their reactions carefully. I had a gut feeling that they were hiding something from me but I didn't want to voice my concerns at this point.

I could see my next revelation hit them all pretty hard. "There is significant evidence to indicate that Jaylin was also murdered." The uncles were initially stunned into silence. After a few moments, they all began speaking and asking questions at once.

I held up my hand. "We can answer your questions and give you details later. The important issues right now are these. First, we can assume that Kalina is in grave danger. It seems logical, for whatever reason, that Kalina is next on the list to be assassinated. Now, we don't know exactly why, but it seems reasonable that the killers are bent on eliminating Thompson's family altogether."

I stood and drained my coffee. "So, we've got to get Kalina to safety and out of harm's way—immediately. Second, we have to get the killers off her trail—permanently. Now, I'd like to turn our meeting over to Colonel Marshall, who has agreed to work as our consultant. He has had a lifetime of expertise in these matters."

The Colonel addressed the second issue first. "Gentlemen, there is only one sure way to get these dogs off her spoor forever," he paused for effect. "That is to convince them that she is dead. I can arrange for her to have new identity papers, but I'll need your help in staging her death. Doctor, you can be of immense help here."

"Yes, yes, I see," said Ngubane.

Johannes offered, "Fire is best. Daht way no one can tell about de body."

"A good idea," the Colonel agreed.

Father Godwin said to Johannes, "Why don't you pick one of the outlying buildings and be sure to create a plausible cause for the fire."

"Yah, I'll do it."

"I'll sign the death certificate to show it was Kalina Sangweeni, sister of Jaylin, and daughter of Alisha," offered the doctor.

Father Godwin said, "I can get it into the newspapers and conduct a proper service."

Colonel Marshall shook his head in admiration. "Now that's teamwork! Thank you, gentlemen. To be on the safe side, there should be some charred remains, at the scene, you agree?"

"Leave it to me," said the doctor.

Colonel Marshall shook his head trying not to think of laws being broken. He exchanged knowing glances with Deacon.

I thought, *what a conspiracy.* I focused on Kalina "Now, how about a safe hole for Kalina—right now."

The doctor chimed in, "My clinic in the Chimanimanis is pretty remote. She ought to be safe there."

"Has she been there before?" asked the Colonel.

"Yes, but only a few times and years ago."

"Then it may be unsuitable. People there know her. They might inadvertently tell others she is staying there."

"I see," said the doctor.

I put forward a proposition. "People are easily fooled. She hasn't been seen there for years and she's grown. We could disguise her somehow, perhaps as a young man."

"How would you do that?" asked Father Godwin.

I paced as I thought it out. "It shouldn't be too hard. Cut her hair shorter. Men's clothes, a cap, boots, sunglasses, and a small theatrical moustache. She can probably find a way to conceal her girlish figure."

Robbie said, "Del could help with that."

Father Godwin asked, "Then what?"

I answered carefully. I still felt a little like an outsider among the uncles.

"I know you all love her and want what's best for her. I think 'next' is….out of the country."

The uncles looked at each other in dismay. I could see they didn't want to lose her.

I understood. Some tactful and delicate explanations were called for. "While she is away I can arrange for Skype conferences and e-mails so you can all keep in contact. I know it won't be the same. But with a different name, and her own maturing, there's a good chance she can return after her schooling and after a few years practicing as a nurse. So it doesn't have to be goodbye forever. Look at it as if she were going to continue her professional schooling abroad." I studied the relief on their faces.

Johannes stood and declared, "Daht seems okay. But I must go to the Chimanimanis and stay wid her."

No one objected. I thought it was a great idea. What better bodyguard?

Ngubane spoke, "But what do we do with Kalina until we can arrange for the fire and her untimely demise?"

I said, "Hopefully, she will agree to wear the disguise and stay with me at Misty Hills until we leave for your clinic in a day or so. I'm not going to let her out of my sight. I'll also be going with the group to the leper colony." The thought of this sent a shudder through me. *Lepers!* Christ, right out of "Father Damien of Molokai."

Our meeting adjourned.

*   *   *   *   *

The uncles were alone discussing their conspiracy.

Father Godwin spoke first, voice quavering. "This has got to end. We are responsible for this tragedy because of the ivory business."

Dr. Ngubane and Johannes exchanged knowing glances. The doctor said in a quiet steady voice, "I know you feel responsible. We all feel terrible, but it was Thompson who violated our trust and stole money from the wrong kind of people—our unforgiving partners. Don't you see? If he had just continued as we were, none of this would have happened. He put his life and that of his own family in jeopardy."

"And what about this drug business--sweet Mother Mary, What's that all about?" Godwin questioned.

The other two shrugged noncommittally. Father Godwin still suspected nothing of the heroin portion of their ivory scheme. He saw the logic in the doctor's words but still felt guilty.

"I can't help it. I think we must stop this ivory operation right away. I've never completely come to terms with it. It's as illegal as hell. If we're caught, all of our work at the mission will have been in vain."

Ngubane responded, shaking his head. "But look around you, and see all the good it has done. I can see how you'd feel this way at this sad time. Let's just shelve this ivory business temporarily and give ourselves time to think. We still have many patients to care for. But I agree we must take care of Kalina above all."

Father Godwin said, "Yes, you're right about Kalina, but to the devil with the ivory. We can increase our fund-raising efforts and still support our work here without profit from the ivory."

Ngubane thought, *naive man*, perhaps we can scratch out some support, but not at the level needed, and certainly not enough to support my lifestyle too. He put his face in his hands.

He knew that their pact with the Columbians was for life. Short of the grave, there would be no getting out of it.

Father Godwin stood and looked up, perhaps for divine guidance, and rushed off to shoot hoops with some teenagers to burn off some of his anxiety. Johannes and the doctor walked off toward the outlying buildings.

Ngubane wasn't sure where Johannes stood in all of this. "Well, my friend, what do you think?"

Johannes, as usual, seemed to have difficulty articulating his thoughts. "First, we save Kalina. I promise Alisha. This I must do. Den, I don't know. We must continue wid de drugs. Dey will never let us go, you know daht, yah?"

Ngubane knew that, despite his rough looks, Johannes was no fool. He had become increasingly aware that they had made a pact with the devil. "Yes, I'm afraid you're right," and he thought, *I'm not ready to give up the good I am doing for my people.* His mind overburdened with the tasks before him, he neglected the usual warm interactions with the staff that he was known for. He couldn't quite admit it to himself, but he wouldn't give up his power and the lifestyle of the Eagle's Lair.

"But," Johannes continued, "If I find who kills Jaylin, dey will die." He clenched his massive fists involuntarily. "Maybe we can continue wid de drugs but not in de ivory."

"I don't know if that will be possible. This system works very well for our partners. We may have to continue both without Godwin knowing or being involved. He's ready to crack."

"Yah, I think so. Too true."

"Well then, to the fire, and Kalina's fake demise."

"Yah, I get to it now. We do it tomorrow morning--maybe?"

"Only if I can get a young woman's cadaver. I'll let you know. Well, I have arrangements to make and a clinic of patients to see. I'll talk to you tonight at your workshop."

"Yah, I have some work to finish up for the next shipment."

The men parted, trusting each other and committed to perform their parts like actors in a grand Shakespearean production.

*   *   *   *   *

I admired Kalina's spirit, but she wouldn't accept the strategy we'd worked out. She argued heatedly with me, and for both our sakes I argued back just as hard.

"No," she said, riding on a long sigh, eyes flashing.

In the end we reached a compromise. She would attend the funeral of her brother in disguise, and away from the other mourners. However, she refused to leave the country after her official "death" in the fire. With the penetrating stare of a cobra she said, "Not until the wicked men are found and punished. But I will stay with you at Dr. Ngubane's clinic in the mountains. I will keep the disguise, and keep to myself while you and the others track down these killers.

I looked out into the colorful landscape and remembered the old saying, "*If you want to see God laugh, make a plan.*"

Her practical nature kicked in and hit me like a blow to the solar plexus.

"Now, I have money, so I want you to use it. Pay for experts, bribe officials, offer a reward. I want the murderers found and punished. I don't care how much it costs." Her firm-o-meter went beyond mine: her eyes blazed in determination. "Use all the money if you have to—the diamonds also."

I had little choice short of kidnapping her. I suspected recent events had led her to grow up fast.

I could only work within the parameters she had laid out.

Thompson would have been proud of his daughter. I certainly was.

Chapter 21

THE FUNERAL SERVICES BEGAN WITH EARLY MORNING MASS. The funeral services began with early morning Mass. Humid, windless and gray, the day reflected the mood of the mourners. Even the birds were quiet in respect. Father Godwin gave a short but moving eulogy in the small, packed rustic chapel. The grief radiated throughout. Jaylin had been a popular lad. Mourners observed him laid out in the uniform of a government game ranger, the profession that he had come to love.

Kalina, carefully disguised as a young man, sat in the back pew near Johannes. She wept quietly, as many were doing. Robbie, Del, Dr. Ngubane and I sat together up front. The Colonel, in civilian clothes, sat near the back door, vigilant as ever, carefully assessing the gathering.

When the service concluded, the entourage processed to a slow drumbeat to a small cemetery at the rear of the property. The shaded glade surrounded by tall eucalyptus trees provided an appropriate setting.

I watched Kalina out of the corner of my eye, standing apart from the others, unrecognized. The large sunglasses helped.

She walked unsteadily in men's boots. Del had done a good job disguising her with a large floppy bush hat and baggy men's clothes. Because of her tears, she had to keep pressing on the ersatz moustache to keep it in place.

Johannes hovered nearby, keeping a careful watch as tear tracks ran unashamedly down his craggy face.

As we moved out of the chapel, Ginger Rose joined us, appropriately attired in black with no emphasis on the curves of her body. She wore a wide–brimmed black hat with a veil and little makeup. She walked over and joined hands with me.

"It's terrible, just terrible," she said quietly. "So young. I've been sent by the paper. They want me to do a human-interest story about the young man, so giving, so close to his aspirations of becoming a game ranger."

"It's good of you to come." Surprised to see her, I felt torn by the grief surrounding me and her electric touch. I couldn't completely slake thoughts of our night together. She let go of my hand. It helped. We didn't speak as we followed the procession to the gravesite.

Altar boys led the way with incense burners, followed by Father Godwin and the casket, carried by six pallbearers. The mourners straggled behind, singing and humming a dirge. The cloudy day held the promise of rain. Somehow I found it appropriate that the heavens should cry too.

*   *   *   *   *

Rose separated herself from Deacon. She recognized Colonel Marshall and nodded in his direction. He acknowledged her and nodded back. *Why is he here?* She wondered. Did he know people here at the mission? She didn't like it. His presence could threaten to expose their operation.

She refocused on the mourners, especially the young women, trying to discern which of them could be Jaylin's sister. None looked any more grief-stricken than the others, and none stood in close proximity to the coffin. A few people, including a young man with sunglasses and a floppy hat, stood off at a distance. She would never fully understand the reasons why the young blacks acted as they did during ritual events. The multitude of tribes all had their own constellations of grieving behaviors.

At the same time, Rose knew that Vicente was watching from a hillock in the distance. She felt sorry for him, knowing he was probably uncomfortable among the bushes and bugs on the sultry day. *Has he observed anything useful,* she wondered?

Prompted by this funereal atmosphere, Rose remembered the few people who had been kind to her and had passed on. Like one of the madams she had whored for—Maria Teresa Abrigon, who had taught her to speak with a more polished accent and vocabulary. Like Sister Claudia who fed her and gave massive hugs during the worst times.

She also thought of those whose death she had welcomed, those who needed to die, and those she helped to dispatch herself: Paulo, her first pimp—Consuella the Peruvian madam who sold her like livestock on both sides of the Amazon and beat her skillfully without ever marking her salable body, and especially her uncle Enrico, who had introduced her to sex in the choir loft of Our Lady of Perpetual Help when she had turned nine. She could still feel his stinking breath and the look of the beamed ceiling as she looked up past him, while he grunted over her. She fervently hoped he was being tormented for eternity in the deepest recesses of hell.

God died for her on that painful sweltering afternoon.

Years later she watched without emotion as her uncle, on her orders had a bleeding pig strapped around his waist prior to being thrown into the murky Amazon. The roiling water around him soon turned red. Satisfying.

She had to negotiate, blackmail, and sex her way into the inner circle of Luis Salazar. He took her in, continued her education, gave her a soft affectionate kind of loving she had longed for—and had only experienced once before with a black South African sailor named Tito Absa.

Tito began their relationship as a customer, then as her lover. He was the first man to treat her decently, buy her nice clothes, and take her out to dinner. Rose, who knew him to be a hard man among hard men, was surprised that he never struck her, not once.

Above all, he made her laugh with his wild stories of South Africa and his misadventures on the high seas. He described in detail animals which she had never seen or heard of, and the lucrative ivory trade. He vividly described his love for the land so rich in gold and minerals. A land which could grow anything, even the poppies for opium and heroin. Rose had always thought this was strange talk for a sailor.

He sailed off one morning, out of her life forever. She wept bitterly, saddened for months. She had tried to find him years later in South Africa but to no avail.

It was Tito Absa's talk of the rich land for growing anything which eventually had become the inspiration for the South African operation. Rose remembered his stories and a few years later, one sleepless night after lovemaking, she relayed his words to Luis Salazar.

Salazar by this time was fed up with fighting the powerful Colombian drug lords for a miniscule share of the cocaine profits. His forces were depleted. There had been much spying, betrayal, ambushes and killing. And for what? Most of the money went into the greedy pockets of the police and politicians. Most of the rest went into the lavish lifestyle of the leaders of the drug families. Very little was left to help the people. Luis needed a new, highly profitable product from a new source.

South Africa provided the answer. There would be no competition from the powerful Colombians. Luis would see to it that the profits would flow into the hands of the right people. However, it wasn't long before Luis couldn't resist taking a huge cut for himself and began to live like the other cocaine princes of the region.

Luis Salazar did not work in half measures. He sent teams of scouts, agronomists, pharmaceutical technicians, and other specialists to first see if it were possible to grow and harvest sufficient quantities of the special poppies in southern Africa. The reports were extremely favorable, especially from neighboring Zimbabwe. Several challenges had to be met and overcome. Among them, cultivation, conversion of the poppies into heroin and distribution.

Rose led the advance team. She had a clever scheme to put herself in a position to gather all the information she could. Through bribery, intimidation, and blackmail, she secured a job as a feature reporter at the Johannesburg Sun newspaper. There she learned of the vast supplies of stored ivory tusks and the CITES (Convention on International Trade in Endangered Species) agreements which banned the international trade in ivory. She also discovered to her delight that there was very little competition in their projected endeavor.

One afternoon, at an elegant luncheon in Salazar's villa, she noticed the wicker cornucopias disgorging fruit and colorful flowers as buffet decorations. When she squinted her eyes and used a little imagination, they resembled short stubby tusks, *colmillos.* They were really hollowed out receptacles. *Why couldn't an elephant tusk be such a receptacle? Could it not hold much precious powder?*

When she presented this idea to Salazar, he became excited at the possibilities. He immediately put Rose in charge of the entire South African operation, and sent Vicente along as her assistant and protector. With this high honor, Rose vowed to make the operation a huge profitable success, no matter what it took.

She snapped back to the present reality. The death of this boy meant nothing. It was part of the business plan, that's all. It could have been avoided if Thompson had kept his hands off money that didn't belong to him.

His greed cost him his life and his hands. *Now to find his daughter and complete the retribution.*

*   *   *   *   *

Father Godwin read from scripture and spoke eloquently of Jaylin's contribution to the people at the mission. The hymns sung in rich harmony were moving. I could carry a tune, but harmony was beyond me. I could produce a pretty good Gregorian chant, however. I appreciated the soft drum rhythms, subtle in their accompaniment. Nearly everyone wore something black, even if only an armband.

Several of the men placed spears and other weapons on the coffin, per Zulu tradition. A tribal chief in full feathers and leopard skin cloak chanted, and threw offerings on the casket. Some looked like bones. Fascinated, I wondered what Father Godwin thought of that.

A high-ranking game ranger placed a photograph of Jaylin with his beloved cheetahs at the headstone. Johannes sank to his knees in tearful prayer.

I've never liked funerals even though I've presided at quite a few. I couldn't help but consider the incomprehensible loss of so many young innocents in Chicago and around the world. A battered woman I tried to help was the last funeral I had attended, just over a year ago. The present ritual dredged up all of my grief again, though admittedly not quite as strong as my original feelings. With God's help, I would endure–without the balm of drugs.

Dr. Ngubane approached and asked me why Ginger Rose was in attendance. "I don't like it. This is a holy time."

I was surprised by Ngubane's reaction to Ginger Rose. "I think the paper sent her to do a feature story," I replied.

Ngubane hung his head and stomped off without another word. *Curious.*

When the simple ceremony concluded, I looked over at Kalina. She remained alone, apart, uncomforted in her sorrow. It had to be this way to protect her identity.

I noticed a flash of a reflection from a nearby hillside. I glanced several times in that direction. As the mourners dispersed, I saw the shape of a man rise up and struggle through the high grass. All I could tell was that it was a white man, heavyset, wearing a bush hat. I could just make out binoculars hanging from his neck. *Why would someone be watching from a distance?*

I saw that Johannes had also noticed the man in the undergrowth. He walked over and whispered to Dr. Ngubane, while observing the man walking down the hill. They had very serious looks on their faces and spoke in hushed tones.

I had no idea what they discussed.

The disguise and lack of proximity to the gravesite proved to be a successful ruse. No one could single out any young woman whose behavior demonstrated that she was especially close to the deceased; especially if that young woman looked like a boy.

As the crowd scattered, I walked away with Rose. We had not spoken for quite a while.

"I hate these events," she said.

"Me too," I agreed.

I looked away, not wanting to share my personal story. "I think it's the weight of the communal grief. It reminds me of loved ones I have lost."

"In my article, I'll mention the priest and clinic, and, of course, Dr. Ngubane. They have done wonders at the mission. I also noticed Colonel Marshall was here. Why do you suppose he attended?"

"I don't know," I shrugged my shoulders and lied. "I met him briefly this morning."

She knitted her eyebrows, "I was given to understand that he was retired."

"I wouldn't know about that. Perhaps he knew the boy or the family."

I didn't like the "reporter" in Rose. As a matter of fact, I recognized my own prejudice against professional women consumed by their work. I don't know why. *God knows, I need to work on that.*

"Were other family members present?" Rose inquired further.

"I don't know. I don't think so. I never met the boy. You'll have to ask Father Godwin."

"Why are you here, if these events disturb you?"

Jesus, won't she quit—a good question, however. Why would I be here? I tried to recover quickly, "Robbie asked me to come along. Maybe he just wanted me to experience an African funeral." I hoped that that would do. It was plausible.

Ginger Rose nodded enigmatically and looked off into the distance. "Now is not the time, I know," she said, "but can we see each other again before you leave?"

"I think so. But you're right, now is not the time."

"When are you leaving? You never mentioned it."

"I'm not sure, really; just not sure at this moment." I was getting irritated by her questions.

She finally stopped her queries. She tilted her head up and looked deeply into my eyes. Magically, she made it an intimate gesture that sent a thrill through me.

She opened her note pad and went over to Father Godwin. I presumed she wanted to ask about the family of the deceased boy.

I couldn't hear her questions but I did hear Father Godwin's lying answers. He was pretty convincing. He said, "I'm not sure if the boy had any family. I know his mother and father are deceased."

"So, is it possible he had siblings?" she continued.

"I really don't know: I doubt it."

Rose finally left him alone and strode off.

Kalina walked alone. Like her "uncles," I wanted to rush to her and comfort her somehow. But the overwhelming priority was her anonymity and safety. She could be comforted later. She had attended the funeral service as she had insisted. I considered it risky, but a necessary part of her necessary grieving process. Now it was time to get her to safety.

*   *   *   *   *

As Rose left the area, she met up with Vicente in the carpark. They compared notes and came up empty.

Rose said, "The priest said the parents were dead and he wasn't aware if the boy had any siblings. The parents being gone was probably true, but about the siblings–*mentira!* I've seen too many men lie, especially priests who are good at it. From that photo I'm sure the boy had a sister. We'll find her soon and be done with this business. It's taking too much of our time. The retribution must be *absoluto.*"

Vicente shrugged. *"Sin Duda."*

Chapter 22

I WANTED TO MAKE SURE I DIDN'T DRAW attention to myself. After the short reception following the funeral, I faded out a side entrance went to my car and sped back to Misty Hills. Perspiring profusely on the sultry day, I set off to find Kalina. As planned, she would be walking along the road so I could pick her up.

As I drove, my gut tightened because I couldn't see her. I looked in my rear view mirror with a bit of paranoia setting in, however I saw no one following behind me.

Finally, I spotted her walking awkwardly in her oversized men's boots on the red-orange clay verge. She was hard to spot because she blended in so well with everyone else walking along the roadside. I felt gratified that Del had done a good job concealing her gender.

I pulled off the road in a cloud of red dust, flinging open the passenger door before the car had come to a complete stop. "Please – get in quickly."

She got in and sat beside me, her face expressionless, her head bowed.

"I'm so sorry," I said, "I know that was tough. You were very brave." I stroked her hair and squeezed her hand.

Her face streaked with tears, and eyes had a hollow, far-away look.

"Now you'd better put your head down, so you won't be seen."

She scrunched down on the seat as I swerved back onto the road.

Previously, Robbie had shown me a delivery entrance at the back of the Misty Hills hotel complex that remained open and unguarded during business hours on weekdays. I turned in and drove up the bumpy dirt road to my cottage. "Now to get you in without being seen." I got out of the car and looked around. No luck. I saw several people strolling about who could see Kalina get out of the car.

I walked quickly back to the car and leaned inside. "We'll have to drive around to the back." I drove around to the rear of my digs, parked in the shade, killed the engine and got out and surveyed the area. No one around. A seven foot wall behind the cottage provided privacy for the small patio and outdoor shower.

"Let's see if I can get you over the back wall and into the small courtyard. Are you game to try it?"

She looked at the wall, then back to me and nodded.

"After we get you over the wall, I'll go around to the front and let you in. Okay, are you ready?"

Kalina nodded again. She hadn't spoken since I picked her up on the road.

"It's going to be all right." I held out my hand to help her get out of the car. She took it with a weak grip. We walked to the high, stucco back wall. I looked around to be sure no one was watching. "Let's try it." I put my back against the wall, bent at the knees and interlocked the fingers of my hands, palms upward, creating a stirrup. "Step in my hands and I'll give you a boost. Can you do it?"

She thoughtfully removed her boots and stepped into my hands. I easily raised her up to the top of the wall. The soles of her feet were hard and calloused. She sat on the wall a moment, swung her legs over, then jumped down onto the soft grass. I threw her boots over the wall to one side.

Grabbing the top of the wall, I jumped and lifted myself up to look over. "Are you okay?" I asked softly.

She looked up and responded, "Yes, I'm fine." She replied looking up at me.

I walked around to the front and let myself in, then hurried to the rear of the cottage and let her inside. Her eyes had that vacant one-thousand yard stare. She looked spent.

During the funeral, Robbie had put another bed into the room as planned. She would be safe here. Thinking of her safety, I absentmindedly looked down to the gun strapped on my ankle. I had used it once; maybe I'd need it again. *Mike Thompson, you devil, look at what you got me into!*

"Are you thirsty?" I asked.

"Yes, I would like some water, thank you."

I went over to the little fridge, removed a plastic bottle of cold water and handed it to her. "I think I'll have an Amstel."

She sat on the side of the bed and stared out blankly. I came over and said all those empty things one says when trying to console the inconsolable. Eventually, after she drank most of the water, she curled up on her side and drifted off.

Sleep, beautiful, sad girl. I kicked off my shoes, finished my beer, turned on the ceiling fan, and leaned back on my bed pillows. Kalina looked peaceful as she slept. *You're going to be all right*, I thought, *I'm here for you and so are your loving uncles.*

Shortly thereafter, I went to the car and pulled out a small battered suitcase and a duffel bag. These contained most of Kalina's clothes and personal items. No one knew how long she'd be staying at the clinic in the Chimanimani Mountains.

*   *   *   *   *

Johannes busied himself using his long auger and special drilling tools. Carefully clamping an elephant tusk into place on his lathe, he began hollowing out the center. It proved to be a long tedious process. He changed drill bits, rearranged his clamps, then drilled deeper into the tusk. He had to be careful not to puncture through to the surface.

Once the tusk had been properly hollowed out and smoothed, he began filling it with small heavy–duty plastic bags of pure, uncut, heroin. The bags shaped themselves nicely into the tubular hollow space. This particular tusk held three and a half kilos of the precious white powder.

To seal off the open end, he mixed the tusk powder from his drilling with a blend of stucco cement, water and finely ground limestone to make a paste. When this mixture hardened no one could tell it from the rest of the tusk. Finished with his task, he turned off his bright working lights, stepped out of his very private workshop, and took a long look around. All was silent except for the wind, the sound of the night insects, and nocturnal noises of far off animals. His hunched over posture exposed his grief, nearly too heavy to bear.

He unclamped the tusk in the dark and hefted it easily onto his right shoulder. The nastiest part of this job he would do outside, and away from any of his work areas. He double-locked the door and walked along the smooth path leading to a storage shed alongside the dilapidated airplane hangar.

He unlocked the shed and lit a Coleman lantern. Its pale yellow light revealed similarly treated tusks, packed with heroin, and ready for shipment. The room had a wretched odor. Soon the light of the lantern filled with dancing insects. While still outside, he stuffed cotton into his nostrils and put a kerchief over his nose and mouth. He opened the sealed can of wild dog urine. The powerful scent of the pack of wild dogs was greatly feared and stopped any animal from coming within twenty-five meters of the place. The scent of a pack of wild hunting dogs was greatly feared. He painted the urine onto the tusk.

Thus treated, no drug-sniffing canine would smell out the heroin. Highly trained dogs would barely get close to the tusks. Putting the lid back on the can, he noticed there was only a little of the vile stuff left.

As he finished up, he thought of Jaylin, and reminisced fondly of their times together. He recalled the young lad's soft facial features. The boy's life had been cut way too short. He would sorely miss Jaylin and their arm-wrestling matches and discussions of his future as a professional game ranger.

Getting back to business, Johannes put the can in a safe place. He would bring it back to the workshop later. When he thought of how to continue to procure the wild dog urine, he fantasized sending that slob Vicente into the wild hunting dog enclosure at the Cheetah Reserve. He could try to coax the urine from the dogs while they tore Vicente apart. A man of no respect deserved such a death.

Johannes locked up the shed, washed in an outside sink with strong soap mixed with lye, and went back to his workshop. As he approached, he could just make out the silhouette of a man standing in the shadows. It could only be one man.

*   *   *   *   *

"*Buenas noches,* Johannes, you *gargola*. Out working late tonight, I see," said Vicente, dressed entirely in black.

Johannes didn't understand the term, "*gargola*" but surmised it to be an insult of sorts. He let it pass. "Yah, for sure. The next batch is ready to go. All you need is de plane to take it the fuck out of here. Oh, I almost forgot, you also need someone else to get the wild dog urine." He raised his chin and had a twinkle in his eye. "Maybe you can do it?"

"We're working on getting the pilot, but what's this about the dog piss?"

"Don't bullshit me. You know dis business. You were watching de funeral, no? You know de young man we buried today used to get it for us from the dogs at the Cheetah Reserve."

"I didn't know. How could I? I knew you used the vile stuff but I didn't know how you got it. Maybe you got wild dogs as pets around here."

"So why were you dere today, watching? Yah, I saw you." Johannes could see that Vicente felt the challenge. He obviously didn't like being questioned.

The air was heavy with the tension between them, billowing like an approaching storm.

"My boss asked me to be there. It's business. It doesn't concern you."

"Why your boss want you dere?"

Vicente had a story ready. "I don't have to, but I'll tell you anyway. We knew Colonel Marshall would be there. What *you* probably don't know is that he used to be the head of the drug enforcement task force. We like to keep an eye on him—especially when he's so close to our products."

"Hummph. So… I never ask you before, but now I ask."

"What now? Ask away." Vicente's mouth was a flat thin line, and his eyes were like gun slits in a World War II bunker.

"What you know about dese killings? Thompson worked for you, yah?"

"*Si´*, we worked together but I know nothing about no killings. My guess is he fucked with the wrong people. Maybe he kept some of their money. Maybe someone got pissed off and killed him. Maybe an old enemy or a lover's husband. How the fuck should I know? All I know is it's a pain in the ass to get a replacement."

"Now," said Johannes, "More important—what you know of the boy Jaylin?"

"Jaylin, who?"

"The boy who we put to ground today. The one who collected the dog piss." He took two menacing steps toward Vicente.

Vicente stood his ground, but held out his hand with the palm thrust outwards. "Far enough, Johannes, you bald *mierde*." He put his hand on the pistol butt in his belt. "I know nothing of the boy. So what of it? One more kaffir dead. I'm sure we can get someone…" before he could finish, Johannes stepped forward.

Vicente pulled out his gun and squatted in a firing position, aiming at one of Johannes' legs.

"Stop! What the hell are you two playing at?" Ngubane said, running up to get between them.

Vicente said, "Nothing. He's *loco*, but if he comes for me I'll shoot off his kneecap. He asked me about Thompson, and the kaffir boy, then he came at me."

Ngubane, smooth as ever said, "We don't like you to use that word. We were all very fond of that boy. Johannes especially."

"Oh, that's how it is, I see now, your *especial* boy." Vicente blew a kiss followed by a grotesque smile.

"You don't know what you're talking about." Ngubane said, maintaining his cool self- restraint while glaring at Vicente.

"I tear your head off and shove it up your arse!" roared Johannes.

"Don't even think about it. I'll drop you where you are, *bastardo.*"

"Enough," the doctor said. "Johannes, back off for God's sake."

"For God's sake maybe, for his sake, no."

"Please, then for my sake." He looked intensely into Johannes's eyes, who reluctantly took a few steps backward.

He turned to face Vicente. "Please, put away your gun."

Vicente did so and said, "He's crazy. What I say is true. He asks me about Thompson and the boy."

"I'd like to ask you, too. What do you know of their deaths?"

"I get sick of this. I know nothing. I told him. I'm telling you. I guess Thompson had a fight with someone. Or maybe he stole something or got into trouble over some woman."

"Why did you say, 'stole'?"

"I don't know, I'm guessing, I told you."

"Why were you watching at the funeral today?" asked Ngubane.

"This is crazy, I keep repeating myself. To keep an eye on Colonel Marshall. That old dog is sniffing too close to our operation."

"That old dog is retired. His teeth have been pulled. We're lucky, his replacement is a baboon. What we do not need is any attention drawn to us."

The three unlikely partners of operation "Happy Tusk" stood silently and ratcheted the tension down a few notches.

Johannes said, "De last of de next shipment is ready to fly dah hell out of here."

"Fine," said Vicente. "Now we have to find a willing pilot."

"Is there anything else?" asked Ngubane.

"No, I guess not. I just come to see if everything is okay after the colonel was here. Keep that shed locked—that stuff inside is worth a queen's ransom."

"No worries. I keep it safe," mumbled Johannes.

Ngubane said, "Tomorrow, I'll be going up to the mountain clinic to look after our operation. I'll be away for a while. I can be reached there if necessary."

"*Claro,*" Vicente turned away and stomped off into the shadows.

When he was out of earshot, Ngubane said, "Please, Johannes, be careful. That one will kill you if you push him. We've had enough killing here."

"I don't believe him. I think he knows something about dose killings."

"I don't know what to believe, or who." Ngubane sighed, "Look, Kalina is safe for now. And I got lucky. A woman was killed and badly mutilated by a crocodile, and no one has claimed the body. I told the authorities I'd take care of it and bury her. Did you find a place to burn?"

"Oh yah, it's a small building, and has a propane tank wid a leak," he winked. "If you're not careful it will cause a fire. It's over by the lepers."

"All right, but it must not spread, and I don't want anyone hurt. Let's get it done, right away."

*   *   *   *   *

The propane explosion that Johannes had rigged broke out just after dawn. The fire brigade came in record time to put out the flames before they could spread. A small concerned crowd from the mission watched nearby.

Dr. Ngubane approached the fire chief after the flames had been controlled. "Unfortunately," said the haggard fire chief, his face smudged with soot, "there was someone in there."

When the body had been brought out, Dr. Ngubane intervened in his official role as regional GMO to examine it. He asked that it be brought to one of the clinic operating rooms. After an inspection, he identified the body as that of a young girl named Kalina Sangweeni who worked at the mission. He explained that he established her identity because part of her face had escaped the worst of the burns, and he recognized the thin scar that ran from her eye to her earlobe which he himself had stitched years earlier.

The next day, the local newspaper noted the tragic coincidence of the young woman's brother having been buried the previous day. There would be another funeral tomorrow, after which she would be buried next to her brother. Father Frank Godwin would say the funeral Mass and conduct the burial ceremony.

*　　*　　*　　*　　*

Ginger Rose got the word through the paper's wire service. Her first reaction: what an incredible coincidence! Her second thought: this was entirely too good to be true.

Vicente sighed and looked relieved. Ginger presumed this was because now he would not be asked to dispose of a young girl.

"I think that the ape, Johannes, suspects me in the killings," he grunted.

"Why?"

"He asked me a lot of questions about Thompson and the boy. Somehow, he saw me watching the funeral."

"We'll have to be more careful," meaning that he would have to be more careful. "I'll look into the death of this girl, but perhaps fate has done our job for us. *Bueno.*"

*   *   *   *   *

The next morning I took some laps in the pool then visited the lavish breakfast buffet and brought a plate of sandwiches, some cereal, bread, fruits and drinks to my cottage for Kalina and me.

"Why is all this happening?" she asked innocently as we ate.

"I don't have good answers." I paused to collect my thoughts. "It seems your father was mixed up with some very bad people. He did something which got him killed. It probably has to do with money. We think these same people want to kill his whole family as a warning to others not to do whatever he did. That's why they killed Jaylin and why we faked your death in the fire so the murderers won't be looking for you."

"I can't believe Uncle Mike did bad things." She continued to refer to Thompson as her uncle out of habit.

"I knew your father for a good many years. In most ways he was a wonderful, good man, but he wasn't a saint. None of us are. Ask Father Godwin who knows more than most, being privy to people's confessions. Sometimes we make bad choices, even for good causes. People fall in with the wrong crowd and get into trouble."

I leaned back and paused to let my words sink in. "Forgive him. He loved you and your mother and wanted the best for you. He even had a backup plan–me. He sent me a letter to bring me to you."

She cried softly and nodded her head. She had only eaten half the food I'd brought for her. "I feel so alone now."

"I can only imagine. But you still have your special uncles and many friends who love you."

I turned on the TV to get our minds off our situation, even if only briefly. I couldn't bear to watch the negative news so we half–watched a cricket match.

I now felt more satisfied now that I was accomplishing what I'd come here to do. We'd developed a plan. And I had help. Kalina was with me and soon we'd be off to another place of safety. I planned to be with her until the ordeal ended. Then hopefully, I'd take her away, after we brought the killers to justice.

We spent the day in reflection, listening to music and reading. I drifted off for a short nap. I loved my afternoon naps when I could get one.

*   *   *   *   *

At one point during the evening, Kalina looked up from a magazine and asked, "Who's the woman I saw you with at the funeral?"

This girl doesn't miss much, I thought. "Her name is Ginger Rose. She's a reporter for the *Johannesburg Sun*. I just met her a few days ago– here at the Carnivore."

"She's pretty." Kalina said unconvincingly, then wrinkled her nose. It made it clear that somehow she didn't like Ms. Ginger Rose. I decided to let it go. How could she feel that way? She hadn't even met Ginger.

What did Robbie say? His wife Del didn't like Ginger either—a girl thing? Intuition? Jealousy?

"Is she American?"

"No, she has an international background. I actually don't know her native country. I'm pretty sure she's from South America. I know she speaks Spanish." Talking about Ginger triggered off a thought that had been rattling around in the backyard of my consciousness.

"She covered your father's death for the paper. Kalina, did you have a picture of you and Mike and Jaylin and your mother?"

"No, but Uncle Mike had one. He carried it in his breast pocket, 'to keep you all close to my heart.'" She started to tear up, again.

"It's okay to be sad. Life is sad sometimes." As usual, I felt hopeless at giving words of comfort.

"Why do you ask about the photo?"

"Because Ginger Rose asked me about it. She said they found it near your father when he died."

"I would like to have it. I have no pictures of us all together."

"I'll ask about it."

*   *   *   *   *

After Kalina took a shower, she put on a light shift and curled up on her bed. She spoke softly as she began to drift off to sleep. "Would you be one of my uncles now?"

"I'd be honored," I whispered, deeply moved.

I sat on the edge of her bed and stroked her forehead gently. I leaned down and assured her, "This will pass. Everything will turn out all right. You're safe now. Be brave. You are loved by so many and God loves you."

I wondered if I wasn't trying to convince myself as well as this young frightened girl. My emotions were bouncing wildly from confusion to terror to anger to pity. The enemy had no face, no form. But it had become real—palpable. I had a search and destroy mission on top of my rescue mission.

As I slipped into my own bed, affectionate thoughts for Kalina again reminded me of Ann, a woman in danger like Kalina, who I'd come to love but could not be with. I hoped she was safe and happy. Then Ginger entered my memory. Was it only two nights ago that we were in this same bed? Thoughts of our interlude began to arouse me. I struggled to put them aside.

I prayed. I hadn't prayed in a long time. Mostly I'd been mad at God and often told Him so. But now I was sincere. *Help me. Help us.*

I fell asleep a few hours later with my gun on the nightstand within easy reach.

Chapter 23

A SECRETARY CUT ROSE OFF ON HER WAY to her cubicle. "There's a Colonel Marshall, retired, waiting for you. I thought I'd give you fair warning."

"Thank you, Ilena."

Rose turned away. *Wasn't that just like her, always working on my good side. Ambitious little toady!* She bit her lower lip thinking, *what loose ends have I left untied?*

As she turned the corner, Colonel Stuart Marshall rose like the old– school gentleman he was.

"*Goeiemore*, Miss Rose." He hadn't mastered "Ms."

"Good morning, Colonel." She smiled broadly shaking his hand. "To what do I owe this pleasant surprise?" As she sat, she artfully crossed her legs, distracting him as designed, then gave him her full attention. "Please sit."

"I'm sure you're busy, so I'll be brief. I'm trying to clear up a few things from my last case—the Thompson murder?"

"Oh, yes. How can I help?"

"You've met the American staying at Misty Hills—Robbie's friend, Deacon Adelius?"

"Oh, yes. I've met him." *And a lot more*, she thought. "As a matter of fact, the other night, he escorted me to a dinner where I was the guest speaker. Interesting man."

"Yes, well, the thing is, he mentioned in passing while we were discussing Thompson's death, something about a photo you said you saw at the murder scene in the Karoo."

Mierde! She remembered telling Deacon about the photo. Vicente had taken it off Thompson's body. No one at the crime scene had actually seen it. Her guard went up. *This slip could be costly. Stick with the truth as far as possible.* "Yes, I recall mentioning it to him," she said indifferently, never dreaming that Deacon would have the opportunity to mention such a thing to the Colonel.

"The thing is, neither I nor my colleagues have ever seen such a photo. I checked; it is not in evidence. May I ask who showed it to you?"

"You know how a crime scene is—people and reporters and photographers all milling about. The picture was being passed around to a few of us in a group. I really have no recollection of exactly who handed it to me."

This old dog was shrewd, she thought. He had done hundreds of interrogations. She could tell he was watching her carefully for non-verbal cues. She never realized that at the mention of the photo she had, for only an instant, involuntarily looked down at her desk.

"I see...do you know where it is now?" he asked.

"No, I have no idea."

"Do you recall what was in the photo?"

"As I remember, Thompson, a black woman and a boy, and a little girl."

"Were there any names?"

"Not that I saw. It was a very old worn out photo." Again, she couldn't resist the briefest of involuntary glances at her desk.

"It's very strange." He fiddled with his moustache. "I've contacted a few of the other reporters who were there and none of them remembered such a picture," he said.

"That *is* strange. But it was a chaotic scene. Maybe you could contact some of the local reporters from the smaller newspapers?"

"That's a good point. I'll follow up on that."

She felt him looking around her office as if he could somehow divine the location of the picture. "Is it important?"

"It could be. I'll tell you this, it can't be a coincidence that in the past few days, both children connected to Thompson have died. Not only did they die, Thompson and the boy were certainly murdered. As yet I don't know about the girl. Right now, it looks like a tragic accident—a fire. I'm tracking down the connection between the murders—and there is certainly a connection."

Ginger cocked her head to the side, "But I thought you were retired."

"It's true, but the commissioner called me in to consult on the Jaylin case," he lied. "I want to see this thing through."

"I see. Well, let me know if I can be of any further help." She stood--a sure signal of dismissal.

He rose with her. "Thank you for your time. I may be seeing you again."

Was that a threat, a promise or just a casual goodbye remark?

*   *   *   *   *

After the colonel left the building, he went to a coffee shop across the road. He didn't believe Miss Ginger Rose. He waited for an hour and twenty minutes, reading newspapers and sipping his third cup of tepid coffee. Years on the force had made him a patient man. Finally, he saw her leave the building. His prey was easy to spot, with her bouncy walk and bright orange sweater matching her hair.

He dashed out of the shop and took a position under some trees on the side of her building where he could observe the entrance and exit of the gated underground parking garage. In a few minutes, a metallic blue Jaguar with a redhead at the wheel roared up the ramp and out of the black maw of the exit. She turned right, quickly disappearing from view.

Marshall hurried back up to Ginger's office. He had timed it well. It was just after one o'clock and most of the office staff were off to lunch. He introduced himself on the run, flashing his badge to the receptionist.

"I was just here and left one of my file folders in Ms. Ginger Rose's office. I'll be just a sec to retrieve it. I'm running late." The receptionist smiled, nodded in agreement and pointed in the direction of Rose's office.

"Danke." He waved thanks to her as he hurried down the hall. There was no one near her office. He quickly looked in the desk drawers, trying to remember the direction of her gaze, when he had questioned her. They contained the usual flotsam and jetsam but no photo.

He tried the file cabinets, but only halfheartedly since that wasn't where she had looked. He did find the file of her article on the Thompson murder, and a copy of the article she had written. No picture, though. Where else?

He rummaged in a file drawer of her desk and located a folder marked "photos"—nothing there. She might have taken it with her. The odds were against it. Now, where else? The photo would probably be small. He looked under her desk calendar, phone, and desk lamp. Nothing!

He couldn't stay much longer. He started looking under anything that would hide a small photo. He lifted her fax machine, almost in desperation, and found a five by seven manila envelope. He glanced around, making sure no one saw him, opened the envelope, and looked at perhaps the only existing picture of Michael Thompson and his family. He recognized Thompson, and surmised the rather elegant-looking black lady, partially covering her face in a veil, was his wife. The young lad was obviously Jaylin in his younger days.

Although she had changed quite a bit from an immature little girl to a beautiful young woman, the resemblance of the girl in the photograph to Kalina was evident.

He took the picture and found a copy machine. Luckily it was a simple older model—easy to operate. He made a copy and returned the photo in the envelope to its resting place under the FAX machine.

So you lied, Miss Ginger Rose, he mused. *What else are you hiding? Time to gather more evidence. Who else is in this with you? And why?*

He left quietly without acknowledging the receptionist.

His mind raced. The connections were coming fast and hard. Often an investigation evolved in that way. Nothing for a while, and then all at once, things began to connect and make sense. Rose, Thompson, drug residue in the plane, the murders, even her Latin background. All circumstantial and certainly more evidence was needed. He would look more deeply into the life and times of Miss Ginger Rose. Then he'd call Deacon and notify him of Ginger's certain involvement.

Chapter 24

WE HAD DRIVEN UP IN TWO VEHICLES. Ngubane and Johannes rode in the truck with the camper shell, and Kalina and I in my rented Opel sedan. I'd asked Kalina to pick out a male name for herself; she had chosen "Jomo." Kalina had said, "He was a warm wonderful man who lived at the mission for many years."

It had been a long hot drive, but the temperatures in the Chimanimani Mountains of Zimbabwe, were noticeably cooler--to everyone's delight. The low veldt had slowly transformed itself into hills, then small mountains. I thought the scenery strongly resembled parts of California. That is, until I saw a giraffe by the side of the road, or a troop of baboons strolling by in their rigid family formation. The redness of the earth, the rocky outcroppings, and trees that seemed to grow straight out of the rocks were as far from the Chicago landscape as the moon. I delighted in the African landscape.

My thoughts ricocheted back to Ann. *Would it always be like this with thoughts of her drifting back to me unbidden? I wished she were here with me. God knows we were in love. She broke it off when I was recuperating in the hospital. Through the pain, part of me knew she was right. I'd probably resent our commitment in time. Confusing, and it still hurt.*

Once we'd arrived in Zimbabwe at Dr. Ngubane's clinic, several introductions took place at once. I could hardly keep track of some of the unusual sounding names. They were almost as complex to my ear and difficult to pronounce as the Polish names in Chicago. Dr. Ngubane simultaneously introduced both myself and Kalina, in her disguise as a boy named "Jomo," to Zekeriah, the doctor's headman and to Muhlukai, Zekeriah's assistant and head of security.

I watched Muhlukai's pupils dilate with interest and could almost hear the young man's heart hammering. He looked Kalina up and down with a hunger in his eyes. Muhlukai obviously believed Kalina to be a boy, and liked the idea very much. I was uncomfortable with his attraction but the disguise was working and that's what mattered.

The staff recognized Johannes from previous visits. Zekeriah said, "We're glad you came Mr. Johannes, 'baas', we got many things here need fixing." We all laughed. Johannes gave a rare small smile and nodded.

Kalina looked very boyish indeed in her disguise. With Del's help, a touch of makeup had also obscured her thin facial scar. I reminded her not to refer to Johannes or Ngubane as her "uncles."

Dr. Ngubane's two-story house on the clinic grounds easily accommodated all of us in separate rooms. Pale stucco covered the thick walls. Tall narrow windows graced every room complimenting the traditional curving Dutch Colonial front. Blue trim around the doors, windows and eves gave the building a homey look.

Unlike the relatively open structure of the Hands of Hope Mission in South Africa, this compound had high walls topped with razor wire. The compound also featured roving security patrols. I wondered, were these here to keep people in or out.

Johannes and I agreed that whenever Kalina left the house, one of us would be with her. Ngubane had patients to see. He told us he had to check with the laboratory to see how various procedures were progressing.

*   *   *   *   *

This is the perfect set-up, thought Ngubane. He surveyed his property with its ideal climate for growing poppies. Because of the steep hillsides, tall trees, and camouflage nets, they were well hidden in case of air surveillance. Local officials had been sufficiently bribed to leave them alone. That, and the natural terror people had of leprosy assured them free rein. There were plenty of signs in English, Afrikaans, Zulu, Xosa, Shona, and Endebele, complete with vivid graphics of horrible disintegrating faces, warning people to "Keep Out—Contagious Lepers." He saw to it that there were only a few trusted and extremely well paid laboratory workers who actually knew what was being produced.

*   *   *   *   *

Although Zekeriah was the headman, Muhlukai headed the Tstsis who guarded the compound. Politically savvy, crafty, and without conscience, he noticed everything. Thugs and local criminals constituted his security force—an unsmiling serious looking bunch outfitted in navy blue uniforms with sidearms and knob sticks.

Muhlukai would report in to his wealthy patron that Dr. Ngubane had returned and brought guests. It was a little unusual that the doctor brought the American and the young boy, Jomo. "Jomo…" even the name excited him. He liked having something to report, so he would be seen as useful and continue to draw a paycheck twice that of Zekeriah, his "superior."

Muhlukai smiled, "*He will be mine. I'll go slow, and be careful. I don't want to spook the lad. Oh, it will be so good. I can't wait.*" Muhlukai had never been so instantly attracted and excited. The lad looked like a dream. Even to the delicate skin and the soft high voice. And that rump! It was all Muhlukai could do not to drool. Unbelievably, the boy also had a familiarity about him.

*   *   *   *   *

Once we were comfortably installed in our rooms, and had eaten a meal of impala steaks and fruit salad, Ngubane pushed back from the table and said, "Tomorrow I'll show you around. Johannes has been here before."

It worked out that Kalina's room was between mine and Johannes'. We all shared one toilet at the end of the hall. The bath and shower room were located at the other end of the hall.

Before she went to bed, Kalina kissed Johannes goodnight on his bald head and came over and whispered to me, "My new uncle, I wish I could sleep in your room again tonight." We hugged briefly, her slender body soft and warm against me.

"I do too," I whispered in return. "But your uncle Johannes would never understand. He might get upset and detach my head from my body. I'll be nearby."

She smiled looking down.

A wave of affection swept through me. I wanted to wrap my arms around her and make her feel safe forever.

*　　*　　*　　*　　*

Muhlukai felt so worked up over his new infatuation, he put off his telephonic report. Except for the visiting American, things were pretty routine anyway. After sunset, he dressed in dark clothes and went behind the big house where the guests stayed. He had done this before and knew the layout well. This would just be a prelude—an appetizer.

The cloudy night hid the moon as he climbed the tree easily and waited. The limb he perched on swayed slightly above the washing-up room and shower, only about twelve yards away. The young, luscious, Jomo would, in all probability, be using it before bed. He jumped when the light went on. It illuminated that muscle-head, Johannes. *God, he was a fright.*

Muhlukai waited impatiently. He considered where he and the boy would meet again, and how to get to know him better. He planned to make Jomo laugh, and get on his good side as a friend--a confidant. A little playful wrestling would be a good start, perhaps followed by a massage. He'd used that ploy before with success. Maybe he'd play the understanding older man and listen compassionately to Jomo's problems, then put his arm around him. Then....the light went on.

It was Jomo. "Oh...I want you." The boy looked in the mirror, with his back to the window. How to describe him? Lean and clean. Yes. That was it, *"lean and clean."* The boy washed his face, and took off his shirt and trousers. What a beautiful, lean back and narrow shoulders. He could only just see the top of his ass, but it looked soft, and round, and lovely. The lad moved out of sight for a few moments. Muhlukai couldn't stop himself. He opened his trousers to release his turgid penis. He just let it bob free while he peeped. When the boy came back into view he had slipped on a nightshirt, then shut off the light and left.

It wasn't much, but more than expected. He stretched out on the limb like a leopard lounging in a tree and let himself relax. He knew he would be back here again—every night until they had made contact.

*   *   *   *   *

After supper, Johannes, Ngubane and I conversed in low tones. We were still concerned, but tonight we contented ourselves with our plan to keep Kalina safe.

I had an idea to suggest. "Just in case, I know it's a long shot, but just in case someone discovers she's here, how about a backup plan?"

"What do you mean?" asked Ngubane.

"Well, rather than react suddenly, if this place is no longer safe, shouldn't we have another safe house somewhere as backup?"

"Yah, dat's a good idea, American," said Johannes nodding.

At the moment the question stumped us.

"I'll call Father Godwin tomorrow," said Ngubane. "Maybe there's a church or another mission he knows of, up this way. He knows them all."

"Good, I'd feel better with a backup." I couldn't help voicing my inner thoughts aloud. "I wish she'd just leave the country with me."

The doctor leaned back, rubbed the bridge of his nose and asked, "What if the murderers are caught? Wouldn't she be safe here and not have to leave? They already think she's dead."

I had to admit Ngubane had a point. "I still think it would be too dangerous. Too many people know her, and would talk of her miraculous return from the dead. You heard what the Colonel said—these killers could track her down here, if they got wind of her being alive. But it would be much more difficult to locate her in the U. S."

A Herrara housemaid brought in a tray of cold Amstels. We sat and continued to pour out our concerns into the night. Johannes smoked a large bowl pipe with a surprisingly sweet- smelling tobacco. Ngubane, busy as always, left first to make his rounds, check on his patients and chat with Zekeriah about clinic operations.

As we went up to bed, Johannes squinted in his unique way and said to me, "I think you be okay. I see you wid the little one and I hear the good in your voice."

I thought, *high praise indeed.* One really wanted to be on the good side of this mountain of a man. "Thank you, Johannes—for your trust."

Johannes grunted and clumped down the corridor to his room.

Alone in my small but clean and functional bedroom, I kept tossing and turning not finding sleep as I rolled our situation around in my mind. *Where the hell else would all of this take me? Is this somehow part of God's plan for me?*

I had much to ponder. I was taking on a commitment for life. *Am I ready? Am I worthy? Can we pull this off?* Such thoughts occupied me for the better part of an hour. I prayed for guidance, then drifted off feeling good that Kalina slept safely in the next room.

She had called me "uncle" I liked that. *Yes my dear, it would have been nice to have you here with me.*

*   *   *   *   *

During the next few days, the Colonel kept busy. Using his contacts on the force, he put together quite a profile on Miss Ginger Rose. He rifled through his notes pinning photos and bits of information on a large bulletin-board. He discovered that her name was Rosa Garcia, and that she was Peruvian, and that she had some minor brushes with the law as a young woman. One particular bit of evidence stood out. An Interpol agent told him that she had been linked in some way, perhaps romantically, to Luis Salazar, an ex-freedom fighter who now had connections in the South American drug trade.

Col. Marshall discovered that she had only been in South Africa for a couple of years. He scoped out the top-of-the-line residence where she lived. Twice he had seen her with a heavy set man with a swarthy complexion and slicked-back hair whose furtive glances were typical of a predator scrutinizing his surroundings. A bodyguard? Colleague? Partner? Relative? He lived in the same apartment complex and his name was Vicente Luna. Apparently, he had entered the country at the same time as Miss Rose. Also Peruvian, he didn't work, but never seemed to lack for funds.

Marshall had discovered enough. He felt certain this unholy duo was somehow involved in drug trafficking. Chances were they'd killed Thompson or had him killed along with the boy. He surmised they were also determined to kill Thompson's daughter. That was their MO. Hopefully, they had bought the story of her death in the fire.

The Colonel was also sure that Thompson's flying was a critical part of the scheme. *Were they smuggling drugs in or out? Were they setting up a sales and distribution organization? What kind of drugs? How did they do it?* He still had a lot of unanswered questions.

# Chapter 25

"I DON'T LIKE IT. I DON'T LIKE IT AT ALL." Ginger snarled as she paced. "That old dog Marshall was sniffing around my office. He knows about the photo. I wonder what else is going through his mind."

"How did he know about the photo?" asked Vicente.

"I let it out to Deacon to help me get information. How was I to know he would ever talk to Marshall?"

"*Claro*," said Vicente. "But let's step back *un momento*. As I see it, you never lied about it. It's, how you say, 'plausible,' someone did have such a photo and was passing it around. Is this not so?"

"Yes, except if he checks with the other reporters and investigators, and no one else remembers seeing the photo, then what?"

"Wait–he couldn't know everyone who might have been there. Also, he isn't active on the force anymore and probably doesn't have access to information he used to. Perhaps this is not a crisis. And if it is, perhaps we can arrange an accident to get him out of our way."

"*Si*, but we have drawn enough attention.... I suppose it may be necessary. I'll have to think about it. Remember, we saw him at the mission, and we have *mucho* product there now." She stalked across the room with purposeful strides.

"We can't let him get any closer," Rose said with a decisive emphasis. She leaned against the railing on Vicente's balcony, staring off into the distance toward Johannesburg. At contemplative times like this, she often visualized her homeland on the outskirts of Iquitos, the great fetid Amazon, and the sailors disembarking from the riverboats looking for a drink and a whore. She smiled with a sweet–sour edge– *looking for someone like who I used to be.*

*   *   *   *   *

For the next few days, we all relaxed a bit at the mountain clinic. Ngubane proudly took me around, showing me the clinic and laboratory. Some areas were off limits for my own safety and prevention of infection. Again I was struck by the modern, state-of-the-art equipment.

"Why the large laboratory?" I asked.

"First of all," explained Ngubane, "We use it diagnostically to better understand how to treat our patients. After the initial cost of setting up the lab, it's much cheaper to do our own lab work rather than rely on other labs. It costs a bloody fortune to send it out, and it takes forever. And the reports we get back are not totally reliable.

"We are also doing some experiments with synthesizing our own medications to help with a variety of infections—and of course, the AIDS virus."

I found the clear explanation, along with some medical jargon beyond my comprehension, impressive and totally convincing.

"And by the way, the land and infrastructure were all funded by WHO, the World Health Organization. This is one of the few Leprosarium's in the world. We treat nearly one-quarter of the Hansens' disease cases in Sub-Saharan Africa."

"Pretty impressive."

*   *   *   *   *

Both Ngubane and I noticed the friendship developing between Kalina, as Jomo, and Zekeriah's assistant, Muhlukai. Ngubane convinced me that it would be good for her to talk to someone nearer her own age. She'd been through a lot and needed to feel young again. I wasn't so sure. I worried more about her identity being discovered than her socializing.

She pulled off the ruse of being a young boy by helping the gardeners. Not only were the grounds a riot of colorful flowers but they also supported a considerable vegetable garden.

Ngubane told me most of the workers at the clinic were Shona, but Muhlukai was Matebele. Muhlukai had been told all of his life that he was related to the great chief Lobengula. He took enormous pride in being kin to "The Earth Thunderer."

*   *   *   *   *

Vigilance at peak levels is always hard to maintain. Quite naturally, one day Johannes became very involved in fixing the brakes on one of the clinic's small trucks. He needed to be useful and work with his hands. He told Kalina, "Now I work here so don't go far from me. Stay close so our voices can reach each other, yah?"

"Yah, I promise." At first she watched him working, but got bored with the mechanical intricacies. Muhlukai chatted with one of the guards. She went over and sat nearby.

He saw her out of the corner of his eye and dismissed the guard.

They eased into relaxed conversation. To her, he seemed full of joy and song. His antics as a natural mimic made her laugh. Even though she thought it was naughty, she enjoyed his imitations of Ngubane, and especially Johannes.

Trees, ferns and rocks combined to form a beautiful nature reserve. The many paths and trails covered with a green canopy invited walkabouts.

Muhlukai said to Kalina, "Come, have a look over this hill. There is a cool stream nearby. We can put our feet in."

"I must stay close to Johannes in case he needs me."

"I see, but it is very close. You could hear him if he calls."

She smiled. "All right then." She went over and told her uncle Johannes that she would be out of his sight but just over the small hill putting her feet in the stream. Being preoccupied, and without looking up, he mumbled his assent.

Muhlukai and "Jomo" walked over a rise and down to a small meandering stream. Both were barefoot. They sat on a large flat rock and dangled their feet into the cool moving water. They splashed each other playfully. Muhlukai was excited beyond anything he had ever previously felt. They held hands which was not unusual between black males in Southern Africa. Jomo's touch, seemed incredibly soft, Muhlukai thought: hands that had never seen hard labor.

They leaned back and closed their eyes, basking in the breezy sunshine. He felt Jomo opening up to him. Now would be a good opportunity to make a move. He said something funny and while laughing, he leaned over and caressed her cheek with his own—a test of the waters. He got no negative reaction.

With Kalina lying prone, Muhlukai began a gentle shoulder massage. His excitement grew. His hands began to move southward. He touched the top of her buttocks under the waistband of loose fitting slacks. It was glorious. Jomo seemed relaxed and voiced no objection. Muhlukai's breathing became deeper and irregular.

"You like my massage?"

"Oh, yes, it's very relaxing. I'm almost drifting off to sleep."

"Yes, this is a good place to relax—to feel good." Humming softly, he gently turned Kalina over on her back as part of the massage. He glanced around quickly, and made sure they were unseen. He looked at the lad closely and noticed the faded thin scar on the side of his face. *Where had he seen such a thing before?* Again, he experienced that feeling of familiarity.

His next step was to slide his hand under the shirt, and do a circular tummy rub. So soft. Finally his hand crept south under the loose waistband of the trousers, and slowly inched down to the crotch. As he did so, he said, "Jomo, you are so beautiful." Suddenly, all hell broke loose. He felt no male genitalia, but the unmistakable feel of a woman. Kalina jumped up and screamed, swatting his hand away. "Stop it, are you crazy?"

"But I thought you were…." Then the realization hit him suddenly: the scar, and the familiarity. This was the girl, Kalina, whom he had seen briefly here a few times in the past. He had hardly given her any notice. But now she pretended to be a boy. He felt stupid for having been fooled about such a thing.

They were both shocked and stood facing each other immobile and silent.

Having heard her scream, Johannes came rumbling over the hill. Muhlukai apologized all over himself. "I'm so sorry. I misunderstood. Please don't tell him. Don't let him hurt me. I meant no harm."

Kalina saw the panic in the face of the young man.

She turned to Johannes laughing. "I'm sorry, we started splashing each other and the water was so cold, I screamed. I didn't mean to scare you and take you away from your work."

Johannes glowered at Muhlukai, and would probably have given him a thrashing if Kalina hadn't been there. "Please come back up by me, I want you to hold de torch so I can see better." He glared malevolently at Muhlukai and turned to return to his project.

"Okay, coming now, now." Kalina said as she walked up the hill to join Johannes. She turned to Muhlukai and said in a sotto voice, "Don't tell anyone about me, please, it's important."

Muhlukai nodded sympathetically.

"Thank you," she mouthed.

His first feeling—overwhelming relief. Next, being embarrassed like this was intolerable. Finally, he felt like a fool. He would surely tell his patron about this charade right away.

# Chapter 26

With the pre-dawn morning mist curling around his knees, Ngubane picked up finished packets of heroin from the lab, gathered several lepers into his truck, and set off back to South Africa. He planned to check in with Father Godwin, supervise the work of a few doctors and interns at the Hands of Hope Mission, then spend some quiet time at his Eagle's Lair with Socorro.

A part-time model of mixed Asian and African blood, she stood as tall as he, with a slender figure, small firm breasts and long fit legs. She often took early morning runs around his compound. Her cheetah-like long strides captured the undivided attention of the guards, who treated her with great deference.

She was meticulously clean and had been paid well with lavish gifts over the last few years to be Ngubane's on-call lover. They had met when he had treated her successfully for a debilitating sinus infection.

She periodically stayed at the Lair. Quiet and compliant, she conformed to all of his wishes. Perhaps, he thought, she even loved him—in a way. He reveled in her ability to take on whatever different personas, or dramatic roles as he wished in his games of intimacy. She was the best he had ever known at this fantasy playing, and he delighted in his time with her.

Kalina was safe now. "Operation Happy Tusk," as named by Rose, could continue as before. Ngubane spent a large portion of his recent profits to purchase the drugs necessary for the AIDS cocktail so badly needed at the clinic. He also sold some of them for a profit to a few of his medical colleagues in Zimbabwe. He saw this whole enterprise as exchanging drugs other people wanted for the drugs he needed for his people. (And of course, he kept a substantial amount of profit for himself.)

Before he left, Ngubane warned Deacon and Johannes to stick to the immediate house area and limit their contact with the outside. "You can rely on Zekeriah and Muhlukai if you need anything at all. Neither of them knows about Kalina, or why you are here."

It would have come as a shock to the doctor to overhear the telephone conversation of one of his trusted lieutenants.

*　　*　　*　　*　　*

Muhlukai made his regular phone call to his secret employer that same morning. He rather formally gave the date and time of the arrival of the two vehicles carrying Ngubane, Johannes, Deacon, and a young woman named "Jomo," who was being passed off as a young man. He had vaguely remembered seeing her a few times long ago at the clinic. He remembered her name was Kalina.

"Anything else?" asked Ginger, barely masking the shock in her voice.

"No, except that the doctor headed back to the mission in South Africa early this morning."

She said, "Thank you for that information," she set the phone down very quietly, as if she didn't want anyone to hear, and smiled wickedly. One thought predominated—Ngubane had lied! She experienced a flood of betrayal, rage and disbelief. He had been sheltering the girl. Bitter questions arose. What else had he lied about? Did he have the money Thompson had stolen? In her anger and frustration, emotional control out the window, she threw the coffee cup she had been drinking from, shattering it against the faux fireplace. Deacon and Johannes were also in on the deception. She felt her carefully crafted operation unraveling. She would have to pull it back together.

First, she had to deal with Ngubane. We'll make his evening return to his precious home one to remember, she thought. She had learned how to instill terror from seasoned guerrillas in the Amazon. She would make him pay. They would all pay!

Yet, she knew Ngubane remained key to their project in terms of providing the raw materials and the conversion process, disguising it, and transporting it to the airstrip at the Hands of Hope Mission.

Yet she still needed him. Being untouchable as the area Government Medical Officer he was nearly impossible to replace. She also knew of his dedication to his medical mission and his need of the money from their operation.

She called Vicente. "Put on some coffee, we have plans to make. I'll be down in twenty minutes." She took off her dress. Yes, she told herself, she still looked good as she gave herself the once-over in the full-length mirror. But this morning, her face would be terrifying to anyone. She would have to control her rage. She had plans to make. She had to show Luis Salazar that she could handle anything—that she could successfully run the entire South African operation. It had all gone so smoothly until Thompson. She felt like screaming his name.

For some reason, as she began to select her wardrobe for the day, she felt very sexy.

Was there a connection between anger and sex for her? If Deacon had been there, she would have insisted they make love, right now. With her on top. What was going on? She absentmindedly stroked her nipples, bringing them to attention. She felt the onset of warmth between her legs. *This was crazy.* Never one for lengthy introspection, but action, she took a shower as cold as she could stand it. The warm feelings passed. She dried herself, avoiding looking into the mirror again. She had business. She dressed quickly and descended to Vicente's apartment.

*   *   *   *   *

With Ngubane gone and Johannes busying himself with practical work, I realized I didn't have much to do. I wrote various things down in a journal to keep up with the scattered bits of information I'd been collecting. I wondered how to make myself useful when Kalina suggested that we take a walk. "I have something beautiful to show you. It will be a surprise."

I strapped on the ankle holster and stripped a machete off the kitchen wall, which I slipped under my belt. The temperature gauge outside the kitchen door registered eighty-nine degrees. I notified Johannes of our walk. As we started out, the birds sang a symphony around us. I followed her lead. Leaving the housing area and the inhabited buildings, the forest again asserted itself. Colorful butterflies and iridescent insects flew up all around us as we walked. Lizards of all sizes scurried about, so well camouflaged I only saw them when they moved.

Remembering the mamba, I kept a wary eye for anything crawling. I felt out of my element. This was about as far from the streets of Chicago as one could get. I saw a large reticulated python draped over a tree limb like a Christmas garland—creepy. There were lacy waist-high ferns, small outcroppings of rock, and in all low areas, streams or ponds which in this part of the world were called, "Dams." Our stroll along a barely noticeable path took us under a high canopy of trees with branches spreading widely, to give dappled shade everywhere.

"What is it you want to show me?" I asked.

"It's unbelievable. It's a surprise, you'll see. I found it by accident. It's just up ahead." Her face lit up with childlike enthusiasm.

We walked for twenty minutes. We were either going up or down, or walking on the sides of hills. Though serene and peaceful, limited visibility made us vulnerable. Someone could watch us or attack us from plenty of available concealment.

My special ops training kicked in. I removed the pistol from my ankle holster, switched off the safety, and tucked it into the waistband of my trousers. I swiveled my head in all directions trying to notice any irregular movement. I remembered the trick to look for *what shouldn't be there.*

In a dip in the trail, we crossed a small flowing creek whose cool water felt refreshing on our feet. As the bank rose on the opposite side, a chain link fence at least seven feet high with razor wire on top blocked our way. A rusted sign slightly askew on a locked gate warned visitors to go no further—DANGER. The sign featured a red skull and crossbones.

"What does this mean? Why a fence way out here?" I asked.

"I don't know. There is no danger. I've been here many times before. We're almost there, follow me."

The gate had a padlock. She turned right and walked along the fence line to a breach where the chain-link had separated from a supporting pole. "Come through here."

The gap was small and the fencing was stiff. I squeezed through with difficulty. We followed the fence back to the path, now narrower and more overgrown. The dense shade mercifully reduced the temperature.

Kalina turned to me with a wry smile and said, "Now, close your eyes."

I didn't care for this request. "Really, do I have to?" But she looked so young and playful—I couldn't refuse. I closed my eyes, held out my hands and said, "Lead on, m'lady." I had to remind myself that Kalina through all of her recent troubles was still a girl.

We proceeded slowly in the uneven footing. After taking a sharp left turn, she announced, "Now open."

A dazzling vision materialized. A scarlet carpet of flowers in the small steep valley splayed out in front of us for as far as the eye could see– poppies, millions and millions of shimmering red poppies. I bent down to take a closer look. "Papaver somniferum."

"What did you say?"

Poppies, I thought—so delicate and beautiful and potent. "That's the scientific, or botanical name for these particular poppies. Somehow the formal name stuck in my head."

"Oh," she said, "You are so smart."

"Not really." I chuckled, "Like most people, I have little pockets of knowledge and odd things I remember." I chose not to reveal to her, that as part of my drug studies in the Army I read about drugs, their origin and how they're made.

Looking up, I said, "Notice the camouflage netting?"

"I think to protect them from the direct sunlight," Kalina responded.

No, my dear, I thought, to protect them from airborne drug enforcement agents. "Is there just this one area?"

"I'm not sure—isn't it beautiful?"

"Oh yes, it is that. Why don't we walk a little farther." I wanted to know the extent of the growing fields.

At nearly every turn, or over every rise, we were met with another field of poppies.

"What do they do with all of these poppies?" asked Kalina.

I didn't answer. I heard voices. "Ssshh, let's move carefully and see what's going on." In a meadow below were stoop workers, some of whom were lepers doing something to the pods beneath the flowers. From this distance I could just make out they were rolling what looked like sap into little balls and placing them in containers attached to their belts.

"What a setup," I said almost to myself.

"What's the matter? What are we looking at?"

"I believe you are looking at a commercial enterprise of growing poppies to process them into ah...medicine." I didn't want to tell her what the "medicine" was.

Dope is everywhere but this was an addict's version of heaven.

"Medicine?'

"I think so, yes. Please, tell no one, absolutely no one, what I've just told you. Promise?"

She tilted her head sideways. "I promise."

*   *   *   *   *

"Let's see where their path leads." We followed a winding footpath the workers used. It led back to the main housing area. I glanced through a window into one of the outlying buildings and saw what looked like a processing laboratory. This was where the poppies would be delivered to be converted into heroin.

We skirted the buildings. Once I made sure Kalina was safely in the main house, I put in a call to Colonel Marshall.

He picked up on the second ring. "Colonel Marshall here."

"It's Deacon. You're not going to believe it, but I believe I've stumbled onto something big out here." I told the Colonel of my discovery.

"It all fits," responded the Colonel. "I also have much to tell you. But I need to see your poppy fields for myself. I'm coming up. I can tell you this much now. Ginger Rose is involved up to her eyeballs."

"Rose! Are you sure?" My stomach dropped.

"And she's not alone. Be careful. You probably don't need me to remind you that we are dealing with people who think nothing of eliminating anybody who even *seems* to stand in their way. Best not to mention this to any of the men from the mission. We don't know who else might be involved. It's probable some of them are in on the scheme."

I saw the wisdom in what he said.

"I'll leave tomorrow morning. I think I can hitch a helo ride to Bulawayo. I'll take a car from there, so I should be there tomorrow afternoon. Meanwhile, try to find out how many guards there are, the number of people working in the laboratories, and the boundaries of the place. I'll need that intelligence in case I have to call in reinforcements."

"I'll do my best, but it's pretty short notice."

"Do your best, then. See you tomorrow. Oh, by the way, is Dr. Ngubane still there?"

"No, he headed back to the mission early this morning."

"I see. Tomorrow then."

"Right, tomorrow."

Tomorrow what? Pieces of the puzzle flew into place quickly. I found it hard to believe that Ngubane participated in the illegal drug trade. Now Rose as well? I supposed that until I knew differently, Johannes could also be suspected. But involved with killing Jaylin and Kalina—never. *And how about Father Godwin?*

Thompson must have known, or found out about the drugs. I recalled the words of the letter—*"insane game, unholy scheme, evil people, began as a noble cause."* Did that refer to the work of the mission? Then I recalled the chilling revelation in the letter—*"they're all involved."*

Thompson admitted that he had tried to skim some money off the top. But he didn't make it. It got him killed. From his letter it also sounded like Thompson initially didn't realize drugs were involved, but found out later. Somehow this thought helped me to feel better about my friend. He must have been desperate to get out.

We had only just managed to get Kalina to safety. Were the cash and diamonds I'd dug up all from this operation, or were they part of legitimate money Thompson had been saving? I knew I would probably never know the answer.

I was shocked at the scope of the enterprise. I could see why these people would do anything to preserve it. They had a fortune in this investment, and it must pay off handsomely—yeah, to the tune of millions of dollars—pure heroin going for about fifty thousand a pound on the street. *Is this where the Hands of Hope Mission got its financial backing?* It made sense.

Remembering the state-of-the-art equipment I had seen at the mission clinic, I would bet that this was where it got the majority of its funding. Could Godwin be in on it? In his letter, Thompson doubted it.

I recalled people's dependence on drugs, and the incredible stories of lives ruined, death and despair I had witnessed first hand. If we could shut down the whole operation....it would have a tremendous impact.

I felt like a warrior again. This was a battle worth fighting. I felt myself shedding my skin of a seminarian, uncovering the warrior beneath.

And Rose! God, I'd slept with the enemy.

Chapter 27

DR. NGUBANE MADE AN APPEARANCE AT THE **MISSION,** checked on his patients, wrote some orders in their charts, and conducted a grand rounds conference. He chatted with Father Godwin assuring him that Kalina was safe.

Later, he took the packets of heroin back to his Eagle's Lair. He felt he deserved some quiet time there.

Ginger called and demanded that they have a short chat late in the evening, after nine. Reluctantly, he agreed. *A short chat?* Now what? He didn't like it.

Socorro would be waiting. They could have some time together. He hated rushing and having sex on some sort of a schedule. However, sometimes one just had to make the best of things. As he pulled up to the Lair, his anticipation of being with Socorro rose like a thunderhead. It had been too long.

He had barely taken two steps from his car when she rushed to him, threw her arms around his neck and kissed him below his ear lobes. She wore a see-through net cover up over a black bikini, whispering *"Bienvenue, mon cher."* Purling sensations like alternating current rippled through his body.

"Oh, it's so good to see you, Gideon. I've missed you."

"I've missed you, too." As they strolled up the winding stone steps he asked, "Please fix me a tall drink with only a little alcohol. I'm thirsty, and I need a shower."

"Whatever the doctor orders. How was your trip?"

Ngubane barely responded, "Fine, as planned." He didn't feel like chit-chat at this moment. A shower, a drink, and Socorro, in that order. He'd think about that witch, Ginger Rose, later. He felt peeved that she had ruined his evening and sorry that he had agreed to their meeting.

Why the hell didn't I tell her "no"? He didn't want to face that answer.

After showering quickly in his ebony-tiled bathroom, he strolled into the great room and with only a towel wrapped around his waist. The Zimbabwe carvings, the colorful paintings, the exquisite ceramic vases and glove-leather furniture were all his to enjoy.

He bent down and stroked the ears of the two beloved show-quality Weimaraners who had the run of the place. From a small fridge on the bar he pulled out two strips of biltong and tossed them to the dogs as treats. They wagged their tails and made appreciative whines as they settled down on their haunches next to him.

Socorro handed him a tall drink. "Rock Shandy with a twist of lime and a tiny splash of vodka—all right?" She giggled in a girlish but sensual way.

Ice cubes clinking, he took two large swallows. "Ahhh, yes, perfect. Come sit with me."

She complied, bringing over her own tall drink.

He had put some soft African-flavored jazz on his state-of-the-art stereo. She snuggled up to him on the huge tawny wraparound couch, with brown and gold speckles that faced a huge bay of floor to ceiling windows affording a spectacular view. "I have something for you," he announced with mock solemnity.

"Ooh, let me see."

"Only if you've been a good girl."

"Do I have to be good?" She pouted, "Being bad with you is much more pleasing."

He gave her a small box containing a gold tennis bracelet with beautifully cut amethyst stones.

Her eyes went wide. "Oh, I love it! I have the perfect outfit to wear with it. It's beautiful, and you are a beautiful man." She kissed him on both cheeks then on his forehead.

"Please try it on."

"Bien sur." She slipped the bracelet on her left wrist, stood and did a few exaggerated modeling poses to show off her new bauble.

"But," said Ngubane with a pained look, "I am distracted by all of your *other* clothes."

She giggled again, and with one fluid motion, she slipped off the black net cover-up, and slowly shed first the top half, then the bottom of her bikini. She resumed the modeling poses, she had often seen in Vogue.

"That's much better. I'm glad you like it."

She twirled around and fell across his lap, still laughing. "I love it, you dear man, *Nyabonga kukulu.*"

"You're very welcome."

She kissed him on the lips, shifted position and kissed him some more down his neck.

"Please don't stop, but listen, I have some unfortunate news." She didn't stop, but he could feel her stiffen somewhat.

"I have a meeting later tonight. It came up suddenly. So, our visit this evening will have to be brief. I'll make it up to you. You can return tomorrow afternoon and we can have the whole night together."

"Oh, I am disappointed, but only a little. After all, you are a powerful man, and I know it must be important."

With one hand he rolled her nipples very gently between his fingers. With the other, he reached down, and expertly touched her between her legs. She sighed and began to reach under his towel. "No. Stop. For now let us stay as we are." She knew it best to follow his instructions. He manipulated her as she kissed him, until she broke away, arched, and pushed into him.

"Oh, Gideon, the waves, one after another, ohhh." After several more shudders, she relaxed.

He stroked her face and hair and neck as she stretched out on the couch with her head on his lap. They stayed this way watching the final rays of the setting sun. Finally, he suggested, "And now it's your turn?"

"Ah, yes." She smiled, turned her head, and lifted his bulging towel. She took off her bracelet with a wicked smile. "Let me try it on here, oh, it fits. Very handsome indeed."

Was there ever a more playful, sexy or giving woman, than Socorro? For a while, he forgot the impending meeting, the drugs, the clinic, Ginger Rose—everything. He quickly built up to his own climax.

They would have more time and be more inventive tomorrow.

*   *   *   *   *

Just before 9:00 o'clock, Ginger and Vicente parked at the gate to the Lair. Vicente told the guard to fetch Nicholas, the chief of security.

Nicholas came at double time. He was tall, and proudly wore a red and black uniform with some form of sergeant's stripes. "Yes, baas? Good evening to you both." Nicholas, a little breathless, spoke to his employers with exaggerated British pronunciation, and very slowly.

Rose furrowed her brow and fixed Nicholas with her gaze. "You will send all the guards away for tonight. Shut down all security alarms. Tomorrow, come back in the morning with guards, several repair men, and a cleaning crew. Understand?"

"*Yabo*, Miss Rose, Ma'am."

"And one more thing before you go," said Vicente "Bring me the two dogs….and not a word to the doctor."

"*Yabo*, I bring de dogs, just now."

"Good man," said Rose with a condescending smile. "What you see here tomorrow, you and your men will forget."

Vicente handed him a wad of folded Rands. "That should cover it."

Nicholas hurried off to do as he was told.

"He's quick. Very efficient," said Rose.

Vicente smirked, "*Si*, he should be for what we pay him, over and above what Ngubane pays him."

*   *   *   *   *

Under a full moon with a gentle breeze blowing in from the south, Ginger and Ngubane sat by the pool. She had dressed casually, wearing black slacks and a stretch knit tube top with horizontal black and white stripes, emphasizing the curves of her breasts. She arrayed her flaming hair cascading to her shoulders and wore large ornamental gold earrings.

Her expression suddenly shifted from pleasant to serious. "I've heard some disturbing news."

"Oh?" said Ngubane, alert warnings bouncing around in his brain.

"Our business is built on trust, is it not?" She had learned from Salazar that it was best to begin interviews such as this, by slowly asking questions. Let the target squirm–let the fear build.

"Yes, absolutely." He began to nervously clean his already-spotless glasses.

"Yet you have been less than truthful with me. For one thing, you have a young girl named Kalina Sangweeni staying at your clinic in the Chimanimani's. Isn't that so?"

Ngubane's heart rate rose, his stomach in knots. There was no sense in lying. "Yes, that is so."

"Not only that, she is disguised as a young man. And you signed a death certificate that she died in a fire at the mission. A serious breach of the law for a doctor."

Ngubane nodded in agreement. *How the hell did she know all of this?*

"My, my, how you have deceived us." She shook her head. "We have been looking for this young woman for our own reasons."

Ngubane tried to cut his losses. "It's true I've lied about her death, and have given her sanctuary at my clinic. But I had no idea you were looking for her. How would I know this? I only knew she was in danger. I love this young girl, practically raised her and tried to protect her."

"But you lied about not knowing her or her connection to Thompson. She was his bastard child, no?"

"Actually, Thompson was married to her mother, but everyone kept it a secret. I'm sorry I didn't tell you. I didn't think it was important. I just didn't want anyone to know."

"Thompson betrayed us, and stole our money. Some of it would have been yours. So, you too were betrayed."

"I don't know anything about the money."

"We run an operation with a delicate balance here. We had to take care of Thompson as a strong warning to others. It is our way to also eliminate family members, to ensure loyalty. Surely you can see the effectiveness of this system?"

Clearly stunned by this revelation, Ngubane asked, "So you were behind Jaylin's death as well?"

She only stared.

"How could you?" A sob broke into his voice. "He was such a fine young boy." Ngubane felt as if his stomach were being pinched by surgical clamps.

"I guess you still don't appreciate the loyalty and commitment we expect. The girl may be spared, but we need to talk to her to try to recover the money. It is a considerable sum." She glared at him to emphasize her point.

Ngubane tried to summon some strength. He jutted his chin forward. "I will not have any harm come to her."

"Very well, but you do need to learn your lessons. All this," she said, dramatically waving her arms around, "everything, your work at the mission, your life, can be brought down in an instant." Rose's breathing rate quickened in anticipation of what was to come.

A loud crash resounded in the still night as Vicente used a cricket bat to break the windows in the glass walkway over the pool. The glass splintered down into the water.

"No, stop him. I'll call my guards."

When she made no attempt to signal Vicente, Ngubane blew a whistle to summon his guards. None came. Ginger grinned broadly without mirth. Ngubane blew on his whistle again, knowing somehow it was useless. He blew on it anyway as if someone would come. The realization hit him that Rose was in total control even to the point of bypassing his own security force.

Vicente heaved two objects out of the broken windows. Both were tethered to ropes–the Weimaraners. They were hung by their necks, eviscerated, with their blood and entrails hanging down and dripping into the pool.

"Oh, no, no! Please God, no." He stared at the horror in disbelief.

"Sit down and be quiet," spat Ginger. Ngubane looked back to see she now had a small pistol in her hand pointing it at him. "Watch!"

Vicente methodically continued smashing windows and tossed vases, carvings and paintings out of the house into the pool, panting from his exertions, but clearly having a good time.

Rose stood and turned to face Ngubane. She yanked down the elastic fabric of her tube top exposing her ample breasts. She loomed over him, still pointing the gun at his face. "Do you like what you see?"

"What? Are you mad? Stop. Cover yourself. Make him stop!" he cried out. Ngubane felt as if he entered another, totally insane world.

In a husky voice, she said, "Don't ever tell me what to do. Yes, perhaps I am mad. And I can make him stop, but first kneel and do as I say."

He obeyed, shaking with fear.

"Now very gently kiss each of my nipples. Gently, or I'll hurt you. After all, I am mad, is that not so?"

"What! No," but seeing the look on her face, he complied. He put his lips on each of her nipples in turn. It was a nightmare. It had to be. His gorge rose.

"Now stay as you are." As she stepped back, her demeanor shifted dramatically. "How dare you look at me, and touch my privates? You will have to be punished." She demurely lifted up her tube top to cover herself. She raised a hand and Vicente ceased his destructive activities.

"While we're waiting for Vicente to join us, you will take off your shirt."

Ngubane began to rise.

"Stay on your knees."

He complied, whimpering now.

"Now, drop your trousers to your knees. Your briefs as well." She instilled a dread so visceral, he knew it would control him forever.

"No, please you've done enough. Please." He pleaded, "Have mercy."

"Don't you ever tell me what's enough. There is very little mercy for liars in our business. It has been known that people who've deceived us have had their balls cut off and have been forced to eat them."

"Oh, God, please, no." Ngubane was screaming, crying, and begging, uncontrollably.

"Silence, and do as I say."

As he knelt with his trousers and shorts down at his knees, she mockingly pointed her pistol at his penis. "Look at that black snake. Yes, you will have to be punished."

Vicente approached, holding two bottles of beer in one hand and was carrying a wicked-looking curved knife in the other. *Buenos noches, medico.* I have been building a powerful thirst." Taking a long swig, he said, "I'm afraid your beautiful house is a mess. Too bad. Someone shat on your big bed. Truly, a shame." Vicente laughed.

"Now," said Ginger, to quaking Ngubane, "Lean forward on your hands." Vicente, if you please?"

Vicente sliced through the night air with his knife.

"No, no, I beg you," cried Ngubane. He leaned forward. His vision blurred by tears and his heart pounding, he saw his beautiful world dissolving into a horrible, surrealistic blur.

Vicente cut down a few long stems from the nearby plants and stripped them of their leaves. With a dozen in hand, he walked behind Ngubane. "What a target." He proceeded to whip the doctor's buttocks.

Ngubane had never been whipped like this even as a child. He could hardly bear it. He was a medical doctor, GMO of the district, wealthy and responsible for two medical facilities, and here he was on his hands and knees being beaten like a dog. Nasty welts striped his skin.

"Enough," said Rose. "Doctor, you are a disgrace. Now say 'thank you,' for sparing my life and my manhood."

Vicente plopped on a chaise lounge and resumed guzzling his beer.

"Oh, thank you, thank you for sparing me," whimpered Ngubane.

"For God's sake pull up your pants, put on your shirt, and sit down—you're disgusting."

"Oh, yes, thank you." He sobbed and winced as he sat.

She knew she had broken him. "Now we will have our chat as I mentioned on the phone. And you will tell me everything you know. Everything. Is that clear? We wouldn't want more unpleasantness, now would we?" She favored him with a tender smile.

"No, no more unpleasantness. I'll tell you everything I know." And he did—even to the involvement of Colonel Marshall and Deacon's connection with Thompson and Kalina.

When he had finished, she nodded and caressed his cheek, "Now, that wasn't so difficult. Quite a little conspiracy. And where is the Colonel now?"

"I have no idea—I swear."

She scowled.

"No, really, at this time, I don't know. Please, I do not know."

"Hmmm. And you say Deacon, Johannes, and Kalina are at the mountain clinic?"

"Yes, staying at the main house."

"Actually, I already knew that. Now, here's what you will do. You will carry on as normal here, and at the mission. You will report everything you hear to me or Vicente. Every tidbit of information, is that clear?"

"Oh yes, very clear," his voice quaking.

"If not, one fine evening, you will surely dine on your own testicles." She waited to let the threat sink in. "You will not tell anyone of our visit and the unpleasantness here tonight. We will not speak of it again. Call it 'a learning experience.' Fear not, everything will return to normal… as it was. The Eagle's Lair can be restored. But, *do* remember what happened here…. It is but a small sample of what could happen."

Vicente walked around the pool area, stretched from his exertions, finished his beer, smirked at his destructive work, and urinated into the aquamarine water.

Rose twisted a strand of her flaming hair and faced Ngubane, "We go now. Do keep in touch. There will be some people coming to clean up in the morning. The expense will come out of your share of the business." She turned to Vicente, "*Bueno esta' lo bueno.*"

"*Si.*"

"If this place were to catch fire, how long would it take to burn down?" Rose asked as if merely curious.

"Not long, especially with an explosion first." Vicente made a gesture with his hands being blown apart.

"Yes, I see. Goodnight, doctor. Remember our visit."

As they strolled away, Rose swung her hips suggestively and waved.

*   *   *   *   *

Ngubane stood to relieve the soreness of sitting on his injured buttocks. As he looked around at the devastation, he knew he could never look at his home in the same way again. The extent of the violation burned into him. He had to confront the fact that he had probably just signed Kalina's death warrant. Revolted by his weakness, his cowardliness, he questioned himself, *what have I done?* Perhaps, he thought, they will not harm Kalina in the end. But, he was alive, and the work at the mission and the clinic could continue.

It was all Thompson's fault. It was he who brought death and destruction on himself and his family. Ngubane wept for Jaylin, for Kalina, for his dogs, hanging dead and bloody over the pool, now attracting swarms of insects. He cried for his wounded Lair.

But he had survived. His manhood was intact.

He knew now for sure, he had sold his soul to a red-haired devil.

Chapter 28

AFTER A HURRIED BREAKFAST of coffee and rusks in the warm old-fashioned kitchen, fragrant with cooking aromas, I sought out Zekeriah.

His eyes wide, he said, "It was good you found me early, baas. Today, I go to Mutare for supplies."

"Good. Do you have a map of the grounds?"

"Yabo, I get it for you."

He went back to his office for ten minutes and returned both a surveyor's map and a sketch of the entire clinic compound. It was exactly what I needed.

"Thank you. One more thing before you go. Can you tell me about the personnel here? How many staff do you have?"

"Yah, surely. We are having fourteen full-time staff, not counting security, and some part-time people to help out."

"How many security?"

He counted on his fingers. "Six, not counting Muhlukai. Dey are on rotating schedules. Always dere are four during de day."

I wondered and asked, "Why are so many necessary?"

Shaking his head, he responded, "Ah, we have many thieves in Zimbabwe. And we have to be here for twenty-four hours. Also we are having valuable vehicles here and of course de drugs in de clinic."

I pointed at the map. "What is this area?"

"Dat is our *kraal*. The *roundavels* are very nice, with toilets and showers."

I'd seen the round structures with the conical thatched roofs from the road. "Who lives there?"

"I am staying dere three or four nights a week, but my home is in Bikita. Muhlukai also stays three or four nights. Our cook, two handymen, and two laboratory assistants live dere full time. Their wives work in de kitchen or at de clinic."

"And why the fence within the compound?"

"For de flowers which grow de doctor's medicine—good *muti*. Dere are many dangerous trails and snakes, so we like to keep people away."

Just what I wanted to hear, "snakes."

"Also it helps keep de animals out."

Zekeriah seemed totally open and without guile. I had everything I needed for now. I thought Marshall would be pleased. "Thank you again. I'll see you later."

"*Yabo baba.*" He took off at a trot.

As I prepared myself to scout the compound, I heard soft singing with intricate harmonies coming from the kitchen workers. This beautiful, peaceful chorus ushered in the misty African mornings—a morning prayer set to music.

I picked up a canteen of water, strapped on my pistol, put some extra rounds in my pocket and took a machete from behind the pantry in the kitchen. With maps in hand I went off at a brisk pace to follow the trails and get the lay of the land. I planned to follow the fence line along the perimeter.

I soon encountered one of the guards who seemed alert and suspicious as his eyes constantly scanned the landscape. He was tall, with a scar on his cheek, and he stood erect, obviously wearing his navy blue uniform with pride. While he asked me a few questions, I noticed he had a rifle and carried a short-shafted spear. I had seen other guards with knob sticks or machetes in addition to their side-arms.

"Just taking a morning hike." I said affably to the dour guard.

"Don't go too far, Mistah." warned the guard glaring at me through deep-set eyes, "It could be danger."

I nodded and walked away, but I didn't consider that there would be much danger. A short walk took me to the little kraal on the edge of the compound. A few cook fires smoldered in the flat dirt area in the center of the mini-village. A few people stared at me unabashedly from the doors and windows of the *roundavels*. A few smiled broadly. I saw no children present. I noticed a large drum of petrol, clothes, a rope or two, cooking utensils, a large oil canister and blankets hanging out on lines. I was unable to see into any of the thatched huts. It was a far cry from the Chicago suburbs. I wondered if these people had ever seen snow.

The path along the fence line was well-worn from frequent guard patrols. Again, my military eye took note of lines of fire. The trees, ground ferns, and lush undergrowth provided excellent concealment.

Tall gray granite outcroppings, were mantled in green foliage which spilled down from the summits. If I were on vacation, I would find this a scenic and relaxing hike. I took photos to show Marshall.

I returned to the break in the fence Kalina had shown me and quickly walked the valley paths among the poppies. Wherever poppies grew, various forms of camouflage netting hung overhead. According to the map, the valleys of poppies were well below the rugged peaks of the Eastern Highlands. A few times I heard something scurry away through the undergrowth. Despite the fences, some small wild game inevitably had set up housekeeping.

I knew I would not have enough time to investigate every trail and complete the perimeter circuit. After four hours, I felt the need to return to the compound. My water was nearly gone and I felt reasonably familiar with the grounds. On my way back I passed by the lepers' huts. They lived in their own compound about fifty yards from the clinic.

I returned to the living area hungry and thirsty and asked the cook for a simple lunch and a cold lager, then sat on the front veranda re-studying the maps and preparing to explain the layout to Colonel Marshall.

I decided to call Father Godwin.

He answered the phone cheerfully. "Hello Deacon. We've missed you here. Hang on a sec. let me close my office door from prying ears. So, how are you getting along out in the wilds of the Chimanimani's my good fellow?"

"Fine, Fine. We had a quiet talk after the *braii* last night and the team thought it would be a good idea to have a fallback place nearby in case this one is compromised. We could use your advice—any catacombs you know of around here?"

"Hmmm. Good idea, another safe haven. I see what you're on about. Let me think." After a short pause he said, "Yes, I have it. A friend, an old mentor of mine, would be certainly able to help you in a pinch. He is now in charge of running the abbey outside Masvingo. It's just near the great Zimbabwe National Monument. Not far from you. I'm sure the chaps at the clinic know of it. The abbey overlooks Lake Mutirikwi. Lovely spot. His name is Father Garrett Stegemann. You may rely on him for sanctuary. I'll call him just now informing him of our discussion. If there is any difficulty, I'll call you right back."

"That's great, thank you, Father."

"Everything else all right?"

No, I thought, just about nothing is all right. Somehow, you and your mission and your friends, the uncles, are either in the drug trade, illegal ivory, or are being used in a most despicable way. But one thought took priority. I knew all of them loved Kalina and wanted her safe. I would trust in their love. And I would trust in the abbey as a safe fallback position. "Yes, everything is fine so far."

"Well then, I'm off. May God bless all of you. Give my love to Kalina."

I left the house, pulled Johannes away from his work, and told him about the abbey and Father Stegemann. We sat on the shady veranda as I spread out some local maps and together we located the abbey on one of the nearby roads. I judged it to be less than ten miles away.

Finishing off a cold Amstel, Johannes said, "Yah, it is good to have dis other place." As usual, a man of few words. We memorized the directions to the abbey to memory in case we had to get there in a hurry.

I needed to prepare him for Colonel Marshall's arrival. "Johannes, a man named Colonel Marshall will arrive soon."

He went very still and fixed me with an intense gaze. "Why does he come?"

I knew I'd had to be careful. "We have asked him to help us find Thompson's and Jaylin's killers."

Before Johannes could respond, we were interrupted by a young Endebele woman who brought us lunch, consisting of freshly baked rolls, a tangy cheese, assorted fruits and a few more beers.

Johannes pierced me with his gaze and leaned forward. "Tell me more."

"He is working to discover who is after Kalina. Robbie Forrester vouches for him. The colonel knows how to protect people and has the right connections to help us with the paperwork to hide Kalina's identity and help us to get her out of the country."

He started swaying his head back and forth like a pachyderm, considering my response. He was clearly disturbed by this news.

I didn't want to push the conversation any further.

Just then, Colonel Marshall arrived. I introduced him to Johannes.

He joined in for cold chicken, a green salad, and some Cape Cabernet. He didn't mention a thing about what he had discovered about Rose, Vicente and the drug connection. I assumed that he didn't want to open up in front of Johannes.

Johannes asked, "You wid de Army?"

"No," replied the Colonel "Newly retired from the SAPS."

"Ach, a policeman." The two men glared at each other.

"I'm here to help," reassured the Colonel.

"Yah, here to help."

Johannes as always, a scintillating conversationalist.

He rose, stepped down from the porch and found a wicker armchair in the yard. He sat heavily and having consumed several beers before lunch and some wine with the meal he stretched out and dozed off.

A sunny, cloudless sky and a soft breeze made for an idyllic day.

Between bites the colonel said, "Not a trusting soul, that one."

"He's a tough old bird but his love for Kalina is real. He doesn't make friends easily." I couldn't help wonder what Johannes' connection was to the drug smuggling enterprise.

I informed the Colonel about the abbey and the fallback plan. He heartily approved.

After a short time Johannes woke and lumbered off to go back to fixing something. Kalina was in the house helping the staff prepare dinner.

The Colonel and I pondered the diagrams of the clinic grounds.

"They have reduced their security risks by having only the one entrance and exit into the clinic compound," said the Colonel.

"Yes, I get it. Everything and everybody comes in and out of the front gate, which is secured every night and has a guard post. I wasn't able to cover the entire perimeter, but I've marked most of the trails and the fence line."

"Well, now is as good a time as any. Let's see your poppy fields."

"Good enough." We rose. I put my lightweight hiking boots back on, checked my ankle gun, and picked up my machete.

"Are you armed?" I asked.

"Always." The Colonel revealed an old Browning automatic under his tunic. I felt safer with someone else who knew how to use a gun.

Before proceeding to the fields, I checked in with Johannes. "I'm just going to show the Colonel around the property. Kalina is in the house—I'll leave her to you, okay?"

"Yah, okay," he said, barely looking up from some piece of oily mechanism he had in his lap. His eyes followed the Colonel. *Guilty, worried or just uncomfortable? Hard to tell.*

"We won't be long."

As I turned away, I felt strong misgivings. I wasn't pleased that so much of Johannes' attention was with mechanical repairs and that he seemed lax in his vigilance over Kalina. For a moment I considered taking her with us, but changed my mind. Perhaps I thought, I'm being paranoid. Then again, some healthy paranoia can save your ass.

As we retreated farther into the interior forest, the Colonel told me more of his discoveries concerning Miss Ginger Rose and her companion Vicente Luna. "It's all beginning to fit together. Drug dealers have their filthy hands spread around the globe. Now they're here in Southern Africa. Miss Rose is Peruvian, and has been connected to Luis Salazar, a headman in the guerrilla movement and drug smuggling consortium. Her partner, Vicente Luna, also Peruvian, arrived at the same time she did. Killing off the family members of those who betray them is their standard operating procedure. Thus far, their enterprise has been under our radar. But after you show me what you've found, we should be able to shut down their whole operation."

I thought of my time with Ginger Rose and her incessant questions; I felt used and dirty. It would be gratifying to kill their project, put them away and get Kalina the hell out of here.

By the time we reached the poppy fields, I was convinced about the drug trade, but still not sure exactly how the uncles fit in, or even how much they knew. The clincher regarding Kalina's vulnerability and Rose's complicity was the copied photograph Marshall showed me of Thompson and his family that he found in Rose's office.

Seeing the extent of the fields and the netting, I could see the Colonel was convinced that this was a major opium growing enterprise. The on-site lab obviously was perfect for converting the opium into heroin. Afterwards, it was somehow transported to a place to be taken out of the country.

"There's no doubt about Ginger Rose and her companion Luna being involved. The project must be destroyed. When we return, we can investigate the others who may be involved and discover their mode of transportation. It would be best to catch Rose and Luna with the drugs."

"What did you say?" I felt as if I'd been slapped in the face.

"I said, it would be best to catch them with the goods."

"Yes, yes, but there was something in the way you said it….I'm sorry, I don't know."

Frantically searching my mind, I knew something was just beyond my awareness. It was maddening not to be able to retrieve it. I let it go. If important enough, it would come back to me soon.

We remained silent for some time as we followed the winding trails in the poppy fields.

"What did you say Rose's partner's name was?"

"Luna, Vicente Luna."

"Luna and Rose. Rose and Luna. Luna and stars." I was free associating word pairs. "Stars and sky. Moon and stars. Rose and Moon. That's it." My eyes widened and I stopped walking.

"What's it?"

"Rose and Moon. What Thompson said in his letter—beware of *'Rosenmoon.'* That was the way he heard it. What he meant was 'Rose and Moon,' Ginger Rose and Vicente Luna. Luna is 'moon' in Spanish. In his letter, Thompson warned me they were killers."

Chapter 29

"PULL UP NEAR THE GATE, but park outside the compound," Rose ordered.

"Si," replied Vicente. The ornamental iron gate was open during the day. Vicente mopped his brow and walked up to the guard's shed.

Rose stayed in the car while Vicente spoke to the uniformed guard.

Vicente ordered, "Get your boss, Muhlukai, out here."

The lanky guard recognized the demanding voice of authority. He expressed no emotion while he stepped back, took a chrome whistle out of his breast pocket and blew it three times. As he had been trained, he didn't leave his post but regarded Vicente warily from behind mirrored sunglasses.

A few minutes later, Muhlukai came jogging up to the gate area. He had met Vicente only once before, but instantly recognized him as his employer's partner.

"This way," said Vicente cocking his head toward the Jag parked nearby in the shade.

Muhlukai slid into the back seat grinning as if he reveled in the sudden air-conditioned atmosphere. Vicente stayed outside, leaning against the car, and lit up a cheroot.

Rose wrinkled her nose. Her first words of greeting were, "You really ought to bathe more often, Muhlukai."

"Yes, *Dumela*, Miss Rose."

"Well, tell me the latest. What's happening?"

He began his report. "Zekeriah has gone to de town for supplies. One of my men saw de American take an older gentleman with big moustache out to de fields."

"That's got to be the nosey Colonel Marshall. Where is this girl pretending to be a boy?"

Muhlukai looked down, remembering his embarrassing encounter with "Jomo." He spoke hesitatingly, "She is in de house maybe helping in de kitchen or in her room, I think."

"And Johannes? That huge bald voortrekker? God, you can't miss him. Where is he?"

"Ah, yes, de big man. He's fixing one of de trucks in de back."

"Good." Rose smiled. "Are the workers in the fields yet?"

"No, not yet."

"Good. Go tell them to stay out of the fields today. It's important." Those will be killing fields this day, she thought.

"*Ya-bo*—no field work today."

Rose smiled and thought, this is as good as it gets. Her quarry was trapped. "How many of your security men are here now?"

"Four on de day watch. One at de gate, and de others on patrol." He was proud that his security force had been hand-picked as men of violence.

"Listen carefully. Here's what I want you to do. Gather your men and send them out to hunt in the fields today."

Muhlukai wrinkled his forehead. "Hunt? There is little game there, except for de birds."

"I happen to know that there are two dangerous vermin prowling there today. They must be disposed of permanently."

Muhlukai's face slowly morphed into a show of revelation. "Ah yes, de two-legged vermin who must be killed." He looked very proud of himself for understanding.

"And as this is a special assignment, there will be a bonus for each man—three thousand Rands when the hunt is finished and the bodies are buried deep in the hills."

"Dey will not come out," said Muhlukai, seriously. Then he went silent, looked up at her and cocked his head sideways.

Rose understood. "And for you, as their leader, five thousand Rands."

He smiled and nodded vigorously. "Dis hunt should be easy. Dey are not suspecting."

"Just don't let your men get too cocky and underestimate their quarry. After you send your guards off, I want you back here at the gate." Rose sensed his relief at not actually being in the hunt.

He went off at a lope to gather his men.

"Vicente, it is time. Go to the *casa* and get the girl. It would be best to do this quietly. Don't harm her. We must try to find out about our money first. *Claro?*"

"*Claro*, I go now."

"I'll wait here in the car. The tinted windows will make sure I'm not seen by anyone. Be quick."

*   *   *   *   *

Returning to the house to get a cold drink, Johannes glimpsed Vicente approaching the house. He scowled and thundered around the side to get a better look. He heard Vicente ask one of the houseboys, "Is there a young boy named Jomo around here anywhere?"

The lad answered, "*Ya-bo*, staying at de house, upstairs."

Vicente thanked him brusquely and proceeded up the hill to the front of the house.

Johannes rushed through the back of the house and lay in wait, holding his breath in a small alcove alongside the front door.

As Vicente entered slowly through the door and walked to the bottom of the staircase, Johannes charged at him from behind with the determination of an Amtrak locomotive. His shoulder hit Vicente in the back, ramming his head forward into a doorframe. Caught totally unawares, Vicente bounced off the doorjamb with a dull thud and lay sprawled motionless on the hall rug, unconscious and bleeding from a gash along his hairline.

Johannes stepped over his body and ran up the stairs two at a time. He nearly ran into Kalina walking down the hall.

"Uncle, what was that noise?"

"No time to explain now, girl, come wid me. Hurry, we are found here." He pulled her by the hand along the upper hallway to the rear of the house and down the backstairs. He didn't want her to see Vicente's body. They exited through the kitchen and ran to the carpark. When they reached the pickup truck Johannes had been working on, he pushed her into the passenger seat. "We must go now."

"Uncle, You're scaring me. Where are we going?" Her eyes were wide with fear, her voice tremulous.

Johannes started the truck, slammed it into gear, and sped toward the front gate. "Father Godwin found us another safe place. We go dere now. Deacon knows dis place. He will know we go dere."

"How do you know someone's found us?"

"A very bad man ask for you."

*　　*　　*　　*　　*

While Ginger Rose sat in her Jag filing her nails, Muhlukai briefed his four-man security team. As he told them of the upcoming hunt and their human prey, their eyes sparkled with anticipation. Blood-lust plus the promise of a substantial reward provided ample motivation for the hunters.

One of his men, Ndiro, a tall Zulu who had often told stories of his warrior heritage, seemed especially eager and insisted upon wearing the ceremonial tufts of tawny lion mane below his knees and around his biceps. His eyes were wide with excitement and he trembled slightly. He refused to wear his navy blue security uniform and insisted on painting his body with geometric figures in white and red. He wanted to adorn himself and go on the hunt separately. He would not carry a gun. Instead he would hunt with the traditional assegais and panga. Wisely, Muhlukai agreed. Ndiro ran off to the krall to attire himself for the hunt.

Muhlukai further instructed the other three. "When it is done, and they are buried deep, come to me and report."

The men smiled, nodded their assent, checked their weapons and headed for the trails at a trot.

*   *   *   *   *

When Rose saw the pickup truck swerve out of the front gate at high speed, she sat upright. She got a good enough look as they passed, recognizing Johannes behind the wheel. She also noticed a light-colored black in the passenger seat, uncertain if it was a boy or a girl. But she'd bet it was Kalina.

Not knowing what had happened her gut instincts screamed at her to follow them. She could come back later for Vicente. Scrambling behind the wheel and with some relief, she spotted Muhlukai at the gate. Driving up to him she threw open the passenger door. "Get in!"

She thought he could be useful and not stand out as she certainly would. Careful to stay a discreet distance behind the truck, her jag easily kept pace. The high profile of the pickup made it easy to follow. After Muhlukai relayed to her that he had sent his men off on their mission, they said very little.

On the outskirts of Masvingo, the truck wheeled into the grounds of an old abbey. They would take sanctuary there, she thought, where they would feel safe. But where they were also vulnerable. She decided to come back for them with Vicente.

Rose drove around the outer stucco walls of the old abbey as far as she could, got out of her car and walked off road with Muhlukai to get to know the area better. She estimated the grounds covered about five acres. Within the walls, a church dominated the compound, surrounded by several outbuildings and walking paths. A large vegetable garden took up one side. One of the paths led to a series of small grottos for worshipers of the Way of the Cross. She remembered this Lenten devotion well from her erratic Catholic upbringing. She spotted the truck in the visitor's carpark but there was no way to tell where Johannes had taken the girl.

An awful rage was built within her. Her breathing quickened and she drove her fingernails into her palms. They had been so close!

She returned to her car to sit in the shade and calm herself. She closed her eyes and willed her breathing to normalize. Soon she would return with Vicente and flush the girl out. As she sat back in the luxurious interior of the Jag, she began to formulate a plan to charm the girl into revealing some things without first resorting to force. If that didn't work, well....

"Muhlukai, I want you to get out and keep watch on the truck, Johannes, and the girl. Stay hidden. They both know you and might recognize you skulking around. I'll be back soon. Then you'll tell me if anyone has come or gone."

"Yes, Miss Rose." He grinned broadly.

She knew that Muhlukai held her in some kind of awe, and would obey her to the letter.

Once she was alone on the highway, Rose reached into her purse and spritzed around some of her perfume.

Chapter 30

THREE RIFLE SHOTS RANG OUT as one continuous sound. In response, a cacophony of screeches rose from the bird population. Feeling painful wasp-like stings on the right side of my face, I realized that one of the bullets had hit the boulder next to me and had driven sharp rock chips into my skin. Luckily, none of them hit my eyes. Another slug sailed harmlessly between the Colonel and me. The third struck the Colonel.

The hunters had picked a good moment. Marshall and I were on relatively open ground, sitting still, while taking a break and a drink of water.

I realized the security guards were still too far away for certain accuracy. These rough looking guys might be good street fighters with knives, knuckles, or knob sticks, but they were not the best marksmen. Probably thinking it might all be over quickly, I heard them raise their voices as though in victory.

We had tumbled over and hit the ground behind the rocks on which we'd been sitting. My heart kicked with adrenalin–a feeling I was all too familiar with. I heard them raise their voices as though in victory, probably thinking it would all be over quickly. I rose carefully and saw them approaching with no apparent hurry.

The Colonel still lay sprawled on his back. I asked in a harsh whisper, "Are you all right?"

"It looks like I took a round in my hip. It burns like hell."

"Here, let me take a look." I crabbed over to where the Colonel lay.

Seeing my bleeding face he grimaced and said, "Hey, you don't look so good yourself."

I felt the blood trickle from the nicks in my face. "Just some ricochet rock chips; they sting but I don't think it's too bad."

I knelt and tore apart his trouser material at the seam near his hip. The bullet had grazed him leaving a long gash. He looked down at his wound. "Only a deep graze, no slug inside, thank God."

I opened my canteen and quickly splashed some water into the bloody wound. Taking off my bush jacket, I tied the sleeves around his hips. "We've got to staunch this bleeding."

The Colonel slipped his belt out of his trousers and cinched it around my shirt, covering the wound to make a pressure dressing. "Okay, that's got it. I'll keep some pressure on it." He spoke with a controlled voice–a tough old bird to be sure.

I looked around, "Now let's get the hell out of here. Higher ground and to their left flank." We scrambled, crawled and ran in crouching postures around the rocks and away from our pursuers. I looked back at the Colonel. The old boy was tough, but he was in his early sixties and his mobility had been seriously compromised.

"How many do you think?" he whispered.

"I'm not sure, three, maybe four. I believe they're part of the security force here. I don't know if Muhlukai is among them."

After we'd covered some ground and were in amongst some large boulders and thick brush, we paused to catch our breath and to assess our situation.

The Colonel said, "We're outnumbered at least two to one, they know the territory, and they're armed with rifles."

Yeah, I thought, but one of our advantages is they don't appreciate who they're dealing with. The colonel and I had skills. My rage overcame my fear. I knew I had to get back to Kalina, but first we had to survive. "We've a few things in our favor. They may not know we're armed, and there's plenty of cover and concealment. We've got to make our shots count. I don't think we can outrun them, so we'll have to take them out."

We took out our guns. "Lock and load," I heard myself saying, almost automatically. "How are you holding up?"

The Colonel's breathing was labored. "Are you familiar with the expression 'DDD'?"

"No, I'm not."

"It means, Definitely Done Dancing."

You gotta love gallows humor.

"Actually, my hip is hurting like hell. I don't think the bleeding will stop as long as I'm moving about. And you?"

"The sweat stings the cuts, but I'm okay. Stay here a few minutes. Now's probably a good time to take a few swigs from your canteen. I'm going to see what we're up against."

I found a tree and dug around the roots until I hit dirt. I used a little water from my canteen to make a paste. Ignoring my facial cuts, I slathered my face, arms and hands. Fortunately I had on a black tee shirt. Next, I plunged my beige-colored cap into the mud. *They can't hit what they can't see.*

I climbed quickly and found a shady space among the boulders. I moved very slowly to spy on our enemies below. They were moving up the slope towards us.

There were three of them, in their midnight blue uniforms. From their countenances and rather casual approach, I guessed they thought they had scored a quick kill. The last man was big, but mostly fat, and lagged behind the others. In addition to his rifle and the long machete in his belt, he carried a shovel. That simple grim reminder of their ultimate task hit me hard. *I won't die easy, you bastards.* Were there more? I assumed the worst—that there were—but God I hoped not. *Bury me this fine day? I think not, you sons of bitches.*

I pulled back slowly and slid noiselessly as I could down to the Colonel. "I saw three of them, for sure. But there might be more out there. Here's my map." I unfolded my map of the area and put my finger on one area. I said, "Here's where we are. I have a plan."

"Let's hear it," growled the Colonel looking at the map.

I recognized distress in his hoarse voice. Although his wound wasn't life-threatening, being close to the bone, it had to be painful.

"If you take the trail to our left, it will lead you to the fence line. Turn left along the fence trail. Eventually, it'll lead you to the little village on the property." I didn't reveal to the Colonel that I thought I'd have a tactical advantage if I faced them alone.

"What will you be doing?"

"I'll go to the right and lure our pursuers deeper into the fields, worse case scenario, maybe they won't all come my way. If that happens, I advise you to set up your own ambush. I'll do my best to draw them off. Once at the little village, chase the people away even if you have to threaten them."

"What have you got in mind?"

"There are cans of petrol and oil in the village. If you're able, set the fucking poppy fields on fire, then get down to the laboratory and torch it as well. I don't know if we'll have another chance. The people and the patients should have time to get away to the road or up to the big house." I began to move, then stopped abruptly, "And for God's sake see if you can find Kalina and Johannes."

"I'll do it if I can. Will you be all right on your own?"

"I'll be fine." I knew he wasn't quite convinced. "I'll find a way to take them down. Be careful. We really don't know who's a combatant and who's a friendly."

"I will."

I raised my thumb, "Good luck and good hunting."

"Good luck yourself."

I watched the older man limp down the trail. I then backed up and made very obvious tracks towards another path which led north into the valleys of poppies. I hoped they would all follow me.

I ran full out for a while to put some distance between myself and the men chasing me; my mind running even faster than my body. I focused on what to do, and how I would take them. I knew I'd have to get up close. I couldn't be sure of my pistol's accuracy beyond forty yards. I still had the machete. *Use your environment. Make use of mobility, surprise, and concealment.* My thoughts were right out of the special ops field manuals.

I heard the hunters guttural cussing when they finally reached the place where we'd been hit. *Your quarry has scampered away, boys. Now what ya gonna' do? Jesus, they'll be coming now. I'd better remember how to do this shit.* I found myself hyperventilating with "shakes." I allowed myself a few precious moments to shut my eyes, bring my breathing back to normal, and focus my thoughts. "That's it, boyo, stay focused and stay alive," I whispered.

On the move once more, I dropped into a valley and crossed a swift moving creek about five yards across and two feet deep in the middle. The bank on the far side was steep and slippery. I made obvious tracks climbing in the mud. I went back and forth to better indicate that there were two men moving along.

Luckily, the rushing water over rocks and debris provided background masking noise. I thought the heavy man would certainly have trouble climbing the far bank. If his partners ran ahead, the big man would be alone and vulnerable. I ran thirty yards down the trail, grabbed an overhanging branch and went hand over hand until I was well off to the side of the path. I dropped down into the deep ferns and doubled back to the creek. I crawled as close as I dared to the side of the steep bank and waited.

Dappled shade being a definite plus, I took a moment to re-cover myself with more camouflaging mud. I swigged a long pull from my canteen. My mouth was the Sahara. The mud I put on my face seemed to have stopped the bleeding. I hoped it wasn't full of dangerous bacteria, or monkey shit, or whatever. *Hell, an infection is the least of my worries.*

I gripped my pistol in my left hand and my machete in my right. I lay in the thick fern cover waiting, while my mind, like a sling-shot took me back to the Middle East with crazy people shooting at me in the dark. *Could I do this?* I was a deacon of the Catholic Church, dedicated to helping others, and now I was being hunted in some damn jungle and planning to attack other men. *"Love your enemies?"* I wanted to kill them. Could I kill again? Probably. Maybe down deep I am a cold-blooded killer. Maybe, deep down everybody is, when it comes to survival.

Considering the present circumstances, this is exactly what I had to be for now. They had tried to kill me. Fuck, they were still trying to kill me. Again, I recalled the shovel that one of the men carried. I would take up the moral questions later. Maybe over a cold beer with Father Godwin. I wondered, Father Godwin's position was on 'situational ethics'? *That's it, you putz, fantasize about a future you may not have.*

In less than five minutes, two of my pursuers popped out of the bush and crossed the creek. They spoke in hushed tones. I heard them calling back for their heavy-set companion to catch up. I could now see them more clearly. They both had rifles. In addition, one carried a machete and the other a wicked knob stick.

They were not patient. As I had hoped, they pressed on, climbed the muddy bank, and continued down the track I'd left for them to follow. I could almost feel their feet hit the ground as they passed within five yards of my position. I was grateful for the gurgling water nearby or surely, I thought, they would have heard my heart beating.

As the footfalls faded, the third man appeared, panting and sweating profusely. He had given up running. He carried a rifle, and shovel, and wore a sheath knife on his belt. The big man lumbered across the creek, moving slowly, making sure of his footing. He stopped to splash water on his head and the back of his fat neck. He actually looked in my direction… but didn't see me.

I crept on the ground like the lizards I'd been watching. I got as close as I dared to the muddy bank that the man had to mount. Finally, he came forward. He looked up at the muddy wall. Seeing no easy handholds or footholds, sighed audibly. He tossed his rifle and shovel up on top of the bank and began to climb.

If I were going to do anything, it would have to be now. While the man concentrated on getting up the slippery bank, I eased down to the water's edge. I knew I'd be exposed for a few seconds, but the man had thrown his weapon away, and was intent on climbing.

I dashed the final ten yards hoping like hell I wouldn't slip and fall on the mossy rocks.

I didn't. As I approached, the fat man turned to face me at the last instant. I had my machete raised, but in that moment decided I couldn't just take this helpless man's life. I brought the blade down in a curved arc aiming to cut the hamstrings on the side of the man's right knee. He howled, his face pure agony. I backhanded the machete severing the Achilles tendon above the heel of the other leg rendering him immobile.

I snarled, "No grave digging for you today! Asshole." The Colonel's expression came back to me. This pursuer was "DDD." I thwacked him on the head with the butt of my machete to knock him out and shut him up.

I stepped on the man and leapt up to reach the rifle protruding over the side of the bank and threw it downstream, where it immediately sank. I didn't think it would be useful to me in close quarters and it would prove cumbersome. Now, at least they wouldn't have it. I did the same with the hated shovel.

The flowing water ran red with his blood. I pulled the knife out of the man's waistband and ran upstream. I'd rendered an enemy helpless to continue. I was exuberant with an adrenalin rush. After what seemed to be only a few steps, I heard the other two come upon their partner. The creek took a turn to the right. Just as I made the turn I heard the shots. I could almost sense the air disturbance around me as the slugs streaked by. I was thankful the security guards were upset, eager, and probably off balance while standing in the moving water.

I scrambled up some rocks and disappeared again into the dense foliage.

One down, I thought. I had a good sense of direction, and knew that I was paralleling the trail, glad I had taken time to study the maps. Once I got to more solid ground, I stood and sprinted to put more distance between myself and those behind me.

I thought as I ran, that they would be more cautious now. Who had sent them? How the hell did anyone know we were here? And as always, what about Kalina? I had to survive for her sake.

I reckoned my pursuers had probably spent years in the countryside. But, I hoped my specialized military training would provide some balance for their bush knowledge.

As I gasped for air, I realized I was not in the kind of shape I had been in while in the service. On the positive side, my motivation was survival. I looked up through the canopy of trees. Darkness would help, but it was too many hours away. How was the Colonel making out? *At least they hadn't followed him.*

Finally, I went down on all fours to suck in some air. My rage continued to merge with my fear. I threw up a prayer. *Help me, Lord.*

*　　*　　*　　*　　*

I slipped off my muddy cap, wiping the sweat from my eyes. In the insanity of the moment, I smiled noticing the golf cap had "Titleist" stitched on the crown. The concept of "golf," under these circumstances seemed to be from another time-space dimension.

I purposely made my spoor easy to follow. I needed to lure my pursuers into some sort of trap, and finish them before I became dehydrated and lost my energy. They still might not know I was armed.

Just beyond a semi-clearing, I put a simple plan into action. I attached my golf hat to a stick and stuck it into the ground amidst waist-high ferns. I pulled down long vines from the trees and tied them together. Once I had a length of twenty feet, I tied one end to the stick, played out the vine, crouched behind a Eucalyptus tree and waited.

If only I could get a clear shot. I might be able to eliminate both of them. Realistically, I felt sure I could get one, thus reducing the odds to even.

I barely detected their approach. They moved swiftly but also very quietly. When they reached the small clearing and stopped to look around, I pulled on the vine moving the stick with the hat on it. Both men raised their rifles to their shoulders and fired.

I knelt ninety degrees to their right side. I thought, perfect-- enfilade fire. If the man nearest me went down I'd have a second clear shot at the other behind him. I braced my pistol against the tree, and aimed for the torso of the man nearest to me.

I squeezed off two shots and the man went down. Unfortunately he staggered sideways into his partner.

Both were down and I couldn't be sure what had happened. One man popped up firing his rifle wildly in my direction. He quickly went down again. I moved back waiting for the man to charge. But this man was careful and held his position.

What would I do in his place? I'd flank my opponent. But on which side? Only one thing for me to do. Keep moving straight back to get further away, regroup and try to outsmart the third man. It had become very quiet; each of us finely tuned to listening.

I belly-crawled as quickly and silently as I could, moving in spurts and frequently stopping to listen. There were three shots left in my pistol. I had put extra rounds in my jacket, which I realized in frustration, was now staunching the bleeding of the Colonel's hip wound. Three shots left—period. And the machete, and the knife I had liberated from the fat gravedigger at the creek.

By now, I'd lost my orientation. The sun was high and I'd made too many turns. *Fuck it*. It didn't make any difference now.

Ahead, the vegetation was less dense and some rocks were piled up like some kid's giant marbles. If I could get there I would have some real cover not just the concealment of the vegetation. I found it hard to crawl, holding the gun and the machete. Any minute I thought I'd look up into the barrel of a rifle. So the last thing I'd see in this world was a little dark hole.

I would need my hands and fingers to climb. I tucked the gun into my waistband on my right side. I put the machete through my belt on the other side, making crawling easier.

I'd minimize my exposure by going to one side of the rocks. I knew if I had picked incorrectly, I might walk right into my enemy. For some reason, the left side looked better. Less to climb, therefore less exposure. I took a couple of deep breaths and ran to the rocks and began to scramble up. Shots rang out from the direction I'd come. So the man hadn't flanked me, but was coming straight on. I felt a hammer blow to my right side. I tumbled over a boulder. I knew for sure I'd been hit. One of the shots hit the pistol in my waistband, breaking it apart and rendering it useless. Useless, except for the fact that it had also probably saved my life.

I was bleeding from cuts on my waist made by bullet fragments or pistol parts being driven into my flesh. I checked the wounds…superficial. Now I was without a firearm against an armed foe. *Just fuckin' great.* Shots ricocheted off the rocks around me. I climbed to higher ground.

I managed to find a depression between large boulders putting me in deep shade. I was spitting cotton–dehydrated. I looked around to see what was available. I found some rocks about the size of grapefruits. They would be small enough to throw with force and large enough to do damage if they hit anything.

Now I had to locate my target. I had to think of my pursuer as a "target." I wasn't going to kill anyone; I was going to hit a target. I wondered about the man I'd shot. *Had I already killed a man today?*

I took a few small stones and threw them into the air, hoping that when they hit, they would draw the man's fire, helping me to locate him. No such luck. The man wasn't biting. I waited and pulled out the machete, which I noticed still bore traces of blood from the man I'd struck down at the creek.

I moved a little to my right not wanting to be cornered in a small space. In my peripheral vision I detected movement of a small snake ringed by colorful bands. The little snake probably saved my life since while I was looking in its direction I saw a shadow moving on the round rock faces. The shadow was tantalizing by appearing and disappearing.

I waited. Finally, the shadow stopped and I could trace it back to a man's foot. The man was close. I felt as if I were shaking inside though I could see I was very still. My nervous system was screaming, danger. Suddenly everything seemed calm. I threw the grapefruit-sized rock where I estimated the man to be.

I heard a grunt and a shot rang out. I charged out of the rocks with machete at the ready, and came into view of a man sitting and rubbing his right shoulder. The rifle was several feet away. When he saw me, he leapt to his feet and held his own machete aloft. So it came down to this. I had never fought with a machete. Had this man?

He was as tall as me, with yellow rheumy eyes and irregular protruding teeth. Sweat was glistening down his craggy face. I felt I had nothing to lose by talking to the man.

"Why are you trying to kill me?" No answer. "What do you want?"

I faked a movement to his right. The man reacted and stumbled slightly. I ran to his left and snatched up the rifle, pointed it at the man's belly and said, "Now we're going to slowly walk out of here. So put your weapon down or I will shoot you." Unbelievably, the man started coming forward.

I shouted for the man to stop. "Don't you understand English? Stop!" I pointed the gun at the man's legs and pulled the trigger. The "click" I heard was probably the worst sound I had ever heard in my life.

The man's lips stretched apart in a skull's grimace. I had dropped my machete to pick up the rifle. The man charged and chopped down with his own machete. I blocked it with his rifle. Actually, I realized, I was more at home and more proficient with an empty rifle than I was with a machete. I had had some experience using a rifle during bayonet training about a hundred years ago. Oh, what I wouldn't give to have a bayonet at the end of this weapon.

It came back to me as if it were yesterday. "What was the spirit of the bayonet?" the drill instructors would shout. The response was "kill."

The man came at me again, yelling in a high-pitched wail. This time when he stabbed at me, I parried and clipped the man's upper arm hard with a horizontal butt thrust. The man wheeled around and came at me again with rapid slicing movements. One of them glanced off the back of my left hand. I involuntarily released my grip and dropped the rifle.

I backed away quickly, and squatted, picking up a handful of loose gravel and sand. As the man charged again, I tossed the gravel up into his face. He only stopped for a moment or two, to wipe his eyes, but in that moment, I extracted the knife from my belt.

I don't know what I was thinking. I didn't know anything about knife throwing, but I threw the knife and got lucky. The knife stuck into his neck. This warrior did a sudden dance of pain. Bright red blood sprayed out as he tugged the knife from his throat and collapsed backwards. In the next two minutes I watched him twitch and die on that pile of rocks.

I glared down at him. It was over. I wondered just when I'd stepped through the looking glass and tumbled down the rabbit hole into this insane world. Probably when I got off the plane in South Africa. Feeling relieved but somehow numb, I sat heavily. My emotions would catch up to reality in a short time. Taking a life up close and personal gripped my heart. *God forgive me.*

I was parched and weary beyond belief. I finished my last few gulps of water. I searched the body but found nothing of use. The dead man carried no water. *Damn.* The combination of the dead man's blood, and loss of his sphincter emitted a God-awful stench. I backed off, sat down and threw up a quick prayer of gratitude. Curiously, I saw the little colorful snake again and threw a salute his way.

My hand was the worst of my wounds. It bled profusely and burned like hell. I tore part of my shirt into strips as a makeshift bandage and wound the strips tightly around my hand.

As I climbed down from the rocks, I saw the vultures circling. They seemed to have suddenly come out of nowhere. How could they look so beautiful in flight and so unbelievably ugly on the ground? *Nature's garbage disposal.*

I picked up my machete and backtracked to where I had shot the other man. I realized that it was this other body that began drawing the birds.

The man I'd shot was lying in a fetal position–dead. He took one wound in the shoulder, the other in the side. Blessedly, this man had a canteen. My thirst overcame any concern of possible diseases this man may have had. I knelt and took two long swallows saving some for the walk back to camp. I hooked the canteen strap over my shoulder, and stood. Was I really clear of this daytime nightmare? I felt like yelling at the top of my lungs and beating my chest in victory. But instead, I began to shake uncontrollably. I surprised myself by bending over putting my hands on my knees and sobbing bitterly.

I felt the urge to vomit. Some sort of relief mechanism, I thought.

These unwelcomed feelings quickly passed.

My wounds were painful, but tolerable. My hand was still bleeding, but more slowly. I hoped no nerve damage had occurred.

I worked my way back to the trail where the walking was easier. Eventually I came back to where the Colonel and I had separated.

I saw no smoke indicating that the poppy fields were not yet on fire as I had hoped. Did the Colonel make it? Had he met resistance? I decided to follow the Colonel's track to the fence line and then on to the village. I had to push myself, suddenly bone weary. A little voice in my head kept urging me to lie down in the lush, emerald grass in the shade and close my eyes. After the terror of the chase and the fighting, I experienced a major drop in energy level.

I pushed on.

As the trail widened, I could just make out the *zareba*—a sort of thorny fence they have around native Kraal. I distinguished the silhouettes of the village huts ahead. The area seemed empty. The petrol cans and the oil drum were where I'd seen them previously.

But where was the Colonel? Could he have gotten lost? Or perhaps he had had a heat stroke or a heart attack?

My questions were answered by my own gasp.

Colonel Marshall had been propped upright against a tree. An assegai pierced his chest, pinning him to the tree like a butterfly on a specimen board. Two other spears had been stuck into the tree under his armpits holding him up. Obviously, he was meant to be found like this. Bastards!

My gut churned.

There *were* more of the enemy around. None of the men following me had carried assegais. I wheeled around listening, sniffing the air and looking for what shouldn't be there. I backed up to the colonel and yanked out the assegais holding him up. I laid him on the ground as gently as I could. This brave old warrior fought his whole life against evil doers. Just retired, now bloody and dead. I should have stayed with him. I pulled him into this. Jesus! I leaned over to close the Colonel's eyelids.

I heard or perhaps felt a faint 'hiss'. A new sound. A sound that shouldn't be there.

I threw myself down alongside the Colonel's corpse. A thud. Just above me, a long assegai was stuck into the tree where I'd been crouching a split second ago. I wheeled around but saw nothing. I detected no movement. Another 'hiss', another spear stuck into the ground next to me. What insanity! I was here to do a favor for a friend. No, I thought, at this moment I was fighting for my life against an unseen spear-thrower—I couldn't help but appreciate the unreality of it all.

I figured no matter how good the spear chucker, a moving target would more difficult to hit than a stationary one as I was now. Taking a couple of deep breaths, and gripping my machete, I got to my feet and did some pretty fancy broken field running for a beat-up tired guy. I plunged into the undergrowth, hit the ground and stopped. No more 'hisses.' I was not going to die today. Not yet anyway. I curled away from the fence to my left, rounding the kraal. I found a slight break in the ferns and looked into the village yard.

There he was, right out of your latest National Geographic African Expose'.

He stood tall covered with red and white body paint and some sort of pale hair hanging from his biceps and just below his knees. His lean, muscled body gleamed like wet obsidian. I'd seen photos like this of traditional Zulu warriors in the airplane magazine.

The man walked almost leisurely to the Colonel's body and picked up two of the assegais he had thrown, and added them to the one he had been carrying. He also had the long hooked blade of a panga hanging from his waist. He looked in my direction and smiled. Great!

I thought he looked like the epitome of a primitive self-assured hunter.

Me, I was prey. But I was a warrior too. Hadn't I disabled one of my enemies and killed the other two? I'd been in a fuckin' bloodbath today. I would not go down to this man. I thought perhaps my enemy was overconfident. That might help.

I drained the rest of the water from the canteen, again hoping its owner didn't have AIDS or TB or some other terrible disease. The liquid was wildly refreshing. It was best to get rid of the canteen anyway because the water made a sloshing noise when I moved.

While crawling away, I suddenly looked up into the softest most beautiful brown eyes I had ever seen. A miniature deer of some sort had stopped grazing in front of me, and was looking at this strange being crawling through the ferns. The small dear had two very tiny horns. It looked like a child's toy. Here we were, two beings facing each other, transfixed and immobile. The little creature turned and bounded away quickly, hardly ever sticking its head above the tops of the vegetation.

It stopped and looked back, almost to say, "Well, are you coming?" It made little noises which sounded like "dik-dik." Then it did a hideous dance of death as an assegai pierced its left side and protruded from the right.

Like any predator, this hunter is set off by movement, I thought. I plunged deeper into the bush, hoping my mind wasn't losing its edge to fatigue. Even the adrenalin rush was wearing thin. My reserves were running low. I would have to figure out something quickly.

I came across another trail and ran down it quickly to put some distance between myself and my pursuer. I soon found myself in one of the poppy fields. Cover was more limited. I looked up into the camouflage netting. Netting! Could I somehow net this guy? It would be pretty damned hard to throw an assegai when you're covered in a heavy net. The net was basically square, being held to four trees by long ropes.

Using my machete, I cut one of the ropes holding the net to a tree. I figured I'd have to plan it so one cut of a rope would bring the whole net down on to the man. I moved ahead, now strengthened by having an endgame. I ran to the second rope and cut it also. Then I cut the ropes from where they had been attached to the edges of the net. The net was now down on one side, and I had two long lengths of rope. The work was especially hard since I was primarily working with one hand. My left hand had started bleeding again. I went across to the other side and cut a third rope, then tied the other two together, and attached them to the rope holding the net and raised that corner of the net again. Now the third corner was up, but all I had to do was release the rope and the third corner would fall. I backtracked to the fourth corner of the net while holding the rope which held up the third corner, and waited. If I had planned it correctly, when my pursuer walked under the net I would let go of one rope and cut the remaining one so the entire net would fall on the man.

Then I realized if the man followed my tracks he might go around the perimeter and never go under the net. And those tracks would lead straight to me. Damn!

I secured rope number three and went back to make very distinct tracks under the center of the net among the poppies. I quickly scrambled to my original hiding place and waited. I'd be a still and patient hunter. I hunkered down low. It had to be now.

Bugs attacked my eyes, ears, and nostrils. My blood had drawn them. My mouth was again sandpaper dry. I settled my breathing and waited.

Without sound, the tall warrior appeared at the edge of the poppy field. He was stooping down studying my tracks. He looked around, studied the net on the ground and seemed perplexed. Instead of going under the net, he was going to one side, as I had feared.

My psyche was screaming inside my head. *Go under the net, you son of a bitch.* I thought, I need a fucking break here. Almost immediately the answer came back. *No schmucko, you make your own breaks, have you learned nothing from your life?*

My pursuer was now on the other side of the net, looking at the obvious trail through the poppies. He didn't move.

Okay, enough of this shit, I thought—all or nothing! I'd make himself the bait.

I stepped out from behind a tree and started moving around, looking at the ground, giving the impression that I was unaware of the warrior's presence. From the corner of my eye, I could see the man coming at me at a crouched trot under the netting. *A little closer, please.* I stood and faced him.

I reached for the tree where the ropes were secured. The man unleashed his assegai as I cut rope number four and released rope number three. The spear flew by, way too close for comfort.

The net fell on the man startling and confusing him. His spearheads faced upwards piercing the net. He began tearing at the confining nets.

On a dead run, I rammed him with my shoulder in the small of his back, knocking him down.

The man tried to use his sharp panga.

I used the loose netting to further entangle the man's arms. Somehow, he twisted the panga, swung and cut into my upper back, but the blow had no real power. I twisted around to get behind the man, wrapped my good arm around the man's neck and bore down forward with all of my weight. He squirmed and struggled, but was tangled in the webbing. I kept up the pressure until he weakened.

I twisted the man's head to one side. When he resisted, I twisted it back in the other direction snapping the cervical vertebrae, with an awful cracking sound.

I let go and I looked up quickly.

Screaming came from somewhere. Then I realized it came from me. God, I prayed, make this the last of my adversaries. I had nothing left. I took one more look at the warrior beneath me in the tangled netting.

I felt no remorse.

Taking the man's panga with me, I half walked and stumbled back to the workers' kraal. I had a job to finish.

*   *   *   *   *

When I got there, I poured the two cans of petrol in a line along the edge of the nearest poppy field. I opened the oil drum and sent it rolling down a hillside, spewing oil from its maw.

I took a glowing ember from one of the cooking fires in the village and set the gas and oil alight. I couldn't be certain, but with luck and a little afternoon breeze which had just come up, the fire hopefully would spread through the valleys burning the poppy crop. *That many fewer drug addicts.*

I screamed obscenities until I was hoarse. I had to get a grip.

I knew the clinic and lab weren't far. I wouldn't leave the Colonel's corpse for the birds or other critters to feast on. I hefted the body onto my shoulder, but when I stumbled and fell, I realized I couldn't carry him. Dragging him wouldn't work either.

I went around the backs of the huts to see if I could find something to help. I found a suitable conveyance--a wheelbarrow. An undignified, almost clownish way to transport a body, but it would work. I hoped the Colonel, from wherever he was, would appreciate the practicality and humor of the situation. With what little remaining strength I had left, I hefted the Colonel's body into the barrow and rolled it along the well-worn path back to the main living area.

I rested briefly along the way and looked back to see pillars of smoke rising from the poppy fields. It just might work.

Handling the barrow was agony because of my injured left hand.

The first person I saw was a young lad who turned and ran from me as if he'd seen the devil himself. I must look like the devil-- wheeling a dead body no less. Mud and blood, my son, but I'm alive. "I fuckin' did it." I heard myself say aloud.

*   *   *   *   *

I crossed the open compound, put down the barrow and went to the house. One of the women saw me and screamed.

Another stood her ground. "Where is Kalina, no, I mean Jomo?" I asked.

"I don't know sah," she answered quietly. "Are you the deacon?"

"Yes, I am, although God knows I don't resemble the man."

She went off and brought back one of the houseboys. "Baas, you are hurt, what happened?" asked the gawky lad.

"Never mind. It's a long story. Where are Jomo and Johannes?"

"I don't know where dey are now. Mistah Johannes took de truck and de boy and got drove of here quick time."

I sighed with a deep sense of relief. Kalina would be safe with Johannes. Whatever had happened here, they had gotten out. My relief touched my heart. Since we had just talked about it, I felt confident they were safe at the abbey. Johannes, you bull, you're a good man. I was sorry I'd doubted Johannes's resolve to protect Kalina.

I staggered into the kitchen and pulled a cold Amstel from the fridge. I poured, rather than drank it down. It was without a doubt the best beer I had ever had in my life. I took out another and some bread and cheese and went up to my room, eating along the way. I took a few bites and another swig of beer, sat on my bed heavily and took off my boots and socks.

Going into the shower room, down the hall, I literally didn't recognize myself in the mirror. I looked like third degree road kill. No--more like an apparition from hell. No wonder the boy ran off.

Though washing very gingerly, I opened a few of my facial cuts in the process. I kept my injured hand out of the shower stream. I was the walking wounded all right, but a damn site better off than the Colonel and four blacks I knew of. The hot shower brought pleasure and pain.

I heard a knock on the bathroom door.

"Deacon, Deacon!" It was a female voice.

"Yes."

"I am Jenny Togambo. I am a nurse from de clinic. Are you hurt? I was told you were bleeding. I have come here to help."

"Yes, Jenny. I am hurt. Just a minute." I turned off the shower and saw the pink water swirling down the drain. Wrapping a towel around my waist, I opened the door.

Jenny was a huge woman with enormous breasts and buttocks. She wore a caftan covered in bright colors of a floral print. Her unique colorful headpiece looked like it had horns or ears. I recognized the costume typical of Herrero women, I'd seen in photographs.

She gave me a brief once-over and said, "Tsk, tsk. Sit down and let me have a look at you."

I complied like a young child while she clinically investigated my wounds.

"Young man, you are a mess, but nuthin' fatal I can see." She opened her bag. "First things first." She applied some ointment to the long cut on my back. It felt soothing for a few seconds, then felt like a hot poker.

"Jesus," I straightened and stood with the pain of it. The towel around my waist fell to the floor. I automatically scrambled to pick it up.

"Leave it for now. There ain't nothin' you got I haven't seen many times before. I'll need that towel to clean up de blood. What a mess you made." She applied some gauze and tape to the gash on my back.

"Stay standing now." She knelt and bandaged the wounds at my waist. Although naked, I realized I felt totally comfortable with her. She was a pro. I allowed myself to be cared for. Sometimes a wounded warrior needed patching up.

"Could I have my beer please, I'm so dry. It's in my room."

"Not now. What you be sayin'?" She mumbled some phrases in her native language somehow criticizing my request, but with a wry smile. She stood laboriously in stages and got me a glass of water from a pitcher on the nightstand. "This is for the thirst, now sit." I obeyed like a lap dog, and drained the glass.

She carefully cleansed the wounds on my face, dabbed on some pale yellow liquid out of a bottle labeled TCP, and applied a few bandages. "De other cuts and bruises will be okay if you keep them clean."

"Now, let me see this hand." With a feather touch, she checked the wound. "This be de bad one. Dis is gonna hurt my big man." She put on powdered latex gloves. "I got to see if there be any bones broken." She moved my fingers, probed the back of my hand and moved my wrist. She wasn't kidding, it hurt like hell. The hand started bleeding again.

"Ah good."

"What's good?" My eyes were tearing.

"Nuthin' broken, I'm pretty sure. But you gonna need some fine stitches." She began to rummage around in her bag.

I thought it best to ask. "Can you do that? Maybe we should go to a doctor or a hospital?"

To say she gave me a dirty look would be a gross understatement. When she dropped my hand, I knew I had courted trouble.

"I been stitchin' up people longer than most doctors' been alive. The smart doctors ask *me* to do their stitchin'." She threw her stuff in her bag and got up to leave.

I felt as if my black angel was about to desert me. "I'm sorry. I don't know what I'm saying. I trust you, please don't be offended. I'd be grateful if you'd patch up my hand."

"Hummph! Well, okay, I guess." She squinted at me, opened a packet and removed a needle. She put several injections around the wound. "There, now you won't feel nuthin'." She hummed softly while she put in four neat stitches to close the wound. "These will need takin' out in seven days. You remember now. Keep it dry my American warrior, even in de shower, you hear Jenny?" She applied a padded dressing on my hand.

"Yes, thank you. Thank you very much. You did a great job."

"That's my duty. I am de nurse here." She hummed and smiled broadly. "Now where is that beer you been askin' 'bout?"

"In my room down the hall, third on the right. The door is open."

As she got up she threw me a clean towel, glancing down at my privates. "Put this around yourself. Have you no shame, in front of lady?" Her teasing eyes twinkled at me. Once she got her considerable bulk upright, she waddled toward my room. I stood to follow after.

As I neared my room, she emerged drinking my beer. "Dis is good beer. I left some pills for you, for the pain. Two for now, two before bed, and two tomorrow mornin' if you need them."

She laughed, waved goodbye, and jiggled her way down the hall, the bottle of beer in one hand and her black bag in the other. Her walk had a lot of side to side movement like a cartoon hippo right out of a Disney animated jungle movie.

She was wonderful, I thought, even though she pilfered my beer. For a precious little while, my mind was on myself, my wounds, and Jenny Togambo.

I dressed carefully, and couldn't help replaying the tapes in my head of the horrific events of the past several hours. The Colonel, the killings, the hunt. I'd made it—just. God forgive me, I'd killed before. That led me to believe I could kill again. Now I had done so. My emotions were bouncing around like the ping pong balls they use in a Bingo machine. I prayed I would be forgiven, but always, was the bottom line of justification—kill, or be killed. It had been quite an initiation to South Africa. It didn't help to assuage my emotional distress one damn bit. *God help me.*

Before leaving the building, I stopped in the kitchen, took some biltong, another cold Amstel, and a large bottle of cold water. I swallowed down two of the pain tablets.

As I walked to my car, I saw the smoke rising from the fields. Some of them were burning for sure. I had two more jobs to do before I left and the authorities arrived with their questions and forms. I drove over to the laboratory, found a few workers, and asked them to please take care of the Colonel's body. They agreed and seemed to know what to do. I also notified them that the fields were on fire and to keep the patients out of harm's way.

Next, I entered the laboratory and shouted at the few people who were there, to leave—now! One look at my black and blue, swollen, bandaged face and hand, and the panga I carried, and they capitulated. I found some alcohol and lamp oil, splashed it around and set fire to it. The lab had to go. It burned to the ground in five minutes flat.

I drove off to the abbey to find Johannes and Kalina.

Chapter 31

"PULL OVER," ROSE SNAPPED, "I left Muhlukai around here someplace."

Vicente brought the powerful Jag to a stop on the narrow red verge in sight of the front entrance of the abbey. Emerging from the shadows, Muhlukai high-stepped over the weeds to the car. Vicente opened the back window.

Rose asked, "Well, Muhlukai, anything going on?"

"No, Miss Rose, nothin' goin' in or out."

"Well that's a break. Stay out here a moment while I talk with my partner." Vicente closed the window.

She stopped to consider the plan that had been forming in her mind. "Vicente, you'll have to get in there and take care of Johannes."

Vicente touched his head wound gingerly. "It will be my pleasure to deal with that *borrico.*"

"But you must let the girl escape. I'll be out here in the car to 'rescue' her. If she sees me as a friend, maybe she'll open up about the money. It may take a while, but we'll have the whole ride back to South Africa for girl-talk."

Rose folded her hands and closed her eyes in thought. "Can you get back to the mission on your own?"

"*Si*, don't worry, I'll go back to the clinic and get a car."

"Good, I'll meet you at the mission late tonight. I have a new pilot ready to transport our shipment of goods up to Namibia. Since it's his first time, we should go with him."

"*Bueno.*"

She opened the window and called Mulukai over to the car. "Muhlukai, you go with Vicente and…"

Vicente winced as he tightened his forehead. "No, I must do this alone. It has been a long time coming."

Rose nodded, "As you wish."

"Muhlukai, stay out of sight out here on the grounds until the girl and I leave. Don't let the girl see you-- understood? Wait for Vicente and then get back to the clinic."

"*Yabo.* I understand, Miss Rose."

"When you and Vicente get back there, make sure Deacon and the Colonel have been taken care of. Then I will take care of you all." She stopped to reflect, making sure she had covered all the bases.

"All right, let's go!"

*   *   *   *   *

Rose drove into the abbey compound and parked the car beneath some acacia trees in a spot where she could see the fronts of the key buildings in the abbey grounds. They still did not know exactly where Johannes and the girl were.

Muhlukai trotted over to the grotto area to mix with some people who were observing the ritual stations of the Way of the Cross.

Vicente set out to find Johannes and the girl. He eased into the chapel and found an old verger fussing with the hymnals for those who would attend the next Mass. His skin was like weathered leather, and his bony frame made dents in the faded black cassock he wore. The shadows, echoes, and the smell of candle wax in the old church reminded Vicente of the Sundays of his childhood in the suburbs of Santa Clotilde on the Napo River, less than one hundred miles from the Colombian border.

Hat in hand and looking penitent, he approached the old man.

"Excuse me."

"Yes," the verger replied without looking up from his work and sounding a little piqued at the interruption.

"Could you help me a moment?"

"What is it?" He looked up and was startled. "You've hurt yourself."

"Oh this," Vicente said pointing to his forehead, "It's nothing, a clumsy accident. Where could I leave a donation for the chapel and the abbey? I had some petitions answered and I need to express my gratitude for all the prayers offered up by the good friars."

The verger brightened. Vicente knew he had him. A little greed goes a long way.

"Well, certainly. There is a box for donations over there by the baptismal font."

Vicente turned, "Ah, yes, I see it now. Tell me, is there a place for separate contributions for you and the others who work here?"

Now he had the man's undivided attention. "Well, we get paid out of the general fund. Of course, it's up to you to designate your donations as you wish."

Vicente handed the man one hundred Rands. "Please take this from a grateful traveler." The man spirited away the money as swiftly as any conjurer.

"You see, when I got into trouble as a young man, I took refuge once in an abbey much like this one."

"Really? How interesting."

"Tell me, do you still give shelter to troubled wanderers?"

"Yes, occasionally we do." He thought for a moment. "As a matter of fact, just this afternoon, a man and a young colored boy came to stay with us."

"Wonderful. God be praised. The work you do is God's work. And do they stay with the monks and eat with them as I once did?"

"They take meals with the monks and acolytes here, but they stay in our guest quarters. We do have visitors from time to time and of course we provide weekend retreats for small groups."

"I see. Marvelous."

"The rooms are in the upper story of the meeting hall." The old man volunteered without having to be asked.

"That's the building outside of the chapel to the right?" queried Vicente.

"No, not quite. The building to the right is the rectory and abbey office. The meeting hall is behind it."

"Ah yes, I see. Are there other people staying there now?"

"No, it's just the two of them at present."

"Thank you, I've taken up too much of your valuable time."

"Not at all. God go with you. *Ambagashli.*"

"*Shalagashli,* and with you. I'll make my donation and pray now. It has been good talking with you." Vicente made a show of going to the donation box, but didn't put anything in. He knelt as if in prayer.

Before he left, he slipped into the sacristy behind the altar and found what he had hoped for. Several monk's cowls and robes hung in a closet. He slipped one of them on and left by the side door, gambling on not running into another monk on the way. Keeping to the shadows, he proceeded directly to the meeting hall with his head bowed. Even if he were to be seen in the open, he was confident that he would blend in with other monks in the area.

Around the entire meeting hall, he noticed only two open windows, their gauzy curtains billowing outside. On a hot afternoon, without air-conditioning, the upper rooms would be like ovens and needed ventilation. He felt sure Johannes and the girl were on the second floor behind those curtains.

He hesitated at the entrance, making sure no one was around, then entered the building. Three quiet minutes went by as Vicente stood still and listened.

Taking out his Berretta from beneath the monk's robe, he screwed the silencer onto the barrel. He checked to make sure his weapon was cocked and fully loaded before creeping up the stairs. On the second floor, he heard soft voices coming from down the hall—a man and a young woman. As he approached he could make out the voice and accent of Johannes.

This was going to be a pleasure. Vicente needed vengeance. He wanted to hurt this man.

He spun into the doorway quickly, aimed and shot Johannes, who was seated and had his back to the door. The bullet entered his right calf with the muted silence of a drawer closing. Johannes reacted as if a bee had stung him. He glared down at the offending pain, his face a furious surprise.

Kalina screamed and stood.

As Johannes wheeled around. Vicente shot him in the left shoulder the report louder than the first. Johannes bent over in that direction while glaring at the muzzle flash.

"Quiet now," Vicente said pointing to Kalina, "Or I'll kill him where he sits."

She backed away biting her knuckles. The smell of cordite filled the small room.

"Now, my bald amigo, let's talk." Vicente purposely walked away from the door, leaving an escape route for Kalina. "You cold-cocked me back there at the clinic. My head still hurts."

Johannes reached out and grabbed at Vicente. Vicente was prepared, but purposely stumbled back out of Johannes's reach, pretending to fall.

"Run, Kalina! Now girl, run!" shouted Johannes.

It had all gone according to plan. Vicente whirled and shot high above the doorway to make it look good. (He loved it when a plan came together so well.) Then he smiled with malevolent good cheer and turned back to Johannes. "Killing you with one shot would have been too easy. How does it feel to be helpless?"

Johannes's face contorted with pain. "You are de helpless one, you prickless coward. I wouldn't wipe dog shit off my shoes on you."

"Big words, muscle head. I've been nursing this headache all day. Now it's your turn." Vicente switched his grip on the gun and began to pistol whip Johannes in the head. The blows rained down piteously. With two bullet wounds, Johannes could hardly move his hands up to protect himself. He couldn't stand, so he remained in the chair, for the most part taking the brutal beating.

"Now you have the big headache, no?"

Thinking Johannes was helpless to stop him, Vicente got careless about the beating. As he swung, at the last moment, Johannes ducked sideways. Vicente missed and his momentum carried him past Johannes. With what reserve strength he had left, Johannes grabbed Vicente's wrist and twisted, breaking his arm. Johannes also bit down on the forearm, tearing away muscle.

Vicente screamed as the gun clattered to the floor. His natural reaction was to pull away.

As he did so, Johannes pushed him, rolled off the chair onto the floor and grabbed the gun. Without hesitation or careful aim, he shot Vicente in the gut.

"*Cingase,* you dumb fuckin' Boer," growled Vicente through clenched teeth as his body doubled up in pain.

Nearly unconscious and seeing the world through a red haze, Johannes crawled a few yards to where Vicente lay clutching his blood- soaked stomach. Johannes jammed the pistol into his right eye and pulled the trigger. Blood, bone fragments and brain matter splattered everywhere.

"Go straight to hell," croaked Johannes. He rolled on his back and as he plummeted into a sea of fading consciousness, repeated, "Run, Kalina, run."

*　　*　　*　　*　　*

Kalina darted outside, right into Miss Ginger Rose, who had been running toward her. Kalina barely remembered her from the mission. In a panic she said, "Oh Miss Rose, we must get help for Uncle Johannes. He's been shot."

"I thought I heard shooting. We'll get help, but first we must get you safe." Rose herded Kalina to the car.

"What are you doing here?" Kalina asked.

"Deacon sent me. He's wounded. He told me you were in great danger. We must get you out of here."

"Wounded? How is he?"

"He's all right—his wound is not life-threatening, but he can't be moved just now. Stay here. I'll get some of the monks to help Johannes."

Kalina remained in the car, trembling, fighting back tears. Rose ran into the nearest building. She timed her stay for two minutes, spoke to no one and ran out again.

"There, I've told one of the monks," she lied. "He'll spread the word. He said they have a doctor on the premises who will see to Johannes immediately. Now we must go." She turned the car around and sped out of the abbey toward South Africa.

"Where are we going?"

"I know of only one place to take you until we hear from Deacon, and that is to Father Godwin at the Hands of Hope Mission."

"Yes, I think that is best. Thank you, Miss Rose."

"De nada. I'm glad I can help." The Jaguar made good time on the nearly empty highway.

*   *   *   *   *

Arriving at the abbey, sore and beat, I pried myself out of the car and walked unsteadily toward the buildings. The whole place seemed solemn and peaceful. The arrangement of the African style buildings with their high, thatched roofs and flower emblazoned walking paths lent itself to prayer and meditation. I prayed that Kalina had found safe haven here.

I heard a demanding voice calling my name.

"Deacon Sah."

I wheeled around to see Muhlukai standing in shadows pointing a gun at me.

"Muhlukai, what are you doing?"

My heart sank again. I had assumed Kalina and Johannes were here and safe, but Muhlukai's presence indicated something else. Even through the madness of the day, I'd never felt quite as helpless and hopeless as I did now with the gun pointed at me. My wounds hurt and my exhaustion had to be put aside. *How the hell did this perfidious Muhlukai know to come here?*

"I don't know how you got away from my men, but now I must ask you to come heah by me." He beckoned with the pistol in his hand.

I approached slowly. "What do you want?"

"Nevah mind dat now."

"Is Jomo safe? Where is everyone?"

"No more questions." Muhlukai's tense voice and wide-open eyes betrayed his tension. "Jomo is gone. Dat young witch lied to me and I am de fool for it."

Muhlukai gestured for me to enter the paths into the grove of olive trees where graphic carvings depicted the Stations of the Cross. We were quite alone. The abbey seemed shrouded in a profound silence broken only by the sibilant wind whispering through the Eucalyptus trees.

I feverishly stalled for time—my mind in hyper-drive. *Look, listen, sense everything. Pick a moment and strike. You didn't come this far to be shot down like a dog in the dirt.* I turned to face Muhlukai. "So now what? Do you plan to shoot me? People will be out here in seconds. You'll be caught for sure and hanged."

"Don't you worry none, baas."

Muhlukai had his back to the abbey buildings. Facing him, I could see his hands twitching. Sweat beaded on his face.

Then, a momentary environmental change. I took advantage of the staccato sound of a door slamming from behind Muhlukai. I looked over his right shoulder and said with a slightly raised voice, "Go back Father, everything is okay here."

It may have been the oldest distraction in the book, but when someone is jumpy, they do not think in cold rational terms. Muhlukai turned his head to see who I had spoken to.

In that instant, I used my wounded left hand to deflect the gun upwards. It discharged. Birds screeched wildly. By reflex, I formed the fingers of my right hand into the shape of a spearhead and drove the points of the joined fingers into Muhlukai's throat.

He dropped his pistol and fell, choking and gasping for air. His body twitched spasmodically, kicking up a small dust cloud.

The roar of the unsilenced gun brought the Abbot and several monks on a dead run, their long robes flapping in the breeze.

I stomped down hard on Muhlukai's gun hand breaking fingers and forcing him to release his grip on the pistol. Half mad with fighting survival skills, I positioned myself to deliver the *coup de grace.*

Only shouts of, "Stop. You must not. Please, for the love of God, don't!" stopped me.

I hesitated, breathing heavily in my rage and snarled at the oncoming monks with bared fangs, but I'd had enough killing. I relented. I was embarrassed to have this happen on holy ground, and to have witnesses to my killing fury. The biblical figures of the Stations of the Cross seemed to look down at me in silent judgment.

"What happened here? Who are you?" demanded the Abbot, his face flushed red with exertions. His bulk and height gave him a commanding presence.

Other monks knelt by Muhlukai administering first aid. I looked down at them, knowing their attempts were in vain.

"I'm Deacon Adelius. I'm a friend of Father Godwin. He called you to ask to keep a girl safe here if need be. This man would have killed the girl. He was trying to kill me."

The Abbot nodded, "The girl is here with a man named Johannes. This is most terrible."

"They're here? Thank God! And thank you, Father! Would you mind taking me to them?"

Despite the best resuscitative attempts of the monks, Muhlukai thrashed in the dirt making piteous gagging sounds and died, his larynx crushed. *Jesus, another death* at *my hands. Will this nightmare of a day never end? Kyrie Eleison.*"

The Abbot looked down at Muhlukai and crossed himself. "May God have mercy on your soul." He looked at me and said the same thing. I hoped his prayer was heard.

Another monk gasped. "Look," said the old priest, pointing up at a carved figure. The errant bullet from Muhlukai's weapon had pierced the wooden figure of Christ, breaking it in two.

The Abbot went over to see for himself, shaking his head in awe. He looked back at me, "Do you know which Station of the Cross this is?"

"No, I'm afraid I don't."

"It's the twelfth—'Christ dies on the cross.' I guess we just keep killing Him." He lowered his eyes and folded his hands.

"Father....please understand...." I looked at the priest as a penitent.

"Not now. I'm sure you had to defend yourself. God understands. I know this man and the security thugs under his command at the clinic. I knew several of them as youngsters. They were troublemakers in this neighborhood—a bad lot."

I didn't tell him of the other bodies I'd left behind in the poppy fields.

After a few words of instruction to the monks, the Abbot turned, "Come, follow me. I'll take you to your friends."

As we climbed the steps to the guest quarters above the meeting hall, I smelled the unmistakable stench of death.

"No, Oh no, Christ, no!" I brushed ahead of the Abbot and ran up the stairs and into the room at the end of the hall. Blood was splattered everywhere. A malevolent odor permeated the room. A dark-haired man in a monk's robe lay sprawled on his back, dead, his face a horrible mass of blood and shattered bones.

Johannes sprawled on the floor next to the corpse, covered in blood. I ran to him, knelt and leaned close.

The Abbot entered muttering, "Mother of God, have mercy."

I felt for a pulse. "He's alive! Get help, please." I looked up, pleading.

"We have a doctor here with us today. I'll get him." The Abbot left on a dead run, his sandals slapping on the wood floors.

I thought I'd been running on empty. I was mistaken. I spoke softly to a battered Johannes. "You're so strong. Hang on. Be strong now, big man. We don't want Kalina to lose any of her uncles."

Saying that made me realize the worst of my fears—Kalina was gone.

I stayed close, afraid to move Johannes. Occasionally, his eyes would flutter and open, but they didn't seem to focus. I kept talking to him in soft, soothing tones.

I could see the wounds in his leg and shoulder but the head injury concerned me much more. And God, there was a lot of blood.

The doctor finally arrived and set to work with bandaging, applying pressure dressings, taking vital signs and doing all the other things doctors do. I threw up a prayer in gratitude that a doctor was available.

The skinny doctor with the pencil-thin moustache looked up through thick glasses and addressed the Abbot. "This head wound is bad. An ambulance is on the way. There is a fine hospital with a neurosurgeon in Masvingo."

I stayed while the paramedics arrived. They rolled Johannes onto a stretcher and with some difficulty got him down the stairs. The doctor going along in the ambulance reassured me.

But what the hell happened to Kalina? Muhlukai had said she was gone. Gone where? And how?

As they pulled out, I addressed the Abbot. "Father, where can I wash up? I'm a mess."

"Yes, my son, you certainly are. Follow me. And throw away that bloody rag of a shirt. I'll find you another." He eyed me with an appraising expression. "Are you sure you shouldn't go to the hospital as well?"

"No, I'm really better off than I look. But thanks for your concern."

"What will you do now?"

My heart sank. "I'll have to find Kalina somehow."

"The girl who came with the big man?"

"Yes. I'll call Father Godwin first and tell him what happened." I looked to the heavens for help. "I'm so sorry all of this violence came to your beautiful, quiet abbey."

The Abbot smiled and nodded, "It wasn't the first time, nor will it be the last. We humans are a violent lot. You'd be surprised how often violence and heartbreak have been visitors to our little abbey." Looking down and shaking his head, he said, "I'm sorry your friends couldn't find safety here."

"I don't know how that thug upstairs learned they were here. By the way, I believe his name is Vicente Luna. He's a killer involved in drug trafficking."

"My God, drugs again! Is there no end to it?"

"There's no time to explain all the details. I promise I'll get back to you. Right now I've got to get back to South Africa." We walked in thoughtful silence. "I'll have to start over. I'll begin at the Hands of Hope Mission and get some help."

"It's nearly evening. You look all in. You're hurt. It's a long drive, and most of it will be in the dark."

"I've got to go."

The abbot was adamant. "After you clean up, sit here in the shade and rest while I get a basket packed and ask Father Gregory to drive you down. He likes to drive, and he's been cooped up here for too long. It will also be good for him to speak with Father Godwin."

He clapped his hands for emphasis, "Yes," he exhaled noisily, "That's it. Done. No discussion."

The Abbot strode off to corral Father Gregory while I washed up. I sensed the man was used to being obeyed. And of course, he had correctly analyzed the driving situation. The thought of a long tedious drive definitely did not appeal. I wasn't even sure I could make it.

I made a brief call to Father Godwin to update him on everything that had happened. Stunned by my revelations, he began asking questions. I answered briefly and told him we could talk more as soon as I had returned. I assured him Johannes seemed to be in good hands.

Soon, the abbot came over. "Deacon Adelius this is Father Gregory."

A short, chubby, middle-aged monk stuck out his meaty hand. "Call me Gregory. Ha, ha, as you see, I'm in civilian clothes for this trip. I haven't driven for a while." He rubbed his palms together. "Where exactly are we going?"

"How do you do, Father. First, to the Hands of Hope Mission." I had the sickening thought that I really didn't know my next step, but felt I needed to talk to Robbie and the team of uncles to gather and share information and make plans.

Just then, a bespectacled monk with a big smile came up with a hamper of sandwiches, fruit, and drinks for the trip.

"Please, both of you, come here," urged the Abbot. He extended his hands onto our shoulders and blessed us in Latin. "We will all pray for you both. Bon voyage, Godspeed."

"Thank you for everything," I said.

"I'll give Father Godwin a call."

"That'd be great. Thanks again, I mean it." I offered my hand.

He gave me a bear hug. "Peace be with you," he whispered, then walked with us to the circular drive in front of the abbey.

As we got into the car, I thought Father Gregory looked like an eager teenager about to take his father's sports car out for a spin. "Let's go," he said. "What will she do, eh? Let's find out."

A sunshower spritzed the windshield as Gregory roared out of the driveway and fish-tailed down the road. I estimated we would make record time getting back to the Hands of Hope Mission.

While Father Gregory put on his sunglasses and tuned the radio to a contemporary rock station, I couldn't resist leaning back to drift off, exhausted. When closer to sleep than wakefulness, I cracked open my eyes for a few moments and saw two lanky giraffes loping alongside the highway.

Boyo, you are not in Chicago anymore.

Chapter 32

SAVVY ENOUGH NOT TO PUSH Kalina with any of the questions she was dying to ask, Rose remained patient during their drive back to South Africa.

After a few hours of casual conversation interspersed with long periods of silence, Rose began her fishing expedition. "I knew Mike Thompson, you know. A terrible tragedy."

"You knew Uncle Mike?" Kalina couldn't stop calling him "Uncle," even though she now knew he was her father.

"Oh yes, Mike loved life. Deacon told me that he and Mike had been friends for years back in the states."

"Yes, Deacon told me that too. Deacon is very brave."

Rose didn't know what the girl was referring to, but decided to let it go. "Yes, he is," she agreed.

Rose felt a pang of regret—a small one—that Deacon was now dead. He and that snoop-nose Colonel had really gotten in the way. The tall *Americano* could have made an interesting playmate for a while longer. She let her mind wander back to their one night together. Yes, she reminisced, with a wistful smile, it had been quite thrilling—a pity to lose him so soon.

A few times, Rose noticed Kalina drift off into restless short-lived naps.

They stopped for a meal in Bulawayo before crossing into South Africa. While they waited for their order, Rose asked, "Have you lived at the mission for very long?"

"All my life. My mother worked as a nursing sister there. I want to be a nurse, too. My Uncle Gideon has taught me a lot. He is a fine doctor."

"Yes, he is. Doctor Ngubane and I have also been friends for several years."

"Really, I didn't know."

"It's because of my work at the newspaper. I'm a reporter, you know. I have done a few feature stories about him and Father Godwin and their valuable work at the mission. You may have seen me around. I have also spoken with them at fund raising events. They really have accomplished amazing things at the Hands of Hope."

"My uncle Mike used to fly them around the country to help raise the monies."

"I'm going to call the abbey to check on Johannes and Deacon." She left the table to make the call.

Instead of calling the abbey, she ducked into a phone booth and called the new pilot she'd recruited; a real *Roineck*. "Be at the airfield later and be prepared to fly a shipment to the Namibian coastline." He agreed readily. She could sense his eagerness to do well. He should be eager, she thought. We're paying him plenty.

Rose returned to the table with her lines prepared. "Deacon is much better, but weak. He sends you his love. He'll come down tomorrow. Your Uncle Johannes has also been patched up at the local hospital. He will fully recover. Deacon will pick him up along the way. He can recuperate at the mission."

As Kalina sighed, Rose could see that she was much relieved.

In different times, they might have enjoyed the incredible sunset as they drove down from the highveldt.

"I have to ask. I guess it's the reporter in me. Why are you in danger?" Ginger sighed, "Deacon asked me to help you anyway I can. Maybe I could help you better if I knew more."

"Deacon thinks the men who killed Uncle Mike also want to kill me." She shuddered, and then spoke softly, "They already killed my brother."

"That's terrible. But why?"

Kalina started to cry. "They want to punish."

Ginger reached over and stroked Kalina's shoulder. "Kalina, I'm sorry I upset you. But please remember that I'm trying to help. My reporter's brain is always working overtime." They drove in silence for a while. The rocky outcroppings gradually were taken over by greenery as they drove toward South Africa.

She paused to change the subject. "I heard wonderful stories about your mother from Doctor Ngubane."

Kalina regained some composure. "Her name was Alisha."

"A beautiful name." *Now was the time to set the bait.* "I saw an old picture of her."

"You did. What picture?"

"Oh, my dear, I'm sorry to bring it up. It was at the investigation site of your father's murder. He carried an old photograph of himself, Alisha and two children; one boy and a little girl. It looked like a loving family photo." Rose tilted her head to one side, and pushed some of her red mane to one side, the picture of approbation.

Rose continued, "At the funeral I learned that Jaylin was Alisha's son, and that he had a sister. It all came together for me. Now with Deacon and all the danger around you, I'm pretty sure that your uncle Mike was more than an uncle." Ginger paused for effect.

"Am I on the right track?"

"You are a very smart lady. Yes, it's true. Deacon told me that Mike Thompson was my real father. Until he came, I didn't know. Could I have the picture?"

"I'll have to ask Colonel Marshall. I think the police have it." She paused thoughtfully and smiled, "But I'll do what I can to get it for you." Rose allowed her thought to be expressed aloud. "So, the uncles got together and tried to fake your death so you'd be safe."

"Yes," Kalina's voice choked up. "But I guess it didn't help, because they found me--and a terrible man shot Uncle Johannes, and chased me, but I got away."

"I'm sure your uncle will be all right. He's pretty tough. You are so young for all of this to be happening to you." They drove on in silence for a few minutes. As they passed a group of schoolgirls walking barefoot along the road, a few of them waved.

"What happened to Deacon?" asked Kalina.

"Oh, child, some other men came to the clinic and tried to kill him. He's been shot in the arm, but he's okay. He sent me to you. A nurse at the clinic was binding his wound as I left."

"That was probably Jenny Togambo." After some thought Kalina asked, "What are you doing in Zimbabwe?"

Rose wasn't quite ready for this simple, abrupt question. But she thought—girl to girl—why not? "I came up just to be with Deacon. Can you keep a secret?"

Kalina nodding gravely said, "*Yabo*, I can."

"Well, Deacon and I went out a few times and I find him fascinating. I think he likes me, too. So we tried to spend some time together to get to know one another better. Who knows...."

"Oh, I didn't know."

Rose noticed the disappointed look, or maybe it was disapproval.

"Yes, isn't it wonderful? But, I'm so worried about him and all this business with Mike and you. I don't know what to do." Rose hoped she was gaining the girl's confidence.

"Deacon and my uncles will know what to do. I may have to go away for a while."

"Yes, that makes sense. But how will you manage? And then there's your schooling."

"Oh, I'll be all right now. My father…" she paused. It was the first time she had referred to Mike Thompson as her father. "He left some money to help me with my schooling."

"But it costs a lot of money these days."

"I think I have enough. He was very generous."

"That's wonderful. Mike provided for you." *That son-of-a-bitch*, thought Rose. *That's my money.* "I hope it's safe."

"I'm sure it is. I gave it to Deacon to keep for me. I don't know how to use money very well, but I told him to use it to find my father's killers."

So, Deacon has the money, Rose mused, *but I have the girl. I should have guessed. I wish I'd known this before ordering him killed.*

Where could he have put the money? Rose considered many alternatives, and rejected them one by one: Hidden in his room? No. Given it to Father Godwin? A possibility. Given it to Ngubane? Doubtful. A bank? Very unlikely. Who would he go to?

Slowly, her sumptuous lips parted in a smile. The best bet—Deacon's old and trusted friend, Robbie Forrester. Sure, Robbie knew how to handle money. He probably had a few good safes around to hold cash from Misty Hills and the Carnivore. Yes, she'd start with Robbie.

"Do you know Mister Robbie Forrester and his wife Del?" asked Rose.

"Very well. I work for them sometimes. Mrs. Forrester took me on a shopping trip. They have a beautiful daughter named Sarah."

"Do they? How wonderful."

Chapter 33

"I DON'T BELIEVE IT," SAID DR. NGUBANE

"You don't? You do underestimate me, my good doctor. Here, I'll put her on the line."

Rose handed the receiver to Kalina.

"*Kunjani*, Kalina, how are you?"

"Hello, is that you, Uncle Gideon?"

Dr. Gideon Ngubane had been holding his breath. Now he knew it was true. Somehow, Rose had Kalina with her. "Yes, it is I. How are you, my dear?"

Kalina spoke in a torrent. "I'm fine now, but it's been terrible. Deacon and Uncle Johannes were shot. I was shot at, but Miss Rose got me away and brought me back." She paused to take a breath and slowed down. "We're staying at a hotel for a while until I can go back to the mission."

Rose beckoned Kalina to give her back the phone, and Kalina complied. "So, Doctor Ngubane, you now know Kalina is safe with me."

The irony didn't escape him.

Rose had registered them into a cottage on the grounds of the Whitehead Country Hotel outside Muldersdrift. It was very close to the Mission and Misty Hills.

Rose turned to the girl, "Kalina, could you bring in some of the cases from the car while I talk with Dr. Ngubane." Kalina nodded and left.

"Where are you, exactly?" he asked.

"Never mind. We are nearby. Kalina is no longer present, so let's make this short. I do not want to hurt this girl, but I do want the money Mike stole from us. Now listen. I want you to make some calls. Disguise your voice. I have it all worked out for you. In about fifteen minutes, call Del Forrester at her home and tell her that her husband has been in an auto accident, but is not in serious condition. Tell her he is at Krugersdorp hospital and has been asking for her and their daughter, Sarah. And no, he can't come to the phone."

She continued, "Wait ten minutes, then call Robbie Forrester. He is sure to be in his office right now--he practically lives there. Tell him that his wife and daughter have been kidnapped. Make him get the money Deacon gave him, put into a briefcase and leave immediately."

"Wait!" Ngubane interrupted, "How do you know Robbie Forrester has the money?"

"A young colored bird as much as told me. Listen, convince him that we have someone watching, and if he's not seen driving out through the gate within five minutes after your call, we'll send him a piece or two of his wife and daughter to convince him we're serious." She lowered her voice a growl. "Make him believe this!"

She could hear Dr. Ngubane suck in air.

"Tell him to turn left out on Drift Boulevard and drive until he sees a yellow blanket on some bushes alongside of the road. He is to pull off and throw the briefcase towards the blanket without getting out of his car. Then he is to drive back to his office and await our next call, where he will get confirmation that his family is safe. That will be your third call. Either tell him, or leave a voicemail that his wife and daughter are at Krugersdorp hospital, waiting for him."

Rose paused, "We just want the money he's been holding. It's our money! Tell him to forget this incident ever happened. Remind him that we can always get to his family if he causes trouble. Have you got all of that?"

"He'll be frantic with worry. How do you know he'll comply?"

"Don't question me, you idiot! "Just do what I say. Convince him. I know what I'm doing."

She switched to her sweetest convincing voice, "Once all of this takes place, I'll drop off Kalina at the Mission with Father Godwin."

The doctor was resigned. "All right I'll do it."

"You damn well better. I'll call you later."

As she hung up, Kalina appeared with the suitcases. "Thank you, my dear." She smiled. "I really don't want to put things away. I just want to change and freshen up after our trip. Then I have to go out for a short while to make sure it's safe for you at the mission. I want you to stay here, but talk to no one. Okay?"

"Yes, okay, I guess. But when can I go back home?"

"If all goes well and it's safe, we'll have you home later this evening. Won't that be fine?" Rose nodded as if agreeing with herself. "Would you hand me that yellow blanket off the bed? I'd like to take it with me."

Kalina didn't question this odd request but took the blanket off one of the beds and handed it over.

Rose stormed out of the cottage. She had a pickup to make.

*　　*　　*　　*　　*

"Hello," said Del in her usual cheery voice, "Del here."

Shaking, Ngubane replied in a gravely voice with an Afrikaner accent, "Mrs. Forrester?"

"Yes?"

"My name is Jonathon. I'm a ward clerk at Krugersdorp hospital. I've been asked to call you to inform you that your husband has had an auto accident and he is here with us."

"Oh my God! How is he? Is he all right?"

"He's fine, a bit banged up. He will be staying the night for observation. It's just a precaution. He's had a nasty knock on his head."

"But he's all right, you're sure?" Del fought back her panic.

"Yes, but he is asking now to see you and Sarah.

"Can I speak to him?"

"No, I'm afraid, not. He's undergoing some tests just now. Will you be coming to see him?"

"Yes, of course, we'll be right there. I'm leaving now-now."

"Fine, I'm sure that that would be good for his spirits. He's in room one-sixteen. Please check in at reception when you arrive."

"One-sixteen, one-sixteen," she repeated. "Thank you so much. Please tell him we're on our way."

Del gathered up Sarah, and trying to speak calmly, told her they were going to see daddy. Without a word to her housemaids, she stormed out of the house and drove her forest-green Land Rover hard down their bumpy drive, and turned toward Krugersdorp.

One down, thought Ngubane. That wasn't too hard. He liked Del, though and he knew he had just caused her much anxiety.

The next call would be more difficult. Why was he doing all of this? He caught himself answering his own question—and he didn't like it.

He hated it! He hated himself.

First, he had sold himself to the witch, Ginger Rose. She had humiliated him. Despite what people saw on the outside, his self-esteem was now shattered. He couldn't shut off the picture from his mind of Rose and Vicente murdering his dogs, violating his Lair, and whipping him like a dog. Now they basically owned him.

Secondly, maybe--just maybe, if he complied, Rose would spare Kalina. After all, the girl really meant nothing to the operation, and Rose would have her money back.

And then there was the money. From his boyhood, seeing his mother work for white people with real money, and lots of it, money had had a grip on Gideon Ngubane. He knew it. This attraction had led to a great accumulation of wealth, his very special Eagle's Lair, and wonderful times with great and interesting people.

He realized money had potential for either good or evil. It was the great "neutral power." It was all in how people used it. His money had given him the power to develop and run the Hands of Hope Mission with its hospital and school, which over time had helped thousands of his people. He also had the leper clinic in the Chimanimanis. But although it also provided a valuable service, it provided an excellent front for the drugs, the ultimate source of big money.

Enough! He quickly dialed Robbie Forrester's number before his courage faded. Forrester's secretary, Karen answered the phone. Once again using a disguised voice, this time with a strong Zulu accent, he asked to speak to Robert Forrester, and that it was urgent. The secretary put him through immediately.

"Robbie Forrester here."

"Sah, we have your charming wife and daughtah."

"What...what are you talking about?"

"Listen carefully. We have taken your wife and daughtah. No harm will come to dem if you do as I say."

"No harm! What is this?" Robbie knew what it was, but was loathe to make himself believe it.

"In exchange for der quick and safe return, we only want de money your friend, de Deacon gave to you—NOW."

"What money?"

"No games, Mistah Forrestah. Put de money in a briefcase and drive out your gates in five minutes, no more, after dis call. We have someone watching. If our man does not see you leave in five minutes, we will send you a few pieces of your wife and little girl, to show you dat we are in earnest. Perhaps an ear, a finger or maybe one of your wife's nipples." He paused to let the threat sink in. "Also, do not try to call her. We have her phone."

Robbie stood, shoving his chair into the wall, his bulk shaking and his muscles tensing. "If you harm them, I'll hunt you down if it takes the rest of my life and I'll kill you, but first you will suffer." Robbie was breathing like a steam engine, his face turning flaming red.

"Now, now. No one wants de unpleasantness. No threats, please. You are in no position to threaten anyone. We do not want any of *your* money. We do not wish to harm your family. We only want what belongs to us."

"Heah are your instructions, turn left on Drift Boulevard and drive until you see a yellow blanket on de side of de road. Pull off dere and throw de case with de money toward de blanket. Do not get out of de car. Drive back to your office and wait for our call."

Ngubane could sense Robbie was skeptical, hesitant. Then he had a flash of something personal that might be convincing. "Your daughtah has her dolls, Jacko and Jenny with her. She is not afraid, yet, but your wife is very nervous." He paused. "Your five minutes starts now." Ngubane hung up.

Thank God that's over, Ngubane thought. He felt sorry for Robbie Forrester. He felt sorry for himself.

*   *   *   *   *

The line went dead. Robbie went numb, as if he'd been body-slammed by a rugby forward. He could see his daughter with her much loved and beat up Zulu dolls, Jacko and Jenney. She took them everywhere. Robbie was perspiring and felt terribly cold at the same time. He knelt and fumbled with the combination of his safe.

"It's only fuckin' money." He said to himself. The voice had said they only wanted the money. He left the diamonds. *It was only money.* He knew Deacon would never hold it against him.

The words, "pieces.... ears.... fingers.... nipples," kept pounding in his ears and in his heart. Could it be a hoax? He would make one quick check. He had spoken to Del earlier about what they were having for dinner and that he would be home earlier than usual. Using precious seconds, he called home.

"Hello, Forrestah residence." Answered Martha, his live-in housekeeper.

"Martha, may I speak to Mrs. Forrester—immediately."

"I'm so sorry, Mrs. Forrestah left here with Sarah a short while ago. Dey were in a wild hurry."

"Thank you," Robbie said automatically and hung up. There was no way of knowing if they were safe at this moment. But, he wasn't going to take any chances. After all, the caller somehow knew that he had the money. Curious, they didn't ask for the diamonds as well.

Taking the cash Deacon had entrusted to him, he filled his briefcase and sprinted to his Toyota 4X4. In one minute he roared out the front gate.

As he drove, he checked the Sig Sauer P-228 he kept in the car making sure it was loaded. He clicked off the safety. He didn't know what would be facing him down the road. He put it on the seat next to him. He vowed if anyone harmed his family, he would shoot to kill them all. He would show no mercy. They were animals. He had never felt such a powerful combination of terror and killing rage.

It was a bright night. Even so, he was worried that he might miss seeing the yellow blanket. There were few cars on the road and he proceeded much slower than his usual speed, while frantically searching for the signal.

Suddenly, draped over some bougainvillea was a light colored blanket. It looked white in the light of his headlights. When he got closer he saw it was yellow. He pulled over, opened his window and threw the case toward the blanket. He looked around frantically but saw no one. He did a U turn, kicking up a shower of gravel and sped back to his office.

*   *   *   *   *

Karen met him coming up the steps as she left the office. "You look terrible. Is something wrong?"

"Yes…no,…nothing."

"Someone just called and said he wanted to speak to you. I think it was the man who called earlier."

"Yes, what did he say?"

"He said he'd call back shortly."

As if on cue, the office phone rang. "I'll get it," he said as he brushed by her.

He lifted the receiver.

"Sah, you did well. Go to the Krugersdorp hospital. You will find your wife and daughter dere waiting for you." The line went dead.

Robbie knew the line was dead but still yelled into the mouthpiece, "Why the hospital? Are they hurt? I'll kill you, you son-of-a-bitch!"

He slammed the phone on its cradle and flew down the stairs. He shouted to his startled secretary, "I'll explain later." His heart and car raced down the road to Krugersdorp.

376

*   *   *   *   *

After Robbie had thrown out the suitcase, Rose waited until his tail lights were out of sight then pulled the Jag over from her hiding place. She quickly stepped out of her car, picked up the case, opened it; saw that it was indeed full of cash. She retrieved the blanket, and drove back to the Whitehead Country Hotel.

"I did it." There was that wonderful glow of satisfaction she experienced after a plan had successfully come together. She now had Kalina and the money.

Deacon, the Colonel, and Johannes were out of the way. She had a new pilot to take a full shipment of tusks stuffed with heroin to the Namibian coast. Ngubane was under control. It had all worked out. "I can handle anything!" She felt lioness proud.

Maybe, she thought, Vicente and I would take a little time off and visit the Seychelles for a short vacation. Or maybe go back home to Peru.

Deacon had whetted her appetite for intimate male companionship. It would be fun to select the right prey, seduce him, and use him. She had a few creative ideas about that.

A few more details to clear up and everything would be back to normal.

She couldn't have been more wrong.

Chapter 34

FATHER GREGORY WHEELED INTO THE HANDS OF HOPE MISSION in a cloud of red dust. I could see it had been an exhilarating ride for him. I guessed that the deprivations of the monastic life could lead one to hunger for the little excitements we all take for granted.

I had relished the opportunity to rest and ratchet down during the trip. Father Gregory wouldn't hear of me taking a turn at the wheel.

The past day had been worse than the trials of Hercules. My wounds hurt, but I felt reluctant to take any more medication--unless absolutely necessary. I wanted my wits about me. The pains were motivating, and reminded me of the seriousness of my mission to safeguard Kalina.

My reverie was interrupted as Father Godwin tramped down the stairs to meet us, greeting Father Gregory with a bear hug. "It was a pretty rough assignment for you to chauffeur, wasn't it?" Godwin obviously knew of Father Gregory's love of driving.

His countenance changed when he saw me. "How do you Yanks put it--you look like you've been rode hard and put away wet."

I blinked, "Father, you watch way too many Westerns for your own good."

"Come in, do come in." He had coffee, juice, sandwiches, and sweet tarts laid out. "Good God, you look much worse in the light."

"You should see the other guys," I mumbled.

"Please, both of you, sit."

Toward the end of the light meal, I said, "We need to talk."

"Father Gregory, would you excuse us please?" He was given a full plate and coffee and ushered to a guest room for the night.

When Father Godwin returned he said without preamble, "Abbot Peter Banks called and told me his end of the story. They haven't had that much excitement there for a decade. Thank God you're safe."

Excitement, I thought. Yes, I guess one could call it that. I would have called it something much more terrible.

"They found us, Father. I don't know how. Possibly Kalina was recognized and word got back to her pursuers." I took a deep breath and plunged ahead. "I'm afraid the Colonel's dead." I tried to shake the image of discovering the Colonel's body pinned to a tree. "And Johannes, I don't know… he was badly injured."

"I can help you there. I received a call from Masvingo Hospital. Johannes lives. The doctors there are not sure how he survived, but he lives. His gunshot wounds will heal, but the surgeon can't be sure how the damage he sustained to his brain will affect him."

"Thank God he's alive. I've never seen a man so badly beaten."

I hesitated, remembering. I was reluctant to tell the priest the worst news—my grand failure. "Father… Kalina's gone."

"Oh God, no!"

I told Father Godwin about the poppy fields and the laboratory operation for conversion to heroin. I also told him of Ginger Rose and her companion Vicente Luna, now thankfully dead. "They killed Mike and Jaylin, and they are the ones after Kalina. Speaking of killing…. Father, I've had to…dispatch a few people."

Godwin looked down, and appeared to me as if he were deep in thought, not knowing how to respond. Finally, he nodded and said, "I'm sure it was necessary. Don't beat yourself up. You're a good man." He put his big paw on my shoulder. "God is a merciful and understanding judge."

"I feel rotten. I'm shaking inside."

"A good sign in itself."

"I came back here because I didn't know where else to go."

Godwin's hands folded as if in prayer, resting on his knees. After a few long moments, the priest said, "I had no idea about the drugs. How are they connected to our mission?"

"I'm still not sure what's going on here. Maybe you should tell me more."   I had always sensed Godwin was holding back information.

"All right. We desperately--'we' being Dr. Ngubane and myself-- needed funds to operate our mission. The need is so great, you understand. Dr. Ngubane met some people who convinced him that a lot of money could be made in the ivory trade." The priest leaned forward, "I know it's illegal, but what does that matter when people have a desperate need for medical care, hygiene, education, and the word of God? Do you know how many people we've literally saved from a life of pain, disease, blindness, and abject poverty?"

I sensed the priest's predicament and his reasoning.

"I assure you. And, we didn't buy from poachers, but from greedy workers at government warehouses full of ivory. The tusks are just sitting there gathering dust. Have been for years. One day soon the ban will be lifted anyway."

"So I went along. Anyway, we were able to buy ivory cheap all over Southern Africa. Mike used to fly around, picking it up. When we got enough, Johannes would prepare it for shipment."

"Mike would fly it up to somewhere along the Skeleton Coast in Namibia for transfer to cargo ships. Yes, we all knew it was illegal, but the four of us thought we were serving a higher purpose. In all of this, nothing was connected to drugs."

I had been listening intently. "You mentioned that Johannes had to prepare the tusks for shipment. What did you mean?"

"I really don't know for sure. I believe he treated them somehow up at his workshop."

"Could you show me? It might be helpful." I would not add, the unthinkable, "*if Kalina is still alive.*" I would not admit to Godwin or to myself that Kalina might be out of my reach. Failure in my mission was just not acceptable. God wouldn't be so cruel as to let me get this close and fail. I had already killed and crippled men on this insane quest.

"Let's go," said Father Godwin, "I'm sure Johannes wouldn't mind, although he's usually very particular about his workshop."

*   *   *   *   *

Trevor Holcroft, rough and ruddy, had been a bush pilot nearly all of his adult life. A tall, broad shouldered, heavy man with a red-gray crew cut and freckles, he had huge forearms, fuzzy with red hair. Flanking a bulbous nose, were small pig-like eyes of pale blue. A red moustache hung over his fleshy lips. He sported the beginnings of a goatee.

He was delighted to have secured his new job. For what they were paying him, he'd fly elephant dung as well as ivory. And there had been a promise of repeat work. He knew he'd have to be tight-lipped about his cargo. He had slipped back and forth across the line of the law before. He'd spent just under a year in prison for assault.

He didn't much like working for a woman, but times change. She was a sexy bird, no argument there. *Who knows?* He thought, I might even get lucky with her. A nice bonus to the work.

He suspected he'd have to be wary of her partner, Vicente. He knew men like Vicente could be deadly. He'd let her make the first move. Yes indeed, she could just come after it. Once she had a taste… he laughed at his own unintended double-entendre… she'd want more. Oh, he'd straighten her out all right, and he knew he had just the tool to do the job.

This part he hated--the manual loading and cargo balancing of the plane. He lifted the heavy tusks, turning his head away from them because they stank to high heaven. He was glad he brought his thick gloves. He couldn't believe that his employer wouldn't pay some bloody kaffirs to do the loading. *What the hell was this country coming to?*

*　　*　　*　　*　　*

Though searching diligently the priest and I found nothing of consequence in Johannes's workshop. A few curious things I did notice were the extremely long drill bits and a state-of-the-art lathe. These might be clues, but I couldn't understand their significance. Something would come to me.

We found no tusks.

I spied an old sepia photo of Johannes in his circus trapeze costume, standing next to what I surmised was his buxom wife and three little blond girls. I thought his torso could have been used by medical students to study musculature.

When I showed the picture to Father Godwin, he said, "Strange, I could have sworn he only had two daughters. They live in Swakopmund on the Namibian coast. He used to visit them every six weeks or so. Mike would fly him up for a few days."

The priest frowned. "I approached him once about his family's odd living arrangements, but his face clouded over and he told me in no uncertain terms, that I was to 'mind my own fuckin' business.'" He sighed and shook his head. "It was very unlike him to speak to me in that way. He apologized for his overreaction for about a week afterwards. I never pursued the issue."

Looking around one last time I said, "Well, nothing else here." I was disappointed and frustrated. I needed something to go on to find Kalina.

Father Godwin stroked his chin and spoke again, "That's odd, because I thought we had just accumulated a load of tusks ready for shipment when Thompson was killed." He paused to think. "Oh, I know, there's a shed next to the landing field. I believe Johannes stored the tusks there before they were flown out."

"So, what are we waiting for? Lead on, Padre."

Chapter 35

BACK AT THE HOTEL, THE WOMEN PREPARED TO LEAVE. "Come Kalina, it's time to go to the mission," Rose urged.

"Oh, yes, I can't wait to see Father Godwin. I have so much to tell him."

"Have you ever been in an airplane?"

Kalina brightened, "Many times, with my...father. He would even let me handle the controls. I was taking lessons. I could take off and fly, but I was just learning how to land when...."

She went silent, and looked up. "Why do you ask?"

"I have a friend named Trevor who might give us an airplane ride sometime soon."

Rose thought how neatly she could tie up the whole business. A flight to Namibia with the new shipment of happy tusks, then an unfortunate accident. Kalina would take the short flight and a long swim. Most people thought she was dead anyway. Didn't they have a funeral service and a newspaper article about her unfortunate death?

Rose took a roll of duct tape from her bag and put in in her purse. On the way to the mission, Rose hoped Vicente would be waiting at the airfield. She always felt more secure with him around.

She guessed that Trevor, the new pilot, could take care of himself. She noticed how he obviously drank in her body with his pale blue eyes. 'Ice eyes,' she thought. He would protect her. Men were so easy.

*   *   *   *   *

Godwin and I walked quickly and silently down a well-worn path. Now that the rain squall had passed, the evening sky was bright with stars and a half moon. A gentle breeze had come up ruffling the leaves on the overhanging trees. As we approached the small airfield, I noticed that the lights were on and someone was moving around. It didn't feel right.

Father Godwin rushed ahead, confronting a dark figure by the plane. "Who are you and what are you doing here?"

"Jesus, you scared me," blurted Trevor.

"I repeat, who are you?"

"I'm your new pilot. Name's Trevor Holcroft. Didn't Miss Rose tell you about me?"

Godwin's eyebrows raised. "Rose hired you? Dr. Ngubane usually takes care of these shipments. And no, I was not aware of your involvement."

I knew Rose ran this operation, so I wasn't surprised.

Trevor continued, "Well, she told me all about you and your set-up of selling off some ivory to support your mission. A *lacker* idea."

Uneasy, I stepped into the light. "So what are your plans here tonight?"

"And who might you be?"

I could see Trevor was not easily intimidated. *Not another tough guy,* I thought. I've had my fill of tough guys. "The name's Deacon Adelius, and you could say I'm part of the operation."

"Fair enough. Well, after I load these bloody, smelly tusks onto the plane, Miss Rose wants me to take 'em up north tonight. I've got a flight plan to the Namibian Coast. Be back easily by dawn. She said she'd be here for the first trip to show me around."

So, I thought, *Rose was coming.* Maybe Kalina would be with her.

Father Godwin said, "You're not going anywhere with that cargo tonight. This operation is over."

A familiar voice arose from the darkness, "A change in plans, gentlemen."

I took it all in quickly. Rose approached quickly and quietly, pointing a gun to Kalina's head. The girl had duct tape over her mouth and around her wrists. Tears streamed down her cheeks. Her eyes bulged as big and bright as an owl's. But thank God, she was alive and looked unhurt. I felt I'd been given a second chance—perhaps my last to save this girl.

"What's the meaning of this, Miss Rose?" hissed Father Godwin.

"Sorry Father, this shipment just couldn't wait. It's too important. We'll be off soon." She turned to the pilot. "Trevor, keep loading, if you please." I noted the sly smile she threw Trevor's way. It was a smile that held promise. I'd seen it before.

I also realized that a moment ago, Trevor looked confused and apprehensive, but with one smile from Rose, he was back into action. This poor *Rooineck* didn't know the serpent he was dealing with. I would have to disarm Rose while Trevor was occupied.

"You look surprised to see me, Ginger," I said.

"Why… I am, a bit." She threw me a crooked smile and cocked her head. "You are a surprising man--a real survivor."

I thought, *why all this for the tusks? And what about the drugs?* I was missing a piece somewhere, and I knew it. Trevor kept loading.

"Let the girl go," I said. "She's not part of this. You have the tusks."

"And more. Oh, don't fret, I intend to let you all go later this evening. We'll just wait a bit for Vicente."

I wasn't sure how to respond, or if I should respond. But now was the time to throw her off balance, and weaken her self-confidence. "I hate to disappoint you, but Vicente won't be coming."

Her face hardened, "Oh, how so?"

I enjoyed giving her my answer. "Because he's dead, of course. As is Muhlukai, at the abbey. So things aren't going exactly according to your plans."

Rose's face dropped. Clearly stunned, her voice…went shaky like a much older woman's. The pistol in her hand rattled. She glared at me. "Tell me what happened."

"Johannes happened."

During our interchange Trevor had stopped working. Talk of people being dead apparently got his attention.

"Don't stop, Trevor my fine boy," Rose interjected. "Nothing's changed." She barked, "Be sure to leave room for passengers in the back of the plane."

I could read Trevor's indecision and angst about this situation. He probably had not signed on for all of this. He had the look of a man torn.

Rose walked over to her new pilot with Kalina in tow. She stroked his face. "I need your help. Will you help a girl? I'm alone now and the night has terrors." She paused dramatically, "Maybe, we can have some time for ourselves later."

She had turned on his switch. Now Trevor was thinking with his little head, just as Rose had intended. He smiled and nodded.

She reached into her voluminous purse and pulled out a roll of silver duct tape. "Now please take this tape and cover the deacon's mouth and wrap his wrists. Can you do that for me?" she cooed. "We don't want any trouble from him, and I don't want to hear any more of his bullshit."

"Yes, I can do that," he nodded.

"Be careful. Deacon has proven to be more resourceful than I had imagined." Then to me, "Not one wrong move, or else...."

I'd thought this might be my chance, but with the gun to Kalina's head and Rose hyper-alert, I didn't dare risk an altercation with Trevor. Hot rage flared within me as I felt the big man apply the tape to my mouth and then my wrists. I realized that never in my life had I been gagged and bound. I felt an overwhelming sense of helplessness and isolation.

"Stop this!" Suddenly. Father Godwin stepped forward, grabbed Trevor by the shoulder and twisted him around.

Trevor shoved the priest backwards.

Father Godwin stepped forward and hit him with a sweeping right cross, staggering the pilot.

A really stupid move under the circumstances, but I reckoned the gutsy priest couldn't stop himself.

Trevor regained his balance and punched Father Godwin with a quick left and right to the face, breaking the priest's nose. Blood gushed from both nostrils, black in the night. Father Godwin staggered back and raised his fists to continue the brawl.

Rose would have no more of this. She spun away from Kalina, pointed the pistol downwards and shot Godwin in the right thigh. He screamed in pain and went down heavily on one knee. The sound reverberating in the countryside brought forth a chorus of animal screeches.

She instantly re-aimed the gun at me. "Not one move out of you."

I stood stone still for the moment.

"Stop. Please God, stop!" Ngubane screamed, running out of the darkness. He looked around and saw that his immediate professional attentions were needed by Father Godwin.

In the excitement of being struck by Godwin, Trevor had not made many wraps of tape around my wrists. And the stupid dolt had bound my wrists in front of me rather than behind. A break? Maybe. I'd have to be careful, knowing Rose was on a knife edge and people could be killed at any second.

Ngubane gave his friend a handkerchief to staunch his bloody nose and put a strong pressure dressing on the thigh wound. "Ginger, please take the money, take the drugs, and let these people go. Please, you know I'll do whatever you want, forever. No one was ever supposed to suffer. Please don't hurt anyone else."

"Of course, you are right, the greedy, intelligent, *Doctor* Ngubane," she mocked. "I never intended to hurt anyone." She looked at the sky and shook her red mane. "But people betrayed me, stole from me, got in my way, and kept things from me." Then much more softly, through clenched teeth, glaring straight at me, "And I've lost my partner."

I saw Rose at this moment as the deranged sociopath that she must have been all along. All of her actions made perfect sense to her. I couldn't help wonder what her past had been like. Now, very dangerous, she could kill us all.

During the conversation, I worked to loosen the tape by surreptitiously flexing my wrists. My left hand started bleeding again.

Kalina screamed even with the tape over her mouth. I prayed that somehow she'd not be hurt. The impact of the last few days on her psyche must have been severe. I threw up a prayer, *God, I need a break here!*

Ngubane jumped to his feet. "Please, go and leave the girl with me. She'll be no trouble, ever, I swear. I guarantee it with my life."

Rose laughed, "Your life is no bargain." She turned back to her pilot, "Trevor get into the plane, if you please, and help me get the girl and this meddlesome American inside."

"No," said Ngubane in a choked voice. "Leave her with me. It will be all right, you'll see. It will be as before. I can help set up the supply for you better than anyone." He was begging now and ratcheting up to a hysterical level.

As Trevor lifted Kalina into the plane, Ngubane shouted, "Where are you taking her? Leave her!" He reached for Rose's gun. She pulled back and instinctively fired into Ngubane's chest. He crumpled to the ground.

"You fool! You just couldn't listen. For a doctor, you really are pretty stupid." She shouted. "I've had enough of all of you and this whole fucking country."

Father Godwin crawled over to Ngubane and took him in his arms. It looked like the Pieta with the priest in the Virgin's place.

Waving her gun at me, Rose said, "All right, Deacon, into the plane."

I climbed up into the plane and sat next to Kalina. Without a look back, Rose boarded and ordered Trevor to take off.

The revs on the Alteris increased to an ear- shattering decibel level. The plane spun around, gathered speed and headed down the runway. The half-moon gave sufficient illumination for the pilot to see clearly. By the moonlight I could see reflections in the pools of water from recent rains and the cook fires around the native roundavels. The plane pulled up steeply, made a long banking right turn and headed north to Namibia.

The four of us and the foul smelling tusks crowded the interior. I looked at Ginger Rose and made pleading sounds from my throat.

"Okay," she said. "You want to talk. We can have a chat. But one wrong move and I'll shoot. Go ahead--pull the tape off your mouth."

I peeled off the tape awkwardly with my bound hands, creating a bleeding crack on my lower lip.

I had to try something. "Thanks. What can I offer you to let Kalina go?"

"Not much, I'm afraid. I have the money."

I went cold. *Not Robbie!* "I don't know what you mean. What money?"

"Oh, God, let's not be coy at this stage," she smirked. "The money you gave to Robbie for safekeeping—the money Thompson stole from me." She produced the briefcase and cracked it open to reveal all the cash I had retrieved from Mike Thompson's cache under the Baobab tree.

I was almost afraid to ask, "And Robbie and his family?"

She waved off-handedly. "They're fine. I have no reason to lie to you now. Robbie Forrester was cleverly duped, even if I do say so myself. With his family threatened, he gave up the money easily. He knows nothing."

I felt immense relief to hear Robbie and his family were unharmed. I couldn't be sure, but I sensed she told the truth. The phrase, "I have no reason to lie to you now," sent a chill down my spine.

"I can't believe you did all of this for a bunch of smelly elephant tusks."

"Hah," She laughed, "Silly boy, of course not. Although ivory fetches a good price, these are very special tusks. I call them *"Feliz Colmillo'*—Happy Tusks. They are worth a fortune—millions."

"What?"

"You see, they're full of one hundred percent pure-grade heroin. It's a perfect supply chain. It begins with the poppies in the Chimanimanis, their conversion at the lab, and transport here to the mission. Then that genius craftsman Johannes hollows out the tusks, fills them with bags of heroin, then seals them back up."

The situation cleared up for me, right down to the long drill bits in Johannes's workshop. "And the smell? It's wretched enough to make a vulture gag."

"Oh that. Yes I agree, disgusting. It's the wild dog urine. Jaylin used to supply it for us from the cheetah reserve. Johannes paints it on the tusks. The odor will dissipate to a large degree over time, but not for the sensitive noses of the drug-sniffing dogs. They stay clear of the tusks and don't signal their handlers that drugs are present." She smiled broadly, spreading her arms out wide. "Isn't that clever?"

I continued. I wanted to keep her talking. "But since ivory transport is illegal, aren't many of these shipments interdicted?"

"My dear, dear Deacon, that's the pure genius of my operation. Some shipments get through—fine, we have the tusks and the heroin. The ones that are confiscated are taken to the holding warehouse of the U.S. Customs Depot at Terminal Island in Long Beach, California."

Rose's eyes sparkled. She clearly enjoyed talking about her scheme. "This is the sweet part." She crossed her shapely legs and smiled, "During the night, a couple of guards who work for us drill out the base of the tusks and remove the happy powder. After they fill the holes with plaster they slip it into watertight containers, and then to a waiting scuba diver along the wharf. He transfers it underwater to a nearby pleasure craft in the harbor. So, in most cases the U.S. government takes our heroin into the States for us." She threw back her head and laughed. "Isn't that accommodating of them?"

Her smile suddenly vanished. "Enough! Slap the tape back over your mouth."

Having no choice, I complied.

Now that she had explained their entire operation, I knew she'd have to kill us.

*   *   *   *   *

Father Godwin watched the plane's lights fade as it climbed into the moonlit sky. He knew his friend and partner of many years was dying. Blood trickled from the corners of his mouth. The priest screamed for help.

Ngubane's speech was labored and came in short bursts. "I don't have much time…. I'm sorry about not telling you of the drugs. It started out…. I swear…. as only the ivory, but when I was presented with a way to earn a fortune by putting heroin into the tusks…. I couldn't resist. We did so much good with the money….But it was wrong….I know it. My friend…I want you to forgive me…. I've brought so much pain."

Father Godwin blessed his friend with his bloody hands. He made the sign of the cross, gave him absolution, and said the prayers for anointing the dying. "I forgive you and God forgives you."

"Please….one more thing….I left my estate and its contents to you in my will…. Please use the profits…. Continue our work at the mission. Promise me." He clutched the priest's shirt front.

"I promise I'll do my best to be a good steward."

"Yes, of course, I trust you…. I'm so sorry about Kalina…and Jaylin. I never meant for anyone to be harmed."

"I know, my friend. You are forgiven. Be assured that our work here will continue. But you will be sorely missed…. I will miss you." Godwin's eyes misted and overflowed with tears.

"Thank you, I…." Ngubane shuddered, exhaled a grotesque deep sound, looked up at the sky with eyes which could no longer see and died.

The priest gently closed Ngubane's eyelids, "May you find peace my old friend." He kissed the doctor on the forehead and yelled for help again, as he painfully crawled back to the mission buildings, dragging his wounded leg.

*   *   *   *   *

Ginger Rose had left us to climb over the tusks and sit up front in the co-pilot's seat. I could hear them talking but couldn't make out what they were saying. I feverishly tugged at the tape on my wrists. Luckily the darkness masked my movements. I could see Ginger had reached across the flight controls and had her hand in Trevor's lap. She knew how to maintain control.

My heart went out to Kalina. I'd failed to protect her again.

But I wasn't beaten yet. I refused to surrender to circumstances. I knew Kalina had been to hell and back a few times since my arrival. For a moment I considered whether it might not have been better for her, had I not been seduced by my friend's midnight letter to come to South Africa.

I quickly dismissed these thoughts. Jaylin and Kalina had been marked for death before my arrival.

By eliminating the poppy fields and the lab, I knew I'd prevented thousands of doses of dope from reaching the mean streets of America. Vicente was gone, and I was pretty sure the whole operation had been halted, if not for good but for a long while anyway.

I wouldn't give up now.

I needed a distraction. If one didn't occur, I'd create one myself. Focus, I told myself. Find the moment. Make the moment, *Goddamnit!*

Rose made her way back to the rear of the plane. "I convinced Trevor to take a small detour over Walvis Bay. The lights around the Bay are exquisite. They should be coming up in a few minutes." I noticed she carried the briefcase with the money by running her hand through the soft handles so it dangled on her wrist like an obscene leather bracelet. I'd have to do something soon. The damn duct tape still held my wrists together.

"There it is," Ginger said, looking down, "Isn't it spectacular? The water positively shimmers below. As a matter of fact, I think it's a great night for a swim. What do you think, Deacon, my sweet love?" She blew me a kiss.

Rose knew enough not to get too close to me. I wished she'd cross over towards my side of the cabin.

"Now, if you would be so good as to open the door next to you."

I had no cards left to play. My mind raced for an opening—any little opening. I didn't move. Rose's intentions were clear and deadly.

"Look," she hissed, "We can do this clean or messy." She tucked the gun under Kalina's right breast. "Do you want this girl to suffer and bleed while you make up your mind?"

I knew I had to be creative—now. *Think, what is available?*

"I know what will help." Rose tore the tape off Kalina's mouth. "Now we can hear her scream when I pull the trigger."

Precious seconds left. I could see no options. I couldn't let Kalina be tortured. I opened the cabin door. As it swung open, I felt and heard the rush of cool air. I stood slowly and yanked the tape off my mouth. "One more thing. Kalina, I'm sorry. Remember how well you're loved. I was proud to become one of your uncles." I knew I was trying Rose's patience, as I stood poised precariously in the open door.

"Very touching. Ach, get on with it!" Rose took a step away from Kalina and lashed out with her foot to kick me out the door.

This was the moment. I reached out, grabbed her ankle and pulled for all I was worth. She fell back and slid towards me. A gunshot went off wildly. The plane suddenly dipped as the pilot must have flinched.

Kalina screaming with her hands tied together fell on top of Rose who shoved her away viciously.

I dove into Rose, gripping her gun with my bound hands.

She scratched at my eyes with her free hand, kicked and screamed but didn't have the strength to fight me in close quarters. The briefcase on her wrist also got in her way.

As the pilot leveled the plane, we rolled toward the open door. I smelled her perfume and sweat and felt the softness of her body as we were joined together as closely as Siamese twins.

My memory flashed back to the last time we were this close. Then as lovers, now in a life and death struggle.

I got purchase with my right leg, stood, lifting Rose and spun around so that she was backed into the open doorway. The briefcase popped open and bills flew out. Some flew back in to the plane but many flew out. In the moonlight, they resembled little bats in flight.

Rose dropped her gun to grab hold of the handle alongside the open door with her right hand. I felt the strong grip of her left arm around my neck.

"If I go, we both go," she shouted, inches from my ear. Then she bit down hard. Exquisite pain shot through my body.

"No fuckin' way," I shouted. With the fingers of my bound hands, I reached up and grabbed all the flesh I could under her left armpit, and squeezed. The sudden pain and numbing effect caused her to lose her grip on my neck. She tumbled backwards out into the slipstream, still holding on to the handle with her right hand.

I had nothing to hang on to. I stood precariously balancing at the edge of the open doorway, the wind working to suck me out of the cabin. I could see the panic in Rose's face as she hung in the air.

Miraculously, I felt myself being yanked backwards, into the plane. I fell on top of Kalina who had grabbed my belt with her free fingers and pulled me back from the brink.

Rose's grip weakened and loosened. I crawled back to the door to pull her in but was too late. Wide eyed, with a wild grimace on her face, she sank into the dark abyss of Walvis Bay. I watched her get smaller and smaller as she silently fell away into the darkness.

"Thanks," I said to Kalina. "I could've gone out at any second." I felt grateful her quick thinking prevented me from being sucked out to join Rose in a death fall.

Kalina was shaiking and crying.

I retrieved Rosa's gun, shut the door and yelled at the pilot, "I know this was your first work with Miss Ginger Rose. It is also your last. She is currently communing with the marine life down in the Bay.

"You will now turn around and fly us back to the mission in South Africa. If you land anywhere else, I will shoot you as soon as you set this bird down. You can walk away from all of this and go scot free. No police. No charges. Now, what's it to be?"

Trevor shook his head, "Sonofabitch! Heading back." He banked the plane back towards the mission.

"Kalina, help me please." She unwrapped my wrists, and I unwrapped hers. I felt compelled somehow, to finish this operation for good. I opened the door again and together, very carefully, we threw every tusk out of the plane to join Rose and the fluttering money below.

Finally, I shut the door and gathered up the currency from within the plane. We sat huddled together for the duration of the return trip. Once again, I found myself making soothing sounds to this traumatized young girl. "Everything will be all right…. It's over." I held her until she gradually stopped shaking.

I thought if I repeated it enough times to her, I'd actually believe it myself. It had been much too close.

Somehow, I felt that now everything would come right. My thoughts retreated back to the mission airstrip. *How badly had Father Godwin been injured?* Ngubane's wounds looked very severe. I doubted if the doctor had survived.

I hurt in more places than I could count. The bleeding from the stitches on my hand seemed to have slowed. My back ached and my face still stung. I felt blood dripping down from my torn ear.

Most importantly, Kalina was safe. *God, what if it wasn't over?* How could I be sure Rose hadn't told anyone else about Kalina? Maybe, there were more people involved in the dirty tusk operation. She might still be in danger. I needed to get her out of this country. My thoughts flitted around my brain like confetti in the breeze.

I felt gratified that the drug smuggling operation had been stopped. Especially gratified also that Kalina and I were alive. The cost had been high. There had been too many lives I had been personally responsible for ending.

I knew that the Jungians had a point. A man could be Ruler, Warrior, Wizard, and Lover according to circumstance and need. I wasn't confident that I could ever turn off my 'warrior' persona. It would always be there, just beneath the surface for me when I needed it. I suspected my life would never be the same. Changes would have to be made. I vowed to take care of Kalina for her sake, Mike Thompson's, her uncles and, of course, myself.

I held her tenderly and pressed her forehead against my cheek as my emotions settled.

Chapter 36

KALINA FLINCHED WHEN THE WHEELS touched down on the hard red earth. "Are we home?"

"Yes, Kalina, sweet girl, we're home." I'd been lightly dozing. Although sore and spent, I felt my struggles were coming to an end.

Once the engine stopped, Trevor said nothing, but glared at me while I had the pistol pointed at him. I watched carefully as the big ruddy pilot threw his jacket over his shoulder and stomped off. I was relieved to have one less confrontation.

I hurt all over and the back of my eyes felt scratchy from lack of sleep.

Kalina and I walked slowly from the small airfield to Father Godwin's house. The lights were blazing. People would be waiting for news. I also had to find out a few things.

As we approached, I could just make out Father Godwin sitting on the porch under a yellow bug-light, holding a basketball, like a child might hold a blanket for comfort. "Hard blues" played on his small stereo. His bandaged leg was propped up on a chair, and a tall pitcher of guava juice was at his side.

When he became aware of our presence, his craggy face lit up. He straightened up in his chair, "I saw the plane coming in. You made it. You're both safe." He raised his arms towards the heavens. "Praise God."

Kalina ran ahead, knelt next to the priest and threw her arms around him.

When I got closer to the porch, I saw the white bandage on the priest's nose spreading like wings of a stingray under his swollen and discolored eyes.

"Yes, we finally made it," I sighed.

"What happened?" Godwin asked.

I took in a long breath, "Details later. Miss Ginger Rose is no longer with us. She and the tusks with the dope are somewhere deep in the waters of Walvis Bay."

I waved my hands, "I let the new pilot run off."

"It's just as well," said Godwin. "The poor bloke probably had no idea what he'd gotten into." Godwin stroked Kalina's hair as she knelt by his side.

To me, it seemed that these two were so in tune they didn't need words. Maybe words got in the way.

"Kalina was very brave. She saved me from a long fall and a hard wet landing."

"Indeed, she is a brave girl." He looked down at her lovingly. "I'm just so happy to see you both. I've been praying for you. Don't let anyone tell me prayer doesn't have power."

I looked over at Kalina who looked totally spent. "Father, if it's okay with you, let's get Kalina settled in, she's out on her feet. Then we have to talk."

"Rightee-o. It's milk and off to bed with you, young lady. You've done a lot of growing up recently. I'm so proud of you."

She looked up at him, "What about Uncle Gideon?"

Father Godwin sobbed suddenly and shook his head. Then, in what I sensed was a role-reversal, Kalina touched her head to his, consoling him. They both wept softly.

Godwin regained control of his voice. "I sat with him to the end. Despite what he'd done, he helped a lot of people here. He loved you, Kalina."

"I know. I'll miss him. He taught me so much."

"You can remember him best by using what he taught you for the good of others."

"I will, I promise. Any word about Uncle Johannes?"

"He's still in hospital. Stable, but in serious condition. They're saying he's a medical marvel of survival."

I wasn't surprised. The man had the constitution of a bull rhinoceros.

I said to the priest, "We'll go in. You stay. You probably should keep weight off that leg. And how's the nose?"

"It's broken, but it's been broken before." He managed a crooked smile, "Maybe this time it will improve my looks."

*   *   *   *

Later, when Kalina was safe in bed, Godwin and I downed several cold beers and talked until the dawn illuminated the ground mist and singing started in the kitchen. We had much to talk about.

Godwin had received word that most of the poppy fields were now nothing but ashes. He had also been told that three bodies were found in the fields. Evidence showed that they had been killed. Godwin lifted an eyebrow and gave me a quizzical look.

I nodded slowly, "Yes father, but I assure you it had to be, or I'd be discovering the glory of the hereafter myself right now."

"And the colonel, too," murmured Godwin.

"Yes, poor brave man. What a way to end his career. Maybe he always wanted it that way—you know, dying with your boots on and all that."

"It's a terrible thing you've endured." The priest put a hand on my shoulder. "May God have mercy and give you peace."

Godwin mentioned the two men at the abbey who were also killed—one by gunshot and one by a ruptured larynx.

The litany of the dead weighed heavily on me--so much death.

Yes, I thought, I may be blameless, but I am responsible, nevertheless. As the memories flooded back to me in vivid detail and color, I abruptly excused myself, stumbled around the building, knelt, retched and vomited.

My brain seemed to throb as I pictured Rose's face getting smaller and smaller as it sank away from the plane into the black night. *Rest in hell, Rose!*

I experienced the familiar sinking into depression I'd felt before when I had killed. Prayer, good friends and throwing myself into activity pulled me back to a more joyous life. *Perhaps the same combination would work again.*

I wondered, however, if my recent experiences had changed me forever. I had faced evil from without and my demons within. I hadn't lost control, but still I was fearful for the future. Would it be easier for me to kill the next time? What would happen if someone got in my face and I felt threatened? My killing skills and rage were a lethal combination. How many people did I know who had actually killed anyone? Not many, I thought, perhaps a few in the army. And I purported to be a man of God.

I sensed that the only way to keep myself from sinking into some emotional quagmire, was to focus on tasks to be done, and to stay active. "You know, Father, I think it's still wise to stick with our original plan and get Kalina out of the country. We really can't be sure if anyone else knows of her or may be after her."

"No, we can't. I think you're right."

"But how the hell do I get her out?"

"I have an idea in that regard," said the priest in a denasal voice, his bandages blocking the passage of sound to his nose.

412

Chapter 37

ROBBIE AND DEL BROUGHT SARAH, who was dressed up in a pink frilly dress and cuter than any of her dolls.

Johannes was still in the hospital. The doctors believed he would recover, but would most likely have some physical limitations. *Fat chance*, I thought. They didn't know who they were dealing with.

Kalina looked spectacular in a beautiful ankle-length white linen dress and a garland of yellow hibiscus in her hair, supporting a short veil. I wore my best black suit, a white shirt and a bright silver tie purchased by Del.

By necessity the church was nearly empty, yet somehow, the blacks working around the mission knew something important was happening this morning. The drumming and harmonious singing had been going on for hours.

The day dawned absolutely perfect. The sun glistened off the plants and flowers enriching their colors. A slight breeze kept everyone comfortable. Big puffy clouds dotted the sky.

Father Godwin stood with the aid of a crutch at the front of the altar underneath the huge rough-hewn crucifix. The bandage on his nose looked terribly out of place.

I enjoyed seeing Kalina being escorted down the aisle on the arm of Robbie Forrester.

Del and her daughter beamed.

Kalina walked with royal dignity holding her head high and looking straight ahead.

Father Godwin began...."Dearly beloved, we are gathered here..."

Kalina and I stood before the priest...and exchanged vows.

Father Godwin had suggested this as a way for me to get her out of the country with the least amount of trouble.

It was only possible because Kalina was of mixed blood. We used the expertly forged documentation that had been provided by Colonel Marshall to give Kalina a new identity.

Father Godwin, Kalina and I had discussed the plan at length. We made sure to explain the necessity for the ruse. I wasn't satisfied until I felt confident that Kalina realized it wasn't a real wedding and that it would never be consummated. I counseled her that this event would in no way interfere with her happiness when she eventually did get married. The poor suitor would have to go through me, Father Godwin and, God have mercy, Johannes Marais.

As soon as she was safe and established in the States, we would have the marriage annulled.

I would see to it that she attended one of the fine nursing schools in Chicago. I promised she would be free to make her own decisions about her future. I was, however, pretty sure she would eventually want to return to the Hands of Hope Mission.

Even though it was a sham, I felt a powerful sense of joy and fulfillment during the ceremony. Del cried openly. Her daughter didn't understand, but she cried too, in sympathy with her mother.

Afterwards, we were congratulated heartily by the small group in attendance. Robbie had a special spread ready for everyone at one of the small banquet rooms adjacent to the Carnivore restaurant.

During the ceremony I had experienced an epiphany. When I got back to the States, I would continue to work for the Church and examine my own future prospects. It felt so absolutely right. Had my experiences changed the course of my life? Time and reflection would tell.

During the meal, Kalina asked me, "Uncle Deacon, will it be hard for you, having me around?"

I liked being called "Uncle Deacon." "No, my sweet girl. It will be a pleasure. And, I've got grand things and wonders to show you in Chicago, but you'll have to get used to very different weather in the winter. There are wonderful nursing schools in my city. But, I *will* be a hard taskmaster and make you study hard."

"Oh, I will. I promise. I want to be a great nurse like my mother."

"Then you certainly will be a great nurse. I know you have a lot to offer."

I had already made my apologies to Robbie and Del for the shock they suffered at the fake kidnapping. Robbie shrugged it off, (typical of him). "Now my darling wife will appreciate me more than ever." Del hit him on the head with a spoon.

I gave Robbie two small packages. One was for Del and the other for Sarah. I made him promise to give them to his wife and daughter after I had left the country. They contained two of the diamonds from the little sack left by Thompson. (I was sure Thompson would approve.) I also gave Robbie two envelopes with a substantial amount of cash in each of them. One was a donation for the abbey in Zimbabwe, and the other was for nurse Jenny Togambo.

I had one of the doctors make a small cast for my injured hand that extended halfway up my left forearm. The rest of the diamonds were embedded in the plaster. This, I figured, would avoid any troublesome inquiries going through customs. I planned to eventually sell the diamonds and put the money into safe investments for Kalina -- and of course, pay for her schooling. With some measure of financial security and an education, she would have a decent start to her adult life.

I was especially pleased that Father Godwin intended to use the proceeds from the sale of Dr. Ngubane's Eagle's Lair and its contents to build a clinic in his name for the treatment of drug addictions. Father Godwin also planned to start a program to visit prisoners who were incarcerated because of drug involvement, and help them with their rehabilitation after they were set free.

The atmosphere of the group had a bittersweet quality.

There was loss.

There was redemption.

There was hope.

Acknowledgements.

I owe a great debt of gratitude to the following individuals for their support and assistance to bring the story of "Deacon's Promise," to life.

Author and mentor Mr. Bruce McAllister who was there at Deacon's birth and provided the guidance to craft a plot and characters worthy of the thriller genre.

Maura Raffensperger who, as in the past, contributed her expertise in all things pharmaceutical, a key ingredient in this story.

Dick Laine who was untiring in reading and re-reading my drafts to provide the necessary critique to successfully shape my novel.

Marianne Stegemann, a marvelous proofreader/editor who spent countless hours doing the detailed work of grammar and syntax corrections.

To my friends and fellow writers in the "Taking Pains" writer's group, (Joyce Melton, Bob Winter April Wursten, and Kevin McCarthy) for many months of critical editing and never letting me get away with anything resembling mediocrity.

Father Paul Johnson OP, who advised me concerning the inner workings of the Catholic Church.

To my South African friends Robert and Adele Forsyth who generously gave me an exciting second home and precious second family half way around the world where I set my story.

To my three sons Steve, Dave and Chris who patiently assisted me in the use of the computer and provided encouragement and useful advice.

Finally, to my wife, Marjorie who was always there as my no. 1 cheerleader.

www.ingramcontent.com/pod-product-compliance
Lightning Source LLC
Chambersburg PA
CBHW032109310726
48972CB00001B/145